Peter Tremayne is the fiction pseud... ... ...
Ellis, a well-known authority on the ancient Celts, who has
utilised his knowledge of the Brehon law system and seventh-
century Irish society to create a new concept in detective
fiction.

An international Sister Fidelma Society has been established,
with a journal entitled *The Brehon* appearing three times
yearly. Details can be obtained either by writing to the Society
at 1643-B Savannah Highway, Suite 396, Charleston, SC
29407, USA, or by logging onto the society website at
www.sisterfidelma.com.

Praise for the widely acclaimed Sister Fidelma mysteries:

'The Sister Fidelma books give the readers a rattling good
yarn. But more than that, they bring vividly and viscerally
to life the fascinating lost world of the Celtic Irish. I put
down *The Spider's Web* with a sense of satisfaction at a good
story well told, but also speculating on what modern life
might have been like had that civilisation survived'
Ronan Bennett

'This masterly storytelling from an author who breathes
fascinating life into the world he is writing about'
Belfast Telegraph

'Rich helpings of evil and tension with lively and varied
characters' *Historical Novels Review*

'The detail of the books is fascinating, giving us a vivid
picture of everyday life at this time... the most detailed and
vivid recreations of ancient Ireland' *Irish Examiner*

'A brilliant and beguiling heroine. Immensely appealing'
Publishers Weekly

THE CHALICE OF BLOOD

PETER TREMAYNE

headline

First published in 2010 by
HEADLINE PUBLISHING GROUP

First published in paperback in 2011 by
HEADLINE PUBLISHING GROUP

1

Cataloguing in Publication Data is available from the British Library

ISBN 978 0 7553 5776 5

Typeset in Times New Roman PS by Palimpsest Book Production Limited,
Falkirk, Stirlingshire

Printed and bound in Great Britain by
Clays Ltd, St Ives plc

Headline's policy is to use papers that are natural, renewable and recyclable products
and made from wood grown in sustainable forests. The logging and manufacturing
processes are expected to conform to the environmental regulations of the
country of origin.

HEADLINE PUBLISHING GROUP
An Hachette UK Company
338 Euston Road
London NW1 3BH

www.headline.co.uk
www.hachette.co.uk

A special token of appreciation for David R. Wooten of Charleston, South Carolina, USA, to mark ten years' devoted service as director of the International Sister Fidelma Society, editor of *The Brehon* and as webmaster.

. . . Abba Pater omnia possibilia tibi sunt transfer calicem hunc a me.

Abba Father, all things are possible for you, take away this cup from me.

Mark 14:36
Vulgate Latin trs of Jerome 5th century

Hic est enim calix sanguinis mei –
For this is the chalice of my blood –

Early medieval Latin Mass

pRINCIPAL ChARACTERS

Sister Fidelma of Cashel, a *dálaigh* or advocate of the law courts of seventh-century Ireland
Brother Eadulf of Seaxmund's Ham in the land of the South Folk, her companion

At Bingium
Huneric, a hunter and guide
Brother Donnchad of Lios Mór

At Cashel
Colgú, King of Muman and brother to Fidelma
Ségdae, Abbot of Imleach, Chief Bishop of Muman
Brother Madagan, his steward
Caol, commander of the Nasc Niadh, bodyguards to the King
Gormán, a warrior of the Nasc Niadh
Brehon Aillín, a judge

At Cill Domnoc
Brother Corbach

At Lios Mór
Iarnla, Abbot of Lios Mór
Brother Lugna, his *rechtaire*, or steward
Brother Giolla-na-Naomh, the blacksmith
Brother Máel Eoin, the *bruigad*, or hosteller
Brother Gáeth former *anam chara* (soul friend) of Brother Donnchad
Brother Seachlann, a physician
Brother Donnán, *scriptor* (librarian)
Brother Echen, the *echaire*, or stable keeper
Venerable Bróen, an elderly member of the community
Lady Eithne of An Dún, mother of Brother Donnchad
Glassán, the master builder
Gúasach, his foster-son and apprentice
Saor, a carpenter and assistant master builder

At Fhear Maighe
Cumscrad, chief of the Fir Maige Féne
Cunán, his son and assistant librarian
Muirgíos, a barge master
Eolann, a bargeman
Uallachán, chief of the Uí Liatháin
Brother Temnen, librarian of Ard Mór

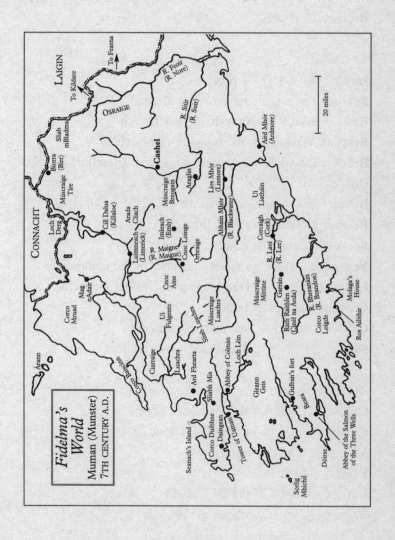

Fidelma's World
Muman (Munster)
7TH CENTURY A.D.

20 miles

LAIGIN

To Fearna
To Kildare

R. Feóir
(R. Nore)

OSRAIGE

CONNACHT

Sliab mBladma

Biorra
(Birr)

Múscraige
Tíre

Loch
Derg

Cill Dalua
(Killaloe)

Arada
Cliach

Luimneach
(Limerick)

R. Maigne
(R. Maigue)

Imleach
(Emly)

Cnoc
Loinge

Orbraige

R. Siúr
(R. Suir)

Cashel

Múscraige
Breogain

Araglin

Lios Mhór
(Lismore)

Abhain Mhór
(R. Blackwater)

Aird Mhór
(Ardmore)

Uí
Liatháin

Corcaigh
(Cork)

R. Laoi
(R. Lee)

Árann

Corco
Mruad

Mag
nAdair

Corco Baiscinn

Uí
Fidgente

Ciarraige

Luachra

Sliab Luachra

Cnoc
Áine

Múscraige
Luachra

Ard Fhearta

Sliabh Mis

Abbey of Colmán

Loch Léin

Gleann
Geis

Seanach's Island

Corco Duibhne

Daingean

Tower of Uaman

Gulban's fort

Bearu

Múscraige
Mittine

Garrán

Ráth Raithlen
(Cinél na Aeda)

R. Bhreanáin
(R. Brandon)

Corco
Loígde

Doíre

Scelig
Mhichíl

Abbey of the Salmon
of the Three Wells

Molaga's
House

Ros Ailithir

PROLOGUE

T he snow had begun to descend in thick icy flakes, driving
into their faces, cold and clinging, obscuring the path
along the river bank and adding another coating to the already
whitened landscape. The low mountains that surrounded them
on both sides of the river seemed to vanish under the white
shroud, for they already had several weeks of snow lying on
them. There was no sound of birds, wisely taking shelter, or
of other animals. The heathland and trees were silent and
even their footsteps made no noise, for the snow was thick
and soft beneath. Only the great river, to their right, announced
its presence with a constant rumble as it cut its tumultuous
path through the white surroundings.

'Is it far?'

The tall, bearded man who was leading the way did not
pause in his measured stride.

'Not far,' he called without turning his head. It was not
the first time that his companion, hurrying in his footsteps,

had asked the question since they had left the little settlement. The second man was slightly built and roughly thirty years of age, wrapped in the dark brown woollen robes of a religieux. The response from his burly guide, clad in a warm badger's fur hunting cloak, was always the same as they trudged along the river path.

It was late afternoon. Just before the scenery had been obscured by the snowfall, the religieux had been gazing anxiously at the grey snow clouds covering the sky to the east. They had been darkening ominously above the low range of mountains and told of the approach of the end of the day as well as the oncoming snow.

'Will we be there before dark?' he asked anxiously, trying to wipe away the flakes that hung from his eyebrows and lids. The light was now completely distorted and the cold had grown intense.

'Before dark,' confirmed his guide. Then the man suddenly chuckled, a deep, throaty sound, and added, 'Do not worry, little Brother, surely your god will protect you in such a place even after nightfall.'

'I am anxious to be able to see the place, that is all.' The other's reply came stiffly.

'A strange place for one of your faith to want to see,' the guide observed.

The religieux did not answer.

The guide shrugged philosophically. It was not his business why this foreign pilgrim had requested his services as a guide. Well, in truth it had been old Father Audovald who

2

had engaged his services for the foreigner. Father Audovald was the aged priest at the chapel dedicated to the Blessed Martin. He was regarded as the leader of the small settlement called Bingium on the banks of the great river Renos. He had told Huneric that he knew no more than that this man had arrived early that morning. The foreigner had come downriver in one of the hardy trading barges, stepped ashore and sought the services of a guide. He had been directed to Father Audovald who, in turn, had asked Huneric to take the new arrival where he wanted to go.

Huneric had a reputation as a local hunter who knew every centimetre of the forests and mountains along the banks of the river. He had several times surreptitiously examined the foreign religieux, trying to work out where he came from. The pilgrim had arrived from the south; that he knew. His face was suntanned in spite of it being late winter. But the man did not sound or look like someone from those southern Mediterranean climes. There were freckles on his cheeks and his hair, so far as Huneric could see, was the colour of copper. The stranger spoke fluent Latin, which was their only common language, albeit a refined and archaic form compared to the rough colloquial language that Huneric used when trading with the Gauls.

The path turned slightly inland towards the shelter of some woodland. Only a slight depression in the blanket of snow actually marked its route. Now and again, the frozen crust of a previous snowfall snapped with a fierce cracking sound under Huneric's heavy tread. The trees gave some protection from the snowstorm and the path became easier. But it was obvious that the wood was little more than a copse and would provide only a brief respite from the driving snow beyond.

'We'll cross the Nava just ahead of us,' the guide offered, shaking the snow from his cloak with a curious dog-like movement of his body. 'It flows swiftly into the River Renos, and the currents are strong and dangerous. Thanks be, there is an old wooden bridge that spans it. We shall cross by it.'

'Another river?' the pilgrim asked, almost in complaint.

'Not as big as the Renos. But an old man once told me that the Gauls, who used to live here before my people came, called it the Nava for, in their language it meant "the wild river". This is the confluence of the Nava and the Renos,' he added unnecessarily.

By the time they came through the patch of woodland, the snow had ceased falling, although the clouds still hung low, dark and ominous. They emerged abruptly on to the bank of a smaller reach of water, across which stretched a long, rickety wooden bridge. The water gushed white and angry underneath the bridge. It looked turbulent as it emptied itself with crashing force into the broader river beyond, creating whirlpools and rapids that would be dangerous to cross in a boat.

The guide halted a moment.

'As you see, the Renos begins to curve through the hills, turning sharply north there.' Huneric pointed. 'The Renos is a broad water highway. In ancient times the Roman legions decided to build their Via Ausonia along its banks to connect

Bingium to the city of Augusta Treverorum, and there was a fortress erected here, by the confluence, to guard the way.'

'But is it far to the necropolis?' demanded the religieux impatiently.

Huneric looked at his companion with a thoughtful frown. Once more he found himself wondering where the man came from and why he wanted to visit an abandoned Roman necropolis.

'The remains of the Roman graveyard are just beyond those trees on the far side of the bridge. It is not far now. Come, but when you cross the bridge, be careful. The snow will have made the wooden planking slippery.'

The warning was well taken for once or twice the religieux nearly lost his footing and only by grasping the wooden rail at the side of the bridge was he prevented from measuring his length on its wet and slushy surface. Once across, he was able to follow Huneric through ankle-deep snow with more confidence. In spite of the snow screen there were obvious signs of ancient habitation here. Remains of walls proclaimed a derelict fortress, much of whose stonework seemed to be missing, perhaps removed by locals to build new habitations elsewhere. Then he picked up signs of a long-abandoned roadway.

Huneric led the way to the edge of what seemed to be another section of forest whose dark foliage was distinctly eerie. The religieux stared at the tall trees. They rose before them like some impregnable wall, with a surrounding girdle of brambles and nettles – nature's own defence against intruders. Huneric seemed to know a path through this dense barrier. The religieux saw yew trees and evergreen oaks; he even recognised the green bark of young holly trees and the smooth grey trunks of the older holly, their prickly lower leaves a deterrent to grazing animals. High among the trees that had shed their leaves for winter he saw strange, round, dark clumps. At first he thought they were birds' nests until he realised they were parasitic masses of mistletoe.

The religieux noticed that these woods were strangely silent even though the snow had ceased to fall. There was no hint of any animal moving nearby, neither wolves nor foxes. The flow of the river could no longer be heard. He grimaced and tried to credit the lack of natural sounds to the cold and the weather. Even so, he could not suppress the apprehensive shiver that tingled on his spine.

Huneric glanced back at him and gave a thin smile, seeming to recognise his anxiety.

'A few steps more, my friend,' he said lightly.

Indeed, a few steps more brought them into what seemed to be a large clearing whose boundaries were marked by the dense barrier of trees and shrubs and almost given a protective canopy by their massive spreading branches. The religieux saw that the clearing was filled with small mounds and decaying stone monuments and markers, many overgrown with all manner of weeds and plants.

Huneric stood aside and let the religieux gaze around him.

'This is where the Roman legionaries, who garrisoned the fortress here, buried their dead,' he announced almost with the pride of ownership. 'This is the necropolis they built many centuries ago.'

The religieux breathed out softly, the cold making visible the vapour of his breath.

'You know what it is that I seek?'

'The graves of the archers, the first cohort,' confirmed his guide. 'Come, follow me.'

He walked across to an area where several stones rose from the ground. He paused before one and with his hand tore away the moss that covered the incised lettering on the ancient surface.

'Is this the one you seek?' he asked.

The religieux went down on his haunches before the stone and peered at the Latin inscription, reading the name softly to himself. Then he exhaled deeply and nodded.

'It is the name I seek,' he replied quietly. He shifted his position to examine it more closely. 'It says that he was from Sidonia . . .'

Huneric had pride in his education, his ability to read the words that Father Audovada had taught him. He nodded in agreement. 'He was a man from Sidon, which is in the country of the Phoenicians.'

'. . . *miles ex-signifer Cohorte Primus Saggitariorum hic situs est*,' the religieux read. 'He was the former standard bearer of the First Cohort of Archers and this is his grave.'

While Huneric looked on with some bewilderment, the religieux delved into the satchel he carried and drew from it a small wooden tablet, hinged in two sections, and a thin bone stylus. He opened the tablet. The wax in the centre of each wooden section was cold and the religieux spent some time trying to soften it with the warmth of his hand. Once pliable enough, he carefully wrote down the five lines of Latin that comprised the inscription. Then he closed the writing tablet with a snap and replaced it and the stylus in the satchel. He stood for a moment looking down at the monument.

'Thank you,' he said in a quiet, almost resigned tone. 'We can return to Bingium as soon as you like.'

Huneric was bewildered. 'Is this all that you came to see?'

'It is enough.'

'Was this Roman one of your ancestors? You travelled a long way just to read a brief inscription.'

The religieux smiled tightly and shook his head. 'He was not my ancestor,' he replied.

'Then who was he?' pressed Huneric. 'Why was he so important that you have made this journey from your country, wherever that is, just to look at a piece of stone under which he lies buried?'

'Why is he so important?' The religieux turned sad, tired eyes on the man. Huneric thought for a moment that he was about to burst into tears. His face was gaunt and white. 'Because that man,' he gestured towards the grave, 'may have been the father of a lie that has changed the world.'

CHAPTER ONE

Although it was not yet the end of summer, there was a
damp chill in the air and Abbot Iarnla drew his chair
nearer to the smoky log fire. No warmth emanated from it,
only grey fumes and the hissing of moisture. He exhaled in
annoyance.

'The wood is damp, Brother Gáeth,' he admonished the
moon-faced religieux whose task it was to bring the wood to
provide warmth for the abbot's chamber.

'Forgive me, Father Abbot,' the man stammered. 'It has
only just been noticed that the thatch on the woodshed roof
was in need of repair. The rain must have come through and
soaked into the wood and—'

Abbot Iarnla made a cutting motion with his left hand.
'*Mox nox in rem*,' he snapped impatiently, 'soon night, to the
business.' The wood-bearer received this sharp reproof with
a bowed head and muttered that he would go at once in search
of dry logs to replace the wet ones. Brother Gáeth was a tall

man with almost ugly features and a permanently crestfallen expression that made the elderly abbot immediately feel guilty that he had spoken so roughly. It was known that Brother Gáeth was not considered robust in mind and his Latin was limited. The abbot forced a sympathetic smile. 'If you can find dry wood, bring it quickly, for I feel a chill.' Brother Gáeth moved obediently towards the door.

When he opened it, he found a tall man with thin, almost gaunt features and pale blue eyes on the threshold, his hand raised as if he were about to knock. Brother Gáeth stood quickly aside, head bowed respectfully, for Brother Lugna was the *rechtaire*, the steward, of the abbey of Lios Mór, and second in authority to the abbot.

Abbot Iarnla had heard Brother Gáeth's soft intake of breath and glanced round to see why he had paused before leaving.

'Ah, come in, Brother Lugna,' he invited, and motioned to a seat facing him on the far side of the fireplace. 'I wanted a word with you.'

Brother Lugna was in his mid-thirties; his long, straw-coloured hair was worn with the *corona spina* tonsure of Rome, which marked him out as one who followed Roman Rule, unlike his abbot who maintained the tonsure of St John, favoured by the Irish clerics. Brother Lugna's features seemed frozen in a disapproving expression. He entered and closed the door behind the wood-bearer. Then he crossed to the chair indicated by the abbot, lowered himself into it and sat without speaking.

Abbot Iarnla was elderly, with silver hair and mournful brown eyes and a figure that indicated a man who had been used to an easy and indolent way of life. He gestured towards the smoking fire.

'The wood is wet,' he explained unnecessarily. There was almost petulance in his voice.

His steward nodded absently. 'I have already reprimanded our *tugatóir*, the thatcher, for letting the woodshed roof fall into disrepair.' His tone indicated that his thoughts were elsewhere. 'He should have known better than to instruct Brother Gáeth to bring wet wood to you.'

The abbot glanced at him thoughtfully. 'I asked you to come, Brother Lugna, because I hear that you are still concerned with the well-being of Brother Donnchad. Or is it the Venerable Bróen who troubles you? I hear that in the *refectorium* this morning he announced that he had seen an angel at his window last evening.'

Brother Lugna's mouth drooped further. 'The Venerable Bróen is old and sadly his mind wanders. But it is Brother Donnchad who is of more concern to the community and me.'

'Such journeys and adventures that have fallen to the lot of Brother Donnchad can leave a marked effect upon the strongest of men,' the abbot commented.

Brother Lugna pursed his thin lips before replying. 'The community is worried for him. I am worried for him. I am told that even before he set out for the Holy Land with Brother Cathal, he was of an introspective nature and prone to moods, spending long hours in lonely contemplation.'

'Surely that is in the spiritual nature of our calling. Why, therefore, be concerned that he displays such tendencies now?' countered the abbot with a wry smile.

'I have every respect for Brother Donnchad's commitment to the Faith and to his scholarship. Nevertheless, his moods cause concern. He has sunk into gloomy contemplation ever since he returned from the Holy Land. Indeed, at times he often displays peevishness with his fellows, especially with Brother Gáeth who, I understand, was once his *anam chara* – his soul friend.' He grimaced and added, 'I always thought Brother Gáeth a curious choice as a soul friend for a scholar of Brother Donnchad's reputation. But I am told that his current attitude to Brother Gáeth is out of tune with his earlier disposition towards him.'

Abbot Iarnla sat back in his chair and clasped his hands together, leaving both forefingers extended and touching at the tips, which he placed against his lips.

'I am reminded that you joined our community just a short time after Donnchad and Cathal set out on their pilgrimage. A pity that you did not know them at that time. Things were very different then.' He paused and sighed. 'Let us consider the facts. In a way, Donnchad has lost his blood brother as well as his brother in Christ. I remember when Donnchad and Cathal first came to join us at this abbey. They were local youths from the fortress by the ford, just a few kilometres downriver from here.'

'I am well acquainted with their story, being, as you know, under the patronage of their mother, Lady Eithne of An Dún,' the steward responded in a flat voice.

'I had not forgotten. She is a most devout lady. Not only is she a staunch supporter of the Faith but has always been a supporter of our community.' Abbot Iarnla refused to be distracted from his reminiscence. 'Her sons, Cathal and Donnchad, were highly intelligent lads and Brother Cathal became one of our best teachers. Alas, it was his very learning that almost became his downfall. Maolochtair, the Prince of the Déisi, who governed the lands this abbey was built on, became jealous of his knowledge and denounced Cathal to the King at Cashel. He claimed Cathal was indulging in magical practices.'

'I have heard the tale and know that Maolochtair was old and twisted by that time,' interposed Brother Lugna.

'He was indeed. But who would dare say it? It was he who instructed Lady Eithne's husband to give this land to our founder, the Blessed Carthach, over thirty years ago, so that he could build this abbey upon it. We had to respect Maolochtair, although, to be frank, his mind was not what it once was. He was filled with suspicion against family and friend alike, thinking they all meant him harm. We tried to send Brother Cathal out of harm's way to administer the church and community at Sean Raithín, the old fortress in the mountains north of here. But Maolochtair soon followed him there with his accusations.

'Maolochtair demanded that the King at Cashel imprison Cathal for a while in order that the grave charges could be considered. The King felt bound to agree, for Maolochtair was kin through his marriage to the aunt of his own father,

Failbe Flann. Thanks to the King's sister, Sister Fidelma, Cathal was cleared. I believe it was her advice that not only secured his release but sent him and his brother, Donnchad, out of the vengeful reach of Maolochtair until that twisted man departed this earthly realm.'

'I know,' Brother Lugna replied, showing his irritation. 'I have heard the story from the Lady Eithne's own lips. Five years ago Cathal and his brother Donnchad agreed to set out on their pilgrimage to the Holy Land. A short time after they left, Maolochtair died from the *delirium tremens*.'

'Our beloved brethren succeeded in reaching the Holy Land. Ah, what joy it must have been to behold Jerusalem and walk the roads where our Lord once walked.' The abbot was smiling, seemingly lost in the pleasure of contemplating such an achievement.

'Except that the joy was not long-lived,' Brother Lugna pointed out. 'On the return journey, they were shipwrecked off the southern coast of Italy.'

'But our brethren survived,' the abbot responded.

'Survived? Indeed they were among the few who made it to the shore when their ship was wrecked. But many others, including the crew of the ship, all perished in the turbulent waves.'

'Cathal was so welcomed by the people of the city where they were brought ashore . . . what was the name of it? Tarentum? Ah yes, that's it. Tarentum. He was so welcomed that he decided to settle there. And the people immediately elevated him to be the bishop of that city.'

Brother Lugna sniffed slightly. 'Their gain was our loss and, indeed, a loss to his own brother as well as to his mother, the Lady Eithne, who still mourns him as one dead. At least Brother Donnchad felt it was his obligation to return here to us in Lios Mór.'

The abbot gazed at his steward thoughtfully and then asked softly, 'Do you imply censure of Brother Cathal?'

Brother Lugna regarded the abbot coldly. 'I did not mean to imply anything of the sort. Cathal remained in Tarentum because he felt that he had been called by the Christ to serve there. However, the point is that he remained there. The Lady Eithne feels a betrayal that he has not returned. She told me so. And his brother, Donnchad, has not been himself since his journey back to us. And it was an amazing journey. North to Rome, where I have studied; from there to our brethren in Lucca and then on to the famous Bobbio, until finally he returned to us here, bathed in glory.' The steward's voice rose with pride. 'How many of our brethren have been on such a glorious pilgrimage? Just to touch the soles of his sandals which have trodden the same earth and stone that was walked upon by our Blessed Saviour, why, that elevates the spirit in each of us.'

Abbot Iarnla's lugubrious expression did not alter, apart from a momentary twitch at the corners of his mouth.

'I doubt that,' he replied in a monotone. 'I am sure Brother Donnchad must have worn out many a pair of sandals since leaving the Holy Land on his homeward journey. The sandals that traversed the roads that were once walked by the Saviour would have long been discarded for more serviceable wear.'

Brother Lugna frowned slightly, examining Abbot Iarnla's features suspiciously. He could not make up his mind whether the abbot was being humorous at his expense or not. Abbot Iarnla's chubby features bore no sign of amusement and the abbot was not usually given to humour. The steward shrugged slightly and dismissed his suspicion.

'So,' the abbot was saying, 'what do you think is the cause of this melancholy that Brother Donnchad has displayed since his return?'

'I cannot say. Brother Donnchad has made little effort to reintegrate with the community. He spends most of his time in his cell in contemplation of some ancient books that he brought back with him, books in languages that I do not recognise. He pores over them, as if searching for something. He has even been known to miss the call to the *refectorium* for meals and, of late, Mass.'

'This is not the first time that we have spoken of his behaviour,' said the abbot with a small sigh. 'I believe that you also spoke to Brother Gáeth about it.'

'I did, but Brother Gáeth has no coherent explanation as to why Brother Donnchad now rejects his friendship as his *anam chara*. I am told that they were the closest of friends before the pilgrimage, a relationship, as I have said, that I consider unhealthy. I am informed that Brother Donnchad has now forbidden Brother Gáeth to so much as approach him.'

'For what reason?' demanded the abbot in amazement.

'That is the essence of the puzzle for it seems there is no reason that can be offered. Had it not been for the fact that

Brother Donnchad was displaying his curious behaviour to everyone in the community, I would have thought the ending of that particular relationship was to be applauded. The fact is that his behaviour is worsening. He has ceased to come to services in the chapel and will not give a reason why. Then, several days ago, he absented himself from the abbey for a full day and refused to say where he had been. To my certain knowledge, he has not eaten since yesterday and the door of his cell remains locked, contrary to the Rule and custom.'

'Yet at your request, Lady Eithne has come twice to see him because of his distressed state,' Abbot Iarnla said.

'It was in the purview of my office to suggest it,' the steward said defensively.

'So what was resolved by her visit?'

'After a short time alone with Brother Donnchad last evening, Lady Eithne met me at the gate. She was in an agitated condition. Plainly she had been reduced to tears by her encounter. I feel that I must insist that we take some action. The Rule of the abbey must be obeyed. Because of Brother Donnchad, many of the brethren are restless and uncertain as to their behaviour. There is an air of anarchy that is spreading. I find that I need your authority to take some action to rectify this situation.'

Abbot Iarnla nodded. 'Yet it is of Brother Donnchad that we speak. He is not only a great scholar but also a hero to the younger brethren, an exemplar to the others . . .'

'All because of his successful pilgrimage to the Holy Land,' pointed out Brother Lugna. 'It is because of this that his behaviour is so destructive. It cannot be allowed to continue.'

The abbot sat upright suddenly, as if making up his mind.

'You are right, Brother Lugna. I am at fault for allowing too much tolerance of Brother Donnchad's behaviour. My excuse for my delay is my respect for his achievements. Now I must confront him and demand his acceptance of the Rule of our community.'

Abbot Iarnla rose abruptly from his seat and Brother Lugna, surprised by his action, followed his example. Without a further word, the abbot turned and led the way from the room. Outside, they passed the wood-bearing Brother Gáeth, now red-faced, as he struggled with an armload of dry wood for the abbot's smouldering fire. He pressed himself against the wall to allow their passage, his head bowed. They passed by without acknowledging him.

Across the main stone-flagged quadrangle, in whose middle a fountain had been constructed around a natural spring, stood a new three-storey building made of stone. It was set in one corner of the quadrangle and two of its grey walls stood on the edge of the abbey complex. From the walls of the building the land sloped steeply down to the dark waters called An Abhainn Mór, The Great River, which marked the northern borders of Lios Mór. It was an unusual building, for most of the others in the complex, except the chapel, were made of wood. But it was clear that there was much new building work taking place across the abbey where the elderly wooden structures were replaced with ones of stone.

Abbot Iarnla moved swiftly for an elderly and rather portly cleric. Without pausing in his pace, he entered the stone building and climbed the flight of stairs to the upper floors with Brother Lugna hurrying after him. The door at the far end of the corridor on the top floor was the entrance to Brother Donnchad's *cubiculum*, literally a 'sleeping room' in Latin. Abbot Iarnla halted before it but did not knock, as was the custom. He seized the handle and turned it. The door failed to open; it was locked.

Irritated, the abbot took a step back and raised his fist, giving three sharp blows on the dark woodwork.

'Open, Brother Donnchad. It is I, Abbot Iarnla.'

He waited a few moments but there was no response.

Behind him, Brother Lugna coughed nervously. 'As I told you, this aberrant behaviour is now usual. He does not respond to any of our entreaties to open.'

Abbot Iarnla raised his fist again and gave several sharp blows to the door. Then he paused and announced in a stentorian tone, 'This is the abbot, Brother Donnchad. You are commanded to open this door.'

There was still no response. The abbot's features grew grim and bright spots of red on his cheeks showed his mortification.

'Brother Donnchad, if you do not open this door, I shall summon the means to break it open.'

As the silence continued, the abbot turned to Brother Lugna.

'Summon Brother Giolla-na-Naomh.'

Brother Lugna hurried off. When he eventually returned with the Abbey's blacksmith, Abbot Iarnla was waiting impatiently.

'Break it open,' he ordered.

Brother Giolla-na-Naomh was a tall, muscular man, as befitted his calling. His strength and willingness to do hard physical work had earned him his name 'Servant of the Saints' soon after he had arrived at the abbey and his original name had long been forgotten. The blacksmith examined the door critically for a moment. Then, waving the others to stand aside, he turned his back to the door, balanced on his left foot and with his right foot gave the lock a powerful back kick. There was a splintering of wood around the metal lock and the door crashed inwards. The lock hung for a moment from the jamb before it slowly fell with a clatter to the floor.

'You may go,' Abbot Iarnla told the blacksmith, before proceeding across the threshold. 'Brother Donnchad, I warned you—'

The abbot's voice stopped abruptly.

Brother Lugna peered into the room over his shoulder.

They could see inside clearly, for a window lit the *cubiculum*. Below it was the wooden cot and on it was stretched the occupant of the room, lying as if asleep, quiet and still.

Brother Lugna squeezed past the frozen figure of the abbot and moved to the bed. He bent down and touched the features of the man who lay there, withdrawing his hand quickly as if he had been scalded. He looked at the abbot.

'Brother Donnchad is dead,' he said flatly.

'*Attende Domine, et miserere . . .*' The abbot began to softly intone the injunction for God's mercy.

To the abbot's surprise, Brother Lugna turned the body

over on to its side so that the back was towards him. He stared at it for a moment and finally let it fall back into its original position.

The abbot paused in his prayer. 'What are you looking for, Brother Lugna? Do you think he took his own life?'

The steward stood upright and turned to the abbot. His face was paler than usual and he wore a troubled expression.

'Took his own life? Not unless he was able to stab himself twice in the back before he climbed on to the bed and lay down,' he rejoined drily.

The abbot's ruddy face blanched and he performed the sign of the Cross.

'*Lux perpetua lucent eis. Qui erant in poenis tene-brarum . . .*' he began to mutter. 'Let perpetual light shine unto them which were in the pain of darkness.'

CHAPTER TWO

'Are you telling me that you are rejecting the Faith, Fidelma?' Ségdae, Abbot of Imleach, demanded in a scandalised voice.

Fidelma stood before the abbot in the private chamber that was always set aside for his visits to the palace of Cashel. By virtue of his ecclesiastical role as Chief Bishop of Muman, Ségdae was always treated with the greatest respect when he came to see his King.

'I am not rejecting the Faith, only the life of a religieuse,' Fidelma replied patiently.

Abbot Ségdae examined her with suspicion. 'This is not good. I know that you have had concerns over the years . . .'

Fidelma raised a hand and Abbot Ségdae paused to allow her to speak.

'When I attended the school of the Brehon Morann and qualified in the study of law, which was my passion, my brother was not then King of Muman, and I needed the means

22

of supporting myself before I could make a reputation as an advocate, a *dálaigh* of the courts. My cousin, Abbot Laisran of Darú, suggested I join the house of Brigid at Cill Dara, because they needed someone with legal ability. It is some years ago since I shook the dust of that place from my sandals for reasons that I think you know well.'

Abbot Ségdae shrugged. 'One bad apple does not mean that the entire crop is ruined,' he commented.

A smile crossed Fidelma's features but there was little humour in it.

'It seems that there are many bad apples in this world. During the seven or so years that I have practised the legal arts, I have come across more than I care to enumerate – even in the palace of the Holy Father in Rome. Anyway, since leaving Cill Dara, I have based myself at my brother's court here in Cashel and sought to serve him and this kingdom, and even the High King, to the best of my ability when my opinion has been sought. The Church has little need of me to serve the Faith, but the law does have need of me.'

'So what are you suggesting?' Abbot Ségdae demanded.

'That I will no longer be a member of the religieuse in name. Many years have passed since I was truly a Sister of a community. Even before I went to Cill Dara, I was never committed to the rules and regulations of the religieuse. It was only a means of security in an uncertain world. Now, my brother often needs me at his side to advise and sit with him in matters of law and this kingdom.'

The abbot frowned briefly. 'I hear what you say, Fidelma.

I hear it and am concerned by it. Is this matter something to do with Brother Eadulf?'

A flush came to Fidelma's face.

'Eadulf? Why do you say that?' she demanded defensively.

The abbot sat back and examined her closely. 'It has been observed, Fidelma, that since your return from the Council of Autun, and the problems you encountered after you left the port of Naoned, you and Brother Eadulf have led separate lives. Why is that?'

'It is . . . it is a private matter,' Fidelma said hesitantly.

The abbot shook his head sadly. 'Anything that affects the well-being of the King's sister, that causes her to withdraw from the religieuse, must surely be of concern to me as the King's chief spiritual adviser.'

'My decision has nothing to do with Eadulf,' she insisted in annoyance. 'I needed time at Cashel while Eadulf wanted to spend some time in contemplation with the community of the abbey of the Blessed Rúan north of here. That is all.'

'All?'

'What else can there be?' she demanded petulantly.

Abbot Ségdae's voice was sorrowful. 'That, my child, is what I am attempting to find out. You and Eadulf had hardly returned here, to Cashel, when he left to go to the abbey of Rúan, while you remained here with your son, Alchú.'

'Is there anything wrong with a desire to spend some time with my son?' Fidelma's voice was fierce.

The abbot ignored her aggressive tone and continued in an even voice. 'Then you come to me and tell me that, after these many years, you wish to leave the religieuse. You must forgive me for thinking that these matters may be connected.'

There was an uneasy silence between them.

'We have known one another a long time, Fidelma,' the abbot began again. 'I know that you are possessed of a sharp mind and it is your questioning ability that stands you in good stead as an advocate in your profession. I know, too, that it often leads you to question some of the tenets of the Faith. The Faith is not something that you can question and always achieve a rational answer – that's what makes it a faith and not an art or science. It is not something that can be proven by evidence as in your law textbooks or even by rational thought.'

He saw Fidelma's lips compress in a stubborn line.

'I have told you, I accept the Faith,' she said softly. 'I am not questioning the Faith.'

'Have you spoken of this matter with your brother, the King?'

'As a matter of fact, I have. My brother Colgú has come to rely on my advice more often than before. It is known that the Chief Brehon of Muman, Baithen, is ill with a wasting sickness and has expressed his wish to withdraw into private life.'

Abbot Ségdae's eyes widened a little. 'And you would aspire to be Chief Brehon of your brother's kingdom?'

Fidelma's chin rose a little. 'Not only aspire,' she replied sharply. 'I feel that the Council of Brehons would support me in that office.'

'Baithen was of the rank of *ollamh*, the highest degree possible in law. Yet you—'

'I am of the rank of an *anruth*, the second highest degree to an *ollamh*,' snapped Fidelma. 'That has never excluded me from being consulted in legal matters even by the High King, let alone provincial kings.'

'I meant no disrespect, my child,' replied Ségdae. 'It is just that there are many others qualified as *ollamh* among the Council of Brehons of Muman. What will be their thoughts at being surpassed in office if your brother nominates you? Would they not say, ah, she is the King's sister, and that is why we have been overlooked? Would that not sow seeds of dissension within the kingdom?'

Fidelma regarded him stubbornly. 'If my brother is happy with the nomination, I cannot see why his people should dissent.'

The abbot once more gave a sad shake of his head. 'There are times, my child, when you surprise me.'

'I have come to you to announce my intention of withdrawing from the religieuse and to pursue my future as a lawyer unencumbered by other interests. As Chief Bishop of the kingdom, do I have your blessing or not?'

'It is not so simple,' the abbot replied firmly. 'I must consult about this; I must talk to your brother, the King. To be truthful, I am not certain that I have been placed in possession of all the facts.'

Fidelma flushed, her body stiffened. 'I do not tell untruths.'

The abbot held up a hand as if to pacify her. 'I did not say that you have told me anything which is not true, merely that you may have withheld some information which, perhaps, might have made me understand your reasoning better. Perhaps you are withholding that knowledge even from yourself.'

Fidelma sniffed in disapproval. 'I have told you that which is pertinent to my request, and if that is not sufficient, then I can do nothing further. By your leave, Ségdae, I will withdraw, but let me say this: I have told you my intention and, with your blessing or no, I will fulfil my design.'

Without another word, she turned and left.

Abbot Ségdae sat motionless for a few moments, staring at the door she had slammed behind her. Then he stirred and, not for the first time, sighed deeply.

'You heard that?' he asked softly.

The curtain hanging over the door-like aperture into the guestroom's sleeping quarters stirred and was pulled aside.

The abbot's steward entered. Brother Madagan was a tall man with thin, serious features and dark, brooding, deep-set eyes.

'I did.'

'And what is your comment?'

'I have a great aversion to placing a wild bird in a cage.'

The abbot frowned and then, as he understood what his steward meant, he smiled at him.

'We have known for many years that Fidelma was her own person. She will not be constrained by anyone. Once she makes up her mind as to the correctness of the course she undertakes, then there is little to be done.'

'Just so.'

'But what if she is choosing the wrong path?' queried the abbot. 'Do we not have a duty to dissuade her?'

'Better that she chooses it than she has a path chosen for her, which she then resents and comes to resent those who chose it. If it is the wrong path, she will find out soon enough and return. If it is the right path . . . well, why should we not encourage her?'

'You are ever a good counsellor, Brother Madagan. I wonder if she has heard that most of the Council of Brehons favour Brehon Aillín of the Eóghanacht Glendamnach as the new Chief Brehon?'

'I do not think that will disturb her ambition.'

Abbot Ségdae sat in thought for a moment or two before making a small grimace. 'I still feel that something is not quite right here. I believe there is more to her decision to leave the religious than a simple ambition to pursue her profession in law.'

'You refer to this separation between her and Brother Eadulf?'

The abbot shifted his weight in the chair. 'Sometimes I think that those esoteric theologists who try to persuade us that celibacy is the best form of life for those who would pursue the religious cause are right. Sometimes relationships within the communities can lead to problems.'

'Fidelma and Eadulf have shown not only their love and devotion to one another over the years but they work so well together on mysteries that would have baffled many. I need hardly remind you how they helped me when Brother Mochta and the holy relics of the Blessed Ailbe disappeared and—'

'If there is anyone more indebted to Fidelma, and to Eadulf, than myself, I have yet to meet with them,' Abbot Ségdae interrupted heavily. 'I am well aware of the debt I owe her. It is that indebtedness that makes me worried. If there is some problem between them, of which this declaration is a manifest-ation, then I must do what I can to see if a resolution can be found.'

'How will you do this?'

'I shall consult the King again. We have heard worrying news from Abbot Iarnla of Lios Mór that might become a solution to this problem.' He paused, and then smiled as if in relief at his decision. 'Indeed, that is what I shall do.'

Colgú, King of Muman, the most southwesterly and largest of the Five Kingdoms of Éireann, ran a hand through his crop of red hair and gazed at his sister with a troubled expression.

'I don't understand,' he said. 'Abbot Ségdae is well within his rights to ask you to explain why you wish to leave the religieuse.'

'And I have answered him,' snapped Fidelma, pausing as she paced up and down in front of her brother, who was seated in his private chamber. 'He should accept my state-ment and not start prying into my private affairs.'

'You gave him your reason but even you must admit that there has been much public speculation since you and Eadulf returned from the kingdom of the Bretons.' He saw Fidelma's lips thin and the fire come into her eyes, and rather than wait for the storm to erupt, he continued, 'You know it is true. It is no wonder Abbot Ségdae questions why you have made this request now.'

For a moment or two Fidelma seemed to be about to give vent to her anger but then abruptly she heaved a sigh and sank into a chair opposite her brother.

'It has nothing to do with it,' she said quietly. 'At least, nothing directly to do with it.'

Colgú was very fond of his fiery sister and he had been increasingly concerned during the past two weeks about her apparent separation from Eadulf. He had also grown fond of the Angle from Seaxmund's Ham. It saddened him to see an apparent rift in the relationship between his sister and Eadulf.

'Can't you tell me what the problem is?' he asked softly.

Fidelma made a motion of her shoulder, a half shrug, but said nothing.

'Since our parents died when you were little, you would always confide your problems to me,' pressed Colgú.

'As far as I am concerned . . .' began Fidelma sharply. Then she halted, compressed her lips for a moment before continuing in a more reasonable tone. 'If you must know, Eadulf wishes to pursue his life as a religieux. He has accepted many of the teachings of Rome and his idea, when we returned here, was to enter a community and settle. He no longer wanted to be involved in my pursuit of law. He wanted us to settle and raise little Alchú in the service of the Christ.'

Colgú nodded thoughtfully. 'He is set on that course?'

'You know he has a good mind and yet he does not realise that he is not suited for a life of contemplation and piety. But he is stubborn. He will become bored with such a life, I know it.'

'And it was over this disagreement of your opinions that he left you and went off to the community at the abbey of the Blessed Rúan?'

'We argued,' Fidelma agreed simply. 'But I told him to go. Better he find out sooner than continue in resentment.'

Her brother grimaced wryly. 'You told him to go? An order to a man such as Eadulf . . .' He left the comment unfinished.

'You know as well as I do that it was our cousin Laisran who persuaded me to join the religious,' she said. 'I am not interested in being committed to spreading the Faith but in spreading the concept of truth and justice under the law and obedience to it. With me, the law comes first and Faith comes second. That is why I have decided to withdraw from the religious and pursue my duties as a Brehon.'

Her brother smiled. 'In the expectation that I shall nominate you as my Chief Brehon when the Council next meet?'

Fidelma flushed indignantly. 'I shall not try to persuade you to do so. You know what work I have done, so I shall let my reputation be my advocate.'

'And what did Eadulf say to this?'

'As I have said, he wanted me to give it up and go to the community of the Blessed Rúan with him. I told him that if that was all he cared about, then he should go on his own. He should respect my wishes.'

'And what of Eadulf's wishes? Should those not be respected?'

'That is not the same thing.'

'Not the same?' Colgú queried sadly.

'Law is the only thing that has really interested me since I reached the *amsir togú*, the age of choice. That is why I persuaded our foster-parents to allow me to attend the school of Brehon Morann. Perhaps if I had not listened to our cousin, Abbot Laisran . . .'

'If, Fidelma? Then what?' Her brother smiled. 'You are the last person to start playing the "if" game. Have you not said before that with an "if" you could put Tara and the High King's palace in a bottle?'

Fidelma did not respond to her brother's humour and moved her hand in a gesture of dismissal.

'It does not alter the facts. I want to devote myself to the pursuit of legal matters. It has been my ambition since a child, what I was trained to do and what I have proved myself adept at. I shall leave the religious with or without Abbot Ségdae's blessing.'

'And with or without your husband's approval?'

Fidelma gazed at her brother, the fire blazing in her eyes.

'If that is the way it must be, then so be it,' she said firmly.

There was a silence and then Colgú stirred reluctantly and rose, turning towards the fire in the hearth. For a moment or two he stood staring down into the flames, one hand on the stone mantel. Then he looked at her over his shoulder.

'Very well. I must tell you that I have discussed the matter with Abbot Ségdae. You are too good an advocate to be allowed to waste your talents. But that does not mean that I am certain to support you in your bid to become Chief Brehon. I will remain neutral and it will be up to the Council of Brehons to make the final decision.'

Fidelma was unable to resist a broad smile.

'I will take the chance that they make the right decision,' she replied.

Colgú frowned sternly. 'Their decision is their decision. Meanwhile, there is something more important to think about.'

Fidelma was already turning for the door but paused now and looked expectantly back at her brother.

'There is a condition that Abbot Ségdae and I have agreed should be put to you.'

'A condition?' Fidelma returned from the door with suspicion on her features.

'You are well acquainted with the abbey of Lios Mór.' It was more of a statement than a question, for Colgú knew the answer.

'Of course. I have sat in judgement in the abbey on minor matters when Brother Cathal was in charge in Abbot Iarnla's absence.'

'But you know old Abbot Iarnla?'

'I do, but not well. I have only met him briefly.'

'This morning Abbot Ségdae and I received a messenger from him asking for assistance.'

Fidelma raised an eyebrow. 'What type of assistance?' she asked.

'Some years ago you may recall that you advised on accusations that were being made against Brother Cathal and Brother Donnchad of Lios Mór.'

'Indeed. The Prince of the Déisi, Maolochtair, had begun to see conspiracy in every quarter. But he was old, though none would dare declare him feeble of mind. He accused Cathal and his brother of conspiracy to overthrow him. Cathal and his blood brother Donnchad were of a princely family of the Déisi. I advised that they should leave on a pilgrimage and not return until a more opportune time. They left for the Holy Land and Maolochtair died while they were away. I remember it very well. I hear that Donnchad returned earlier this summer, while Cathal decided to settle in some city south of Rome.'

'That is so. Brother Donnchad has returned to Lios Mór.'

'So what is Abbot Iarnla's problem?'

'Brother Donnchad was found yesterday dead in his cell. He had been stabbed twice in the back. Yet he lay on his bed, on his back, as if in repose, and his door was locked from the inside. The abbey is in uproar.'

Fidelma's eyes widened a fraction at the news.

Colgú continued, 'Ségdae and I have sent a message, telling Abbot Iarnla that you will be setting out tomorrow for Lios Mór.'

Fidelma did not conceal her sudden excitement. During these last weeks she had found nothing to pit her intellect against and she found herself bored with doing nothing. She felt a momentary pang of guilt at dismissing her daily play with Alchú as 'nothing'. But it was Muirgen who usually nursed the child. She had also gone riding, of course, and for the occasional swim, but – she had to admit it – without Eadulf, there seemed little enjoyment in these diversions. She had even taken to asking Brehon Baithen if there were any courts in which she could sit. That was when she had learned that Colgú's Chief Brehon was ill and was resigning his office. In eighteen days, the King and his Council of Brehons would meet to make a decision on his successor and Fidelma had decided that she would put herself forward for the office. Now she could hardly contain her excitement at being offered such an investigation; if handled well, it could only enhance her reputation.

'Thank you, brother, for choosing me,' she said with a happy smile.

'It was, frankly, not my choice,' Colgú said, with a shake of his head. 'It was Abbot Iarnla who specifically requested you,' he replied dourly. 'He remembered that you had resolved the problem with Maolochtair.'

'It is still well,' Fidelma replied, undeterred.

'Then there is the condition that Ségdae and I would impose on you before you accept this undertaking,' her brother added. 'In sending to Abbot Iarnla and saying that you would attend him, we have presumed your acceptance of this condition.'

An expression of uncertainty crossed her features. 'I shall not withdraw my request to the Council of Brehons,' she said firmly.

'I did not expect you to. The condition is that you are to be accompanied by one other.'

Her expression grew dark and ominous.

'After all this time, you do not trust my experience?' she said sharply.

'On the countrary, I do trust your experience. Sometimes, however, I do not trust your emotions.'

'Who have you foisted on me to investigate this matter?' she demanded aggressively.

'Someone you have worked well with in the past and to whom my kingdom owes a great debt. I have asked Brother Eadulf to be here by this afternoon.'

Fidelma stood for a moment, saying nothing. Colgú watched the emotions chase each other across her face until she brought them under control.

'I had not imagined that you were a matchmaker, brother,' she finally said in a tone of irony.

Colgú resumed his seat before responding.

'Neither am I, sister. In such a matter as this, where the community of Lios Mór now speak of dark, supernatural deeds, I felt that I should send those best qualified to bring about a rational resolution. Do you deny that you and Eadulf have worked on such mysteries in the past and come to a logical resolution of them?'

'I do not. Yet it seems that you have not accepted what I have said about Eadulf.'

'I have understood exactly, Fidelma.'

'He will not accept this,' she said firmly. 'He will not come.'

'In that case, you are absolved from the condition and you may go alone.'

Fidelma hesitated. Her brother's words suggested that he had no doubt Eadulf would come.

'We shall see, then.'

Later, in her chamber, Fidelma sat alone and reflected on the situation. She had to admit to herself that she did hope Eadulf would come but Eadulf was a stubborn man and she had been particularly caustic with him during that last argument. She gazed moodily at the fire in the hearth as she remembered their parting. He had called her arrogant and accused her of being too concerned with her own wishes and having little or no concern for others. He had even told her that she was unwilling to tolerate other people's opinions or beliefs. That was partially untrue. She knew her own faults.

It was when Eadulf had said that she had too much pride in herself and scorned others that she had lost her temper and told him to leave. It was true that she would not tolerate ignorance or false pride in others but her own pride . . . she did not think of it as pride to have faith in her knowledge of law and to pit that knowledge against others. She did not tolerate fools gladly. That was not arrogance. She was not full of unwarranted pride or self-importance. It was only when she came up against those who would not treat her with the respect her knowledge of law warranted that she was forced to remind them that she held the second highest degree it was possible to obtain from the law schools. If they had no respect for that, then she reminded them that she was the daughter of a king and the sister of a king. It was so easy to be overwhelmed by the dictates of others that she was determined to repulse anything that she saw as an infringe-ment of her independence. Was that being overbearing and haughty, as Eadulf pointed out?

Fidelma sighed deeply. She was aware that she was trying to justify her faults and that made her more irritable. At the same time, she tried to examine her feelings for Eadulf. He was only the second man she had allowed into her life. The first had been a young warrior called Cian who had awak-ened her sensuality as a girl and then brutally discarded her for another. She had barely been eighteen years old when she had met the handsome warrior of the High King's bodyguard, the Fianna. Cian's pursuit of her had been frivolous and her life had become a turmoil of conflicting emotions. The memory of Cian had haunted her until she had met him again on a pilgrim ship and events had caused her to realise the folly of the bitter-sweet intensity of her youthful affair.

And Eadulf? Eadulf was very different to Cian. When she had first met him at the great synod held by King Oswy at Streoneshalh, she had not liked him but, by the end of the council, she reluctantly felt that he had become a friend. It had taken a long while before she had come to accept that friendship could become the basis of a partnership in marriage. Even then she had been cautious, first agreeing to a trial marriage of a year and a day, as was the custom of her people – to become his *ben charrthach* under the law of the *Cáin Lánamnus,* and see if things worked out. She respected Eadulf's intelligence; after all, he had once undertaken her legal defence when she was accused of murder and he had shown her to be innocent. She trusted him. They had been through much together. It hurt her when he did not realise just how much the profession of the law meant to her and out of this hurt she had been bitter in her attack on his proposal that they should remove from Cashel and join a community solely devoted to religious pursuits.

She stirred again and sighed.

And there was their son, little Alchú. She suddenly felt guilt as she recalled her emotions following his birth more than three years ago. They had bordered on the resentful. Initially she had felt confined by the presence of the child and a responsibility she did not want. When she was called to investigate a series of murders at the great abbey of Finnbarr, she had had a wonderful feeling of freedom and then, returning to Cashel, of depression. She loved her child; she declared it fiercely to herself. Too fiercely? After his birth she had had all manner of depressive thoughts. She even began to question whether she was ready for marriage – marriage to anyone.

Her mind turned quickly back to Eadulf. She had concerns for him. She was concerned that, under the law of her people, theirs was not a marriage of equals. She was of royal rank and Eadulf, being a foreigner, did not have equal property rights with her. Did Eadulf still feel resentment because of this? She knew that she could not really contemplate an existence without Eadulf's support. Who else would tolerate her sharp temper, which she accepted was her biggest fault? She enjoyed Eadulf's company, his friendship and his tolerance.

Perhaps she had taken it all for granted and when, a few weeks ago, he had proposed his idea of a withdrawal from Cashel . . . well, bitter words were exchanged. After he had left Cashel, she had felt a curious isolation, a loneliness, which she had tried to cover with her fierce determination to pursue the law.

She wanted to apologise to Eadulf for her temper but, at the same time, she felt that she was right; that she should be allowed her individuality and the freedom to pursue her own path in life. She had no wish to dominate but she wanted a supportive partnership. Would Eadulf see an apology as surrender? She was growing more confused than ever.

There was movement outside that caused her to look up from her meditation.

Fidelma knew who it was as soon as she heard the footfall outside the door. A smile of excitement came to her lips, which she immediately sought to control. Before she could do so there was a knock and she had called out, 'Come in, Eadulf.'

Eadulf stood uncertainly on the threshold.

In spite of her misgivings, Fidelma rose and moved towards him, both hands outstretched.

'I've missed you,' she said simply.

'And I you,' he replied slightly stiffly, although he responded to her embrace. She drew back, her eyes searching his.

'You should know at once that I have asked Abbot Ségdae for his blessing on my withdrawal from the religious.'

He was silent for a moment, his face expressionless.

'I did not doubt that you would follow that course once you had set your mind to it. I assume that you are sure that this is what you want?'

She turned back to the chair she had risen from, near the fire.

'Close the door, Eadulf. Come and sit down.' She waited until he was seated before continuing. 'I am sure,' she said simply. 'This is what I must do.'

'The status of a religious is not to be abandoned lightly,' Eadulf observed with some sadness.

'You know that I have never had any inclination to be a proselytiser of the Faith, to preach or teach, nor to spend my days in isolated contemplation or worship. I am a lawyer, Eadulf. That is my role in life.'

'But being of the religious gives one security and status,' he protested in a half-hearted fashion, aware that they had had this conversation many times.

For a moment her eyes flashed. 'I am a princess of the Eóghanacht. I am a *dálaigh* of the law courts of the Five Kingdoms. You know that I am no longer in need of such status.'

Eadulf nodded slowly. 'And soon you will be claiming the office of Chief Brehon of your brother's kingdom.'

'Who told you that?' Fidelma's voice was sharp.

Eadulf smiled briefly, without real expression. 'If you have taught me nothing else, you have taught me how to make a logical deduction. Once I heard that Brehon Baithen was ill and that the Council of Brehons will soon meet to discuss his successor, well . . .' He ended with a slight motion of his left shoulder as if to dismiss it. 'Has Abbot Ségdae given you his blessing?'

Fidelma shook her head. 'Not immediately. He suspects my leaving might have something to do with us.'

Eadulf's brow wrinkled. 'With us? I do not follow.'

'Because we have separated he thinks . . .' It was her turn to shrug.

'He looks for cause and effect,' Eadulf reflected. 'That is logical.'

'But not accurate,' replied Fidelma. 'Anyway, whether I have his approval or not, and whether I secure the office of my brother's chief legal adviser or not, I am determined to follow my career in law.'

'I suppose it was silly of me to think that I could change you,' admitted Eadulf. 'During these last weeks, I have come to realise that the cause of most of the problems in this world is the desire to change other people, to make them think as we think, or behave as we do. *Quid existis in desertum videre . . . hominem mollibus vestitum?*'

It took her a moment before she realised that he was paraphrasing the Gospel of Matthew: 'What went you out into the wilderness to see? A man clothed in soft raiment?' In other words, one shouldn't judge others by one's own standards.

'I will not attempt to put any further constraints on you, Fidelma,' he went on. 'You must do what you think best. And I . . . I must give thought to what I must do to fulfil my path in life.'

She stared at him in surprise. And suddenly she felt sorry for him. He looked very tired and resigned.

Then she mentally shook herself. She did not want to go down the path of discussing what thoughts he might have – at least, not yet.

'Have you seen my brother yet?'

'I have seen him and Abbot Ségdae.'

'And you were interested enough in their proposal to come back to Cashel?'

'Your brother is King and his proposal was more of a summons than a request. I think I have been able to reassure Ségdae that his suspicion was wrong. That your decision to leave the religious was made a long time ago.'

'So what do you think of their plan that we undertake the investigation at Lios Mór?'

'At first I was inclined to think that your brother was hatching some plot to bring us together but apparently the news of the murder of Brother Donnchad of Lios Mór is true.'

'There still might be a motive in my brother's thinking.' Fidelma grimaced. 'Nevertheless, you are right. It is true that Brother Donnchad has been murdered and the abbot has requested help in resolving the matter.' She hesitated. 'Are you prepared to work with me on this mystery?'

'I came here in answer to your brother's summons,' said Eadulf. 'But whether I work with you or not is entirely your decision. I have told him that I will not impose myself where I am not wanted.'

She glanced at his determined features and suddenly smiled softly. 'In these matters, we have always worked well together, Eadulf. I am not averse to your aid; in fact, I would more than welcome it.'

There was a moment of embarrassed silence.

'Then I shall accompany you,' Eadulf said after a while. 'If we are to set out for Lios Mór tomorrow at first light, I must find somewhere to sleep.'

'Muirgen will fix you up a bed in little Alchú's chamber,' Fidelma replied. 'He has been asking for his father this last week and will be pleased to see you. Did you come here by foot or by horse?'

'By horse, as it was the King's summons.'

'A good horse? It is a long ride tomorrow and, as you will recall, there are some steep mountain roads to climb before we reach Lios Mór.'

'You know me and horses, Fidelma,' Eadulf returned. 'I had a loan of this animal from a local farmer to whom I have promised to return it.'

Eadulf knew that Fidelma was an expert horsewoman. She had ridden almost before she had begun to walk, and so he was happy to leave the matter in her capable hands. Eadulf was never comfortable riding, although he had greatly improved in recent years but he still knew little about horses.

'Then you go to see Alchú and tell Muirgen to make you up a bed. I will go to the stables to look at your animal. We have several horses that can replace it if it is not suitable.'

They rose together and Fidelma went to the door and

opened it. She paused and suddenly turned with a quick smile.

'I am glad that you are coming with me,' she said softly.

For the first time in weeks Eadulf felt happy. He realised that he felt comfortable, at ease, being back in the familiar apartments they had shared for so long. He had a momentary feeling of having come home. That was stupid, he reminded himself. Cashel was not his home. Yet there was no denying how he felt. He regretted the argument that he had had with Fidelma, which had developed out of proportion to what he had wanted to say to her. Yet once heated words were exchanged, matters seemed to be out of his control. In the years he had been with Fidelma he had come to realise that she would never do what she did not want to do, what she thought was wrong. He regretted his attempt to make her do so. He had felt contrition for his action almost from the moment he left Cashel.

What had it all been about?

Pride, he supposed. He had never fully accepted that he was not considered equal in law with Fidelma in her own land. He had once been an hereditary *gerefa*, son of a magistrate of his own people, the Angles, and Fidelma would not have been considered his equal in the land of the South Folk, had they settled there. He had known this long before he entered into a relationship with her and had been happy to make the decision that they would settle in her brother's kingdom. But that pride, that resentment, had become a small quibbling voice at the back of his mind. He had begun to think that if they retreated into some religious community where all were regarded as equal, this would resolve matters.

Of course it would not. He should have known that better than anyone. Fidelma was not a person to be constrained in any community with rules and regulations. How many times had he seen her chafe against such confines when she encountered them? And he had been trying to confine her. That was stupid. He just hoped it was not too late to make amends.

He turned towards the door that led to little Alchú's room with a lighter heart than he had felt for a long time. He was looking forward to seeing his son again – *their* son.

CHAPTER THREE

The white light that heralded dawn had only just begun to spread over the jagged tops of the eastern hills when Fidelma and Eadulf came into the courtyard at Cashel. The stable lads were patiently waiting with their horses, already saddled for the journey. They were surprised, however, to find the young warrior, Gormán, also there, with his horse saddled and obviously prepared for a long journey. Gormán was a warrior of the Nasc Niadh, the warriors of the golden collar, élite bodyguards to the kings of Muman. He was also the son of Fidelma's friend, Della, a former *be taide,* or prostitute, who lived in the township beneath the Rock of Cashel on which the palace of the Eóghanacht rulers was situated. Fidelma had successfully defended both Della and Gormán from accusations of murder. Gormán had become one of Cashel's most trusted warriors and had shared several adventures with Fidelma and Eadulf.

'Where are you off to?' Eadulf asked after they had greeted one another.

'Off to Lios Mór with you,' grinned Gormán before turning to Fidelma. 'The King, your brother, lady, has instructed me to accompany you and put myself at your service,' he explained.

For a moment, a frown crossed her face. Then she dismissed the objection that had sprung to her mind, realising that Gormán was never intrusive and often helpful in their quests.

'Very well, we have a long ride ahead and I would like to be in the abbey of Lios Mór before nightfall.'

'Shall we go directly by way of the Rian Bó Phádraig, the old highway that takes us across the mountains?' queried the warrior.

'We shall,' affirmed Fidelma.

Eadulf noted that his horse had been exchanged for a roan-coloured cob with a luxuriant mane and tail. It was a powerful and muscular animal, well proportioned and with a proud head. But at least the breed was known for its docile and willing nature, Eadulf thought thankfully. As they mounted, Colgú suddenly appeared with Caol, the commander of his bodyguard, at his side to wish them good fortune.

'Remember that this is an important matter.' Colgú's tone was soft but serious as he addressed his sister. 'Brother Donnchad was recently back from a pilgrimage to the Holy Land and his brethren stood in awe of him, regarding him almost as a saint. That he should be killed in this mysterious manner is likely to cause alarm and dissension throughout the entire kingdom, if not beyond.'

'You know me well enough, brother. I treat all matters involving unnatural death as important,' Fidelma replied quietly, looking down at him.

'I do not doubt it,' returned Colgú, 'but truly, Brother Donnchad was no ordinary scholar. He has walked on the ground where the Christ has stepped and preached. That makes him venerated throughout the kingdom.'

'I understand, brother,' Fidelma assured him. With a quick lifting of her hand, she set off through the gates of the palace. Eadulf and Gormán urged their horses after her.

They trotted down the slope that led into the township nestling in the shadow of the grey walls that rose on the great limestone outcrop. For a while, until they were well beyond the township, they did not travel at more than a walking pace, nor did they engage in any conversation. Then on the open road beyond, Fidelma urged her grey into a quick trot. She was riding her favourite horse, a gift from her brother bought from a Gaulish horse trader. She called it Aonbharr, 'the supreme one', after the magical horse of Manannán mac Lir, the ocean god, which could run across sea or land and could not be killed by man or god. It was an ancient breed, short neck, upright shoulders and body, slight hindquarters with a long mane and tail. The Gauls and even the Romans had bred the type for battle. It had a calm temperament, displayed intelligence and, more importantly, had agility and stamina. It could easily outrun the cobs ridden by Eadulf and Gormán.

Fidelma and Eadulf had not talked further of their quarrel or the matter that had led to it since the previous day and both felt, in their own ways, grateful for Gormán's presence, which restricted a return to any such conversation. Eadulf was happy to examine the countryside as they took the main highway running south towards the distant mountain ranges, which stood as a barrier between the plain of Cashel and the abbey of Lios Mór. They passed several disused fortresses that had once guarded the ancient highway; each of them had names, such as the *rath* of blackthorns or Aongus' *rath*. The most impressive of these forts, in Eadulf's opinion, rose on a great mound called the Hill of Rafon. Fidelma had pointed it out on several previous occasions when they had passed it. She did so with an air of pride because, she had told him, it was the former seat of the Eóghanacht kings of Muman, a place where they had been inaugurated and took the oath of kingship in ancient times, before they transferred their capital to Cashel.

By trotting and cantering over the flat plain they made good time in reaching the banks of the broad River Siúr where a settlement had risen around the ancient fortress appropriately named Cathair, the stone fort. Just south of here, Eadulf recalled, were caves in the limestone cliffs overlooking the river, in which he and Fidelma had sheltered on a journey back from the far west. It was there that he had been worried about Fidelma's depressive moods following the birth of Alchú. And here the old road turned slightly to the south-east, following the banks of the Siúr towards the distant hills. They kept the river to their right before moving away to follow the old road through good, flat farming country before swinging back south-westerly to return to the barrier of the Siúr again. The hours sped by and no one spoke beyond an occasional remark on the scenery through which they passed.

It was time to rest and water the horses, and to eat something. Rath Ard dominated this area, the fortress seat of one of the powerful nobles of the Múscraige Breogáin. Gormán wondered if it was Fidelma's intention to seek hospitality at the fortress. Fidelma replied that she preferred to press on rather than undergo the rituals of hospitality that would be undoubtedly forced on them and perhaps delay their journey by another day. For the same reason, she did not want to call at the nearby abbey that Fionán the Leper had established near the banks of the River Siúr which was named after him – Ard Fhionáin, Fionán's Height.

The abbey stood by a natural ford across the river and a small settlement had sprung up around it. It was a good location, set in pleasant scenery and provided a base for traders coming upriver to transfer their goods to smaller barges or pack animals before coming to the more inaccessible reaches of the kingdom. But the ford had always presented a problem, for the currents were fairly strong. In fact, the abbey of Fionán provided a 'watcher by the ford' to ensure that no accident went unobserved. A bell hung ready to be rung to summon help if needed. But, as they rode beyond the abbey walls, both Fidelma and Eadulf were surprised to see a new bridge, its timbers hardly seasoned, now spanning the river.

'It was only recently built,' explained Gormán, when Eadulf

commented on the fact. 'The members of the abbey community built it.'

Fidelma did not seem to hear, her mind was occupied with
other thoughts. In fact, she was reflecting that it was here, at
this very spot, that she and Eadulf had first heard that their
nurse Sárait had been murdered and their son Alchú had been
kidnapped by the evil leper Uaman, Lord of the Passes of
Sliabh Mis. Gormán had been in love with Sárait and was
initially accused of her murder. She glanced anxiously at
Gormán but there was no reason he would know of the connection. She wondered if Eadulf remembered and if he would
mention it, but if he did remember, he gave no indication of it.

A tavern stood just before the new bridge. Gormán cleared
his throat anxiously. He knew that Fidelma wanted to press
on but they had been riding for some hours.

Fidelma took the hint; she realised that the horses did need
watering. But she insisted that they did not stop long, only
time enough to have their horses watered and to take food
and drink in moderation for themselves.

They sat outside the inn, for the day was cloudless and
warm. A stable lad attended to their horses while the innkeeper
brought them their refreshments. The man had no other
customers, so he remained with them and talked about the
possibilities of a good harvest, the fine summer and the number
of newcomers who were building their homes around the abbey.
Fidelma was clearly impatient to continue the journey.

'Is the bridge safe to cross?' Eadulf inquired of the
innkeeper as he was finishing his drink.

'The bridge safe to cross?' The innkeeper was a burly man, with balding head and slightly protruding eyes, and his jowls shook with laughter. 'Bless you, Brother, an entire troop of the king's horsemen could ride back and forth several times without disturbing one beam of it.'

'I am not concerned with a troop of cavalry but only with my well-being,' replied Eadulf dourly.

Before the conversation could be prolonged, Fidelma stood up and signalled to the stable lad to bring their horses. Gormán settled with the innkeeper and soon they were crossing the new bridge. Indeed, the bridge was built strongly, as it had to be, for the rushing waters of the Siúr beneath them pounded against its supports with alarming ferocity. The great sawn tree trunks on which the crossbeams rested had been driven deep into the river bed and there were about fifteen on each side. The width of it, like the Irish roads, according to Brehon Law, was broad enough to take two carriages, with room to spare between them. It was an easier crossing than last time, Eadulf remembered, when he had had to ford the rushing waters on horseback.

'Well, a bridge certainly makes the old roadway easier to traverse,' Fidelma observed. 'We should make better time now.'

In fact, it was hardly any time before they came to the next natural obstacle across the track. This was a smaller river called the Teara, a tributary of the Siúr that they had just crossed. The ford here was easy, for there was an island in the middle of the river that divided it into two small crossings.

'This is where they say the road took its name,' Gormán suddenly said, tired of the silence of their journey.

'I have travelled this road several times,' Eadulf replied, 'and never once worked out why it is called the "Track of Patrick's Cow".'

'Why it is called Rian Bó Phádraig?' Gormán hesitated and glanced at Fidelma. 'There is an old legend.'

'You may as well tell it,' she invited. She had heard the legend before.

'Well, the old folk say that the Blessed Pádraig, who helped bring the Faith especially to the northern kingdoms, had a cow and this cow had a calf. The cow and her calf were peacefully grazing on the banks of the Teara, this very river we are crossing. The story is that a thief from near Ard Mór stole the calf. The cow was consumed with anger at the loss of her calf and chased the thief all the way across the mountains to Ard Mór, and its tracks made this road.'

Eadulf pursed his lips sceptically.

'But doesn't this road lead from Cashel to Lios Mór?' he pointed out in pedantic fashion.

'And continues all the way on to Ard Mór,' Gormán added, with a grin at his puzzled companion.

'It is a legend,' Fidelma intervened impatiently. 'It is not to be taken literally. The road is far older than the time of the Blessed Pádraig. It joins the Slíge Dalla, the Way of the Blind, at Cashel, which, as you recall, is one of the five great roads that lead to Tara. There is no way of knowing why legends come about. The Blessed Ailbe converted our kingdom to the new Faith long before Pádraig arrived here and before Declan built his abbey at Ard Mór. Why would Pádraig have a cow grazing on the banks of the Teara River of all the rivers in Ireland? It makes no sense.'

'Legends,' Gormán solemnly announced, 'are often the result of half-understood events, or events that have become embroidered out of all proportion by their retelling.'

'Yet they are usually founded in truth,' observed Eadulf.

'The question is, how do you find that truth?' Fidelma retorted.

'Doesn't the legend become its own truth?' asked Gormán.

Eadulf chuckled. 'You are becoming a philosopher, Gormán.'

The young warrior turned to him and, without warning, lunged forward, knocking Eadulf off his horse with a single blow of his hand. As he fell, Eadulf was aware of a curious whistling sound in the air. Something thudded into a tree just behind his horse. Gormán yelled to Fidelma to take cover and at the same time drew his sword. He urged his cob forward towards a group of trees a short distance away along the side of the highway.

Fidelma had time to see a figure with drawn bow release a second arrow before she slithered from her mount and crouched down. She heard it whistle past, wide of its intended target.

'Stay down!' she cried, as she saw Eadulf trying to rise from the dust in the road where he had fallen.

'Has Gormán gone mad?' he protested, not having seen

the arrow that had nearly embedded itself in him but was now stuck in the tree.

'He just saved you from being shot,' Fidelma replied grimly, peering forward. She ignored Eadulf's exclamation of surprise as she saw Gormán, sword swinging, attack the man who was trying to place a third arrow into his bow. The sword struck him on the side of the neck and he gave a cry and went down. A second man was already mounted on a horse and was urging it away at a gallop. Gormán pursued him for a short distance but it was clear the man had a fresh, and therefore faster, mount. In fact, Gormán was also handicapped by an unwillingness to abandon Fidelma and Eadulf in case there were other attackers on the road. He wisely reined in his horse and gave up the pursuit. By the time the young warrior resheathed his sword and returned to them, the second man had disappeared.

'I am sorry, I didn't catch him,' he said as he rejoined them. 'I might recognise him again, though. He was a thin man with long hair as white as snow.'

'Elderly?' asked Fidelma.

Gormán grimaced briefly. '*Bánaí*,' he replied, using a word that meant someone whose hair, skin and eyes lacked normal coloration. Fidelma had only seen such a person twice before and remembered the whiteness of their hair and skin and the pinkness of their eyes.

'Robbers, do you think?'

'Hard to tell. Assassins certainly, for if their arrows had struck home . . .' He shrugged.

'I have you to thank for my life, Gormán' Eadulf began awkwardly.

'That is my duty, Brother Eadulf,' he replied quickly, walking across to the tree and extracting the arrow. He examined it with a shake of his head. 'Nothing to indicate an origin. Well crafted, though, but any one of a hundred fletchers could have made it.'

'Let us see if we can get any explanation from our would-be killer,' Fidelma said.

Gormán's mouth drooped cynically. 'I doubt it, lady. My sword bit deep.'

When they reached the body of the assailant, they could see that the man was certainly dead. He was not old although his hair was streaked grey. It was cut fairly short and his face was closely shaven. The man was tanned, which proclaimed he led an outdoor life. Regarding this, Fidelma bent to look at the hands of the man. They were neither the rough callused hands of a field worker nor the soft hands of someone unused to hard work. His clothes were nondescript, a field worker's clothing of furs and leather. The clothing indicated someone who was neither wealthy nor poor. There was no purse on him, nothing to identify him.

It was Fidelma who pointed out that the sword that still hung from his belt was of good-quality workmanship, a warrior's sword rather than some cheap ornament. It would not be chosen by someone who had little means to purchase it. There was also a dagger with an embossed handle, which was unusual for a field worker. He had a quiver of arrows hanging on one side of his belt. His bow lay where it had been discarded when he received his death blow from Gormán. Fidelma picked it up and turned it over in her hands. It was well made of yew wood, a war bow rather than one used just for hunting. She turned and handed it to Gormán, asking a silent question with raised eyebrows.

'A professional warrior's bow,' he muttered, having given it a quick examination. 'Well strung.' He paused and tested the pull on it. 'It would take a trained bowman to pull it. There is good tension on it and a secure grip.'

Fidelma knelt again beside the body and examined it closely.

'He wears no ornamentation, which is unusual. There is nothing decorative on him. But see here, what do you make of this, Eadulf?' She pointed to the neck where there was a slight discoloration, like bruising or an abrasion. Eadulf's mind went back to the customs of his own people.

'The mark of a slave collar?' he hazarded. 'The slaves among my people are often given iron collars to indicate their position.'

An expression of distaste crossed Fidelma's features. Then she turned to Gormán.

'What do you think?'

The young warrior pursed his lips in thought for a moment and then replied, 'Brother Eadulf has a point. I have seen Saxon slaves at the seaports wearing iron collars. But I doubt this man is a Saxon. Given his weaponry, and despite his clothing and lack of ornamentation, this might be the mark of a torc.' His hand went automatically to the circlet of gold at his own neck, showing that he was of the élite warriors of the Nasc Niadh.

'You think he was a warrior of rank?' demanded Eadulf in surprise.

'The thought that he was a professional warrior did not escape me,' Fidelma affirmed.

'But he is not of the Nasc Niadh, lady,' pointed out Gormán.

'We are not the only people whose élite warriors wear the torc of gold. It is an old custom, even among peoples in Gaul and among the Britons.'

'Are you saying that this person is some élite warrior in disguise?' repeated Eadulf. 'I do not understand.'

Fidelma shook her head. 'We are not saying anything except that this man poses several questions. Why would he and his companion be waiting here on this road? Were they robbers lying in wait for any passer-by? Why did they attempt to kill us first? They could have simply threatened us if the intention was to rob.'

'Given the quick retreat of the second man, perhaps they did not have sufficient courage to do so and thought to rob us after we were killed,' Gormán offered.

'Or was it us in particular they were waiting for?' mused Eadulf.

'You mean that they might have been waiting specifically to ambush us?' Fidelma queried. She gave a shake of her head. 'That's absurd.'

But Gormán was frowning thoughtfully. 'Perhaps not, lady.

After all, you and Eadulf have made many enemies these last few years. There's no denying it. Uncovering guilt and meting out justice inevitably causes one to gather enemies like a bee gathers honey. This man was lying in wait out of sight with a good bow. Had I not spotted him move forward to release his arrow and pushed Brother Eadulf from his horse, that arrow would have surely transfixed him. He drew quickly, this man, and his next arrow was already on the way to you, lady, when I cried to you to take cover. This archer was no novice when it came to the use of the bow.'

'In other words,' Fidelma said quietly, 'you think these men were professional assassins whose aim was to kill Eadulf or myself?'

'Or all three of us,' added Gormán with a grimace. 'I have gathered enemies as well. Although you were his first targets.'

'This might have been a means to prevent us going to Lios Mór,' Eadulf suddenly remarked.

Fidelma stared at him a moment and then turned thoughtfully to Gormán.

'When my brother, Colgú, asked you to accompany us, did he say that he suspected something like this would happen?' she asked.

The young warrior shook his head quickly. 'Your brother, the King, felt that you might have need of me. That is all. If he had such a concern, then surely he would have suggested I bring a couple of companions with me. As I have said, lady, you have gained many enemies in your career. Those whose crimes are found out always think they are hard done by when caught and punished. They often swear to exact revenge on those responsible for their undoing.'

Fidelma glanced down at the face of the dead man. 'If he is an enemy, I do not recognise him. Anyway, we are speculating without knowledge. He and his companion might just have been robbers. But we will keep a careful watch in case his companion doubles back. We'll take this man's horse and weapons. Perhaps we will eventually be able to identify him by them. There is nothing else. We will have to leave the body in this ditch. I'm afraid the wolves and other scavengers will have to dispose of it.'

Gormán bent swiftly to the task of removing the weaponry from their assailant and tied the bundle up before placing it on the brown pony that was tethered nearby. He glanced quickly over the beast before he did so and said, 'The horse is unmarked as well. Nothing to tell where it came from other than the breed is popular in these parts.'

Fidelma compressed her lips in annoyance at herself. She should have considered that the horse might have carried an identifying brand. Gormán had diplomatically reminded her of the question that she should have asked.

'Shall we continue on this road?' asked Eadulf uneasily, distracting her. 'If this was an attempt to prevent us reaching Lios Mór then it might be better to choose another route.'

She remounted her horse and turned to him. 'It is the quickest route and, as I said, we want to be at the abbey before nightfall. The road swings to our left towards the Gallagh, the river that passes through the glen of stones. You may remember it. We shall follow it through the glen. At the head of the glen is the little chapel of Domnoc where we can rest the horses and refresh ourselves at the hostel before starting the climb through the mountains. We will follow the track up Cnoc Mhaol Domnaigh. It will not take us long to reach Lios Mór once we are through the mountains.'

Eadulf remounted and glanced at Gormán. 'Can you manage leading that pony?' he asked, indicating the dead man's mount.

'I can,' the young warrior answered cheerfully. He knew well that Eadulf was not a good horseman and when it came to climbing through the mountains he felt he would be better able to handle their newly acquired pony.

'Then let us start out again,' Fidelma called, already moving off. 'But this time let us proceed with caution.'

They rode on with senses alert but saw no one until they reached the little chapel of Domnoc, which stood by the road-side at the head of Glen Gallagh. A thickset man was working with a hoe in the field nearby and, at the sight of them, he stopped his work and approached them with a cheery greeting. He turned out to be the brother in charge of the chapel, Brother Corbach. His cheeks were red and he had bright sky-blue eyes. He recognised Fidelma immediately from previous trips she had made along this road, acknowledged Eadulf and noted Gormán's gold torc. With some deference, he set about offering what hospitality he could. 'I can provide good beds for the night, lady,' he added but Fidelma shook her head.

'We mean to cross the mountain and be in Lios Mór before nightfall if the weather stays fair,' she said.

Brother Corbach glanced up at the sky. 'It will be a fine evening.' He paused before asking: 'Is it because of the news from Lios Mór that you are journeying there?'

'The news?' asked Fidelma, curious at the man's question.

'Why, the news of the murder of Brother Donnchad,' replied the man. 'Travellers passing on this road have told me of it.'

'And have there been many travellers today?' Fidelma asked, deflecting his question.

'Not many today. Why do you ask, lady?'

It was Gormán who pointed to the horse that he had been leading, the bow and quiver hanging from its saddle.

'Did two men pass here, one being an archer riding this horse with those weapons on him?'

Brother Corbach looked puzzled but examined the horse and weapons more closely. Then his eyes widened and he nodded slowly.

'Two men passed early this morning and halted only for some water. What happened to the archer who rode that steed?'

'I killed him,' replied Gormán quietly.

The religieux looked shocked. 'That is not a good jest, my friend.'

'It is not meant as one,' Fidelma intervened solemnly. 'The man and his companion tried to ambush us. My companion here killed one assailant and chased the other away. Did you know either of them? Had you seen them before?'

The man shook his head slowly. 'Both men were strangers to me. They came over the mountain from the south.'

'And their speech? Could you tell where they came from by their tones of speech?'

Brother Corbach reflected a moment or two. 'I would say that the one who rode this horse might have been of the Uí Liatháin. The other man, who had strange, white hair, could have been a foreigner.'

Gormán frowned. 'Uí Liatháin? They are always causing trouble,' he muttered softly.

The clans of the Uí Liatháin dwelt to the south, beyond the river An Tuairigh. They claimed to be Eóghanacht but not of the line of Corc who had founded the royal dynasty at Cashel. Instead, they claimed that an ancestor called Bressal had been King of Muman. It was a claim that the genealogists of Eóghanacht of Cashel did not recognise. They were also boastful that the daughter of their chieftain, Tasach, had been wife to Laoghaire, who had been High King when Pádraig had arrived. It was said that she had converted to the new Faith and ensured her son, Lugaidh, was raised as the first Christian High King.

'What made you think the other was a foreigner?' asked Fidelma.

'He never spoke but his appearance was strange.'

'And did they say anything to you when they stopped for water?' pressed Fidelma.

'Simply to ask if there had been any travellers on the road, but that is a question everyone asks, just as you have.'

Fidelma noticed the religieux hesitate. 'You have remembered something else?'

'It is just that I recall that they were specific. They wanted to know if there were any travellers going south from Cashel.'

'South to Lios Mór?' Gormán pressed, with a meaningful glance at Fidelma.

'If you go south from here, then any traveller would come to Lios Mór,' Brother Corbach pointed out pedantically.

'That is true, Brother,' Fidelma agreed. 'And now we shall avail ourselves of your hospitality, although we must be brief for we must continue our journey soon. Can you fodder our horses as well?'

'That I can, lady. Perhaps I may have some help . . .?' He glanced from Gormán to Eadulf.

'I will help you with the horses,' Gormán offered.

A short time later they were all seated round the table in Brother Corbach's little *bruden*, or hostel for travellers, eating cold meats, cheeses and bread, washed down with local ale.

'So,' Fidelma said, after a while, 'what have the travellers been saying about the death of Brother Donnchad? You mentioned that you have heard news of his murder from them.'

Brother Corbach's features assumed a worried expression. 'Most were shocked by the news. Brother Donnchad was a venerated scholar who had recently travelled to the Holy Land in the east.'

'And did anyone have an opinion about his death?' asked Eadulf.

'They say that Brother Donnchad was found stabbed to death in his cell, but the door was locked from the inside. They speak of some supernatural vengeance.'

Fidelma could not refrain from a cynical sniff.

'What sort of supernatural vengeance?' Eadulf queried quickly.

Brother Corbach shrugged. 'I merely relate what the travellers say. They ask how the blessed man could be slain in this fashion. How could he be killed while the perpetrator could pass through stone walls as though they did not exist?'

'Usually one finds that the perpetrator in fact passed through the door or the window,' Fidelma replied firmly. 'I have never come across a murder committed by a wraith or any other spirit.'

The hostel keeper frowned glumly. 'Of course, lady. I merely echo what travellers say.'

The conversation turned to other local gossip, mainly on the current condition of the roadway over the mountain, for each section of road, by law, had to be maintained in good order by the local chief or noble responsible for the land through which it passed.

A short time later, the three were testing the conditions themselves. The roadway was now no more than a well-kept track, over the broad shoulder of Cnoc Mhaol Domhnaigh. The track led through a small gap in the mountains, with the summit of the mountain to the west of them and another peak to the east, called Cnoc na gCnámh, which Eadulf interpreted as the Mountain of Bones. On the southern slopes, the track dropped, winding through a wooded valley that was called the Caoimh, which meant 'gentle' and 'calm', after the name of the clan who dwelt there. They descended sharply, keeping a gushing stream to their right and crossing it before it was joined by a larger river descending from the left. Fidelma explained to an inquisitive Eadulf that it was called the river of the rough glens. From here they could now see southwards to the broad stretch of An Abhainn Mór, The Great River, and beyond it to where a complex of buildings, surrounded by wooden walls, rose on its southern bank.

'Lios Mór,' Fidelma remarked in satisfaction. 'We shall be within the abbey long before nightfall.'

Gormán was frowning. 'It is some time since I was last at Lios Mór, lady,' he said slowly, 'but there appear to be a lot of changes.'

Fidelma looked again towards the complex. Then she nodded. 'There seems to be a great deal of new buildings.'

'There are men still at work there,' pointed out Eadulf as he gazed at the distant abbey. 'New buildings suggest that the abbey is prospering.'

'Not just new buildings either,' Gormán observed. 'They seem to be replacing the wooden buildings with ones of stone. Someone must have endowed the abbey with wealth.'

CHAPTER FOUR

Fidelma and Eadulf were relaxing in chairs before the glowing fire in the chamber of Abbot Iarnla. One of the brethren who attended the abbot had presented them with the traditional cup of mead to refresh themselves after their journey, before withdrawing. Now they were alone with the Abbot and his dour-faced steward. The abbot reclined in his comfortable chair to one side of the hearth while his *rechtaire*, Brother Lugna, sat upright in his chair on the other. He was clearly not at ease. But it had been the steward who had greeted them, albeit somewhat stiffly, at the gates of the abbey before he brought them to the abbot's chamber. They had left Gormán in the hands of the *echaire*, who looked after the stables, so that he could help attend to the horses and ensure their comfort.

'It is some time since I have visited Lios Mór,' Fidelma was saying. 'It seems that the abbey is prospering.'

'How so?' inquired the abbot.

'I see that much building work is going on here.'

'We have to move with the times,' Brother Lugna intervened defensively. 'The old wooden buildings were fine for our founders over three decades ago but our community has grown quickly and now we must put up buildings that will last and proclaim the importance and purity of the community.'

'As you say, it is some time since you were here,' the abbot added, 'and it is sad that your coming now is caused by the death of a distinguished member of our brotherhood.'

'Other than yourself and your steward, who knew that we were coming to Lios Mór?' Eadulf asked.

The elderly abbot frowned for a moment, considering the question. 'I did not think it a secret,' he replied. 'I suppose the word has spread through the community, and I certainly informed the Lady Eithne, the mother of poor Brother Donnchad.'

'Is there something the matter?' asked Brother Lugna. 'Should your coming have been kept quiet?'

'We were attacked on the road here,' explained Eadulf. 'It was almost as if the attackers were lying in wait for us.'

Abbot Iarnla registered his surprise. 'Are you saying that this attack had some connection with your coming to investigate Brother Donnchad's death?'

'Perhaps there was no connection at all,' Fidelma replied quickly. 'They could simply have been robbers waiting to attack any passer-by. But it does seem curious that they attacked with the obvious intention of killing us rather than merely threatening and robbing us. They had the advantage of the ambush.'

'What happened to them?' Brother Lugna asked.

'Gormán, our bodyguard, killed one and the other ran off.'

There was a silence. Abbot Iarnla looked shocked. His steward frowned as he considered the matter.

'Therein is the answer to your question,' Brother Lugna's tone was dismissive. 'They saw you had a warrior with you, a member of the King's bodyguard, and rather than pit their strength against his, they decided to attack first. They were just cowardly robbers, no doubt. I will be frank with you, Sister Fidelma. I was not in favour of the abbot's decision to bring you here.'

Fidelma regarded him with surprise at his abrupt change of subject. She smiled thinly. 'May I ask why not?'

'I believe—'

'My *rechtaire* believed that the matter should be resolved within the abbey community,' Abbot Iarnla intervened hastily, with an uncomfortable glance at Brother Lugna. 'He believes that, as abbot, I have the power of judgement and punishment in such matters. But this abbey does not subscribe to the Penitentials.'

The steward gave a disdainful sniff and Eadulf noted the tension between him and the abbot. 'So I take it you believe in the Penitentials, Brother Lugna,' he observed. 'I see that you wear the tonsure of Saint Peter and so favour the Rule of Rome.'

'As do you, Brother Eadulf. I studied five years in Rome.'

'Where do you originate from, Brother Lugna?' asked

Fidelma. 'I do not hear the local accents of this kingdom in your voice.'

'I am from Connachta, of the Uí Briuin Sinna of the Plain of the Sea.' The announcement was a simple statement of fact, without pride.

'Then you are a long way from home, Brother Lugna.'

'The Faith is universal and whether one is in Rome or Lios Mór, or even in Connachta, one is among brethren if they follow the true teachings.'

There was an uncomfortable silence for a moment. Eadulf was aware of a growing dislike for the arrogant young Brother Lugna.

Abbot Iarnla gave a hesitant smile. 'Well, we are glad no harm befell you and your companions on your journey here, Fidelma. The news of the attack on you, for whatever cause, is alarming. We will offer a special prayer of thanks in the chapel tonight for your safe arrival. I believe your coming here to preside over this important matter is necessary. I would trust no one else with it.' He glanced at his steward with a curious expression they could not interpret. 'That is why I have overruled the advice of my steward. Your judgement, at the time when Maolochtair tried to harm both Donnchad and Cathal, saved them from a greater harm as well as saving Maolochtair from his own fantasy. That is why I requested that you come to help us.'

It sounded almost as if he were trying to explain his reasons to his steward.

'I understand that Brother Cathal remains in Tarentum and may never return to Lios Mór,' Fidelma observed.

'Cathal has accepted the *pallium* offered by the people of Tarnetum. They call him Cataldus now,' Brother Lugna replied. The sour tone in his voice made it clear that he did not approve.

'I remember when Cathal was acting abbot. It was when I was sitting in judgement at the court here,' Fidelma continued.

'Ah yes. I was away at a Council at the abbey of Imleach at the time and appointed Cathal to take charge in my absence,' replied the elderly abbot. 'Brother Lugna, of course, was not with us then. He did not join us until three years ago.'

'Three years? A short time to have risen to be *rechtaire* of the abbey,' commented Eadulf softly.

'Blessed are those who can recognise talent in others,' Brother Lugna replied almost pugnaciously.

After a quick frown of disapproval at Eadulf, Fidelma turned her gaze to the abbot. 'But you have been abbot here a long time, Iarnla,' she said. 'You must have known Cathal and Donnchad since they were young lads.'

'I came here when our blessed founder, Carthach, whom we lovingly refer to by the pet name of Mo-Chuada, was still alive. He died in the very same year as your own father, King Failbe Flann. Sadly, you did not know either of them, Fidelma.'

A momentary melancholy crossed Fidelma's features. 'I was a babe in arms when my father died,' she replied quietly. She had often expressed regret that she had never known her father and barely remembered her mother who had also died when she was young.

'Your father and the Blessed Carthach were good friends. When the Uí Néill drove Carthach and his community out of Raithean, they fled south here to the Kingdom of Muman. Your father offered Carthach lands near Cashel to set up a new community but that holy man had a vision to come to this place, for he had passed through this country some years before. Did you know that Carthach actually healed your father of an ailment in his eye?'

Fidelma looked surprised. 'I have not heard that story.'

'Your father was distressed, for the King of Laighin was hard pressed by a revolt led by a distant relative, Crimthann mac Aedo Díbchíne, who had gathered support to challenge him for the kingship. King Failbe had concluded a treaty of friendship with King Fáelán, son of Colmán of Laighin. He promised that he would lead his warriors to assist him in times of crisis. Your father's ailment caused him to be blind in one eye. To his anguish this meant he could not lead his warriors into battle. The Blessed Carthach treated him and cured the disease in his eye. Your father and his warriors joined Fáelán's army, together with those of Conall, lord of Clann Cholmai, whose sister was married to Fáelán. They defeated Crimthann and his rebels at the Ford of the Smith, Áth Goain, on the River Lifé.'

Fidelma smiled sadly. 'I knew of the victory of Áth Goain. It is a story told by the bards of my family. But I did not know of Carthach's intercession with my father.'

'It happened four years before your birth, the death of your father and the death of the Blessed Carthach all occurred in that one fateful year. It was just before those events that I heard that Mo-Chuada, the Blessed Carthach, had been offered this land by Maolochtair of the Déisi, and I came and joined him. Carthach was a great man, a great educator.'

'But you say he died in the same year as my father. Is that when you became abbot?'

Abbot Iarnla chuckled with a shake of his head. 'Bless you, child, I was still a young man. I could not have risen to such a height as abbot. Mo-Chuada's maternal uncle, Cuanan, became abbot here. He died twenty years ago. That was when I took over.'

'So there is little about the community here that you do not know,' Fidelma said seriously.

'I admit to the sin of pride in that,' confirmed the abbot.

'Then perhaps you can answer a question that has puzzled me. Is it usual in this community for a member to have a key to their *cubiculum* and to lock it?'

The abbot shook his head immediately. 'It is not usual but there are exceptions.'

'So Brother Donnchad was an exception? Why was that?'

There was some hesitation before Abbot Iarnla replied. 'He requested a key because he had returned from his pilgrimage to the Holy Land with some relics that he wished to keep safe.'

Fidelma's brow furrowed as she considered his reply. 'You mean that he was worried there might be thieves among your brethren?'

'That is an insult to our community,' intervened Brother Lugna, whose cheeks had coloured.

'It is not I who am insulting them,' Fidelma pointed out. 'What other interpretation can be placed on why Brother Donnchad wanted a key to lock his cell?'

Brother Lugna's mouth closed firmly. Abbot Iarnla was also silent for a moment while he seemed to consider the answer.

Fidelma looked from one to the other. Then she insisted softly, 'How can I investigate this matter if I am not in possession of all the facts?'

Abbot Iarnla lowered his head. 'Perhaps my steward should explain matters,' he said in resignation. 'He dealt with them.'

Brother Lugna hesitated. Fidelma faced him, waiting. Then he sighed. 'It is true that, when Brother Donnchad came back, he returned with some things which he said he had picked up on his pilgrimage. He wanted them kept safe while he considered them.'

'Considered them?' queried Eadulf.

'They were supposed to be mostly manuscripts rather than objects,' explained the steward. 'Like his brother, Cathal, Brother Donnchad was a scholar of many languages, of Greek and Hebrew as well as Latin, and also Aramaic. I never saw the documents, for he kept them hidden.'

'The abbey here has a renowned *scriptorium*, a great library containing many such manuscripts,' Fidelma pointed out. 'Why did he not simply place the documents there? Surely the library is secure enough? What made these manuscripts so precious they had to be locked elsewhere?'

Brother Lugna raised his shoulders and let them drop in a resigned gesture. 'As I say, I never saw them nor were they found in his cell after his death.'

Fidelma's eyes narrowed for a moment and she looked at the abbot. 'Did you see them, Abbot Iarnla?'

The abbot had not.

'Anyway,' the steward continued, 'Brother Donnchad seemed so concerned, so anxious, that we decided to humour him and have a lock made for his door.'

'Not simply a bolt on the inside?'

'He was specific about a lock and key.'

'Who made the lock and key?'

'Our own smith, Brother Giolla-na-Naomh. He holds the rank of *flaith-goba*,' he added with a note of pride.

Fidelma knew that smiths had three distinctions of rank according to their qualifications, and the *flaith-goba*, or chief smith, had knowledge of all metalworking. The other two ranks were limited in both the metals they worked and the artefacts they could produce.

'How many keys to this lock did he make?'

'He was instructed to make only one and I presume that he made only one,' replied the steward.

'Presumption is not fact,' observed Fidelma.

It was Abbot Iarnla who said: 'When we could not gain entrance to Brother Donnchad's cell, I summoned Brother Giolla-na-Naomh to help us. He had to break down the door.

76

Had he made an extra key, he would have fetched it to save breaking the door.'

It was a good point but Fidelma was not entirely satisfied.

'You say that you decided to humour Brother Donnchad in his demand for a key. "Humour" seems a curious word to use.'

Abbot Iarnla and Brother Lugna exchanged an uncomfortable glance.

'Brother Donnchad was—'

'He had begun to behave in a curious fashion,' interrupted Brother Lugna.

'In what way? How did this manifest itself?' asked Eadulf.

'He became reclusive,' the abbot explained. 'He shut himself away from his oldest friend in the community.'

'He even stopped going to Mass,' pointed out Brother Lugna. 'When we found that he had shut himself away and would not communicate with anyone, I sent for his mother, Lady Eithne, to see if she could find out what was vexing him.'

'And did she?'

He was about to speak when he was interrupted by the noise of several horses arriving in the quadrangle of the abbey. With a muttered apology, he rose and went to the window to peer out. Then he turned back.

'You may ask the question of Lady Eithne herself, Sister Fidelma, for she has just arrived with an escort.'

He left the room to greet the newcomers.

Lady Eithne was imposing. Tall though Fidelma was, she had to look up into the face of the woman. There were still traces of a youthful beauty in her features. She wore a slightly austere expression. The sharp blue eyes bore few of the tell-tale marks of age; only when one came nearer was age discernible, for she used berry juice to darken her brows and hair. The person who dressed her hair was clearly skilled, for it was elaborately done. Three dark-brown braids curled and wound round her head, held in place by gold circlet pins called *flesc*, while a fourth braid was left flowing between her shoulders and down her back. On top of her head was a kerchief arranged to show that she was a widow. Her only jewellery was an ornate cross of gold worked with semi-precious stones, the like of which Fidelma had never seen before. It was clearly of foreign workmanship. Lady Eithne wore a bright green dress of *siriac*, or silk, with a bright blue cloak of *sróll*, satin, edged with badger's fur.

She took a pace forward and held out both hands to Fidelma in friendly greeting.

'You are welcome here, lady. I have been expecting your arrival ever since I heard that you had been invited to come to the abbey.'

'Lady Eithne,' replied Fidelma, bowing her head, not to the rank of the woman but to her age and reputation. Lady Eithne was the chieftain of the local territory, being a *banchomarbae* or female heir, as well as widow of a Déisi prince.

'And this is Eadulf of Seaxmund's Ham?' Lady Eithne turned to Eadulf with a smile. 'I have heard much of you. You are both welcome in the territory of the Déisi.' Then she greeted the abbot with a surly nod.

Looking troubled, the abbot invited her to be seated in the chair he had vacated, which surprised Eadulf for it was not often that an abbot abrogated his rank to the local nobility. Brother Lugna produced another chair, and the abbot reseated himself next to Lady Eithne.

'Your visit is unexpected, lady,' the abbot commented, when the steward had served mead to the newcomer.

'Not so,' Lady Eithne replied firmly. 'As soon as I was informed that Fidelma of Cashel was here, I rode here to greet her. I am as much concerned with the resolution of this matter as the abbey of Lios Mór. Perhaps more so.'

It was a clear rebuke and a reminder that it was her son whose murder they were speaking of.

'Let me say at once, and on behalf of my brother, the King, and our family, that I am sorry for your great loss, lady,' Fidelma began after a few moments of awkward silence. It was no more than a ritual opening.

'Your condolences are appreciated,' she replied automatically. 'Do you hope to resolve this matter quickly?'

'We were speaking of the circumstances of your son's tragic death when you arrived,' Fidelma replied, not answering her question.

Lady Eithne gazed sadly at her. 'There is no need to tread carefully with my feelings. I have mourned sufficiently in public. My grief is now for myself. I hope you will be able to discover who is responsible for his death.'

'We understand that you may have been the last known person to speak with him. We are told that since his return from his pilgrimage, Brother Donnchad had been growing agitated about something.'

'Agitated?' queried Lady Eithne distantly.

'Agitated enough for the steward of the community, Brother Lugna here, to send for you that you might come to the abbey and speak to him. I am told that Brother Donnchad had withdrawn from his companions and was no longer attending the services of the abbey.'

'That is correct,' confirmed Lady Eithne.

'You acceded to the steward's request and, therefore, you were probably the last person to see your son before his death.'

There was a silence for a while as Lady Eithne took a sip of her mead. Then she replaced the glass on the side table with a quick nod.

'Apart, that is, from the person who murdered him,' she replied. 'When Brother Lugna sent for me, I was much disquieted by his message. Brother Lugna asked me to come here and speak with my son and perhaps discover the reason for his behaviour.'

'And did you?' asked Eadulf quietly.

'Donnchad told me he was in fear for his life. He told me that he was apprehensive of certain intrigues and jealousies in the abbey. He knew someone was envious of him and the precious manuscripts he had brought back from his travels.'

Fidelma saw a tinge of red colouring Abbot Iarnla's neck and spreading up his cheeks. The abbot opened his mouth to say something.

'He told you this clearly?' Fidelma interjected quickly.

'He did so.'

'I am told that no manuscripts or artefacts have been found in his cell.'

Lady Eithne met her eyes steadily. 'Precisely.' The tone was emphatic.

'I see,' said Fidelma, understanding her implication. 'Then you believe whoever killed your son also took these precious manuscripts?'

'I do.'

'And you saw these documents when you visited your son?'

'I did. On that very day just hours before his death.'

Fidelma sat back and glanced quickly from Abbot Iarnla to Brother Lugna, before returning her gaze to Lady Eithne.

'There was some doubt whether these manuscripts actually existed.'

Abbot Iarnla stared at the fire while the steward flushed. Lady Eithne's lips parted in a humourless smile but she said nothing.

'When your son told you that he feared the theft of these books, did he mention any specific threat?' asked Fidelma.

'He did not.'

'Then perhaps you could repeat his words – his exact words – so that we might try and interpret them?' Eadulf suggested.

There was a perceptible tightening of Lady Eithne's jaw and Fidelma, anxious that she should not take this as questioning her veracity, said hurriedly, 'Eadulf is right. If you can give us his exact words, there might be something in them that could lead to the root of his fear.'

Lady Eithne relaxed and paused for a moment as if trying to recall.

'He told me that the Faith was under attack from those who would deny its very message. He feared that these attackers would destroy it.'

'People who would destroy it?' echoed Eadulf. 'He was not specific about names or where they could be found?'

'Those were his words. I believe my son was killed because of his scholarship and the manuscripts he had brought back with him from the Holy Land.'

'If possible, lady,' Fidelma said, 'let us turn to your last meeting with him. When you arrived here, had he locked himself in his cell?'

'He had.'

'But he let you in to speak to him?'

'I am his mother. Of course he did.'

'I am told that he had one key to that chamber. The locksmith had made the lock specially.'

'I asked my son who held the keys to his room, since he was in such fear for his life. He told me that he had the only key.'

'While you were in his cell and saw those precious manuscripts, did you know what they were? What sort of works were they?'

Lady Eithne sniffed, her chin rising a little.

'My son was a great scholar. I can read and write my own language and I have a little Latin learning, but not much. I could scarcely understand the varied and unusual works that

he had access to. I would not know Greek from Hebrew.'
Lady Eithne gave a shake of her head. 'My son had several
works in his room.'

'Could one person have carried the manuscripts away with
them?'

'I suppose so. After all, he had to carry them himself on
his journey from the Holy Land.'

'He was also supposed to have brought back some artefacts,' Eadulf said.

Lady Eithne's hand went to the strange, ornate cross which
hung round her neck.

'Indeed. He brought back a piece of the True Cross for
the abbey and he brought me this. It was a gift from both
my sons, bought for me in the very town of Nazareth where
Our Saviour grew up and began his work.'

'Anything else?'

'Not that I know of. Brother Lugna, surely you know what
gifts he brought for the abbey.'

Brother Lugna shifted his weight and made an odd gesture
with one hand, palm outwards. 'A piece of the True Cross,
which is now in our newly built chapel. A few icons and trin-
kets for decorative purposes, but that is all.'

'So now . . .' Lady Eithne suddenly rose, and they all
followed her example. 'It was merely my intention to come
to greet you, Fidelma, and extend a welcome to this territory.
I must return to my fortress. It is only a few kilometres to the
east of the abbey but the sky is darkening. I would welcome
your visit there. If there is anything else I can help you with,

I shall be most willing. It is hard to lose both my sons . . .'
She smiled quickly. 'Cathal is lost to me in a foreign land and
now . . . now Donnchad . . .' She ended with a shrug.

'You have already been more than helpful, lady,' Fidelma
replied gravely.

Lady Eithne inclined her head to Fidelma and then to
Eadulf, glanced at Abbot Iarnla in an almost disapproving
way, and then turned towards the chamber door which Brother
Lugna held open for her.

CHAPTER FIVE

After Brother Lugna had followed Lady Eithne down to the courtyard where two warriors of her escort were waiting, Abbot Iarnla reseated himself. He looked ill at ease.

'Do I detect some tension between Lady Eithne and you?' asked Fidelma, also sitting down again.

The elderly abbot looked up at her and his expression was not happy.

'I preside over this abbey where her son has been murdered. In fact, I presided over it when her two sons were falsely accused of plotting the murder of her cousin, Maolochtair, Prince of the Déisi, and thereby forced them to go on pilgrimage to avoid his attentions.'

'At my suggestion,' pointed out Fidelma.

'Nevertheless, I feel that I am the one she blames for all the misfortunes that have befallen her family.'

'And do you feel that you are to blame?'

'She believes that I am. That is enough.'

'How powerful a person is Lady Eithne in this area?' asked Eadulf. 'Usually a . . .' he fought for the right word, 'a *baintrebthach* . . . a widow . . . does not exercise much power.'

The abbot gave a quick shake of his head. 'Lady Eithne was also a *comthigerna*, a co-lord, of the area, so that when her husband died, even with her two sons living, she continued as lord of the area. While she answers to the senior Prince of the Déisi, Maolochtair's successor, she has total command in this territory.'

'A chieftain in her own right,' Eadulf summed up.

'That is so,' confirmed the old abbot. 'A *bancomharba*, female heir, to the lordship of this territory.'

'Do you know what she means by these intrigues and jealousies in the abbey? Intrigues that would concern Brother Donnchad?' Fidelma asked gently, returning to the main point.

'I have no such knowledge. It is the first I have heard of it from Lady Eithne. But I fear that she accuses me.'

Eadulf was thoughtful. 'Surely Brother Donnchad had an *anam chara*, a soul friend, with whom he discussed matters and made confession? We might be able to learn more of this from him.'

The *anam chara* was not exactly like the confessor priest in the Roman Church. The soul friend was someone with whom one could discuss one's deepest and most intimate thoughts and problems; someone who shared one's very soul and provided support and, where possible, guidance along the spiritual path. It was a concept that was ancient long before the coming of the new Faith and, Eadulf admitted, a better practice than merely the confessing of certain sins as defined by the rules of others, for which a priest could then issue punishments as penance.

'Before he left on his pilgrimage, his soul friend was Brother Gáeth,' replied the abbot. 'Donnchad seemed to spend much of his time with Brother Gáeth. They had known one another since they were children.'

'Then Brother Gáeth should be able to tell us what it was that troubled Brother Donnchad,' Eadulf said.

Brother Lugna re-entered the room. Fidelma caught the uncomfortable glance that Abbot Iarnla cast at him as he entered. Brother Lugna had picked up on the last remark.

'I am afraid you will not get much help from Brother Gáeth,' he said firmly. 'Since Brother Donnchad's return, their friendship ceased. Brother Gáeth was forbidden even to approach him.'

'Forbidden? By whom?' queried Fidelma.

'By none other than Brother Donnchad himself,' replied the steward.

'Nevertheless, we shall speak to Brother Gáeth,' said Fidelma. 'When did Brother Donnchad become so solitary? Presumably there was a period between the time he came back to the community and when he became reclusive.'

'He arrived back in early summer. The problems really began about three or four days before his death,' replied Brother Lugna. 'I only knew him after he had returned from the pilgrimage, so I am not able to judge any differences in his character. All I can say is that he always kept himself and his thoughts to himself.'

The abbot nodded. 'It is true that, after his return, he often seemed preoccupied. He was – how should I put it? – of an unfriendly disposition. He confided in no one, kept himself to himself and moved in a secretive way. But three or four days before his death, he locked himself in his cell and refused to see anyone.'

'And you have no idea what caused him to do that?'

Brother Lugna was shaking his head but it was the abbot who replied. 'There is no reason that I know of. All I know is that four days before his death, he returned to the abbey and shut himself in his cell.'

'He *returned* to the abbey?' Fidelma asked quickly. 'I am not sure what you mean.'

Brother Lugna, who had compressed his lips in a reaction to the abbot's words, now spoke awkwardly.

'The abbot refers to the fact that Brother Donnchad left the abbey for an entire day without our knowledge. We ascribed this breach of our rules to his peculiar behaviour generally. As steward, I was going to reprimand him for that disobedience in not seeking our . . . the abbot's approval. That day I noticed he did not attend the early morning service. Then Brother Echen, our stableman, mentioned that Brother Donnchad had taken a horse from the abbey stables and ridden off before dawn, saying that he would return that evening. Brother Echen naturally assumed that he had the permission of the abbot and myself.'

'And did he return when he said he would?'

'He came back well after dark, left the horse in the stable and went straight to his cell, locked the door and refused to communicate with anyone. The following day I sent for Lady Eithne. I never saw him alive again.'

'Did you do anything in response to this curious behaviour, apart from allowing his mother to attempt to reason with him?'

'On the very morning before we discovered his body, we discussed the best way of dealing with the matter,' replied the abbot. 'Rightly or wrongly, I had previously decided that he needed more time to settle back after his momentous journey. But that morning I decided to confront him. I went to his cell with Brother Lugna. When we could not get in, I sent for our blacksmith and he broke down the door. That was when we found him. Murdered.'

'Let me get this clear.' Fidelma was thoughtful and spoke quietly. 'Before he became reclusive, did you discuss with Brother Donnchad any matters that were bothering him?'

'We had a few discussions immediately after his return but not since his behaviour became strange and certainly not during the last week.'

'What were the subjects of the discussions on his return?'

'Varied. About the sights he had seen in his travels and the gift he brought back. Also about the changes to the abbey, the new building. But he was very preoccupied, as I said. It was as if his heart was not in such matters and his interests lay elsewhere.'

'So where do you think he went on the day that he left the abbey? Do you think he went to see his mother?' asked Fidelma.

Brother Lugna shook his head immediately, saying, 'It was something I asked Lady Eithne but she had not seen him that day or for some time prior. I am afraid that we have no idea where he went on his last journey from the abbey.'

Fidelma sat silently for a few minutes before summing up the facts she had been told.

'So, in short, what you are telling us is that when Donnchad returned from his pilgrimage, he was troubled by something. He feared that someone would steal the manuscripts he had brought back with him and asked for a lock and key on his door. We hear now that he also feared for his life. His attitude was such that you felt he should be "humoured", your word, in this matter.' She glanced at them to emphasise the point. Brother Lugna nodded slightly. The abbot did not meet her eyes. 'Then he disappeared from the community for an entire day, without permission and without telling anyone where he had been. When he returned, he locked himself in his chamber. Having felt that his behaviour was becoming even more abnormal, Brother Lugna sent for his mother to speak to him but she had no effect. So, finally, you both went to remonstrate with him and found him dead, murdered in his cell, yet the door was locked, and you maintain that it could only have been locked from the inside. Am I right?'

'Those are the essential details,' agreed Abbot Iarnla.

Fidelma continued, 'We will go to examine the cell shortly

but you have told me that there was only one key. How do you know it was turned from the inside?'

It was Brother Lugna who answered without hesitation.

'Because the only key was lying by Brother Donnchad's body. Therefore it had to have been turned from the inside.'

'Logical enough,' muttered Eadulf. 'But a lot seems to rely on your assertion that there was only one key.'

'It is no assertion. As I said, our blacksmith was told to make the lock specially and only one key was provided to assure Brother Donnchad of his security.'

'And these manuscripts that he guarded so diligently, only his mother seems to have glimpsed them.'

'Lady Eithne says she saw them, so they must have been stolen by whoever killed him,' asserted the steward firmly.

The abbot said nothing and Fidelma turned to him.

'You seem uncertain, Abbot Iarnla.'

'I cannot comment. I never saw the documents.'

'Do you doubt Lady Eithne's word?'

'I would only point out that Lady Eithne admits that she does not know Greek from Hebrew. How can we rely on her word that the manuscripts that she glimpsed were the precious documents that Brother Donnchad claimed they were?'

'Did anyone else see these valuable manuscripts apart from Lady Eithne?' Eadulf asked.

'I imagine that our *scriptor*, Brother Donnán, would have seen them,' Brother Lugna replied.

'Did you question the *scriptor* about them?' Fidelma asked. 'After all, as the head of your *scriptorium* in this abbey, he should surely have known about such precious manuscripts being brought here.'

'We have questioned no one,' replied Brother Lugna, a little sourly, avoiding looking at the abbot. 'It was felt that such matters should await your arrival.'

'We will speak with your *scriptor*,' Fidelma said gently. 'And we will examine Brother Donnchad's cell. I presume the obsequies have already been conducted?'

'As you know, it is our tradition to bury the body within twenty-four hours,' replied the abbot. 'He was laid to rest in our burial ground just outside the abbey walls, after the day of watching in the usual custom.'

'But your physician will be able to report on the manner of his death?'

'He was stabbed in the back,' stated Brother Lugna. 'That's how he died. Surely that is enough.'

'Just so, but there are details that only an apothecary or physician would notice. I presume your physician examined him?'

'Naturally.' Again there was a defensive tone in the steward's voice. 'Brother Seachlann is our physician.'

'Then we will need to see him.' She rose, as did Eadulf, but the abbot remained seated as if lost in thought. Then he suddenly realised they were leaving and gestured to his steward.

'Brother Lugna will see to all your needs. However, the hour grows late. Perhaps tomorrow would be a better day to begin.'

Fidelma realised that a distant bell was ringing to mark the end of the day's work, calling those who tilled the fields to return to the abbey and cleanse themselves before the evening meal.

'You are right, Father Abbot,' she conceded. 'It has been a long day.' She glanced at Brother Lugna. 'Has our companion, Gormán, been accommodated and our horses seen to?'

'They have,' the steward said. 'And I have asked our *bruigad*, our hosteller, to make a chamber ready for you in our *tech-óiged*, our guesthouse—'

'Separate chambers,' interrupted Fidelma softly.

'But I thought . . .' Abbot Iarnla frowned and then went on hurriedly to avoid embarrassment, 'Of course. See to it, Brother Lugna. And perhaps you will join us in the *refectorium* for the evening meal when you have had your evening bathe.'

'I have ordered your baths to be made ready,' added the steward.

Eadulf had felt a little embarrassed when Fidelma ordered separate chambers. But he realised that life could not continue as before and there was much to be sorted out between Fidelma and himself. He said nothing as the hosteller, who identified himself as Brother Máel Eoin, guided them to the wooden building that was the guesthouse. Their chambers were separate but close to one another. A tub of hot water was waiting for him when he entered. Eadulf had long grown used to the custom of Fidelma's people of taking a daily bath, usually in the evening, in a large tub called a *dabach*. Guests in any hostel or inn had the baths prepared for them with scented warm water and oils. After guests had washed, combed their hair and put on fresh clothing, they could attend the principal meal of the day, called the *prainn*, which was taken in the evening.

Eadulf had noticed that Brother Lugna used the Latin term *refectorium* instead of *praintech*, the usual word for an eating house. Eadulf had noticed that in many abbeys Latin terms were replacing native words for functions and places – the use of the Latin *cubiculum* for chamber instead of the usual *cotultech*; of *scriptor* for librarian and *scriptorium* for library in place of *leabhar coimedach*, keeper of books, and *tech-screptra*, library. It seemed that the abbey of Lios Mór, too, was changing. Perhaps Brother Lugna's Roman tonsure was more significant than he had previously thought.

It was a short time later when Brother Máel Eoin came to show him and Fidelma the way to the *refectorium*. At the doors of the *refectorium* they found Gormán about to enter.

'Are you being looked after well?' Fidelma greeted the young warrior.

'I have a good bed, lady,' he replied with a brief smile. 'I am quartered above the stables with the *echaire*, the stableman. I have been looking around at the new buildings. It seems the abbey is growing rapidly since last I came here. A chapel in stone and two other buildings already completed. The abbey appears to have come into great wealth.'

He was interrupted by a gesture from Brother Eoin as he

opened the doors and showed them into the great hall where
the community was eating. He steered them through the rows
of long tables to a table set to one side of the *refectorium*.
Many of the brethren raised their heads to observe their
passage with undisguised curiosity. A low murmur arose from
them. Fidelma noticed that there were few women in the hall,
although there were some. Lios Mór had, she recalled, initially
been a *conhospitae*, a mixed house, where men and women
cohabited, raising their children to the service of the new religion. She remembered the story of how Carthach had come
to Lios Mór with Flandait, the daughter of Cuanan, and several
other women to help form the community. They found a holy
woman named Caimel already living by the river. Caimel had
become the head of the community of women at Lios Mór.
She wondered whether Abbot Iarnla was gradually leading
the religious community towards celibacy, for there was little
evidence of women being co-equal as they had been when
she last visited.

The fact that there were few women in the hall had also
occurred to Eadulf. He had also noticed that the women
who were present had been placed at the lower end of the
refectorium. The abbot's table was at the far end on a raised
platform and here Abbot Iarnla, his steward and several others
were seated at their meal. Eadulf presumed that the abbot's
table was filled with the hierarchy of the abbey and they were
all male. Then he realised that Brother Eoin was leading them
to a table to one side of the hall. Eadulf knew from experience that Fidelma, as sister to the King, was usually seated

as a distinguished guest. He saw that Fidelma gave no sign that she was insulted by what seemed a breach of natural courtesy. One or two of the brethren bowed their heads towards them in obvious recognition as they passed between the tables.

At the table to which they were guided they found two other guests, who introduced themselves. Glassán was a man of middle age, with even features, bright blue eyes and wiry brown hair, and a firm chin with a cleft jaw. He looked used to being outside in the elements and his clothing did not hide his well-muscled body. He seemed to assume a natural command over his companion who was introduced as Saor. He was thin and sinewy, a swarthy fellow with close-set eyes.

'Are you guests in the abbey?' Fidelma asked as they seated themselves. She was interested by their appearance, for neither seemed like men who would choose life in an abbey.

'That we are,' replied Glassán with a broad smile that was almost patronising. 'Fairly permanent and important ones.'

'Permanent *and* important?' Gormán's query seemed to be without irony, but his eyes were glinting. 'What manner of men are you who honour us with your company?'

'I am an *ailtíre*,' the brawny Glassán declared without any modesty. 'Saor, here, is my carpenter and assistant.'

'Ah, you are a . . . a master builder?' Eadulf tried to translate the technical office.

'I am in charge of the rebuilding of the abbey,' confirmed Glassán. Clearly he was not a man who believed in humility.

'We saw that there had been changes,' Gormán replied. 'A

lot of new stone buildings have appeared where I remember buildings of wood.'

'Quite right, my young friend,' agreed Glassán. 'For three years now the abbey has employed me to oversee the new building work.'

'That must be an enormous task,' Eadulf commented. He was genuinely interested.

'I have several men working under me, including some of the finest *caisleóir*, stonemasons, of the south.'

'The abbey must be rich to engage in such rebuilding,' observed Gormán.

The master builder grimaced. 'That you would have to ask Brother Lugna. For my part, each fee for services is specified by the Law of the Fénechus, as is compensation for craftsmen injured in the pursuit of their work.'

Eadulf looked surprised and Fidelma explained. 'A master builder is considered on the same level as the intended successor to a *bo-aire*, which would mean his honour price is worth twenty *seds* – the value of twenty milch cows.'

Glassán was looking at Fidelma with interest.

'You know something of the law, Sister?' Then he smiled. 'Ah, of course. You are the *dálaigh* that the brethren here have been talking about. Someone who is going to make a report about the cleric who died.'

'Did you know him?'

'Know him? We are too busy to socialise with the brethren here, even if they were sociable.' He grinned at his quip. No one laughed.

'Twenty *seds* is a large sum, indeed,' observed Eadulf, filling the awkward silence.

'Small compensation for the many years of study and apprenticeship, as in all arts and crafts,' pointed out Glassán in an almost defensive manner. 'There is a lot of responsibility in superintending the construction of these buildings, and one has to be a master in many different things, stone-masonry, carpentry . . .' He suddenly shot a condescending look at his quiet companion. 'Thankfully, Saor here takes many onerous tasks from my shoulders. He is my chief assistant.'

'But if you are building in stone, surely you need stone-masons rather than carpenters,' queried Gormán.

Saor's chin came up defensively and he spoke for the first time. 'Even with stone work, wooden frames must be made and carpentry must be employed,' he announced with a tone of annoyance.

'Of course.' Glassán smiled, regaining the conversation. It was clear that he was enthusiastic about his craft and not loath to expand on the problems and skill that faced him and the rest of his team of workmen. As master builder, Glassán was provided with accommodation in the guest-house, while his assistant and his workmen lived outside the abbey, along the river bank, in a collection of huts they had erected for the purpose. For the rest of the meal he continued to talk of the problems of replacing some of the wooden structures of the abbey with buildings of stone. He had a habit of talking in a low droning tone, almost without stopping, so that there was little dialogue.

Gormán's expression quickly took on a slightly glazed look, as if he had shut off his mind from Glassán's interminable details and technical explanations. Throughout, the thin-faced Saor sat in almost moody silence, apart from one or two muttered comments. At the end of the meal, Fidelma and Eadulf rose hurriedly, thankful to be able to escape.

Outside her chamber, in the *tech-oiged*, or guesthouse, Fidelma turned apologetically to Eadulf.

'I did not mean to embarrass you earlier about our accommodation,' she said softly. 'But there are many things we must discuss in case we fall back into old habits which are no good for either of us.'

'I understand,' Eadulf agreed. 'I realise that it is your brother who is trying to mend fences; it was not your doing to bring me back to Cashel.'

'It is not that I regret his interference, Eadulf,' Fidelma said quickly. 'I welcome it as a means whereby we might try to rebuild our relationship on a better footing. I am firm in my resolve to pursue the course I have set myself. I would be a hypocrite to do otherwise. How that will square with whatever else must be taken into consideration . . . well, we must talk more clearly when there are no other problems to distract our thoughts.'

'Agreed,' Eadulf replied with a smile. 'Let us give our minds completely to the current problem.'

She answered his smile. Then said, 'Gormán made a good point this evening.'

'You mean his ability to switch off his mind while our builder friend was chattering on,' Eadulf observed wryly. 'I swear the man did not even pause to eat his food, yet his plate was clean at the end of the meal. How did he talk and eat at the same time?'

'That is not what I meant.' She laughed. 'I meant the point he made about the abbey being rich to embark on all this new building work.'

'That observation was made before. Many communities are building and expanding. Why not Lios Mór?'

'As you know, Lios Mór was only established a little over thirty years ago, Eadulf. It was levelled and fenced in with the members of the community building it with their own hands. They sought no help from outside. The material was the timber from the surrounding woods. The community have barely had time to establish themselves, let alone start to rebuild from stone.'

'I have seen many communities in the Five Kingdoms putting up buildings of stone,' Eadulf pointed out.

'Usually in the west where stone is more easily accessible than wood,' replied Fidelma. 'But here, wood is plenty and varied. I know that the community is expanding, but to bring in a professional builder and his men is surprising. Glassán was right when he said that the law lays down strict rules, regulations and fees for professional builders and craftsmen. If the community here can afford to pay those rates, it means they have the finances to do so. How have they achieved such wealth in so short a time?'

'Perhaps Glassán and his men are donating their work to the Faith,' suggested Eadulf.

'You heard him speak of his fees. I don't think he will forgo them for the sake of the Faith.'

'Well, perhaps that is something we should ask Abbot Iarnla about.'

Fidelma nodded absently. 'Anyway, we have more to concern us than how the abbey has raised the means to pay craftsmen to construct stone buildings.' She opened the door of her chamber, then turned back to him with a smile. 'Sleep well, Eadulf. We have much to do in the morning.'

For a moment Eadulf stood gazing moodily at the closed door. Then with a deep sigh he turned and walked slowly to his own allotted chamber.

If Fidelma was so convinced of her future, Eadulf knew that difficult times lay ahead for him. There would be no easy reconciliation, no easy getting back together, as it seemed Fidelma's brother had hoped.

Eadulf lay down on the straw palliasse of the wooden framed cot and drew a blanket over himself, but it was a long time before sleep came to him.

ChAPTER SIX

The next morning the sky was cloudless and the sun bright. 'It is going to be a hot day,' announced Brother Lugna, moodily, after he had greeted Fidelma and Eadulf. They had just emerged from the *refectorium*, where they had taken a light breakfast.

'In that case, we should avail ourselves of the early morning freshness to begin at once,' Fidelma replied.

They had emerged to a cacophony of sound at odds with the usual meditative quiet of an abbey. They could hear the ringing of hammers on stone, the grating of wood being sawn and the harsh shouts of men issuing instructions.

'That's the building work,' explained Brother Lugna. 'The disturbance of our peace is but a small penance for the reconstruction of the abbey into a monument that will last forever.'

He led them across the stone-flagged quadrangle, past the *tipra*, the small fresh-water fountain splashing in a basin carved from limestone. Facing them on the eastern side of the quadrangle was the large three-storey stone building which contained Brother Donnchad's cell. Brother Lugna told them that the *cubicula*, or individual cells, of all the senior members of the community would eventually be housed in the building.

'So it is a very new building,' Fidelma commented, observing the still immaculately polished stonework.

'Less than a year old,' Brother Lugna agreed. 'It was the second of the new buildings to be finished. The first, of course, was our chapel. I regret that the *tech-oíged*, the guest-house, will be the last building to be replaced in stone as it is the least important of the complex. But I hope the current building is comfortable enough for you.'

Fidelma wondered whether there was some humour behind his words. But she did not think that Brother Lugna was given to humour.

'Comfortable enough,' replied Fidelma. 'So comfortable that I wonder why the abbey should spend so much on replacing buildings that are well built and still fairly new anyway?'

'It is the ambition of the abbey that Lios Mór should become one of the greatest centres of the Faith and of learning not only in the Five Kingdoms but beyond the seas as well. The abbey of Darú claims that this year they have attracted pious students from eighteen different nations. To achieve our ambition it was decided that our buildings should reflect our abilities. Great structures of stone will last longer than poor buildings of wood.'

It was the first time they had seen the usually dour steward almost in a state of excitement.

'But surely wood or stone is merely an outward covering,' Fidelma suggested. 'The fame of an abbey lies in the deeds of its community and its scholars.'

Brother Lugna flushed a little and did not respond. Instead he pointed to the upper floor of the building. 'Brother Donnchad's *cubiculum* is on the top floor.' The steward guided them up a stone stairway to the upper floor before leading them along a corridor and halting before a door. They could see immediately that the lock on the door had been smashed open. There was no sign of the lock but splintered wood marked the place where it had been fitted. The steward reached out and pushed the door open.

'Where is the lock and key?' Fidelma asked.

'They were handed back to the smith who has been told to keep them for your examination.'

'So this door has not been secured since you found the body?' asked Fidelma.

'Even if it could be, there was no need to secure it,' replied Brother Lugna primly. 'Brother Donnchad no longer had need of the lock.'

'And Brother Donnchad had no possessions to keep safe?'

'There was little of value here but the abbot ordered that nothing be removed until you came. I can assure you that nothing has. As the abbot and I have told you, there were no precious manuscripts here.'

'What happened after you found the body?'

'The abbot and I remained here to examine the room even after the body was taken by the physician for examination and preparation for burial.'

'The physician did not examine the body here?'

'He saw Brother Donnchad was dead, so there was little need to do anything further here.'

'Would you ask the physician to join us here?'

Brother Lugna hesitated.

'Is there a problem?' Fidelma asked.

'There is little he can tell you that I cannot,' replied the steward.

'But you are not the physician who examined the body,' Fidelma said.

Reluctantly, the steward turned and hurried off on his errand.

Fidelma entered the *cubiculum* and halted just inside the door. She looked round at the small room. It was lit by one narrow window to which Fidelma immediately went. It was high up in the wall, the sill on a level with her head. She turned round, seized a chair and drew it to the window. She looked out at the walls below the window. They were smooth and obviously could not be scaled without a ladder. The ground beneath appeared muddy, evidence that this had, until recently, been a building site, although here and there a few bushes had sprung up since the building had been constructed. Then she turned her head and glanced upwards. There was an overhang to the roof that made it practically impossible for anyone to descend in order to gain entrance through the window, even if they had been small enough.

'Well, unless the murderer was a midget, an acrobat, or had wings, I cannot see anyone gaining entrance this way,' Fidelma announced, climbing off the chair and returning it to its place. 'Even if they could scale the wall, and perhaps that is possible with all this building work going on with ladders lying unattended. But an intruder would have to squeeze through the window and would have given his victim plenty of warning. We are told there were no signs of a struggle.'

'And we are told that he was stabbed in the back,' Eadulf pointed out. 'That means he had his back to the intruder and was not expecting the attack.'

The next thing that struck Fidelma was how bare the room was. For a scholar of Brother Donnchad's reputation, and one who had travelled on such an important pilgrimage to the Holy Land, it was decidedly empty.

Eadulf agreed. 'And if we accept the word of the abbot and his steward, nothing has been taken from here except the body.'

The wooden bed, with its straw palliasse and blanket, still lay in turmoil. The mattress and woollen blanket were stained with blood. They had certainly not been touched. Some shelves contained a few odds and ends of writing materials, goose quills and a small knife to cut them. There was a broken stylus and an *adarcín*, part of a cow's horn used to contain *dhubh*, a black ink made from carbon. But there was no sign of any material to write on, vellums or parchments, nor a writing stand or maulstick to guide the hand of the scribe. Indeed, there was no sign of any books, scrolls or manuscripts at all.

'Curious,' murmured Fidelma.

'Not even a *marsupium* or *tiag luibhar*, no bags to carry even a small book,' added Eadulf, reading her thoughts.

Fidelma pointed beneath the bed. Just at the foot, barely visible, was the end of wooden box.

'Bring that out, Eadulf. Perhaps we'll find something inside.'

Eadulf went on his knees on the floor and dragged the box out. It was not secured and so he lifted the lid. It contained nothing more interesting than a pair of sandals, a robe, and underclothes.

'Well, I am quite sure that there is nothing here. Even aside from the question of any precious manuscripts, a scholar of his reputation would have had some documents in his room. But there are no papers here at all.'

'Then we must work on the assumption that the murderer stole them,' Fidelma suggested. She was moving around the small *cubiculum*, examining the walls.

'What are you looking for?' Eadulf asked.

'Another way in. We are told that Brother Donnchad was murdered here. Stabbed in the back. We are told that the door was locked from the inside because there was only one key and that key was found by the body on the bed. It looks as though no access could be made from the door or the window there.'

'This accounts for a mood of unease and stories of

supernatural entities,' replied Eadulf. 'I was told this morning in the *refectorium* that one of the brethren claims he actually saw an angel flying by the building.'

'I think that, too, can be discounted,' replied Fidelma coldly. 'So how did the human agent enter here, kill the victim and leave with a bundle of manuscripts without a trace of entry or exit?'

'There might be another key, of course,' he offered.

'The smith who made the lock and key would be able to answer that and we will ask him. In the meantime, let us see if we can eliminate any other means of entry.'

'You believe there might be another way of entering here?' He was sceptical. 'If there were another means, Glassán the builder would surely have known about it and informed the abbot. After all, he must have built this place.'

'Better we should check ourselves,' she replied.

Eadulf looked on with some cynicism. 'If someone popped out of a secret door or tunnel, the sound of it opening would have alerted Brother Donnchad. This place is small and he would have put up a struggle with the assailant. Indeed,' he continued warming to his reasoning, 'he would have been equally warned if someone had come to the door and opened it with another key.'

'You are right, Eadulf.' Fidelma paused, standing thoughtfully for a moment. 'Even if he was fast asleep in bed and slept through the sound of the assailant's entrance, how would his killer have been able to stab him in the back without a struggle?'

There was a movement in the corridor and a moment later Brother Lugna entered with a tall, dark man whose sour expression seemed to fit his saturnine features.

'This is Brother Seachlann, our physician,' the steward announced, standing aside.

'As I am unable to examine the corpse for myself, you must explain to me the nature of the man's death,' Fidelma said.

'Little to explain. He was stabbed twice and died.'

Fidelma smiled thinly at the man's offhand manner which bordered on insolence.

'I think a little more information is in order,' she said gently. Eadulf recognised her dangerous tone. 'Where was he stabbed?'

Brother Seachlann frowned in annoyance. 'In the back. Haven't you been told?' His voice was full of arrogance. 'I cannot understand why you must waste my time with such questions. I am a qualified *liaig*, a physician, and am to be treated with respect and not summoned to answer questions that have no need of an answer.'

Eadulf waited for the explosion. It did not come.

'Brother Seachlann,' Fidelma spoke very softly, 'so far no one has treated you with disrespect. I am a *dálaigh*, an advocate of the courts, qualified to the level of *anruth*. I accept that you are a qualified physician. As such, you ought to know enough of the law to realise that you must respond to my questions. Failing to provide satisfactory answers to me can result in censureship and a fine. I have the power to take away your *echlaisc*. So I hope you will save me the trouble of having to drag from you every little piece of information that I want. Do I make myself understood?'

What Fidelma meant by taking away his *echlaisc* was that she could have him disbarred from medicine. A doctor usually went to visit his patients on horseback and thus an *echlais*, a horsewhip, had become the symbol of a physician.

Brother Seachlann flushed, swallowed and glanced at Brother Lugna, who stared expressionless before him.

'Brother Donnchad was stabbed twice in the back. He died from those wounds.' The information was given almost between clenched teeth.

Fidelma ignored his apparent petulance.

'Eadulf, come here and stand in front of Brother Seachlann with your back to him. Good. Now, Brother Seachlann, can you show me where these two wounds were?'

The physician leaned forward and tapped Eadulf under the ribcage on the left-hand side of the back and then again on the left-hand side of the neck, just at its base.

'Can you say anything more about the wounds?' pressed Fidelma.

'The lower one was struck in an upward manner and the one at the neck was struck downwards.'

'And was there much bleeding?'

'There was blood over the bed and floor.'

'Do you have any further comment about the wounds?'

'Only that they caused his death.' Brother Seachlann barely concealed his contempt.

'Eadulf, what do you say?' Fidelma asked.

'The vital organs are fairly well protected by the bones in the back, according to Galen's works on anatomy,' he began. 'There are many bones covering the back. It occurs to me that the upward thrust and the downward thrust are indicative of someone who has a rudimentary if not expert knowledge of such matters. They knew they had to find soft tissue between the bones to strike at a vital organ that would result in death, and instantaneous death at that. A warrior would know that or a good physician.'

Brother Seachlann's irritation increased. 'And what would you know of such matters, Saxon?' he snapped. 'I am the expert here.'

'Eadulf spent some time at our great medical school of Tuaim Brecain,' replied Fidelma sharply, before Eadulf could respond. 'It seems that his eye is much more discerning than your own, physician.'

The physician swallowed hard. Again, a tinge of red came to his cheeks.

'I am fully qualified in all the healing arts and no one has questioned me before in this manner. I am qualified to the level of—'

'I heard you the first time,' interrupted Fidelma with emphasis. 'Where were you qualified?'

'I am of the . . . I studied at Sléibhte.'

'Well, Seachlann of Sléibhte, I have never heard that the people of the Kingdom of Laighin were disrespectful to their Brehons.'

The physician glanced uneasily towards Brother Lugna as if expecting him to say something.

'Brother Seachlann has only recently joined our community,' the steward belatedly intervened. 'We have found him an excellent physician.'

'Then he should also know how to give evidence to a Brehon,' replied Fidelma.

Brother Seachlann seemed flustered. He said nothing.

'Tell me, physician,' Fidelma spoke slowly and deliberately, 'having seen the wounds that caused the death of Brother Donnchad, would you agree with my husband, Eadulf of Seaxmund's Ham? Do you concur that they were delivered by someone whose intention was to kill and were delivered with some foreknowledge of where to strike a death blow? Or do you argue that they were delivered in a frenzied attack born of anger or some other emotion?'

Brother Seachlann seemed to consider the matter and then he said sullenly, 'I would say that the blows were struck with some foreknowledge. The person knew that striking upwards, under the ribcage or downwards into the neck, would produce the desired result.'

'And being made in the back, this was done in stealth? The victim was unaware that he was about to be attacked?'

'That is beyond my conjecture but it would seem to be the case,' agreed the physician, 'otherwise Brother Donnchad would have swung round to face his attacker in order to defend himself.'

'Could the blows have been struck as he lay asleep, face down, on the bed?'

'They could not.'

'Why?'

'I do not think there would be enough power behind either blow if the victim were prone. Not enough power to achieve the damage inflicted. He had to be standing upright, his back to his assailant. Further, I would say the blow to the neck was received while he was sinking to the floor, or else the assailant was a very tall person.'

'Yet the body was found lying on its back on the bed.'

'I was told that was how the abbot and Brother Lugna found it. They told me that they had not moved it.'

'Except that I lifted the body a little to discover the wounds and blood,' added Brother Lugna pedantically. 'But I made sure the body went back into the position I found it in.'

'Just so,' said Fidelma. 'So what did you make of that, Brother Seachlann?'

'That Brother Donnchad must have fallen to the floor, having received the wounds standing up. But given their nature, he could not have raised himself on to the bed of his own accord.'

'People can do astonishing things in the moments before death, but I agree it seems unlikely he had such a capability,' said Fidelma solemnly. 'Once the knife had plunged downwards into his neck, he would probably have been dead before he reached the floor. Which means . . .?'

'That the killer must have then lifted the body on to the bed and placed it so that it was in a position of repose,' finished Eadulf. 'Would you agree, Brother Seachlann?'

'That would be a logical deduction but, of course, I could not swear to it,' replied the physician.

'Of course not,' agreed Fidelma. 'Nevertheless, as you say, from your medical knowledge, it is a logical deduction.'

'It is.'

'Then we have no need to detain you further, Brother Seachlann. You see, it was no hard task to answer the questions of a *dálaigh*, was it?'

The physician hesitated as if to say something but then decided against doing so and turned for the door.

When he had gone, Brother Lugna shifted his weight uncomfortably and appeared apologetic.

'We have found our new physician a little . . .' he paused, searching for the right word.

'A little lacking in social graces?' suggested Fidelma. 'Well, his rudeness is a little mystifying – there must be a reason for it. Yet it is of no consequence for the moment. We will discover what ails the man later.'

'Have you seen all you wanted?' asked the steward, indicating the chamber.

After a quick glance at Eadulf, Fidelma nodded. 'We have, but tell me, Brother Lugna, we are in the last room on this level, so who has the cell directly next to this?'

'No one,' replied the steward. 'In fact, three of the cells on this floor are not even allocated as yet.'

'And directly below?'

'The Venerable Bróen. He was one of the original members of the abbey when the Blessed Carthach founded it. He is old and a little confused now and prone to seeing visions.'

'Ah, the one who sees angels,' said Eadulf. 'Well, we won't bother him. There are no secret trapdoors in the floor of this room, are there?'

Brother Lugna did not share his humour. 'There is no way into this *cubiculum* other than through the door,' he said drily.

'Nevertheless, I would like to see the next one to this,' replied Fidelma.

They went out into the passage and the steward opened the door. Apart from the fact that there had been a lock fitted on Brother Donnchad's door, the *cubiculum* was exactly the same. It had the same high window. What was missing was any form of furniture, there was no bed, chair or table. Fidelma entered and moved along the wall that divided the cell from the one Brother Donnchad had occupied. There was certainly no secret mechanism to open a way into the next cell so that an attacker could enter in stealth. She turned and smiled at the frowning steward.

'You'll probably want to see our smith next, Brother Giolla-na-Naomh,' Brother Lugna suggested, when she declared that she had seen enough. 'Alas, I do not have time to show you the way. I have a meeting to attend with the master builder. But if you make your way to the stables, you will not be able to miss his forge.'

At the entrance to the building they watched Brother Lugna

hurry off across the quadrangle. Then Fidelma caught Eadulf by the arm.

'Before we find the smith, there is something else I wish to see.'

Puzzled, he followed her along the gap between the side of the building and the old wooden wall that surrounded the abbey. She halted at the back of the building, looking up at the windows. Fidelma paused when she judged them to be underneath the window of Brother Donnchad's chamber three storeys up.

'Careful,' she said to Eadulf and stood still. Fidelma examined the ground carefully. Then she shook her head. 'I can see no sign where anyone might have placed a ladder, nor can I see any other means of reaching the window above.'

'Well, you were sure that the window was not a means of ingress anyway,' Eadulf said.

'These things have to be checked and checked again,' returned Fidelma. As she turned her eye caught a scrap of white almost buried in the mud. 'What's that?'

Eadulf was nearer to it and bent down, carefully extracting it from the mud. He wiped some of the clinging earth from it. Then he held up a tiny piece of torn parchment in his hand. It was crumpled as if it had been discarded.

'It's nothing,' he said, looking at it. 'It must have been out here for some time and it is damp.'

'Be careful with it,' she said. 'There is still some writing on it.'

He gently stretched it out so that the few words were readable although the ink had started to run.

'Anything of interest?' asked Fidelma.

Eadulf shook his head. 'I think this is a line from one of the gospels – *si vis transfer calicem istrum a me*. It is followed by three words, the same word written three times over – *Deicide! Deicide! Deicide!* There is nothing else on it.'

'The last word means "god-killer" in Latin.' Fidelma peered at the text over his shoulder. 'To *Dei*, the word for god, is added *cide* from the verb *caedere* to cut down.'

'Why would anyone write that out several times? Was someone trying to remember how to spell it? Maybe it was Brother Donnchad and having captured the word he threw the parchment out of the window.'

'A scholar of Brother Donnchad's ability could surely spell a simple Latin word.'

'God-killer is what some of the early Christian Fathers claimed the Jews were because they demanded the crucifixion of Christ,' Eadulf said. 'But where does that first line come from? Something about "remove this chalice from me".'

'Chalice or cup. It depends on your translation,' replied Fidelma. 'I think it is from the gospel of Luke.'

She frowned, took the parchment from him and examined it again before placing it in her *ciorbholg*, which she always carried attached to her *criss*, or belt. The *ciorbholg*, or comb-bag, was carried by all women and usually contained items such as a *scathán*, a mirror, *deimess*, scissors, *sleic*, soap, a *phal* containing a favourite fragrance – Fidelma preferred honeysuckle – a small linen cloth and other personal items.

Eadulf was impatient. 'Let us find the smith and see what he can tell us about the lock and maybe a second key.'

Usually, they could locate a forge by the sound of the hammer smashing down on the *inneoin*, or anvil, but with the sound of the building work it was impossible. Before they came to the forge they passed another tall building being erected with stone blocks and suddenly Eadulf nudged Fidelma.

'There is a means of entrance to Brother Donnchad's *cubiculum* and someone small enough to pass through the window.'

A tall ladder was resting against the building to allow the masons to climb to the upper walls. Seated by it was a small boy who was busy sharpening a chisel with a honing stone.

Fidelma regarded the boy critically for a moment. 'I'll grant he's probably small enough but he would need two conspirators to help lift the ladder in place.' So saying, she strode across to the boy.

'Hello,' she greeted him. 'I haven't seen you before.'

The boy was no more than ten years old, with fair hair, a ruddy face and wiry limbs. He glanced up at her with a shy smile.

'Nor I you, Sister,' he replied pertly.

'My name is Fidelma and he,' indicating Eadulf, 'is called Eadulf. What's your name?'

'Gúasach. Why does he have a funny name?'

Fidelma chuckled. 'Because he comes from a place across the sea which is called the Kingdom of the East Angles. Are you working on this building?'

The boy smiled proudly. 'I am. I am apprentice to the master builder.'

'How long have you—'

Her question was interrupted by a loud shout from a rough-voiced man on the other side of the new wall.

'Gúasach! The chisel immediately!'

The boy sprang up with the chisel, gave them a grin of apology and disappeared through a gap in the wall.

Fidelma turned to Eadulf. 'I doubt we have found the killer in that lad.'

'Conspiracy?' mused Eadulf. 'Several people carried the ladder to the wall, the boy went up, killed Brother Donnchad and took the papers and books they wanted . . .' Eadulf halted with a wry chuckle. 'You are right. It is not a likely story.'

The *cérdcha*, or forge, of Brother Giolla-na-Naomh was located near the main gate of the community but just beyond the stables. It was after several wrong turns that they finally found the way behind the stable block. A young man stripped to the waist was gripping a glowing piece of metal in a *tenn-chair*, a pair of tongs. He struck the metal with an *ord*, a heavy hammer, causing sparks to fly as each ringing blow descended. An older man, also bare to the waist, though with a buckskin apron covering his chest and front, was clearly overseeing the young man's work. He caught sight of their approach and said something to his apprentice. The young man turned from the anvil and plunged the piece of metal he was working into a *telchuma*, or water trough, next to the anvil.

'Greetings, Sister Fidelma,' the older man boomed. His voice was as deep and resonant as one might expect from his tall and muscular appearance. 'I saw you and Brother Eadulf in the *refectorium* last evening. I am Brother Giolla-na-Naomh.'

Both Fidelma and Eadulf recognised the smith as one of those who had been seated at the abbot's table the previous night. A smith of the rank that had been ascribed to Brother Giolla-na-Naomh would of course, take precedent among the hierarchy of the abbey after the abbot, his steward and librarian.

The big man smiled through his shaggy black beard and examined them keenly with his blue eyes. He thrust out a massive hand to each of them in turn.

'While I am pleased to welcome you here,' he said, 'it is sad that it is the death of Brother Donnchad that brings you.'

'We share your sadness, Brother Giolla-na-Naomh,' replied Fidelma solemnly, 'and appreciate your welcome.'

The smith turned to his apprentice. 'Bring me the metal lock that is on the shelf behind you.' When the young man had passed it over, the smith added more instructions. 'Stoke up the furnace with the *cual craing* and keep it hot.' Eadulf knew that *cual craing* was literally 'coal of wood', the term applied to charcoal.

The smith turned back to them and pointed to a stone bench that stood under the canopy of a yew tree a little way from the forge.

'The furnace is too hot to remain in comfort near it on a day like this,' he said. 'We may sit in the cool shade of that tree. The bench is comfortable. Brother Lugna advised me last evening that you would be wishing to question me.'

'About the lock,' confirmed Fidelma. She sat down on the stone bench while Brother Giolla-na-Naomh lowered himself to sit cross-legged on the ground in front of her. Eadulf simply stood to one side against the tree.

Brother Giolla-na-Naomh glanced round as they made themselves comfortable and said, 'I expected the steward to come with you.'

'For what purpose?' asked Fidelma, intrigued.

'No purpose.' The man grinned. 'Our steward simply likes to know everything that is happening. He is young to have reached the office of *rechtaire*. He has been here barely three years and already thinks he is in charge of all of us.'

'Tell us about the lock,' she invited the smith, mentally noting that he was obviously no big admirer of the steward.

The smith shrugged his massive shoulders and handed her the metal lock. She saw at once that Brother Giolla-na-Naomh was no novice at his art. It was a fine piece of work.

'Not much to tell, really,' the smith said. 'It was Brother Lugna who came to me with the request. Brother Donnchad desired a lock and key to be fitted to the door of his *cotul-tech* . . . beg pardon, *cubiculum*. Brother Lugna insists on using these new Latin names.'

'Did you find that a strange request?' asked Eadulf.

Brother Giolla-na-Naomh smiled briefly. 'I have had

121

stranger requests. But, I suppose it was unusual in our community where trust is our faith and a way of life.'

'There is usually no need to lock anything away? There are no other locks in this community?'

'Of course not. We are a poor community. Does not *The Didache* say, "Share everything with your brother. Do not say it is private property. If you share what is everlasting, you should be that much more willing to share things which do not last." Is that not right, Sister?'

Fidelma regarded him in surprise. 'You have read *The Didache*? It is a rare book, which I have seen only once.' There was envy in her voice.

'Our *tech-screptra* has a copy of the Greek text. It is regarded as one of the central texts of the Faith.'

Eadulf was looking bewildered.

'It is an ancient Greek text,' explained Fidelma quickly. 'It is called *The Didache*, or *The Teaching*, but its full title is *The Teachings of the Twelve Apostles*, and it is said to have been written shortly after their deaths.'

'Anyway,' the smith went on, 'the quotation sums up how our community should live. As the Blessed Tertullian taught, we, who share one mind and soul, have no misgivings about community in property.'

'Very well, let us return to the subject of the lock and key,' Fidelma said. 'You were asked to make them for Brother Donnchad.'

Brother Giolla-na-Naomh nodded.

'Tell me about it.'

'As you see, Sister, the lock was to be *glais iarnaidhi* – an iron lock. I understood from Brother Lugna that it had to be unlike any other lock. I think I achieved that.'

'It is true that I have not seen one like it,' she agreed. 'And the key?'

'I was told that one key only was to be made.'

'And was it?'

'Of course.'

'You fitted the lock yourself?'

'I did, and I gave the only key to Brother Donnchad.'

'I was told that the key was found with Brother Donnchad's body. I hope that it is not lost?'

'I still have it.' Bother Giolla-na-Naomh reached into the leather pouch on his belt. He took out a metal key and handed it to her. She glanced at it. It was made of iron and was nearly seven centimetres in length. It, too, showed good-quality workmanship, with several teeth of varying lengths and spaced irregularly. The other end of the key, the part held between thumb and forefinger, was impressively worked with spiral designs. There was a slippery quality about it.

'And you confirm that this was the key that you made for the lock and found by the body?'

'I do confirm it.'

'No one could open the lock without this key, is that right?' she asked.

Brother Giolla-na-Naomh shrugged. 'No one can guarantee that, for what a man can make, another man can unmake. Isn't that the old saying?'

'But it would take time to unpick the lock and such a method would leave behind markings to show that it had been tampered with.'

'Abbot Iarnla asked me to examine the lock after I had broken in. I had done no damage to the lock, only splintered the wood of the doorjamb where I kicked it open. There were no signs that it had been tampered with.'

'That's fair enough,' Fidelma sighed, examining the key on the palm of her hand. 'What accounts for the quality of the surface? Do you have to oil it to make it work?'

The smith frowned and looked at the key carefully.

'The key should need no oil,' he replied. 'The lock, when I tried it, was working perfectly. But this is not oil. More like wax . . . maybe Brother Donnchad spilt some candle wax on it. It can easily happen. A candle by the side of the bed, a key resting nearby . . .'

Fidelma placed the key in her *marsupium*.

'Keep the lock for me and I will keep the key,' she said.

'I will do so,' Brother Giolla-na-Naomh replied. 'But I would be glad if you did not tell Brother Lugna unless you have no other choice.'

Both Fidelma and Eadulf looked at him in surprise.

'Brother Lugna asked me this morning, before the morning meal, if I would give him the key. I told him that I had mislaid it.'

'He probably meant to hand it to me when we were examining Brother Donnchad's cell.'

Brother Giolla-na-Naomh looked uncomfortable. 'Perhaps.'

Then he added, 'I tell you this strictly between ourselves, Fidelma of Cashel. I am a loyal servant to Abbot Iarnla. Loyal to the abbey and to this kingdom. I will say no more except that our steward told me that I should be frugal with the information I gave you. I have refused to obey his instruction and have provided you with what information is in my knowledge. I say to you, be careful. I suspect our steward has given the same instruction to everyone in this abbey whom you may wish to question.'

Fidelma and Eadulf exchanged a glance.

'Thank you for the warning,' said Fidelma. 'I shall do my best to keep what has passed between us strictly to myself unless the time comes when I must use it in my task to uncover who killed Brother Donnchad.'

'That is fair enough,' said the smith. 'All I wish is for the abbey to prosper and peace to follow my craft.'

'Are we keeping you from the work of rebuilding the community?' Fidelma smiled, glancing round at the building works.

The burly man shook his head. 'Glassán, the master builder, has his own team of workmen,' he said with some resentment in his voice. 'They even have their own forge and smithy outside the abbey for their work. My skills remain for the brethren and not for the new building work.'

'The abbey will be truly magnificent once the new buildings are erected,' Eadulf observed. 'When will that be?'

'Glassán and his men have been working here for two years or so. We estimate that another three years will see all the main buildings in place.'

'The fees for such professional work must be high,' Fidelma remarked innocently.

'I suppose so. Such matters only concern the abbot and Brother Lugna.' Brother Giolla-na-Naomh rose to his feet. 'If you will forgive me, I must tend my forge.'

Eadulf sat down beside Fidelma and they watched him walk back to his forge.

'Well, well,' said Eadulf. 'The steward of this abbey does not want to cooperate with us at all, it seems. Strange that he doesn't want people to speak to us.'

'It is curious,' Fidelma agreed.

'Perhaps he murdered Brother Donnchad?'

'If he did, then he is very stupid to go around trying to stop people speaking to us. It would arouse their suspicions if not ours, and eventually it would get back to us. As it is, I thought the physician's performance was bizarre and now the smith has explained it. The man was probably trying to obey the steward's orders. We will have to watch Brother Lugna very carefully.'

A bell started to ring in the distance.

'What is that?' demanded Eadulf, raising his head.

'Judging from the position of the sun,' Fidelma said, looking up, 'I would say that it is the bell to summon the community for the *eter-shod* – the midday meal. It has been an interesting and exhausting morning and I, for one, would welcome some refreshment.'

CHAPTER SEVEN

Abbot Iarnla walked across to their table as they were rising to leave when the midday meal had finished. The community took three meals a day. The custom was to rise at dawn, wash one's face and hands, and break one's fast with a light meal. The *eter-shod*, or 'middle meal', was taken when the sun was at its zenith. Thankfully, it appeared that Glassán and his assistant Saor ate their midday meal on site and so they were spared another monologue on his craft. Gormán was happily occupying his time fishing along the banks of The Great River. Only Fidelma and Eadulf had been seated at their table.

'I hope you have had a productive morning,' Abbot Iarnla greeted them anxiously. 'Have you reached any conclusions?'

'We are far from any conclusions yet,' replied Fidelma. 'There are many questions that still need to be asked before we can proceed to judgement.'

Abbot Iarnla looked about almost furtively and then, as if

assuring himself that no one was observing him, dropped his voice and said, 'I trust you will forgive me for seating you here, Fidelma. As sister to our King, I considered it more appropriate for you and Eadulf to sit alongside me. However, Brother Lugna informs me that Church customs in Rome . . .' He hesitated, not sure how to proceed.

'We are content here, Abbot Iarnla,' Fidelma replied softly. 'Brother Lugna has made no secret of his resentment of our presence here. We would not wish to impose on him more than we have to.'

'I apologise for him. He is inflexible when it comes to the rules that he has drawn up for the community.'

'Rules that he has drawn up?' Fidelma was surprised. 'I thought the drawing up of rules for the community was the prerogative of the abbot?'

'He believes that the brethren were too lax and free of discipline and order,' the abbot confessed. 'Times change, I suppose. I have tried to run things in the spirit of our blessed founder, Mo-Chuada, but, as you know, the Faith is changing. New ideas are coming in from Rome. So I have been persuaded to let Brother Lugna pursue his course of action to strengthen the community.'

Fidelma was about to say that perhaps he was abrogating too much authority to his young steward but the abbot suddenly turned and motioned to a man who was helping an elderly member of the community along the aisle between the tables towards the door. The younger man hesitated and then guided his companion towards them.

The elderly man could barely walk without the help of the young man's arm and a stout stick he carried in his other hand. His skin was stretched tight on his face, which was white as parchment. His grey eyes were wide, staring and watery. The lips were thin and almost bloodless. He had no hair at all save the white stubble over his chin and upper lip where he had been badly shaved. Flecks of spittle adhered to the corners of his mouth. He could have been any age from four score to a century.

His companion was at no more than three decades in age, with features Fidelma would have described as ugly. His skin was sallow and although he was clean-shaven, the cheeks and chin had a bluish hue, suggesting a thick beard would result if no *altan*, or razor, were applied. His blue-black hair was closely cropped, which was unusual, as both men and women usually wore their hair long, as a mark of beauty. He wore the tonsure of the Irish. The eyes were dark and it was almost impossible to discern the pupils. He had a bulbous nose and thick lips, with a protruding lower lip. The half-open mouth displayed badly kept teeth. Fidelma's eyes dropped to the man's hands and, as she suspected, the man had unkempt nails which were a sign of ill-breeding. It was the custom among the wealthier classes of her people to keep fingernails cut and carefully rounded. He was not a tall man nor well built. He looked like someone whose meals were sparse and infrequently come by. His whole appearance gave the impression of melancholy subservience.

The abbot introduced him. 'This is Brother Gáeth. He was

Brother Donnchad's *anam chara*. I know you wanted to talk to him.'

At that moment the elderly man peered at Fidelma, his eyes narrowing, and he moved closer to her. There seemed a look of hope on his thin features. Then he sighed, shook his head and said in a disappointed tone, 'You are not an angel.'

The abbot appeared embarrassed but Fidelma merely smiled at the old man.

'I am not. I am Fidelma of Cashel.'

The old man was still shaking his head.

'No angel,' he muttered.

'This is the Venerable Bróen, Fidelma.' The abbot offered the introduction in an apologetic tone. 'He was with Mo-Chuada when the abbey was founded. Alas, he is a little . . . a little . . .'

'I have seen an angel,' the old man interjected, speaking in a confidential voice.

Fidelma humoured him. 'That does not fall to the lot of everyone,' she replied solemnly. 'You must be blessed.'

The Venerable Bróen sighed deeply. 'I saw an angel. The blessed one of God flew in the sky. I saw it.'

'Forgive me, Fidelma,' Abbot Iarnla said hurriedly. 'I wanted to introduce you to Brother Gáeth. Brother Gáeth, remain here with the *dálaigh* and I will take the Venerable Bróen back to his *cubiculum*.' So saying, he took the old man's arm and began to lead him away.

They heard the Venerable Bróen's petulant tone. 'I did see

the angel. I did. It came to take the soul of poor Brother Donnchad. I saw it flying in the wind.'

Brother Gáeth remained standing before them with down-cast eyes. To Fidelma, he did not look the sort of person to become the soul friend of an intellectual and scholar such as Brother Donnchad had been. Then she remembered the words from Juvenal's *Satires* and felt guilty: *fronti nulla fides*, no reliance can be placed on appearance.

Fidelma waved to the table they had just risen from.

'Be seated, Brother,' she instructed, reseating herself. Eadulf followed her example, while Brother Gáeth moved slowly to the far side of the table and lowered himself on to the bench, his eyes still downcast.

'I am afraid I know nothing of Brother Donnchad's death,' he volunteered. The words came out in something of a rush. 'He had not spoken to me in days and told me to leave him alone.'

'So when was the last time you spoke to him?'

'About two or three days before his death.'

'How long had you known him?'

'Twenty-five years.' The answer was without hesitation.

'That is a long time,' commented Eadulf. He had estimated Brother Gáeth's age at no more than thirty-five.

'I was his soul friend . . . at one time.'

'Tell us about him,' encouraged Fidelma. 'Firstly, though, tell us something of yourself and how you met him.'

'I was a field worker of the class of *daer-fudir*.'

Eadulf looked surprised for he knew that a *daer-fudir* was

someone who had lost all their rights because of some great crime and had to work almost in a state of bondage to redeem themselves. They were considered untrustworthy and were not entitled to bear arms and had no rights within the clan. The third generation of *daer-fudir* was automatically reinstated, given their rights back, and could be eligible for election to any office within society. But usually a *daer-fudir* was a stranger, perhaps a fugitive from another territory who had sought asylum; often they were criminals or captives taken in battle.

'It was my father who caused our family's downfall,' muttered Brother Gáeth as if in answer to Fidelma and Eadulf's unasked question.

'Tell us more of this,' invited Fidelma.

'It was simple enough. My father killed a chieftain of the Uí Liatháin. He fled with my mother and me and sought sanctuary with a lord of the Déisi called Eochaid of An Dún.'

'You mean the father of Brother Donnchad?' Eadulf asked in surprise.

Brother Gáeth nodded. 'I was very young. Eochaid could have handed us back to the Uí Liatháin for punishment but he decided that he would grant my family asylum on the land but as *daer-fudir* to work and toil for him. My father died after several years of labour, my mother soon after. Eochaid died and Lady Eithne took control. She was a hard mistress.'

'But you are now a member of the brethren here,' observed Fidelma. 'How did this happen?'

'How did I become a member of this community rather than still toiling in the fields for Lady Eithne of An Dún?'

'Exactly so,' replied Fidelma.

'Through the intercession of Donnchad,' Brother Gáeth said.

'In what way did he intercede?'

'Although I was servant to Lord Eochaid and Lady Eithne, I was treated well by their sons, Cathal and Donnchad. We almost grew up together. It was through them I learnt something of reading and writing. It was Donnchad who spent most time with me, teaching me how to construe words and form letters. And he would speak about the Faith and tell me wondrous things. One day he told me that he and his brother Cathal would be joining the community here at Lios Mór. I felt devastated. Abandoned. I said that I wished I had the freedom to go with him if only to be his servant.

'At that he laughed and said none of the brethren of the community had servants. Then he paused with a strange look in his eye and left me. A few days later, he found me in the fields and said he had spoken with his mother. She had agreed to release me to the community. So it was,' he ended with a shrug.

There was a short silence between them.

'So you came with Cathal and Donnchad and joined the community.'

'And have been here ever since.'

'And what tasks do you perform in the community?'

Brother Gáeth chuckled sourly. 'I exchanged life as a field

worker for Lady Eithne to become a field worker for the abbot of Lios Mór. I am still of the rank of *daer-fudir*.'

Fidelma was surprised. Such ranks did not exist among the brethren of an abbey.

'You sound bitter, Brother Gáeth,' she said.

'Before my father's crime, he was a chieftain of the Uí Liatháin, he was Selbach, lord of Dún Guairne. He led some of his people, with a band of missionaries, across the great sea to a land of the Britons called Kernow. A ruler called Teudrig massacred most of them there. My father and some others escaped and returned home. He found his cousin had usurped his place as chieftain in his absence and he challenged him to single combat. In the combat that followed my father killed his cousin. His enemies persuaded the people that it was *fingal*, or kin-slaying. The Brehon, also an enemy to my father, declared the crime so horrendous that my father should be placed in a boat without sail or oars, and with food and water for one day only. He should be taken out to sea and cast adrift. That night he managed to escape and took my mother and me to seek refuge with the Déisi.'

Fidelma gazed at him. 'What you tell me does not seem to be justice. Surely it could be shown that the Brehon was biased and the punishment a harsh one? Why was this matter not appealed to the Chief Brehon of the kingdom? Why was it not brought to the attention of the King in Cashel? There is provision in law for these things.'

Brother Gáeth shrugged. 'I only know what I know. I was

but a boy at the time and this was over a score of years ago.'

'And is the current chieftain of the Uí Liatháin related to you?' asked Eadulf.

'Uallachán is the nephew of the cousin my father slew,' said Brother Gáeth.

'What happened after you joined the community?' prompted Fidelma.

'Donnchad continued to treat me well. He became a great scholar and his time was spent mainly in the *tech-screptra* while I worked from sun-up until sun-down in the fields outside the abbey.'

'But you became his *anam chara*, his soul friend.'

'As I said, he was kind to me. He continued to talk to me as he had when we were boys. He told me much about the wondrous things he was learning from the great books in the library. He insisted that I be officially regarded as his soul friend.'

'Did the abbot approve of this?'

'Not entirely. He felt that Donnchad should have a soul friend who was his intellectual equal.'

Fidelma's eyes widened at the phrase. It sounded alien to the man.

'You overheard him say that?' she asked quickly.

'Yes. That is what the abbot said to Donnchad. But Donnchad told him that he felt comfortable telling me his problems. So, every week, before the start of the Sabbath, we would meet and he would tell me of the events of the week and I would listen. I often wished I had learning to read the works of the great saints as he did and the very words that our Lord spoke when he walked the earth.'

Eadulf could not help but glance at Fidelma. Surely a soul friend was more than someone to talk at but a friend who could understand and exchange ideas and spiritually guide their friend, saving them from making mistakes.

'I presume this stopped when the ruler of the Déisi accused Cathal and Donnchad of plotting against him,' Fidelma said.

'Yes,' said Brother Gáeth with a sigh. 'They had to leave the community and go into hiding. I did not hear from Donnchad until he passed through the abbey for a single night with his brother en route to Ard Mór and lands beyond the seas. He told me he and his brother were going on a pilgrimage to the Holy Land, the very land in which our saviour walked and taught. Ah, but I wanted to go with him. But I was merely a *daer-fudir*, a field worker.'

'And so you stayed here,' Fidelma said patiently. 'When did you next see Donnchad?'

Brother Gáeth smiled at the remembrance. 'On his return. His return here was triumphant. The community, even the abbot himself, turned out to welcome him.' He paused and shook his head sadly. 'But Donnchad had changed. I went to greet him but it was as if he did not know me. After that first day, I left him alone for a while, thinking it was just the strangeness of his return that had made him seem preoccupied and distant. After he had had time to settle, I went to see him again. He was no longer preoccupied but he was harsh and cruel to me.' Brother Gáeth lowered his head, as if trying to conceal his emotion.

'How was he cruel?' pressed Fidelma.

'He told me that he did not want to know me.'

'Did he explain why?'

Brother Gáeth shook his head. He reminded Fidelma of a dog who had been badly treated for no reason by his master and could not understand it.

'He gave you no explanation at all?'

'He said, cast off your robes and escape from this place into the mountains. In the mountains there is solitude and sanity. There is no sanity among men.'

Fidelma sat back, her eyes a little wider than before. 'Those were his exact words?'

Brother Gáeth nodded. 'I remember them as if they were spoken but moments ago.'

'When did this conversation take place?'

'That was a day or two before his death. He told me that he did not want to see me ever again. He told me to leave this community and seek sanity. I still have no idea what he meant.'

'You never spoke to him again?' asked Eadulf.

'I have said so,' Brother Gáeth replied.

'Did you know that just before he was found dead, his mother came to see him?' asked Eadulf.

'I saw her riding to the abbey while I was in the fields but I think that was a few days before he was found dead.'

'Had you met her again since she gave you leave to join the community here?'

'Not exactly.' There was bitterness in his tone. 'She would pass me by on her visits. Whether she even saw me or not, I do not know. That was how it was when I worked on her lands. Perhaps she would not have recognised who I was anyway. I was just another field worker.'

'Do you know how she felt about her sons?' asked Fidelma.

'Oh, she idolised them. She was very proud of them. It is thanks to the Lady Eithne that there is all this building work at the abbey.'

Eadulf's head came up sharply. 'Is it?'

Brother Gáeth looked at him as if surprised he did not know. 'Of course. When word came that her sons, Cathal and Donnchad, had reached the Holy Land, she came to the abbot. The whole community knows that she offered to help fund the replacement of the wooden buildings with great structures of stone that would last forever and help the abbey become one of the great beacons of the new Faith in the west. The condition she made was that the abbey should be a memorial to them.'

'I see,' Fidelma said softly. 'So all this work is not being paid for by the abbey but by Lady Eithne of Dún?'

'That is so.'

'What did Donnchad say about it on his return?' asked Eadulf.

'He never mentioned it but, as I have said, he hardly spoke to me.'

'Do you know if he confided in anyone else?'

'I do not.'

'But you observed that something was disturbing him. Could it have been connected with this matter?' asked Eadulf.

'All I know is that his face was black as a storm from the moment he rode back through the gates.'

'Do you think that this was because his brother, Cathal, had decided to remain in Tarantum and accept the *pallium* as bishop of that city?' asked Fidelma. 'After all, they were close as brothers and had come to this place together to be members of the community. And they had undertaken that arduous pilgrimage to the Holy Land together. That must have affected Donnchad.'

Brother Gáeth thrust out his lower lip for a moment. He appeared to give the question some thought and then shook his head slowly.

'Among the things that he said when he last spoke to me was to curse his brother, calling him a fool and worse.'

Fidelma could not suppress a look of surprise in Eadulf's direction.

'Everyone is calling Cathal blessed, that he is one of the saints. Yet you say his own brother called him a fool and cursed him? Why so?'

'I can only repeat what Donnchad said,' Brother Gáeth replied stubbornly. 'That is what he said.'

Fidelma sat back reflectively. 'You have been most helpful, Brother Gáeth. Thank you for answering our questions.'

Fidelma and Eadulf sat in silence for a few moments after Brother Gáeth had left the *refectorium*.

'Well, I had the impression that Brother Gáeth was

supposed to be a simpleton,' Fidelma said. 'He seems intelligent enough but just constrained by circumstances.'

'There are a lot of sad people in this world,' Eadulf commented. 'Didn't Horace write, *non licet omnibus adire Corinthum* – not everyone is permitted to go to Corinth?' In Horace's day, Corinth was a centre of entertainment and pleasure that not many people could afford. It had come to mean that circumstances deny people certain achievements.

'But who altered his circumstances?' Fidelma wondered.

'What do you mean?'

'His father is forced to flee from what, most likely, was an unjust death sentence. Such a sentence is only given to the incorrigibles who will not pay compensation or be rehabilitated. So such a sentence is suspect. He flees from his clan territory and ends his life as a *daer-fudir*, which involves two generations of bondage. Why did no one among his people take up his cause? Did he not have a friend in the world?'

'Apparently not,' said Eadulf. 'At least we have found the answer to one mystery.'

'Which is?'

'Who is providing the funding for the rebuilding of the abbey.'

'Lady Eithne is committed to the Faith and proud of her sons and their achievements, so that is natural.'

'What is our next task?'

'To go to the *scriptorium*. We must see if we can find out anything more about the missing manuscripts.'

'So what do we know so far?' asked Eadulf.

'Let's enumerate the facts. You start.'

'Very well. Brother Donnchad, a well-regarded scholar, returns to this abbey after a pilgrimage, which has made him something of a hero. He starts behaving in a curious manner. He is reported to have some precious manuscripts with him. He becomes reclusive and even tells his soul friend that he does not want to see him. He says he fears that his manuscripts will be stolen and then he fears for his life. He is reported as cursing his brother for a fool and advising his former soul friend to leave the abbey and take to the mountains. A few days later he is found in his cell stabbed to death.'

'And the curious facts about that are . . .?'

'He is stabbed twice in the back but the body is lain on the bed in a position of repose. The door is locked and there is only one key that locks the door and that is found by the body. That poses the question of how did the murderer enter and how did they exit taking, we presume, the manuscripts?'

'That is so,' agreed Fidelma. 'Then we have to consider the reason Donnchad gave for requesting a lock on his door with only one key, which you have mentioned. He was fearful someone might rob him of these valuable manuscripts. Yet no one ever saw them . . .'

'Except Lady Eithne,' pointed out Eadulf. 'Why would she lie?'

'Therefore we presume that the murderer stole them but how?'

'And so we shall question the *scriptor* of this abbey as, if anyone in the abbey knows about such things, it would be the librarian.'

Fidelma rose and turned to the door of the *refectorium* with Eadulf following. To their surprise they found Abbot Iarnla waiting outside the door for them. He seemed a little self-conscious.

'How did you get on with Brother Gáeth?' he asked anxiously.

'As you thought, he could tell us little,' Fidelma answered. 'It seems he has not been in the position of a soul friend since Brother Donnchad's return.'

'I thought he would have little to add,' said the abbot. He stood awkwardly, looking at the ground, as if he wanted to say something more.

'Brother Gáeth seems to have led a sad life,' supplied Eadulf when the silence became awkward.

'Ah.' Abbot Iarnla looked up and sighed. 'He told you he was of the *daer-fudir*?'

'I was under the impression that once a person passes through the portals of a community, such distinctions no longer existed. A king who abdicates to enter an abbey is regarded as being on the same level as a *céile*, a free clansman, or a *daer-fudir*. There is no difference in class between them.'

'Not exactly so, Brother Eadulf,' returned the abbot. 'Fidelma will confirm this. An abbey comes under the patronage of nobles and the kings, who present the community with the land on which they build. It cannot be alienated and if the community seek to dispense with it, they can only do so with the permission of the noble or king who granted it to them. In this, as in all things, they are subject to the Law of the Fénechus and the judgement of the Brehons.'

'Yet there is a new movement developing,' Fidelma pointed out. 'The adoption of Roman ideas, where communities take the land in full ownership and are bound by the Penitentials rather than our own law. Abbots often regard themselves as powerful as kings within these communities.'

Abbot Iarnla flushed. 'My abbey obeys the laws of this kingdom, Sister, in spite of . . .' He was obviously about to say 'Brother Lugna's rules' but he stopped himself. 'You may assure your brother, the King, of that fact. When Brother Gáeth entered this community, he was released into our charge by the Lady Eithne as a *daer-fudir*. She said that the initial judgement came from the Uí Liatháin and it must stand; that was the condition. Only Gáeth's death will absolve him from the liability that his father placed on him.'

'Or by dispensation of the abbot,' pointed out Fidelma.

'Who can only act with the approval of the lord of the territory.'

'Doesn't Brother Gáeth resent the fact that he continues to be condemned by Lady Eithne and yourself?' asked Eadulf.

'He told you that?' asked the abbot sharply, for the first time showing anger.

Fidelma shook her head. 'We detected a certain resentment but he did not say so outwardly. I think he may have hoped that his life would change when he entered the abbey, as it has for so many others.'

'You were told his story? How his father Selbach slew a chief of the Uí Liatháin and how he fled to Lord Eochaid of An Dún from whom we received this land?'

'He told us.'

'The Lady Eithne, the widow of Eochaid, allowed him to come here at the earnest request of her son Donnchad, but the law still applies. I have tried to treat him with understanding as I would any other brother here, but clearly he continues to feel resentful.'

'Can you expect any other attitude given the circumstances?' demanded Fidelma.

'I suppose not,' Abbot Iarnla reluctantly agreed.

'And you say you cannot change his status because of Lady Eithne.'

'She will not discuss it.'

'Couldn't a *daer-fudir* be given work other than digging the fields and similar drudgery? He seems sensitive enough.'

'Sensitivity is not education.'

'He says that he reads and writes and has some Latin.'

'We have tested him and, alas, he is not proficient enough to undertake anything more responsible.'

'Have you given him an opportunity to improve his ability?'

Abbot Iarnla nodded. 'We are not insensitive ourselves, Fidelma. Indeed, we have tried. He has reached the level that we expect in a young boy. His ability to read is impaired. Beyond a simple level, he does not proceed. He used to get frustrated. Sometimes he threw tantrums like any child would. Brother Donnchad used to be able to calm him.'

'He did tell us that Brother Donnchad taught him his basic reading and writing,' said Eadulf.

'You must have been worried that Brother Donnchad determined on Gáeth as a soul friend,' Fidelma remarked.

'It did seem strange that a man as intelligent and scholarly as Donnchad would insist on such a person as his spiritual guide,' admitted the abbot. 'But then they had been boys together and playmates. But I saw no benefits in Gáeth being able to give spiritual guidance to Donnchad.'

'It seems a curious relationship. Did Cathal ever enter it?'

'Cathal was older than Donnchad and did not have much to do with Gáeth.'

'What happened when Cathal and Donnchad left on their pilgrimage to the Holy Land?'

'What happened?' The abbot did not understand.

'What was Brother Gáeth's reaction at the loss of his friend Donnchad? How was Gáeth managed if he had tantrums that could only be calmed by Brother Donnchad?'

'Ah, I see. Certainly we had some trouble with him. He continued moody and uncommunicative. Once or twice I even thought he might try to abscond from the community. But Gáeth has been constrained by the law and by tradition most of his life, and in the event he knew he could not break with it.'

'You mean he just accepted the legal obligations of being a *daer-fudir*?' Eadulf asked incredulously.

'I think he knew his place in the scheme of things.'

Eadulf was about to say something else when he caught a warning glance from Fidelma.

'I am interested, Abbot Iarnla, as to why you seemed concerned that we should talk to Brother Gáeth,' she said.

Once more, Abbot Iarnla became embarrassed. 'I wanted you to have a chance to meet and discuss matters with Brother Gáeth.'

'And now that we have?' demanded Fidelma sharply, when he hesitated again.

'Now that you have, did he mention when he last saw Brother Donnchad?'

Fidelma saw that there was some meaning behind the question.

'He said it was two or three days before Donnchad's death,' Eadulf answered.

'Then he did not tell you the truth. It was the day before Brother Donnchad died,' said the abbot. 'I saw him hurrying away from Donnchad's cell. Brother Lugna wanted to start allocating the accommodation to some of our senior clerics here and I felt that I should inspect them. I was in the next *cubiculum* but one to Brother Donnchad's when I heard his door open. I heard Brother Donnchad's voice say, "I rely on you, Gáeth." Then I heard Gáeth exit into the passage.'

'Did Brother Gáeth reply?' asked Eadulf.

'He did. He said, "It shall be put in the place of the dead. Have no fear. It will be just as you say." Then I heard the door close and the key turn.'

'It shall be put in the place of the dead?' repeated Fidelma. 'Did you confront Brother Gáeth?'

Abbot Iarnla shook his head. 'I did not. As I said, Brother

Donnchad shut the door and I heard Gáeth walking past the cell door where I was. When he had passed by I peered out and saw him heading towards the stairs. There is a window overlooking the quadrangle and so I went and leaned out to watch him come out of the building below. He was putting something under his cloak, for he was wearing one.'

'Something? What sort of something?'

Abbot Iarnla shrugged. 'I suppose it could have been anything. I had the impression it was a scroll.'

'What sort of a scroll?'

'It might have been a parchment.'

'I wish you had told me this before we spoke to him. I might have been able to draw him out on this matter,' Fidelma said irritably.

'I had hoped that he would volunteer the truth rather than have to be confronted by it. One thing is certain, if Brother Donnchad entrusted Gáeth to undertake this task for him, then we must assume there must still have been some friendship between them,' the abbot concluded.

'Perhaps,' replied Fidelma. 'This place of the dead that Gáeth mentioned, was it a *relec*, a graveyard, or was it an *otharlige*, a specific sepulchre? His exact words might give a clue as to where he was going to bury this object with which Donnchad had entrusted him.'

Abbot Iarnla brightened. 'You are right, Fidelma. I had not thought of that. Gáeth chose an unusual word. He said *dindgna*.'

'That is a mound, a small elevation,' Fidelma translated. 'The mound of the dead? Does that mean anything to you?'

'Not at all. Our cemetery to the east, where Donnchad himself is now buried, is a low-lying flatland surrounded by trees. But our chapel was originally built on a mound because our founder wanted it to overlook the community. The only people buried there are our founder, Mo-Chuada, and his successor, Abbot Cuanan. No one else.'

'I will not pursue this matter with Brother Gáeth for the moment, for I need to gather a few more facts,' Fidelma said. 'It shall remain a secret between us.'

'You are a discerning person, Fidelma of Cashel. I know that. Otherwise I would not have invited you here to investigate this case.' The abbot fidgeted, as if trying to formulate words to express what was on his mind, 'You said that you detected some resentment in Gáeth. Now that you know he has lied to you about the last time he saw Brother Donnchad, what do you think?'

'I think you should tell me what is on your mind,' prompted Fidelma.

'While Brother Donnchad was in this community, he seemed to exercise a control over Gáeth that calmed him and made him at peace with his lot in the scheme of things.

'And when Brother Donnchad was due to set out on his pilgrimage, Gáeth at first wanted to accompany him and his brother Cathal. That concerned me and it was explained that such a thing was not possible.'

'What reason did you give?'

Abbot Iarnla shrugged. 'Simple enough. Cathal was against it and so was Lady Eithne.'

'Since when does Lady Eithne pronounce rules for this community to obey?' queried Eadulf.

Abbot Iarnla looked uncomfortable. 'I have already explained to you that this land is under her jurisdiction according to the law of the Fénechus.'

'We appreciate that. And this accounts for her control?' asked Eadulf.

'Under the law and with the judgement of the Brehons,' confirmed the abbot patiently. 'On the matter of the pilgrimage, Cathal probably made his views known to his mother and she made her views known to me. Gáeth was to remain here in the abbey while Cathal and Donnchad proceeded on their pilgrimage. Gáeth was not happy to see his lifetime's friend and companion leave, especially in view of the fact that Donnchad was the only person among the brethren who seemed to have time to sit down and talk to him.'

'But then Donnchad returned.'

'Donnchad returned,' sighed the abbot. 'But not the same Donnchad who left, as has been explained to you. Can you imagine what his rejection of his former soul friend meant to Gáeth?'

There was a silence.

'I once knew a man,' said Eadulf suddenly in a reflective tone. 'He had a dog whom he petted and fussed over. The dog went everywhere with him, even slept on his bed. Then the man met a woman. They married. The dog was no longer important and was chased out of the bedroom and when it whined and howled, it was chased from the house. When it continued to whine and howl, the man chased it from the village, throwing stones at it. As he did so, the dog, angered by the rejection and hurt by the flying stones, leapt for the man and bit him in the throat. The man died.' Eadulf regarded the abbot expectantly. Finally Abbot Iarnla stirred.

'You must draw your own conclusions,' he said. 'I am just recounting the facts. I will see you in the *refectorium* this evening.'

They watched him walk away and then Fidelma turned to Eadulf. 'I cannot see Gáeth having the ability to carry out this killing. The lock, the manuscripts . . . no. It is too complicated.'

Eadulf pulled a face. 'But the motive is there. Gáeth could have killed Donnchad in resentment and retaliation for his rejection. It's a logical suggestion.'

Fidelma shook her head but did not answer.

Chapter Eight

The *tech-screptra*, or *scriptorium*, was a large wooden structure located next to a muddy area from which a new stone building was rising. Several men were at work on the site, some carrying stones, others sawing and nailing wood. There was no sign of Glassán, the master builder, but they presumed that he would be somewhere in the construction. The wooden *scriptorium* was the most imposing of the old buildings in the abbey complex. It was imposing not because of its size but in its design. It was an oblong two storeys high, with a frame of large oak timbers and covered with red yew planking decorated with intricate carvings of symbols and icons.

As they entered through large double oak doors, the first impression was of one great room that rose up to a high vaulted ceiling. The second floor, accessible by steep stairs at both ends of the room, was a gallery that ran round the building halfway up. The walls of the library were entirely covered by *pels*, or racks, from which hung *tiaga lebar*, leather

151

book satchels. Each satchel contained one or more manu-scripts, whose titles were labelled on the outside. The satchels were also used to carry books, especially by missionaries on their travels. They were regarded with great veneration. It was famously told that when Longarad of Sliabh Mairge, a friend of Colmcille and the most eminent scholar of his age, died, the book satchels of Ireland fell down from their racks.

At the far end of the *scriptorium*, underneath two large windows that were designed to let in as much light as possible, were six desks. Each had an elaborately edged flat top placed on a carved wooden plinth shaped like a tripod. Six young members of the brethren were bent over books placed on these. One hand used a maulstick to support their wrists while they wrote industriously with the other.

A fleshy-faced man who had been overseeing one of the busy scribes looked up and saw them. He came waddling towards them, for he was overweight and moved awkwardly. His heavy flushed jowls seemed to move of their own accord but there was a friendly smile on his features.

'Sister Fidelma! You are most welcome. Welcome. As soon as I heard you were in the abbey, I knew that you would come to visit me before long.'

Fidelma held out both hands to take the fat man's great paw between them.

'Brother Donnán, it is good to see you again.'

The man beamed happily at her remembrance of him. 'It is some years since you were here last and then sitting in judgement in the court . . .' he began.

'And you were my clerk and helped to keep the court in order,' responded Fidelma. She turned to Eadulf. 'Brother Donnán is the *leabhar coimedach* here,' she said, using the Irish term. 'This is Eadulf.'

'Greetings, Brother Eadulf.' Brother Donnán smiled. 'I am called the *scriptor* these days. Brother Lugna, our steward, prefers us to use the Roman titles rather than our own Irish ones.' He suddenly chuckled. 'Yet he finds it difficult to get people to call him *Œconomus* instead of *rechtaire*.'

'Brother Lugna is the only senior member of the community I have seen here with a Roman tonsure,' Fidelma remarked.

'That is true,' agreed Brother Donnán. 'And true again that our *rechtaire* is keen to adopt the ideas agreed at the councils at Streonshalh and at Autun. He wants the abbey to bring in Roman usage and the Rule of Benedict. He has already brought in several new rules.'

'And what does the community say?'

'We elect to follow our own liturgy. But Brother Lugna, as steward, makes small changes here and there, such as our titles of office. These changes can be tolerated. But he has begun to discourage the old concepts of the *conhospitae*. He is one of the aesthetes that favours celibacy.'

'I had noticed that there were few women in your community now,' murmured Fidelma.

'Indeed, and they will not be here long for already arrangements have been made for them to move. This idea of celibacy among us seems to be spreading quickly now.'

'Brother Lugna appears very involved in the proposals to rebuild the abbey.'

'Indeed, he is. When he arrived here he was always boasting of the great stone buildings he had seen in Rome. He felt that this abbey should be built in their image.'

'But I thought it was Lady Eithne's idea as a tribute to her sons. Are you saying that it was Brother Lugna who persuaded Lady Eithne to rebuild the abbey?'

'Brother Lugna is a strong personality and no doubt when Abbot Iarnla is taken to the heavenly pasture, Brother Lugna will be his succesor,' replied Brother Donnán glumly. 'At that time, I have no doubt that as abbot he will introduce the Penitentials and Benedictine Rule. Let us pray that Abbot Iarnla may have a long life before him.'

'I suspect that you do not approve of Brother Lugna?' Eadulf remarked with humour. 'Do I detect that your steward is not entirely popular?'

The fat librarian grinned. 'You have a keen eye, Brother Eadulf,' he replied.

'Brother Lugna can only enforce his changes if he is elected abbot and the community approve the changes,' pointed out Fidelma more seriously. This was the custom of all the abbeys and of the native churches. Abbots were chosen and elected in the same way that chieftains and kings were chosen. In the abbeys the community were considered the family of the abbot and therefore it was the *derbhfine*, the electoral college, who chose and endorsed his successor.

'True enough, Sister,' agreed the *scriptor*. 'But, as I say, let us hope that the day when Abbot Iarnla stands down as abbot is a long way ahead of us. But enough gossip. I am sure you have come to speak to me about the death of poor Brother Donnchad. How may I serve you?'

'I am sure that you must have known him well,' said Fidelma. 'His reputation as a scholar was well known.'

'I thought I knew him well enough. I joined the community shortly after he and his brother Cathal did. Both of them spent most of their time in our *scriptorium*, as did I.' He gestured with his podgy hand around the hall. 'They were both scholars of considerable merit. And a great asset to the reputation of this library.'

'You certainly have a magnificent library, Brother Donnán,' agreed Eadulf.

The fat librarian seemed to appreciate the praise. 'We have a great many books here,' he said with satisfaction. Then his expression changed into one of seriousness. 'But it is not for books that you have come here.'

'Would you know Brother Donnchad's handwriting?' Fidelma asked.

The *scriptor* nodded. 'I believe I would. He wrote with a distinctive style.'

Fidelma produced the scrap of parchment they had found below Donnchad's window.

'*Si vis transfer calicem istrum a me ... Deicide! Deicide! Deicide!*' muttered Brother Donnán as he studied the text.

'Is that his hand?' pressed Fidelma.

'It is not much of a sample by which to judge,' he said. Then he glanced at it again and shook his head. 'I would say that Brother Donnchad did not write this.'

'What subjects was he interested in?'

'Arguments on philosophical matters mostly. But that was before he left on his pilgrimage.'

'Did he continue to research here after he returned from his pilgrimage?'

The *scriptor* shook his head immediately. 'He did request parchment, ink and quills and I provided him with what he wanted. Such writing materials are getting expensive these days,' he added.

'And where are his writings now?'

'I had assumed they would be in his room but I have heard a rumour that there was nothing there.'

'Did he leave anything in the library, anything at all?'

'He lodged several of his early works here as well as copies he made of other scholars' work. He was a good copyist and his own commentaries were excellent. But that was, of course, before he went on his pilgrimage and I suspect you are more interested in the period following his return.'

'Your suspicion is correct, Brother Donnán.'

'Well, he came here several times. I think he was checking references in other works. But I never heard of anything he was writing.'

'Some libraries keep a record of what books their scholars examine,' Eadulf said. 'Do you?'

Brother Donnán glanced towards a desk in the corner. 'I

pride myself on the way I run this library. I do keep a list of the items that members of the brethren ask for in the library.' He smiled briefly.

'So what manner of manuscripts was Brother Donnchad interested in?' asked Fidelma.

'Works on the philosophy of the Faith mainly, particularly the works of the founding fathers.'

'Can you be more specific?'

Brother Donnán hesitated, thinking, before he said, 'He asked to see the works of Origenes.'

'Origenes?' Eadulf frowned.

'A Greek from Alexandria who was one of the great early theologians of the Faith,' explained Brother Donnán. 'He lived many centuries ago. He was nicknamed Adamantios – the unbreakable one.'

'And do you have copies of his works here?' Fidelma asked.

The *scriptor* smiled. 'Not everything of his, I grant you, lady. But we have some of his important works such as *On First Principles*, some of his many commentaries on the books of the Bible, essays on prayer and on martyrdom . . .'

'Do you remember what work Brother Donnchad was particularly interested in?'

Brother Donnán shrugged. 'Not offhand.'

Eadulf glanced across to the desk in the corner. 'Then perhaps your lists will provide an answer,' he suggested, moving towards it.

Brother Donnán hurried forward to the large side table on which a ledger rested. Near the table was a member of the brethren deep in study of one of the manuscript books. He looked up as they approached and smiled briefly. It was the *bruigad*, the keeper of the guesthouse, Brother Máel Eoin. They exchanged a smile of recognition before he returned to the work he was reading. Brother Donnán started to turn the pages of the ledger. Fidelma and Eadulf peered over his shoulders. The pages consisted of lists given under various names. The *scriptor* halted at a page headed with Donnchad's name and began running his finger quickly down the list.

'Origenes,' Fidelma said sharply. 'You ran past the name, Brother Donnán. See there? It says Origenes, eight books entitled *Contra Celsum*, and you have marked it as a specific request. Isn't that date only a few days before Brother Donnchad was killed?'

The *scriptor* flushed, apparently embarrassed at nearly missing the entry. 'Indeed, I believe it was a week before he died.'

'*Contra Celsum*? What is that?' asked Eadulf.

'Arguments against Celsus; he was a pagan writer.'

'I have to admit, Brother Donnán, that I have never heard of Celsus.'

'Better that no one hears of him,' replied the *scriptor* in disapproval. 'He was a great opponent of the True Faith. However, Origenes pointed out the error of his ways so that people could see his arguments were false.'

'And do you have this work here?' asked Fidelma.

Brother Donnán shook his head indignantly. 'How can you

ask if we have the work of Celsus, a pagan, in a Christian library, Sister? For shame.'

'I meant the work of Origenes, the work that Brother Donnchad requested.' Fidelma chose not to point out that most libraries were filled with the works of Greeks and Latins who had lived long before the coming of the Faith.

'We do – or rather we did. The abbey at Ard Mór requested that we lend them the copy. We frequently exchange books with them. As soon as Brother Donnchad had finished with it, we sent it to the abbey of Ard Mór with someone who was making the journey there.'

'I wonder why Brother Donnchad would be interested in reading the arguments of Origenes against Celsus?' She posed the question rhetorically, not expecting an answer.

'Little is known about Celsus except that he was probably a Greek who lived during the reign of the Roman Emperor Marcus Aurelius.' The *scriptor* seemed to pride himself on his knowledge of his books and he liked to share it. 'That is, he lived about two centuries after the birth of the Christ. His main work was called *Alethos Logos*, which is Greek for *The True Word,* and he showed himself to be an implacable opponent of the Christians. He tried to ridicule Christians for what he claimed was their advocacy of blind faith instead of reason.'

Fidelma stirred uncomfortably. In the many years that she had served both the law of the Fénechus as well as the Faith, she had always been uncomfortable when her questions could not be answered. On every difficult question she was told one simply had to have faith; one had to believe and not question the belief. She wondered what Origenes had argued if Celsus had brought up similar questions.

'And what do you know of the book *Contra Celsum*?'

'I have not read it.'

'A pity,' sighed Eadulf. 'And you never had a copy of Celsus's original work? If you had the refutation, it surely would be logical to have a copy of what it refuted.'

'Brother Donnchad made the very same point,' replied Brother Donnán. 'As I have said, our library is filled only with books by the faithful. Indeed, Brother Lugna now insists on obedience to this rule. I was told to discard the works of any that are critical of the Faith.'

'Sometimes one learns and receives strength by studying the arguments of those of contrary opinion,' Fidelma said. 'Do we know what matters Celsus raised that needed to be refuted?'

'The important thing is that we know he was wrong,' said Brother Donnán with a pious air.

'But how do we know that?' asked Fidelma.

Brother Donnán looked shocked. 'Because Origenes tells us it is so.'

Fidelma sighed softly but did not bother to pursue the argument.

'Did Brother Donnchad mention why he was researching this work?'

'He was never much of a conversationalist, unlike his brother Cathal. Cathal was always the talkative one but Donnchad was very introspective, and preferred his own company or that of the simpleton.'

'Simpleton?' Eadulf's tone was sharp.

'Brother Gáeth,' the *scriptor* said, unabashed. 'He is a field worker who can barely write his own name. You will meet him no doubt and will be able to judge for yourself.'

Fidelma shot a warning glance at Eadulf who was obviously about to admit to their discussion with Brother Gáeth.

'But he was Brother Donnchad's *anam chara*,' she pointed out.

'That was before he went on his pilgrimage,' replied the *scriptor*. 'Anyway, Brother Donnchad had no need of such a soul friend.'

'Do you know if the brethren ever discussed why Brother Donnchad became reclusive?' she asked, ignoring the remark.

Brother Donnán hesitated before lifting one shoulder and letting it fall to signal his lack of knowledge. 'I do not listen to gossip.'

'Yet sometimes gossip leads to truth,' Fidelma encouraged.

'I would not know,' the *scriptor* replied. Then, realising they were waiting for him to make some further reply to the question, he added, 'Some said that he was not right in the mind because of the hardships encountered on his journey. Others opined that he felt abandoned by his elder brother Cathal because he remained behind, having been offered the *pallium* of some foreign city.'

'But what did you think?'

Brother Donnán was reflective. 'To be truthful, I thought he had become a little crazy.'

'In what way?'

'He became furtive, secretive, felt people were hatching plots against him or about to rob him of things. I heard that he demanded a lock to the door of his *cubiculum* – a lock and key!' The *scriptor* raised his arms in a gesture of helplessness. 'Now I realise that perhaps he wasn't so crazy after all because of the manner of his death. But I thought at the time that his fears were part of his dementia.'

'As you say, now that he has been murdered, perhaps he wasn't so crazy,' Eadulf commented.

The *scriptor* remained silent.

'We are told that he brought back manuscripts from his travels and other artefacts,' said Fidelma. 'Precious manuscripts.'

Brother Donnán smiled and turned to her eagerly. 'I was looking forward to seeing them. I heard there were some valuable manuscripts which our library could take a pride in owning.'

'But you have not seen them?'

'Brother Donnchad, as I have said, was scared of someone stealing them and so kept them in his *cubiculum*.'

'So he did not deposit any of his manuscripts with the library?'

Brother Donnán shook his head. 'Not since his return from the pilgrimage.'

'And the artefacts,' Eadulf said. 'Who were they given to?'

'He brought back a sliver of the True Cross, of course. That is now in the recess of the altar in our chapel.'

'Anything else?'

'I think he brought some gifts for his mother Lady Eithne.

One was a lovely ornate cross from the east. The jewels are magnificent. When he presented them at the fortress . . .' The *scriptor* suddenly hesitated.

'You were there?' prompted Fidelma.

'I have visited several times to take manuscripts to Lady Eithne,' admitted the librarian.

'Brother Donnchad used to visit his mother, then?'

'Her fortress is not far from here. You passed it on the road that crosses The Great River before you turn along it westward to the abbey.'

'I know it,' said Fidelma quickly. 'So you saw him recently at his mother's fortress?'

Brother Donnán shook his head. 'He went to pay his respects to his mother the day after he arrived back. That was early summer. I think he spent several days with her before returning to the abbey. It was a coincidence that I was there at the time.'

'He was not there more recently?'

'Not that I know of. I often take books to the fortress.'

'Did you know that his mother was sent for when it became clear that all was not well with him?'

'It is now well known among the brethren,' Brother Donnán said. 'The master builder, Glassán, told me. He spoke to Lady Eithne when she was leaving the abbey just a few days before he was found murdered. Glassán is a talkative fellow.'

'Well,' Fidelma said, after a moment's further thought, 'that seems to be all . . .' Then she hesitated. 'One thing does strike me. Do you know of any library that holds the original work of Celsus? Have you ever heard of any library holding such a work?'

Brother Donnán thought deeply before replying: 'Never.'

'So Brother Donnchad visited the *scriptorium* to read some works but you knew nothing of what he was working on apart from the fact that he spent long hours over the text of Origenes. Is that correct?'

'It is.'

'But you knew he was behaving oddly in the days before his death.'

'I have already said it was well known among the brethren. He was always very quiet—'

'Except that last day he was in here, a day or so before his death.'

They looked round. Brother Máel Eoin had risen from the table, where he had been reading, to put away his text and had overheard Brother Donnán's last remark. Fidelma turned to him with interest.

'What do you mean?'

'I was in here that day. You must remember, Brother Donnán,' the hospitaller said. 'I like to come, when time permits, and read some of the hagiographies of the saints that we have here.'

'Go on,' said Fidelma. 'What happened?'

'Well, Brother Donnchad came in. It struck me that he was behaving very out of character. I don't mean his reclusive change since he returned to the abbey. Not at all. He came roaring into the library.'

'Roaring?' For a moment Eadulf had to think about the word that the hospitaller had used. The word was *bláedach* and not one that Eadulf had heard used of a person before.

'He was in an angry temper, shouting, his face red. He had mislaid something and was convinced that it had been stolen from him. Don't you remember, Brother Donnán?'

'Stolen?' demanded Eadulf. 'What was it? A manuscript?'

'Not as such,' replied the librarian, entering the conversation for the first time since Brother Máel Eoin's interruption. 'It was his *pólaire*. I had forgotten the incident.'

Eadulf looked blank. 'A *pólaire*?'

'In Latin it is called a *ceraculum*, from the word for wax,' explained the *scriptor* pedantically.

Brother Máel Eoin nodded. 'Just so. It is a wooden writing tablet whose surface is hollowed out and filled with wax so that one can write on it, making temporary notes. You can re-warm the wax, smooth it out, and re-use it.'

'And he had lost his?' Fidelma asked.

'Indeed. He claimed that it had been stolen from him. I denied all knowledge of seeing it, which was only the truth. He had not left it in the library.'

'And you told him that?' asked Fidelma.

'I did. I had seen him looking at it several times during his former visits here. He was making notes from the Origenes book. But I swear he had taken it with him. I am sure of it.'

'He went away, but still in a great temper,' confirmed Brother Donnán. 'That was the last time ever I saw him.'

'Let me be clear about this,' Fidelma said. 'This incident happened when exactly?'

'On the day of his death. I am sure of it,' the hospitaller confirmed.

Fidelma glanced at the *scriptor*.

'I suppose it was that day,' he affirmed after a moment.

'Had he not been away from the abbey the entire day before?'

'You are correct, Sister,' Brother Máel Eoin said. 'He had, indeed. He might well have left it wherever it was that he went.'

'You have no idea where he went?'

The hospitaller shook his head.

'Perhaps he went to visit his mother again,' offered the librarian.

'Very well, Brother Donnán,' Fidelma nodded. 'Thank you for your information. And thanks also to you, Brother Máel Eoin. You have both been most helpful.'

CHAPTER NINE

Outside the door of the *scriptorium*, Eadulf shook his head. 'Brother Donnán has presented us with more questions than he has answered. We can't even identify the manuscripts that Brother Donnchad was afraid might be stolen.'

'The assumption that the murderer sought to steal them remains the only motive for the crime,' replied Fidelma. 'One thing I do find worrying is that Brother Lugna seems to be more in charge of this community than the abbot.'

'But he is the steward and surely the steward does have charge of the running of the community?'

'What I mean is that he seems to have some extreme ideas that are contrary to those of the abbot and are disapproved of by some of those we have spoken to. Yet he seems to be able to dominate them. How did he get to be chosen as steward?'

'I find it worrying that he has ordered the destruction of pagan books.' Eadulf's eyes widened as he thought about it. 'Brother Lugna is a natural suspect.'

'It is too early to suspect any particular person yet. He is making himself obvious by his behaviour and that makes me think the opposite. The guilty try to hide their guilt and make themselves inconspicuous. We must not speculate without information,' she said, voicing her favourite maxim. 'The sad thing is that there are many clerics who think it helpful to the Faith to destroy pagan works. They think that the exhortation to go out and turn people from darkness and idols to the light of the living God means they should destroy everything their ancestors thought and wrote, and they do so without a second thought.'

'Whatever was in those books that Brother Donnchad was protecting must be something very powerful if they were the cause of his murder,' Eadulf reflected.

At that moment the sound of a shout and a loud bang from the direction of the new building caused them to glance in that direction. Loud and angry voices rose. Someone had apparently dropped something heavy and was being rebuked by another of the builders. Eadulf caught sight of a small figure dodging among the debris. As he turned back to Fidelma, he saw Brother Lugna appear round the corner of the *scriptorium*.

'*Lupus in sermone*,' muttered Fidelma, 'the wolf in the story', whose colloquial meaning was 'talk of the devil'.

The *rechtaire* of the abbey greeted them without expression.

'How goes your investigation? Is there progress?'

'We move slowly,' replied Fidelma.

'But we move surely,' added Eadulf, whose dislike of the man had hardened.

Brother Lugna looked at him, as if trying to decide what the tone in his voice implied.

'I am pleased to hear it,' he replied flatly.

'Did Brother Donnchad report to you that he had lost his *ceraculum*?' Fidelma asked.

A frown passed quickly over Brother Lugna's features before they re-formed without expression.

'As a matter of fact I do recall encountering him one day on his way back from the *scriptorium*. He mentioned that some thief had taken it. I pointed out that it was a serious accusation, especially if he was accusing someone among the brethren. He called me a fool and walked away. That was shortly before his mother came to the abbey to speak to him about his behaviour. After that visit he refused to open his door to anyone. What makes you ask?'

'He apparently flew into a rage when it went missing. We wondered why that was. Surely he could obtain another such notebook easily within the community?'

'Brother Donnchad's behaviour was always curious insofar as I was concerned. I presumed that he had important notes still on the writing tablet and that was what annoyed him. That would be a logical conclusion.'

'Of course.' Fidelma smiled, as if the problem had been solved. Then she glanced around. 'I see the building work is going well,' she remarked, changing the subject. 'The new chapel looks truly magnificent.'

'It is indeed.' Eadulf could almost swear that the steward's chest expanded with pride. 'Soon our name will resound throughout Christendom for the purity of the abbey and its teachings.'

'The purity of its teachings?' queried Fidelma softly, as if the words had a special meaning.

Brother Lugna gazed sharply at her before replying: 'There is a difficult task before us, to cleanse the lax and impure ways that have been allowed to develop among the community. That is my task, as I see it. Absolution is given too freely to those who do not adhere to strict obedience to the disciplines of the Faith. Those who turn away from the truth and then think they can return and be immediately forgiven for . . .' He halted, as if he realised he had said too much. With a curt nod of his head, he left them, striding quickly away. Fidelma looked long and thoughtfully after him.

'There is something about that man,' muttered Eadulf.

'He is not the most likeable of people,' she agreed. 'Come, let us follow up the matter the abbot told us about. The matter of Brother Gáeth placing something in the "mound of the dead". We'll start with the chapel.'

The *daimhliag* – the usual term now applied to churches built of stone – was quite imposing, built of substantial stone blocks, carefully cut and smoothed. Like many churches, it was built on an east–west axis, the entrance being at the west end and the altar at the east. Already, the brethren had begun to plant trees around the new building, mainly yew for ornament, so that a symbolic sanctuary encircled it, called the *fidnemed*, or grove of the sanctuary. It was considered sacrilege to cut down or despoil these sacred groves. It was a custom that had been adopted since the days before the Faith had arrived in the Five Kingdoms. They wondered whether Brother Lugna approved of this ancient custom.

The stone church was not as big as many abbey chapels that Fidelma had seen. It was twenty-five metres long and six metres wide. From base to apex the long sloping roof was about nine metres. Beside the main door at the western end was a bell and a rope, used to summon the congregation to services. The oak door was well built; as was usual, the jambs of the door and the windows were angled so that the bottom of the opening was wider than the top. Round them were set large stones, with a horizontal lintel. The windows were long and narrow with a triangular top. The steep, sloping roof was covered with flat, thin stones.

Inside, the walls were hung with woollen tapestries depicting scenes from the life of the Blessed Carthach, or Mo-Chuada, the founder of the abbey. At the eastern end, the altar was of carved oak, behind which, as was the custom, the priest would face the congregation to conduct the services, although some of those now following the Roman liturgy performed the service facing the altar, with their back to the congregation. The congregation stood; there were no benches, unlike some continental churches that Fidelma had seen.

Fidelma and Eadulf stood gazing around.

'This seems a curious place to hide something,' Eadulf remarked.

'Let's find the tombs of the abbots,' replied Fidelma.

In fact, the tombs lay beneath their feet. The memorial stone to the Blessed Carthach lay immediately in front of the altar. The stone was part of the flagged flooring, with a Chi-Ro symbol engraved on it and the single name Mo-Chuada. The foot of the slab was at the eastern end and the head at the western end, in accordance with the custom that one should be buried with one's feet towards the east. The memorial to the second Abbot of Lios Mór, Mo-Chuada's maternal uncle, Cuanan, was placed in similar fashion but on the southern side of the chapel. They searched around the tombs for a while and Eadulf even examined under the altar but there was no sign of any place where anything could be hidden.

'I suppose we will have to ask Brother Gáeth what it was Donnchad gave him and where he put it,' sighed Eadulf.

'Do you really think he will respond to such a question?' snapped Fidelma irritably. 'He did not volunteer the information for a reason and will never do so if we confront him with the fact that he was not open with us. Use your sense, Eadulf.'

Eadulf coloured hotly at her rebuke.

'One of the things I find difficult about you, Fidelma, is that there are two people in you.' His words flooded out in reaction.

She turned to stare at him in surprise. She had never seen him lose control of his tongue before.

'There is the person I fell in love with,' the words continued to rush out, 'the companion who is humorous and sensitive. Then there is the person who is arrogant, with an acid-sharp tongue; a confrontational and aggressive person whose attitude I do not like; the person who is ready to chastise, to criticise without listening to the reason for my comments or actions. It is as if I do not count when you are undertaking these investigations. My opinions may be just as valid as yours, sometimes more so. I do not criticise you because I take the trouble to understand what you are thinking, even if I disagree with your thoughts. I prefer to ask the question why, although you always take that as censure of your ability.'

Fidelma stood still, as if she had been slapped in the face. There was shock in her expression. Then her jaw tightened. Her eyes flashed dangerously.

'So, perhaps we are getting to the truth of your views about me.' Her voice was cold and hard.

Eadulf, red in the face, was now in control of himself.

'Do not react until you have considered what I am saying. I am not so uncaring that I cannot see both sides of you. But I have to tell you that I am weary of being a . . .' He tried to think of an Irish term. 'I am weary of being an *idbartach.*' He chose the word for 'sacrifice' and hoped that it would convey the idea of someone who was used as a victim.

Fidelma's face had become a mask. He waited for the explosion he presumed would come. Then, amazingly, her frozen features seemed to dissolve into a troubled expression. She said in a quiet voice, 'What is it that you want in life, Eadulf?'

He did not reply immediately, too surprised by the softness of her tone.

'What do I want for the future? I don't want to live without you or our son, Alchú. But I want to be regarded as someone whose feelings should be considered as equal.'

'Do you think that forcing me to give up the law, as you tried to do, and move to some enclosed community would be a recipe for happiness?'

'Perhaps I was wrong to think it. But I don't want to be a mere appendage of Fidelma of Cashel,' he replied firmly. 'I want to be my own person. I want to be regarded for my own worth and not for your sake.'

'You don't think that you are already?' she asked with a frown.

'I certainly do not,' he returned immediately. 'Although I have spent many years here, I am not of your country, Fidelma. I rely on your charity for my subsistence.'

She shook her head with a sad smile. 'We knew that life together would not be easy. That was why I insisted on pursuing our custom of living with each other for a year and a day before we took our final vows of marriage.'

'I know, I know. Perhaps it was my fault. There was little Alchú to consider,' he muttered angrily.

'Eadulf, all I can say is that I am sorry you feel that you are not regarded for your own worth. I know I am cursed with a temper. I cannot stop the criticism that springs from my tongue when I am distracted. But let me tell you this. As far as I am concerned, without you, your advice, your ability to

analyse, I would not have succeeded in many of the investigations we have undertaken. Remember the time when you were
able to understand the Law of the Fénechus to the level where
you were able to successfully defend me when I was unjustly
charged with murder. Who of importance in this kingdom has
not shown you respect? My brother, the King, respects you,
as does the nobility of Muman. Abbot Ségdae of Imleach
respects you, and so do most of the religious of Muman. Indeed,
even the High King himself knows and respects your abilities.'

Eadulf was silent for a moment.

'I suppose,' he said uncertainly, 'I sometimes feel that I
am not respected by the one person I really want respect
from.'

Fidelma looked long and hard at him and there was
suddenly a brightness in her eyes.

'For that I am truly sorry. I know I must try to curb my
temper, yet I cannot change my life or my ambition. I have
explained many times that my cousin, Abbot Laisran, acted
for my benefit when he told me to join the community at
Cill Dara. It seemed a good idea at the time but I soon discovered it was not. For some time, because I was young and
inexperienced, I did not know what path I should take. But
finally, I know what I should do. My whole being is involved
with law and the administration of justice. Not pursuing this
will mean the death of my soul. No sacrifice that involves
me giving this up is possible.'

'Do you regret your time with me, as you regret your time
in the community at Cill Dara?' asked Eadulf.

Fidelma shook her head vehemently. 'It tortures me, Eadulf, to think that we have come so far along our path in life together and may not continue on. I do not want to lose you. You will forever be my soul mate, my *anam chara*, and if you go, my soul will die. But if I am constrained from doing what I need to do in life to be fully alive, my heart will die. So what is my choice?'

He did not know how to answer or, indeed, how to sort out the thoughts that crowded into his mind.

'What would you do in a religious community, Eadulf?' Fidelma pressed when he did not answer.

'In a religious community there is security.'

'Security?' Fidelma actually chuckled. 'Look at this community and at the many communities to which we have been called when our talents are needed. Little security here, I'm afraid.'

Eadulf found himself smiling for it did seem a contradictory thing to say.

'I mean in terms of position,' he added, 'of putting food on the table.'

'Have we not security enough in Cashel? Are not our talents in demand far and wide? One day, we find ourselves summoned to Tara to investigate the death of the High King; another day our path takes us to Autun in Burgundia to advise at a council. Now, here we are in Lios Mór, where our talents are required yet again. Who knows where our footsteps may take us? But let us remember the saying from Horace – *vestigia nulla retrorsum* – no steps backwards. We have much to do to finish this investigation and once we have, I swear we will talk about our future. We know what we each want; we must see if we can reconcile our wants to some compatibility of purpose and, of course, the welfare of our son.'

Eadulf forced a wan smile. 'Very well. And let me also quote Horace, as advice for both of us: *ira furor brevis est: animum rege: qui nisi imperat.*'

Fidelma laid a hand on his arm. 'Well considered, Eadulf. Anger is a momentary madness, so we shall both control it before it controls us. And now I think it is time to return to the guesthouse and prepare for the evening meal.'

She turned and was leading the way from the chapel steps when she halted abruptly, causing Eadulf to cannon into her.

'Eadulf, I think you have made an excellent suggestion.' She turned excitedly.

He stared at her in bewilderment.

'About controlling anger?' he asked.

'Is there not a saying, in anger there is truth?'

'I have never heard it,' he replied.

'Then perhaps we shall invent it.' She suddenly gave that mischievous grin that he had fallen in love with. 'I have an idea . . .'

Before she could explain, they were hailed by Gormán who was crossing the quadrangle and had spied them.

'I was looking for you,' he announced as he came up to them.

'Is anything the matter?' inquired Fidelma, observing the excitement in the warrior's expression.

'I've been chatting with the *echaire*, the stableman, about the builders,' he said.

'Haven't you heard enough about builders after Glassán's eloquence the other night?' Eadulf had reacquired his sense of humour.

'In fact, it was Glassán we were chatting about. Did you know that Brother Echen is originally from Laighin?'

'We did not,' responded Fidelma solemnly, 'but it is good to know that he has an appropriate name for a stableman.' Echen meant a 'steed'.

Gormán ignored her humour and went on, 'It seems that his cousin is actually the *táisech scuir*, the man in charge of the King of Laighin's stables.'

'There is a point to this?' Fidelma pressed gently.

'Of course. Did you know that Glassán was of the degree of *ollamh*?'

An *ollamh* was the highest degree in any of the professions within the Five Kingdoms.

'I am only surprised that he neglected to tell us,' Fidelma said wryly. 'He was quite eloquent about his merits and the merits of his profession. It seems perfectly reasonable for the abbey to employ a master builder of his degree.'

Gormán smiled without humour. 'Well, it might surprise you to know that our friend, Glassán, was once master builder to the King of Laighin.'

'Was?' queried Eadulf. 'I did not think that master builders to kings resigned their office unless they retired. And he is not old enough to retire from such a position.'

'He does not have to have left that position,' Fidelma corrected quickly. 'Usually the *ollamh* builder is employed in direct service to the King, and answers to him for a fixed annual payment of seven *cumals*, equivalent to the value of twenty-one milch cows. However, he is also permitted to exercise his art for general commissions from members of the public. He has probably taken on this work as extra to his service to the King of Laighin. Although, I grant, it does seem odd that he has crossed into the kingdom of Muman for employment.'

Gormán was shaking his head. 'You are wrong, lady. Brother Eadulf raises a good question. Brother Echen grew quite loquacious after I shared a flagon of *korma* with him. He was told, by his own brother, who serves the King of Laighin, something that is quite interesting about Glassán.'

'I wish you would get to the point of this tale,' Fidelma said irritably. Then she glanced at Eadulf, grimaced and added, 'If you don't mind.'

'Simply that some years ago Glassán was dismissed from the service of the King of Laighin's in disgrace. It turned out that he had been asked to construct and oversee the work of a guest hostel at the fortress residence of some relation to the King. It was badly constructed and the roof fell in, killing several people, including one of the builders.'

Eadulf whistled silently and then glanced nervously at the chapel behind them.

'What happened?' Fidelma was now interested.

'He was taken before the King's Brehon. It was argued

that, while his task had been the design of the building, and he should have been there to oversee its construction, he had not actually followed through. He had left the work to an assistant who had not placed the supports correctly or strongly enough.'

'So was he judged responsible?'

'On the contrary, it was his responsibility to have overseen the building at every stage. While the assistant had to pay the bereaved families the honour price of the persons killed, Glassán himself was deemed culpable and had to pay court fines to the King and was stripped of his rank of *ollamh*.'

'Yet he is here rebuilding this abbey,' breathed Eadulf in amazement.

'Does your friend, Brother Echen, know how this came about?' asked Fidelma.

'How Glassán was commissioned to build here? He seems to have come here at the invitation of Brother Lugna.'

'Did Brother Echen tell Abbot Iarnla about Glassán?'

'He said he told Brother Lugna who, as steward, is in charge of the building on behalf of the abbey. Brother Lugna as good as told him that he should remain silent, for judgement had been passed and Glassán had paid the fines.'

'That, of course, is true,' Fidelma agreed. 'A person cannot continue to be punished after they have made reparation in the eyes of the law. But one thing intrigues me. What defence did Glassán present, if any, at the hearing? Did Brother Echen know?'

'His defence was why the Brehon imposed a heavy penalty

on him,' Gormán said. 'He tried to throw all the blame on his assistant who had overseen the work when Glassán should have been doing it. He said that he had undertaken other commissions elsewhere in the kingdom and so had had to go and oversee them. He said he had trusted his assistant and the entire fault lay with him.'

'Glassán had agreed the contract and therefore the responsibility was his own,' Fidelma said. 'I would have made him pay the honour prices of the dead to their families as well. The Brehon was lenient. I find it difficult to accept that Abbot Iarnla and Brother Lugna can feel confident employing such a man to be in charge of this great building work.'

'When did this disaster happen?' Eadulf asked Gormán. 'Did the stableman say?'

'About ten years ago.'

'Ten years? That is a long time. And he started on this work two or three years ago, soon after Brother Lugna arrived here from Rome,' mused Fidelma.

'I wonder how Brother Lugna knew him,' Eadulf said thoughtfully.

'I can tell you that.' Gormán smiled. 'Or at least Brother Echen had the information. There was talk that Glassán went into exile in Connachta and was doing building commissions.'

'And Brother Lugna comes from Connachta,' Eadulf added.

'Glassán was apparently specialising in making underground storage areas. He became a master of *uamairecht* – cellar-making.'

'Cellar-making?' Fidelma swung round and headed

determinedly back to the chapel. 'That is something I totally forgot,' she said over her shoulder. 'Come on. We neglected to finish our search.'

Eadulf, with a wary glance at the high roof of the chapel, went after her. In some bewilderment, Gormán followed them into the chapel.

'Is someone going to tell me what I said?' he asked plaintively.

'We need to find out if this building has a cellar or vault to it. If there is, the entrance is concealed,' Fidelma told him.

It was some time before they re-emerged. The floor of the chapel was solid. There was no sign of any entrance leading to vaults beneath the building. Disappointment showed on Fidelma's features. Once again she had to conclude that this was not the 'mound of the dead' where Brother Gáeth might have hidden whatever it was Brother Donnchad had given him.

She look up at the sky and sighed.

'We just have time to prepare before the bell sounds for the evening meal,' she said. She walked rapidly to the guest hostel. Eadulf hurried after her while Gormán stood watching them, totally bewildered.

CHAPTER TEN

E adulf knocked gently on Fidelma's door to escort her to the evening meal. His eyes widened as she opened it.

Fidelma was not wearing her simple and practical robes; she had put on the clothing that was hers by right to wear as both daughter and sister of a king of Muman. Eadulf had not seen her wear such finery since she had made a plea before the *Airechtais*, the Great Assembly of the High King, at Tara a year before. He had, of course, seen her wearing such clothes several times before but never when a guest in an abbey.

Her gown was of deep blue satin with intricate gold thread patterns. It fitted snugly at the waist and then flowed out into a full skirt that came to her ankles. The sleeves were of a style called *lamfhoss*, tight on the upper arms but spilling out just before the elbow in an echo of the lower part of her dress. Over this was a sleeveless tunic, called an *inar*, which covered the top of the dress but ended at the waist. From her shoulder hung a short *lummon*, a cape of contrasting red-coloured satin edged with badger's fur. The cape was fastened on the left shoulder by a round brooch of silver and semi-precious stones. On her feet were specially decorated sandals, sewn with pieces of multicoloured glass, called *mael-assa*.

She had put on bracelets of complementary coloured glass around her wrists and round her neck she wore her golden torc which proclaimed not only her royal position but that she was of the élite Nasc Niadh of Muman, the bodyguards of the Eóghanacht. In her fiery red hair was a band of silver with three semi-precious stones at the front – two emeralds from the country of the Corco Duibhne, in the west of the kingdom, and a glowing red stone which reflected the stones in the silver brooch that held her cape. The headband served to keep in place a piece of silk that covered her hair but left her face unobstructed. It was called a *conniul* and indicated her married status.

'Are you being wise?' Eadulf finally asked, having found some difficulty articulating his thoughts.

Fidelma had that mischievous look on her face. 'Firstly, I need to prove something. Secondly, I need to assert something. Have no fear, Eadulf, I know what I am doing. And now, the support of your arm, please. I suspect that I may need the support of more than your arm before the evening is over.'

Eadulf sighed. He felt incongruous clad as he was in a simple religious robe. But he said nothing.

The *bruigad*, Brother Máel Eoin, was waiting for them outside the *refectorium*, with Gormán. The hosteller registered some surprise and then bowed his head in acknowledgement to her. The young warrior grinned broadly and straightened a little as if to salute her.

'It is good to see an Eóghanacht reassert their presence,' he said simply.

He preceded Fidelma and Eadulf into the *refectorium* and led them to the table they had been assigned. As they passed by the tables of the brethren, a silence fell throughout the hall and glances of astonishment were cast towards Fidelma. Then a muttering began to rise from the lines of seated brethren. Ignoring it, Fidelma and her companions reached the table where Glassán and Saor sat open mouthed at her change of appearance. Then a sharp voice cried from the table of the abbot, 'This is an affront, a sacrilege!'

Fidelma, with Eadulf and Gormán at her side, turned slowly to face the abbot's table. It was not Abbot Iarnla but his steward, Brother Lugna, who was on his feet. His face was red and almost quivering in his indignation.

'Sacrilege, Brother Lugna?' Fidelma's voice cracked like a whip.

'How dare you come into this *refectorium* in . . . in those shameless garments?' cried the steward.

Fidelma drew herself up a little. 'Do you insult the Eóghanacht? You have been too long in Rome, Brother Lugna. You are now in the kingdom of Muman and in the presence of an Eóghanacht princess.'

'What . . . what did you say?' demanded the steward, taken aback.

'I am Fidelma of Cashel,' she went on in the haughty

manner that Eadulf knew she could assume at will. 'I am sister to Colgú, King of Muman. Have I not been requested to come to this place as the guest of your abbot, the Abbot Iarnla, who presides over this abbey and this *refectorium*? Am I not an honoured guest in this abbey . . . an abbey that, I must remind you, is part of my brother's kingdom? For his is the ultimate authority over all the chieftains, nobles, abbots and bishops of this land. Am I not here as sister to your King as well as a *dálaigh,* come to investigate a matter on behalf of my brother your King. If Abbot Iarnla wishes to withdraw his request for my presence, let him do so and I will return to Cashel and report this insult to the King and his advisers.'

The blood had drained from the face of Abbot Iarnla, sitting at the side of the risen figure of Lugna. He seemed mesmerised, as if he had no part in the scene being enacted before him.

'There are rules in this abbey—'

'There are rules everywhere. Usually, the rules are agreed upon by the community and not imposed on them,' Fidelma cut across him.

'We are talking about the rules of dress among the religious,' spluttered Brother Lugna. 'For you to enter our *refectorium* in those clothes . . . that dress . . .' He seemed at a loss for words.

'You object to my dress which distinguishes me as the sister of your King and a *dálaigh*?' challenged Fidelma.

'I object to it as you are a member of the religious and should obey the edicts of the Faith.'

'Indeed I do. The edict on dress is very clear. The Holy

Father wrote to the bishops of Vienne and Narbonne that all the religious should be distinguished by their Faith and not by their clothing. We have it from the Holy Father himself that it does not matter what a person wears but how he lives his life and what his beliefs are.'

Brother Lugna frowned. 'What Holy Father wrote such words?' he sneered. 'Name him!'

'He was Celestine, the first of his name to sit on the throne of Saint Peter,' replied Fidelma. Only Eadulf detected the barbed innocence in her voice.

'Celestine?' barked Brother Lugna as if she had uttered an obscenity. 'Celestine was but a . . .' He struggled to find the words. 'He was no credit to the throne of Saint Peter. Had it not been for that manipulative woman, the Empress Galla Placidia, he would never have been elected Bishop of Rome. He persecuted many of the True Faith because they held different ideas to himself.'

There was absolute quiet in the *refectorium* as the brethren tried to understand the meaning of the exchange.

'I know who he regarded as heretics to the Faith,' Fidelma replied. 'And those he regarded as heretics are still regarded as heretics by the current Holy Father in Rome.'

Brother Lugna sat down suddenly in his seat. His mouth snapped shut and a series of emotions chased one another across his features; the predominant one was anger. A hum of voices began to rise across the hall. Fidelma had clearly made some point that had reduced Brother Lugna to silence but no one was sure what point had been made.

Abbot Iarnla took the opportunity to rise to his feet and bang his staff of office on the floor beside him.

'*Tacet!*' He commanded silence. 'This is a *prainntech*.' He flushed, glanced at his steward and corrected himself. 'A *refectorium* where we gather to feed our bodies just as we gather in the chapel to feed our souls. It is no place for debates on the Faith.'

'In view of the objections raised by your steward,' Fidelma said, not letting the matter go, 'does the request you sent to my brother, the King, remain your request, or do you wish me to return to Cashel?'

Abbot Iarnla glanced quickly at Brother Lugna before he replied. 'Fidelma of Cashel, you and your companions are guests here at my invitation as abbot, by special request to your brother, the King, and his advisers. Be seated with your companions but I would urge you, for the future, to seek an accommodation of compliance with the rules of our community.'

Fidelma bowed gravely to the abbot. 'I will do my best to do so. We will discuss the matter after the meal in your chamber in, of course, the presence of the steward.'

She turned before he could reply and seated herself. Her companions followed suit. Suddenly the silence erupted into loud conversation. Glassán, the builder, was still staring at her open mouthed. At his side Saor watched her nervously.

'Are you truly the sister of King Colgú?' Glassán stammered after a moment or two. 'Are you Fidelma of Cashel of whom we have heard so many stories?'

'Yes, this is Fidelma of Cashel,' Gormán announced proudly

before she could answer. 'And you have also doubtless heard of her companion, Eadulf.'

'I did not know,' confessed the builder. 'I heard only that an advocate of the law was coming to investigate the death here.'

Fidelma was about to say that it was of no consequence, but of course she had made it of consequence in order to find out what she wanted to know. Her action had been overly dramatic but perhaps it would bear fruit in the long run; it had already provided an answer to her suspicion about Brother Lugna.

Glassán now seemed nervous. He glanced at his plate, pushed it away unfinished, then rose quickly and glanced at his assistant, Saor.

'Forgive us,' he mumbled, 'there is something we must examine at the works before the light totally fades.'

He turned from the table. Saor, apparently unwillingly, followed, but not before he had grabbed a piece of bread and a lump of cheese.

Gormán watched them leaving with a broad smile. 'What a pity we did not tell him who you were on the first evening, lady. We might have been spared the lecture on the joys of being a master builder. He obviously has an aversion to relatives of kings. Maybe his former association with the King of Laighin is to blame.'

Fidelma was looking thoughtful. 'Perhaps you are right, Gormán. But remember this, there is much to be learned from a conversation with even the most boring of people.'

Eadulf cleared his throat. 'Speaking of which, I am not sure I learnt anything from your exchange with Brother Lugna. That is, apart from what we had already realised, that poor Abbot Iarnla seems to be totally under his thumb.'

'The abbot does occasionally show flashes of his old self,' Fidelma replied. 'We must hope that he has not abandoned himself entirely to Brother Lugna's control.'

'But what about this pantomime of your dress? You do not usually assert your rank and authority of birth so blatantly. In fact, you only do so when you feel that the person needs to be put in his place . . .' Eadulf paused and smiled. 'So you were attempting to put Brother Lugna in his place?'

'Not entirely. But I have a suspicion about Brother Lugna that I wanted to put to the test,' she replied, helping herself to a bowl of hot vegetable soup.

'And did that exchange confirm it?'

'I think it did,' she said. 'Between us, my exchange confirmed to me that he is of a heretical sect. But I will keep the detail to myself a while longer. The main thing to remember is that Brother Lugna is a fanatic and tolerates no dissension.'

'I dislike the man anyway,' muttered Eadulf. 'I still think we should be treating him as a suspect.'

'Dislike him or not, suspect or not, Brother Lugna is steward of the abbey. It is best that he knows where he stands with us.'

After the meal and the blessing from the abbot, Gormán leaned forward.

'Shall I come with you to see the abbot, lady?' he asked quietly. 'You may need . . .' He tapped a finger on his belt where his sword should have hung.

Fidelma pretended shock. 'Heavens, no! I do not mean to start a war. This is simply an essay in diplomacy.'

'Diplomacy?' Gormán grunted in surprise. 'I did not think so, the way you responded to the steward.'

'Don't worry, Gormán. If you are needed, I will call you. But Eadulf will be with me.'

Eadulf had no understanding what was in Fidelma's mind. He felt it better to hold his peace and see what happened rather than show his ignorance by asking her what she intended.

The abbot and the steward had disappeared by the time Fidelma and Eadulf left the *refectorium*, so Fidelma led the way to the abbot's chambers. Outside, lurking in the shadow of the building, they found Brother Máel Eoin. The hosteller came forward, until the light of the lantern hanging over the door illuminated his features. He placed a finger against his lips. With outstretched hand he drew Fidelma and Eadulf aside and spoke in a whisper.

'I just wanted to warn you about Brother Lugna, lady,' he said. 'He is not a . . . nice person. You made an enemy of him tonight in the *refectorium*. You made him back down in front of the brethren, and he knows they do not like him.'

Fidelma smiled and laid a hand on his arm. 'Take comfort, Brother Máel Eoin. We are aware of Brother Lugna's temperament.'

'Before he came to the abbey,' the hosteller went on, 'Abbot Iarnla was strong and independent. Then Brother Lugna came with his strange ideas. Whenever anyone questions them, he says this is done in Rome or that is the rule of Rome. We cannot argue when we are also told that Rome is the centre of the Faith and where the Holy Father dwells. Brother Lugna persuaded sufficient numbers of the brethren to support him in becoming the steward of the community. It was afterwards that things began to change.'

'And these changes are not liked?'

'The changes have upset many of us and, I have to be honest, lady, it has been sad to see how he is usurping Abbot Iarnla's position. The abbot seems unable to stand against him. We feel that it is Brother Lugna who is in control and not the abbot.'

'Do you know why that should be?' asked Eadulf.

'It is as if Brother Lugna has some power over him,' replied Brother Máel Eoin. 'What it is, I do not know. But I felt I must warn you to be careful, lady. Be very careful.' The hosteller turned and left them.

After a few moments, they rapped sharply on Abbot Iarnla's door and entered.

Abbot Iarnla was seated in his usual chair, while Brother Lugna was standing to one side and a little behind him.

'What was the meaning of your exchange in the *refectorium*, Fidelma?' the abbot demanded at once. 'I have no understanding of it.'

'I think your *rechtaire* understands,' replied Fidelma coolly.

Brother Lugna scowled, shifted his weight but said nothing.

Abbot Iarnla looked up at him with a trace of his old assertive self.

'Well, Brother Lugna, will you explain?'

When the steward remained silent, Fidelma said, 'Brother Lugna was kind enough to inform me, when we arrived here, that he did not favour my coming. He believed that this investigation should be an internal matter.'

'I did not hide my view,' Brother Lugna said sullenly.

'You did not,' Fidelma agreed. 'But when the abbot over-ruled your objections and insisted I came here, that should have been an end to the matter, should it not?'

Abbot Iarnla appeared troubled again. 'Of course that was an end to it. You have complete authority to make your investigation.'

'Yet I do not think Brother Lugna shares that view.' Fidelma was looking straight at the steward.

'Explain,' demanded the abbot.

Brother Lugna's mouth was a tight, thin line.

'What Brother Lugna is going to explain,' went on Fidelma, 'is why he went round to those I wanted to question and told them not to cooperate with me. He told them to answer questions as sparsely laden with facts as possible.'

Brother Lugna's jaw rose aggressively. 'I suppose the simpleton has been telling you a story,' he sneered.

'If you refer to Brother Gáeth, it was certainly not he who revealed this to me. And we find that he is no simpleton. I shall not tell you who it was who told me but be assured it was not Brother Gáeth. I shall not be happy if I hear some punishment falls on him because of such a suspicion.' There was no belligerence in her quiet voice. She made a statement of fact.

Abbot Iarnla looked scandalised. 'Of course nothing will happen to Brother Gáeth.' Then he paused, again uncertain and nervous. He turned to his steward. 'Are you admitting that what Fidelma says is correct, Brother Lugna? Did you tell members of our brethren not to cooperate with her?'

When the steward hesitated, Fidelma went on, 'I thought the manner in which the physician responded to my questioning was extraordinary. A physician trying to avoid questioning by a *dálaigh* of the courts is unprecedented in my experience. I soon found out that he had been told to behave in that manner.'

'But why, Brother Lugna, why?' demanded the abbot.

The steward shrugged. 'My views have not altered since you rejected my advice, Abbot Iarnla,' he said defiantly. 'This abbey has no need of outsiders poking their noses into the affairs of the community.'

'This abbey is not independent of the kingdom,' Eadulf observed. 'It has to conform to the laws of the kingdom.'

'What would you know of this, Saxon?' The steward's voice was taunting.

'Eadulf of Seaxmund's Ham is my husband and stands foremost among those whose advice is sought by my brother, the King,' snapped Fidelma. 'And he advises correctly. This abbey is not above obedience to the law.'

'Many abbeys adopt the Penitentials and claim a right to their own rules,' replied Brother Lugna.

'The Penitentials again?' snapped Eadulf. 'They do not run in this abbey.'

'There should be no husbands and wives among the religious,' retorted the steward.

'But there are. There is no rule of celibacy in the Faith, even in Rome.'

'Not yet.'

'And it is to be hoped there never will be, for that would be to reject our human condition created by God,' Eadulf returned angrily. 'And isn't that an insult to God's creation rather than a happy acceptance of it?'

Fidelma suddenly smiled and laid a hand on Eadulf's arm. 'Indeed,' she agreed. 'But we are not talking about how we interpret the Faith. We are talking of the law, of which I am a representative. There is a set list of fines for those who try to conceal evidence from a *dálaigh* in a case of murder, Brother Lugna.' Fidelma turned to address the abbot. 'Perhaps Brother Lugna did not realise that a person who conceals or gives false evidence, or persuades others to do so, according to the *Din Techtugad* text, loses their honour price. Of course, if Brother Lugna can convince a Brehon that he acted in ignorance, the fines will be halved and he may keep half his honour price.'

Brother Lugna's mouth was a thin line again, his eyes staring maliciously at her. He said nothing.

Abbot Iarnla spread his hands helplessly. 'I am sure that

if Brother Lugna did do what you accuse him of, he must have acted without appreciating the law of the kingdom.' The abbot's voice was almost pleading.

'I am sure he did,' Fidelma replied solemnly. 'No one would be so stupid as to put his honour price in jeopardy. The fact that he went against your ruling as abbot is a matter for your internal discipline. I will accept that it was his adherence to his belief that made him think he was above the law and your decisions as abbot. So we will leave it with a simple reminder of the law. But now we would be grateful to Brother Lugna if he would accompany Brother Eadulf and me across the quadrangle to the guesthouse.'

Brother Lugna moved forward unwillingly. Then frowned. 'Why?' he demanded.

'Because,' Fidelma said softly, 'a *dálaigh* has requested you to do so.'

They left the abbot gazing in dismay after them.

The waxing moon was now bright and they had no need of lanterns to cross the stone flags.

'He is a sweet old man,' Fidelma remarked as they reached the fountain in the centre of the quadrangle where she suddenly halted. 'I do not want him to be troubled unduly over this matter of Brother Donnchad's death. In order to spare him, I am sure you will cooperate with me now that my position here is clear.'

Brother Lugna breathed out slowly as if in resignation.

'The sooner this matter is resolved, the better,' he replied.

'Then a few questions. How did you come to choose Glassán as your master builder?'

Whatever questions Brother Lugna was expecting, it did not appear to be that one. There was a momentary stiffening of his shoulders. He had his back to the moon and it cast too many shadows for them to make out his expression.

'He was a master builder in my own land, in Connachta,' he replied firmly.

'Oh? I thought he was from the Kingdom of Laighin?'

There was an awkward silence.

'What is it you want, Fidelma of Cashel?' Brother Lugna asked sharply. It was the first time he had acknowledged her rank.

'I?' Fidelma sounded surprised. 'I want nothing more than to fulfil the task that my brother, the King, asked me to fulfil.'

'I will not stop you,' replied Brother Lugna ungraciously.

'But, hopefully, you will also help me and advise others to do so? Simply not stopping someone do something is not the same as helping them do it.'

'As I have said,' repeated the steward, 'the sooner this is over, the better.'

'Then I think we have an understanding.' She paused. 'There was once a learned man, centuries ago, in another country, who had convinced opinions and felt that no one should disagree with those opinions. When his superior disagreed, he tried to overthrow his superior and set himself up in his stead. But his superior spoke for the vast majority of people. The man himself was eventually overthrown instead of his superior. His opinions were denounced as not conforming to what everyone else agreed. They were considered heretical and punishments were drawn up for anyone who followed the man and tried to force his opinions on others.'

Brother Lugna seemed to be watching her in the semi-light like a hunter watching his prey.

Eadulf found he was barely able to repress a shudder, a cold feeling ran along his spine in the darkness as he sensed the malignancy in the man.

'I acknowledge my mistake in opposing your investigation, Fidelma of Cashel,' the steward said in a begrudging tone. 'You will have my support.' Then he added, 'There can be many paths to the same belief and each are entitled to their own path.'

'That is precisely my point,' agreed Fidelma vigorously. 'We should be tolerant of one another; conformity of opinion, by its very nature, cannot be enforced.'

'Is there anything else?' Brother Lugna's voice was almost sullen.

'Do we have an agreement?'

'We do.' With that the steward turned and left them standing in the middle of the quadrangle.

'I don't trust him,' muttered Eadulf as they walked to the guesthouse. 'When he says the sooner the investigation is over, he really means that the sooner we leave the abbey, the better for him.'

'At least we have made a little progress today,' Fidelma said. She turned at the door of her chamber and wished Eadulf a good night.

Eadulf could not sleep. His mind kept thinking about the last few weeks; of the arguments he had had with Fidelma and the cause of them. What was it that Aeneas said about leaving Dido, the Queen of Carthage? *Varium et mutabile semper femina.* Was that it? Woman is ever fickle and changeable. But Fidelma was not really capricious, it was just that she had a low tolerance of faults in others. She had a low tolerance of her own faults, too. He knew that, she had allowed him close enough to know it, still her sharp criticism frustrated and angered him.

She had been right to demand to know what he wanted. It was true that he wanted to be with her and their son Alchú, but did he really want to force them to go into some religious community and settle down? Did he really think that this meant security, a means of avoiding the complexities of the world? Or was it merely a means of trying to exert his individuality? As a youth he had met the missionary called Fursa in his village of Seaxmund's Ham, who had persuaded him to journey across the sea to the land of Éireann. He had studied in the great teaching abbey of Tuaim Brecain, a celebrated medical school of the religious, founded by Bricin. There were two other colleges in the abbey, one of poetry and one of law.

Eadulf had arrived there many years after its founder Bricin had died. Cennfaeladh ran the school. As a youthful warrior Cennfaeladh had fought in a battle at Magh Rath and received a dangerous wound in the head. He had been taken to Bricin's medical school where his skull had to be trepanned. It was an ancient surgical procedure that had long been practised among the Gauls as well as the Britons and people of the Five Kingdoms. As soon as he recovered, Cennfaeladh had devoted himself to studies there and eventually became head of the school.

It was Cennfaeladh who had taught Eadulf the language of the country. Then he urged Eadulf to go and study in Rome. While he was in Rome, he had been chosen to attend the great Council in St Hilda's abbey at Streonshalh in Northumbria. Had he not been at that Council he would not have met Fidelma. Since then, he had been back to Rome, travelled extensively among the Five Kingdoms of Éireann and been to the Kingdom of Dyfed, to Burgundia, Frankia, Gaul and Bro-Waroch.

Surely he could not be accused of hiding from the world and its complexities. Maybe it was just that he was tired. Tired of the rigours of travel. And now, here he was in another strange abbey. He had been here once before but only briefly. There had been no new buildings then. New buildings . . .

Eadulf suddenly sat upright. That was what was worrying him. The ladder and the young boy – what was his name? Gúasach. Fidelma had not pursued the idea of the ladder and boy being the means of gaining access to Brother Donnchad's locked cell. Yet it seemed the obvious answer. The ladder had been easily accessible on the building site. Young boys had been known to kill people before. Didn't Fidelma always say that the obvious answer, even if unpalatable, was often the right one?

Eadulf swung off his bed. He would take a look at that ladder lying by the new building. He would at least see if it was long enough to reach Brother Donnchad's cell. He would do it now. He would not wait until morning, as he did not want Fidelma to know that he had not accepted her dismissal of the idea. If he could argue from knowledge then . . .

Impatiently he lit the candle at his bedside with his *tenlach-teined*, the tinderbox with its steel and flint. Eadulf had, over the years, become more adept at creating the *tenlam*, or hand-fire, as it was called, for he had taken instruction from Gormán. Warriors prided themselves on being able to create a fire by means of steel, flint and tinder faster than most people. It was part of their training. Eadulf pulled on his robes and sandals and, taking the lantern, made his way quickly and silently down to the abbey courtyard. The dark shadows of the abbey were shrouded in silence. Here and there he saw the flicker of lamps that were kept burning all night by the main gates and outside the doors of the main buildings.

Eadulf peered around, judging his bearings and checking to see if anyone was about, but all was quiet. The moon was now sheltering behind clouds. He was thankful for the light of the lantern. He made his way quickly across the quadrangle, wishing his leather sandals did not slap so noisily on the stone flags. The splashing fountain appeared to provide a muffle to his footsteps. It seemed that the entire abbey and its occupants were blissfully asleep. Not even the lonely cry of a distant wolf outside the abbey gates seemed to disturb their slumber. As he passed the library building and reached the building site, the clouds parted and a nearly full moon provided an ethereal light. The stone walls of the lower part of the building had been built to window level; the windows needed lintels to cap them before the walls could rise higher. But the main door seemed to have its lintel in place although it appeared to be at a curious angle.

Eadulf paused and listened. He thought he had heard a sound. But it was only an owl perched somewhere in the wooden framework above him.

Eadulf looked around, trying to locate the ladder. He could not see it and moved forward, towards the doorway. Then he heard a creaking noise, a rasp of moving stone. As he lifted his lantern to identify the sound, he heard a loud gasp behind him and something slammed into his back. It was such a force that the lantern flew from his hand and he was flung forward. His head smashed against something solid and unyielding. There was a moment of bright light and then utter blackness.

CHAPTER ELEVEN

W hen Eadulf swam reluctantly back to consciousness, his head was pounding with pain. He registered that it was daylight and realised that he was lying on a bed and someone was bending over him. A voice he could not identify said, 'Ah, good. How do you feel?'

Eadulf's mouth was dry and he tried to lick his lips. His voice was a rasping whisper.

'Like a building has fallen on me.'

'Do you know who you are?'

'Eadulf.' He had no hesitation. 'Eadulf of Seaxmund's Ham.'

'Do you know who I am?'

He peered up at the man. The face swam into focus and he recognised it.

'You are the physician . . . Brother Seachlann.'

'Excellent. Now, there is something I want you to drink that will make you feel better.'

'Where am I?' he asked, easing himself up. He was not in the bed in the guesthouse. There was a pungent smell of herbs in this place.

'This is the *bróinbherg*, our little hospital in the abbey.' The word meant 'house of sorrow', the name often given to hospitals.

'How did I get here?'

'You ask too many questions. Come, drink this down, it will help ease your headache.'

'What is it?' asked Eadulf suspiciously, as a small cup was held beneath his nose. Its odour was pungent.

Brother Seachlann frowned for a moment. 'Of course,' he said, 'you were trained at Tuaim Brecain. This is *deoch suain*, a sleeping draught that is an infusion of valerian mixed with wild mint and rosemary.'

Eadulf allowed Brother Seachlann to hold the cup to his lips. He knew it was the sort of medication that was prescribed for a bad headache.

As he lay back, he realised his forehead was bandaged. He raised a hand uncertainly to it as the physician stood up from where he had been perched on the side of the bed.

'What happened to me?'

'I made a paste of comfrey root and spread it over the abrasion on your forehead. It should heal in a few days.'

'I meant, how did it happen? How did I get here?'

'I brought you here.'

At that moment, the door burst open and Fidelma came in, her face drawn and anxious. She hurried to Eadulf's side.

'I've just heard. Are you all right?'

Eadulf managed a lopsided grin. '*Non omnis moriar*,' he joked. He could not remember where the line came from. It meant, 'I shall not wholly die.'

Fidelma made an impatient sound and asked, 'What happened?'

'I was just asking Brother Seachlann the same question. I have no idea.'

She turned to the physician. Brother Seachlann placed the cup he was holding on a nearby table.

'I cannot tell you much. I was passing by the new building, the incomplete one. It was late last night. I heard a moaning sound. I went towards the sound. I couldn't see much even though I had a lantern. I almost tripped over Brother Eadulf, who was lying in the rubble. It looked as though he had tripped and struck his forehead, for there was blood on it. The fall had knocked the senses from him. Having checked that he had not broken any bones, I lifted him up and carried him here, dressed his wound and put him to bed. As soon as it was light, I sent a message to Brother Máel Eoin to inform you.'

Fidelma looked at Eadulf. His eyes were closing but he was breathing regularly. Seeing her anxious look, the physician said, 'That will be the effect of the infusion that I gave him. He will sleep and when he wakes again his headache should be gone.'

'Why didn't you send for me earlier? It was only a short time ago that the hosteller woke me with this news. You say Eadulf has been here all night?'

'I could not leave him in case of complications,' protested the physician. 'It was best to stay with him. It was only moments ago that he recovered consciousness. It would have served no purpose to rouse you in the middle of the night. Better only one person should lose a night's sleep than several.'

It made sense to Fidelma but it was frustrating that she could not question Eadulf immediately. She knew it was unlike him to go wandering about without informing her and he was certainly not one prone to accidents.

At that moment Gormán entered, looking anxious.

'I heard . . .' His eyes went to Eadulf lying on the bed. 'Is he . . .?'

Fidelma turned to the physician without answering the warrior. 'Are you sure he is out of danger now?'

Brother Seachlann shrugged. 'The physician who says he is sure of anything is a physician to be wary of. When Brother Eadulf wakes he should be fine apart from a bruise and a gash on the forehead which he needs to keep bound for a few days.'

'Then if Gormán will stay with Eadulf, perhaps you will show me the spot where you found him.'

Brother Seachlann looked surprised. 'For what purpose?'

'For my own satisfaction,' Fidelma replied firmly.

Brother Seachlann led the way across to the site. One or two men already at work regarded them with curiosity. The physician halted and pointed to a spot close to the supporting columns of a door. There was no lintel on it; the lintel stone was lying on the ground close by, ready to be hoisted into place.

'I found him lying there, by that wooden post,' the physician said.

Fidelma moved forward and inspected the thick wooden post beyond. There was a dark discoloration on it. She licked the tip of her finger and ran it over the stain.

'Dried blood,' she muttered. 'So this is what Eadulf encountered with his forehead.'

'He must have tripped and hit his head,' suggested the physician. 'A place like this is dangerous in the darkness.'

'Well, one thing is certain,' Fidelma replied, 'he did not walk up to the post and bang his own head against it.'

'Hey! Be careful!' They turned at the shouted warning to find Glassán hurrying towards them with Saor, his assistant, at his side. 'What are you doing there? It is dangerous to wander around a building site like this.'

'That has already been discovered,' Fidelma replied drily.

Glassán spotted the lintel. 'What happened there?' he demanded. 'Surely that was secure and in place when we finished work last evening.'

Saor looked uncomfortable. 'I swear it was. Maybe it was not fitted properly.'

'Even so, it would need a push to get it off its resting place,' Fidelma observed, looking thoughtfully at the door supports.

Glassán glanced at the lintel and then at her.

'What do you mean?' he demanded. 'Pushed off?' There was a note of unease in his voice.

'It could have fallen down,' Saor suggested as he examined it.

'It seems Brother Eadulf tripped over something last night. Perhaps that stone,' suggested the physician.

Glassán's bewilderment increased.

'Brother Seachlann found Brother Eadulf last evening,' Fidelma explained. 'He was lying unconscious at this spot. It seems he tripped and knocked himself out on that wooden post there.'

Glassán's face paled; his jaw muscles tightened. Then he turned to Saor. 'Better be about the work. There is much to do to refit this lintel.' When Saor had left, he turned, licking his lips nervously. 'How is your husband, lady?'

'He is recovering,' intervened the physician. 'He has a bad gash on the forehead and a headache. Nothing more. Now I should like to get back to my patient.'

Fidelma dismissed him with a motion of her hand.

'What was Brother Eadulf doing here last night?' Glassán asked. 'I am truly sorry to hear that he has been hurt but I must point out that I cannot be held responsible for anyone entering a building site without permission and injuring themselves.'

'No one is accusing anyone of culpability just yet. We do not know the facts and will not know them until Eadulf has recovered enough to tell us.'

The master builder hesitated. Then he said quickly, 'Just so, just so. Well, there is much to be done.'

Fidelma continued to examine the scene carefully. When

she had seen everything she wanted to see, she finally turned and picked her way from the area of the doorway. Glassán followed her. As they came to the edge of the new building, she saw the young boy, Gúasach, hurrying round the corner. He saw them and smiled a greeting to Fidelma and then spoke to Glassán. 'Good morning, *aite*. Where am I to work this morning?'

Fidelma gazed at him in surprise. The term *aite* was one that denoted foster-father.

Glassán answered gruffly, telling him to report to Saor. The lad nodded, turned and hurried off across the building works.

'You have young workers here, Glassán,' commented Fidelma.

'The boy is my *dalta,* my apprentice, under fosterage,' the master builder replied. 'In another six years he may be able to leave fosterage and start a career of his own in this art.'

'Has he been with you long?'

'Since he was seven, as the law prescribed.'

Most male children were sent away to fosterage, or *altram*, between the ages of seven and seventeen, when they reached the *togu aismir*, the age of maturity, when they had full responsibility under the law. 'Fosterage' was a keystone of society and practised in all the Five Kingdoms since remote times and by all social ranks. Fosterage in this context denoted education, since the fosterers were supposed to teach their charges the skills necessary for their adult life. Some were fostered for affection, usually because they were kin, and some for payment determined by law, depending on what class and degree the child was.

'He seems a bright boy. Is he a relative?'

'I am paid an *iarraith*, a fee, for his fosterage,' Glassán said shortly. 'Now, if you will excuse me, lady.'

Fidelma nodded and turned to make her way back to Brother Seachlann's little hospital. Gormán was still there, sitting anxiously by Eadulf's bedside; the physician was mixing some potion at the table.

'I doubt if he will be awake before midday,' the physician said as she entered. 'Better to let him sleep naturally and deeply. Do not worry. I shall take care of him. After a good sleep he will be able to go back to his own *cubiculum* this evening.'

Fidelma motioned to Gormán to accompany her and left the physician with Eadulf.

'Have you found out what happened?' asked the warrior.

'Only that something took him to the building site last night, that he tripped and hit his head on a post, knocking himself unconscious.'

They were making their way across the quadrangle when Abbot Iarnla came hurrying across to them.

'I have just been told of Brother Eadulf's accident. Terrible! Terrible!' The elderly abbot was distraught. 'How is he?'

'Your physician tells us that he will make a good recovery after rest. There are no bones broken,' replied Fidelma.

'*Deo gratias*,' intoned the abbot. 'But how did it happen?

I am told he was on the building site in the middle of the night.'

'Who told you?'

'Brother Lugna. I think he was told by Brother Máel Eoin.'

She was about to speak again when she saw Brother Lugna himself approaching.

'I am distressed to hear the news of Brother Eadulf. I trust he is recovering well,' he greeted them. His voice was entirely without emotion.

'He is,' Abbot Iarnla replied impatiently before Fidelma could respond.

'That is good,' Brother Lugna replied, still looking at Fidelma. 'But what was he doing at that place in the middle of the night? Doesn't he understand that it is dangerous to be wandering about such a construction site?'

Abbot Iarnla nodded in agreement. 'That is just what I was asking.'

'We think that Eadulf was looking for something and fell, that's all.'

Brother Lugna was puzzled. 'Looking for something? In the middle of the night and on the building site?'

'I can only say that Eadulf had good reason to be there.' She felt compelled to defend Eadulf. 'You must indulge us while we investigate.'

'I fail to see what stumbling about the new buildings in the middle of the night has to do with the death of Brother Donnchad.' Brother Lugna's tone was critical.

'By time everything is revealed,' smiled Fidelma, airing the old proverb.

Brother Lugna seemed about to speak further but then compressed his lips into a thin line and turned away.

Abbot Iarnla looked anxiously after him. 'I hope you will be able to come to some conclusions soon, Fidelma.'

'One cannot hurry truth, Abbot Iarnla,' she replied in a philosophical tone. 'There is more to be done and more to be asked.'

The abbot stood hesitantly. 'You will keep me informed as soon as you know anything positive?'

'You will be informed,' she assured him solemnly.

As they watched Abbot Iarnla walk across the courtyard to the main abbey buildings, Gormán heaved a deep sigh.

'I would say that he is a worried person, lady,' he remarked softly.

'I would agree, Gormán,' she replied. 'I think there is much to be worried about in this abbey. Keep your eyes open, Gormán. It might be helpful if you can pick up any gossip from the builders' encampment. I am going into the *scriptorium* as I have a mind to ask a few more questions of Brother Donnán.'

She walked towards the abbey library. Behind her the work on the new buildings had recommenced. The crash of hammers against stone, the sawing of wood and the shouts of men filled the air. Inside the wooden *scriptorium* the noise was barely muffled and the *scriptor* Brother Donnán was wringing his hands in despair. He came forward quickly as the door opened but the hope on his face faded a little when Fidelma entered.

'I was expecting Brother Lugna so that he could order the workmen to stop a while. My copyists and scholars cannot concentrate at all. I have had to send them all away.'

Fidelma gazed around the empty library room. 'So I see, Brother Donnán.'

Brother Donnán seemed almost about to burst into tears. 'This is frustrating. Brother Lugna has made it a rule that no book or manuscript should be removed from the library so that I cannot ask my copyists to carry on the work elsewhere.'

'But finding you here alone is good for me.' Fidelma smiled. 'I wanted a further word with you on your own.'

'Is everything well?' The *scriptor*'s tone was suddenly anxious. 'Brother Máel Eoin came by and told me the news of Brother Eadulf. I hope he is not badly hurt.'

'He is resting. He has a bad gash and bruises, but that is all.'

'Well, that is bad enough but thanks be that he is no worse. It will be good for all of us when this building work is finished. It is so dangerous. But you wanted to speak with me?' He gestured to a nearby chair and took another facing her.

'Dangerous?' asked Fidelma, sitting down. 'In what way?'

'During recent weeks there have been several accidents on the site. Indeed, I heard that Brother Lugna had to remonstrate with Glassán to take more care that no harm came to any of the brethren.'

Fidelma was thoughtful. 'What sort of accidents?' she asked.

'Falling timbers. Timbers that were not secured. Oh, and a stone fell from a wall and nearly hit Glassán himself. He was very angry.'

'He was not hurt?'

'No, but the stone narrowly missed him.'

'How many such accidents have there been?'

Brother Donnán thought for a moment and then shrugged. 'Four, as I recall, during the last few weeks. Five with Brother Eadulf's accident.'

Fidelma raised her eyebrows. 'Five? Has anyone else been injured?'

'Two of the workmen. A grazed arm and cuts, that's all.'

'Has anyone been found responsible?'

Brother Donnán looked surprised. 'Responsible?'

'Have any workmen been censured for negligence?'

'No one. Glassán put it down to shoddy workmanship. Oh, yes, now I come to think of it, he did fine one of his men for slackness.'

'That is helpful, Brother Donnán.' Fidelma was solemn. 'But that was not what I wanted to speak to you about.'

'I am at your service, as always.'

'Indeed. You and I are old friends, Brother Donnán.'

The *scriptor* preened himself a little. 'There were some tough cases to be heard by you that day you sat in judgement here as a Brehon. The witnesses needed to be sorted out. Do you remember the case of the son of Suanach, and

Muadnat of the Black Marsh? That was a very complicated case. I was amazed how you worked it out.'

'I could not have accomplished half of those judgements without someone to keep the witnesses and the court in proper order.' Fidelma leant forward confidentially. 'That is why I turn to you now, to ask your help. Information is what I need.'

'If I have that information, it is yours.'

'When did Brother Seachlann join the abbey?'

'Brother Seachlann? The physician? He came here about a month ago.'

'Only a month?'

Brother Donnán nodded.

'Do you know anything of his background?'

'He is a physician from Sléibhte. I know little else about him.'

'Is it known why he came to join this abbey? Has there been any speculation?'

The rotund librarian shook his head slowly. 'I certainly never gave it a thought. Our abbey is beginning to have a reputation for learning and I suppose that was what attracted him.'

'What happened to the abbey's previous physician? I presume that you had one.'

'We did not have one for several months after poor Brother Siadhail died of some coughing paroxysm. He was elderly. Brother Seachlann came along at the right time.'

'Is he considered a good physician? Is he well liked among the brethren?'

'I have heard no complaints,' Brother Donnán replied. 'But as for being well liked, well, he keeps himself much to himself and does not venture friendship with anyone.'

'So he is not close to anyone among the brethren?'

'Perhaps that is the way a good physician should be,' ventured the *scriptor*. 'Then he can treat everyone equally and without favour.'

She smiled and nodded assent. 'That's probably how things should be.' She paused and added, 'You will remember that we were talking about Celsus the other day and Origenes' answer to him.'

The *scriptor* frowned. 'An interesting work. Origenes' work, that is.'

'It sounds a very fascinating work,' Fidelma said. 'I wonder why Brother Donnchad was so interested in it.'

'I can tell you no more than I said before. He was a great scholar. And he often argued that one must understand the origins of the Faith. That was in the old days, of course, before he set off on his pilgrimage.'

Fidelma sighed. 'I was hoping that you might know something of the work or someone who might have read it.' She rose from the chair. 'But you have helped a lot, for which I thank you.'

Brother Donnán seemed disconcerted for a moment. Then the door opened and a strange warrior stood hesitantly in the doorway. He cast a glance at Fidelma and then turned to Brother Donnán.

'I am sorry to disturb you, Brother Donnán, but Lady Eithne has sent me for the books she requested.'

The librarian actually flushed and cast a nervous look at Fidelma. Then he hurried to a side cupboard and took out two leather book satchels and handed them to the warrior without a further word. The man thanked him and left immediately.

'I thought you said Brother Lugna had a rule against books being taken from the library,' Fidelma remarked as the door shut.

'In the case of Lady Eithne an exception is made,' Brother Donnán replied quickly. 'She is, after all, the patroness of the abbey.'

'What books has she requested?'

'She is very supportive of the Faith,' countered the librarian.

'I do not doubt it.'

'She has been reading some of the epistles of the Blessed Paul of Tarsus.'

'Really? The original texts in Greek?'

'Some Latin translations.'

'Ah, of course. She said she did not know Greek, although I thought she had only a little knowledge of Latin. Well, no matter.'

She bade farewell to the librarian. Outside, the sun stood high in a cloudless sky and it was very warm, almost oppressive. Her forehead was moist. She felt uncomfortable in her woollen robes. She decided to return to the guesthouse to splash her face and wash her hands before the midday meal.

As she entered, she found the hosteller, Brother Máel Eoin, cleaning the entrance hall.

'How is Brother Eadulf, lady?' he asked, pausing in his sweeping.

She gave him the now standard reply.

'I saw one of Lady Eithne's men coming from the *scriptorium*,' he went on. 'Ah, that lady must love books.'

Fidelma, who had been about to pass on, paused. 'Why do you say that?'

'The number of times she has either sent her men for books or asked the steward or librarian to take them to her at her fortress.'

'Really? It is a frequent occurrence then?'

'Brother Lugna and Brother Donnán often go to her fortress at her bidding. Brother Lugna, in particular, seems to be a close adviser to her.'

'Has she been interested in reading for long?'

The hosteller thought for a moment. 'I suppose it was after her son, Brother Donnchad, returned from the pilgrimage. That must have been what stirred her interest in such matters.'

'Such matters?'

'I have heard that she is particularly interested in what manuscripts and books are kept in our library relating to the principles of the Faith.'

'And so she has come to an accommodation with the abbot to borrow such works from the library from time to time.'

'The abbot?' Brother Máel Eoin smiled thinly. 'I don't think he knows about the arrangement. No, it was probably made with Brother Lugna. She even had Brother Donnán running after her when she could have taken the books herself.'

'What do you mean?' Fidelma was curious.

'After she spoke to Brother Donnchad on the evening before he was found dead, she had poor Brother Donnán taking manuscripts to her.'

'How do you know this?'

'I heard it from Brother Gáeth. He was working in the fields by the roadside and saw the Lady Eithne riding back to her fortress. Then, not long afterwards, he saw Brother Donnán trotting down the road bearing some manuscripts from the library for her. I suppose it is her right as lady of this territory but I feel sorry for the librarian having to act in the manner of a messenger.'

A bell chimed. It was the summons for the *etar-shod*, the midday meal.

Fidelma joined Gormán in the *refectorium*. Glássan and Saor were obviously taking their meal with the workers again, so only the two of them were seated at the guests' table. Fidelma was in no mood to talk. After the meal, she made her way to the *bróinbherg* and found only Brother Seachlann there. The bed on which Eadulf had been sleeping was empty.

'I could not stop him,' Brother Seachlann told her. 'He has a strong will. When he awoke, he determined to go back to the *tech-oíged*. I insisted that he have some soup and bread to sustain him. At least he had that before he went. I prepared a salve for his forehead and a jug of an infusion that should ease any residual headache. Try to ensure that he uses both. He should have remained here the rest of the day.'

Fidelma thanked the physician quickly and hurried across to the guesthouse and Eadulf's *cubiculum*.

Eadulf was lying on his bed but in a semi-upright position.

'Can you tell me what happened to you?' Fidelma asked after he had assured her he felt well enough to talk.

'Not really,' Eadulf grimaced wanly, 'apart from getting knocked out. I seem to be making a habit of it.'

She smiled at his reference to the falling masonry that had nearly killed them both at the old abbey of Autun earlier in the summer. That masonry had been deliberately set to kill them both.

'Come on, Eadulf,' she prompted. 'Give me the details. What were you doing on the building site at night? You know it is dangerous.'

'If you must know, I was following up an idea.'

'Go on.'

'I was lying here thinking about the long ladders that were being used on the building site. I wanted to check to see if any had the length to reach up to Brother Donnchad's window.'

'Didn't we discount that?'

'You said only a midget would be able to get through the window.'

Fidelma sighed. 'You think that small child Gúasach could have entered through the window and killed Donnchad?'

'I did so and then . . .' He stopped and shrugged. 'I thought

about Glassán's story. What if Brother Donnchad had discovered Glassán's background secret and threatened to tell
the abbot? Glassán would have a good motive—'

Fidelma stopped him with a shake of her head. 'I don't
think it is much of a secret. I am sure Brother Lugna knows
about it, judging by his reaction when I mentioned Laighin
the other evening. I'll grant you that the abbot has not been
kept fully informed but I don't think Brother Donnchad would
be bothered about the master builder. His behaviour suggests
that he had something else on his mind.'

Eadulf looked disappointed.

Fidelma continued. 'However, I'll grant you that Glassán
is not beyond suspicion and the fact that young Gúasach is
his foster-son makes it all the more essential that we should
not forget them. However, are you telling me that, seized by
this idea, you set off into the night?'

A corner of Eadulf's mouth turned down and he sighed.
'It seemed a good idea at the time.'

'So you arrived at the building site. Then what happened?'

'I found the spot where they had left their ladders and I
had a candle with me. I was going towards it when I heard
a rasping noise.'

'Rasping? Like stone on stone?'

'Exactly.'

'And where did the sound come from?'

'I wasn't sure. Overhead, I thought. I raised the candle to
see then . . .' he hesitated, frowning. 'I think I heard someone
gasp. Suddenly I was flying forward.'

'Did you trip?'

'I did not. Something, or someone, pushed me hard in the small of my back. It sent the candle from my hand and I pitched forward. The next thing I knew I was in Brother Seachlann's hospital.'

'Well, if you were pushed, whoever pushed you saved your life.'

'Saved my life? How?'

'You just missed having a heavy lintel stone come down on top of your head.'

'You think that was the rasping sound I heard?' asked Eadulf.

'Yes, I do. The lintel was on the ground when I went to look at the spot where you were found.'

'Then whoever knocked me out of the way must have seen the person who was pushing the stone so that it would fall on me.'

'A logical conclusion. Yet why?'

'Because they knew that I was going to discover Donnchad's murderer?'

'Perhaps. Perhaps not. Maybe they did not even know who you were. I have heard from Brother Donnán that there have been several so-called accidents on the building site in recent weeks.'

'Isn't that usual? You cannot have several workmen building these large constructions of stone without accidents, can you?'

'Did you see anything else before you were pushed?'

'I only had the candle. When I heard the rasping, I raised

it in order to ascertain where the sound came from. But I saw nothing at all.'

'You raised the candle when you heard the rasping?'

'As I said, I was trying to identify the sound. But before I could focus on anything, the push came and blackness.'

'The candlelight would have fallen on your face. Perhaps you were not the person they wanted to kill,' she speculated.

'If it wasn't me they wanted to kill, who was it?'

'If we knew the answer to that question, we might have an answer to the whole conundrum.'

'Perhaps it was Glassán and his foster-son who pushed me?'

'I doubt the boy is strong enough to either push you over or move the lintel. We can rule them out, I think. Or the boy, at least.'

Eadulf realised she was right.

'Maybe we should have a talk with the child?' he suggested. 'He might know something even if he isn't directly involved.'

'I agree that he might be able to tell us something more. However, I would rather do it when he is on his own. We especially don't want Glassán or Brother Lugna about.'

'There is one question I would like answered,' said Eadulf. 'What was the physician doing on the building site last night? How did he come to see me lying there and carry me back to his hospital?'

'That is more than one question,' Fidelma pointed out with humour. 'But you are right. They are questions that need to be answered. I think I shall go and ask them now.' She rose.

'Is everything all right with you? Do you want for anything? You are taking the potion that Brother Seachlann gave you?'

Eadulf nodded at the jug by his bedside. 'Brother Seachlann has provided me with a noxious brew and a salve. I just hope they work.'

Fidelma picked up the jug and sniffed cautiously. 'I smell mint. Do you know what is in it?'

'Don't worry. I do not think he is trying to poison me,' replied Eadulf. 'From what I know of the contents, it is the sort of mixture that most apothecaries would mix up in the circumstances. I'll try to sleep off this headache, though. I know there is much to do.'

'I'll ask Gormán to stay near in case you want anything.'

When she glanced back from the door, Eadulf was already lying back, exhausted, his eyes closed.

CHAPTER TWELVE

Fidelma found Brother Seachlann in the *bróinbherg* treating a member of the brethren who glanced up shame-faced as she entered.

'Am I disturbing you, Brother Seachlann?'

The physician shrugged. 'I am just finished with this one,' he replied. Turning to the obviously embarrassed man, he gave him a small earthenware jug. 'Take this mixture and drink a small cupful at frequent intervals and if there is no relief you must come back to me.'

The man nodded quickly, rose and left the chamber.

Brother Seachlann grimaced. 'A case of food poisoning, I think. He is suffering the *buinnech*. When he first came yesterday I treated him with meadowsweet but it was not strong enough, so I have made an infusion of agrimony which is stronger and should work within three days.'

'*Buinnech*?' Fidelma queried. 'That's . . . flux.'

'Diarrhoea,' agreed the physician. 'Since no one else has

succumbed, I suspect the Brother has been eating something that he should not have been. Some of the brethren do tend to cheat on the meals as laid down in the rules drawn up by our resolute steward Brother Lugna. He believes in frugality.'

'Agrimony has a bitter taste,' commented Fidelma. 'I much prefer boiled sorrel with red wine.'

'Fine for those who can afford red wine,' the physician retorted. 'Now what can I do for you? I hope Brother Eadulf has not taken a turn for the worse.'

Fidelma offered him a reassuring smile. 'I came to thank you for all that you have done for Eadulf.'

'It was no more than my profession calls on me to do.'

'But it was lucky that you were passing by where he lay.' When he did not respond, she went on, 'How did you come to be there so late at night?'

The physician frowned and began to clear away the dishes in which he had been mixing his last patient's medication.

'I always like to take a walk before preparing myself for repose,' he said. 'It helps to clear the mind.'

'But so late?'

'I am no slave to the motions of the sun and moon,' he replied shortly. 'If I were, then I would not be a physician because sickness and injury do not take account of night or day.'

'That is true. What made you become a physician? Are you descended from one of those families of hereditary healers?'

Brother Seachlann flushed. She saw a glimpse of some emotion she could not recognise cross his features.

'I went to study the healing arts when I saw there was a need of them among my people.'

'That is very laudable, Brother Seachlann. It is this abbey's good fortune that you decided to leave your people and come here.'

'The physician should serve all people, irrespective of who they are.'

'So you saw there was a need among your people but, having qualified, you decided that others had greater need of your talents?'

'That much is obvious as I am here,' he replied waspishly.

Fidelma merely smiled and waited.

'I qualified among the religious and thereafter I considered them my people,' he tried to justify himself.

'Indeed, so you came here to my brother's kingdom,' she said, reminding him that she held power in the land. 'In this kingdom,' she went on, 'as I think that you learnt from our first meeting, a *dálaigh* has particular authority, especially when that authority is backed by the rank of birth. Usually, rank of birth does not enter into matters until someone attempts to usurp the authority of the law.'

There was a moment's silence and then he dropped his gaze to the floor.

'I beg your forgiveness, lady,' he said thickly. 'When you first came here, I was told that I should be careful about what I said to you. I was told neither your rank nor your position.'

'And it was Brother Lugna, of course, who said that to you.'

He seemed nervous at the suggestion.

'Do not worry, Brother Seachlann. I presume that you were not in the *refectorium* for the evening meal last night?'

He frowned and shook his head.

'Can I ask you where you were? Even a physician has to eat.'

'I was called earlier that evening to attend to a patient. I did not return to the abbey until after dark.'

'Who was the patient?'

'A warrior at a nearby fortress.'

'Which fortress?'

'Lady Eithne's.'

'What was wrong with the warrior?'

'An ulcerated wound. It was easily treated and there was no cause for me to be called to her fortress. A herbalist, or even Lady Eithne herself, could have done as much as I did. I saw she was quite knowledgeable about healing herbs and anatomy. However, she believed it beneath her dignity to treat one of her own warriors.'

'You say that it was an ulcerated wound.'

'I was told that the man had been practising with his sword and sustained a cut on his arm which he simply washed. I mixed some sorrel and apple juice and applied it to the wound with the white of a hen's egg. If he keeps the wound clean, then there should be no problems.'

'So you were kept at the fortress and returned here after dark.'

'That is so.' He hesitated and asked, 'And if I had been here for the evening meal what then?'

'Then you would have witnessed the steward of this abbey having to acknowledge my authority. I had already learnt that he had given some bad advice to you and others.'

'I suppose I should have known better.' The physician sighed.

'You should,' agreed Fidelma. 'But as you have been here only a few weeks . . .' She shrugged. 'What made you choose to come here?'

Once again a guarded look spread across his features. 'Much praise has been given to Lios Mór for its scholars and learning. It is good to be associated with such a community.'

'Where did you study? I think you mentioned Sléibhte.'

'Indeed. I studied at the medical school attached to the abbey at Sléibhte in Laighin.'

'I know it, for I was once at Cill Dara, which is not far distant. Aedh is abbot at Sléibhte, is he not?'

Brother Seachlann gave a grunt of assent.

'It is a small world,' Fidelma said pointedly.

'It is,' he responded, 'and so you will know that there is regular contact between Lios Mór and the abbey of Sléibhte. It is surely not strange that it would bring me here.'

'That is true,' Fidelma agreed. It was clear that the physician was determined to provide as little information as possible while seeming to answer her questions. She thanked him for his help and left him to his herbs and potions.

Fidelma made her way slowly towards the building site again. She realised that it would have been quite a distance for the physician to carry the inert body of Eadulf by himself in the darkness. She was almost tempted to demand that Brother Seachlann reveal who his companion had been. He seemed to be hiding something but she knew she would not find out what by directly confronting him.

It was late afternoon now and Fidelma was surprised to find the site deserted. There was no shouting, no sounds of hammering, sawing or the clash of stone on stone. She hesitated before the half-built door whose lintel had so nearly put an end to Eadulf's life. A cold shiver went down her spine. She realised that she would not have been able to continue had anything happened to Eadulf. She felt a sudden desire to cry. Then she sniffed and drew herself up, trying to chase the thought from her mind.

The lintel had been replaced in position on top of the door and a line of stones had been laid to secure it. Fidelma looked round at the deserted site and shook her head. She was about to turn away when suddenly a young voice started singing from beyond the walls of the half-built construction.

> *Hymnum dicat turba fratrum,*
> *hymnum canos personet . . .*

> Band of brethren raise the hymn,
> let our song the hymn resound . . .

Fidelma picked her way towards the sound of the singing.

It was the young boy Gúasach, busy piling up loose pieces of wood.

'Hello,' Fidelma called.

The boy turned with a frown and then, on recognising her, smiled broadly.

'Were you looking for Glassán, Sister?' he asked.

'Everyone seems to have vanished except you,' countered Fidelma. 'Where have they gone? It is surely early to stop work for the day.'

The boy shook his head. 'They have not stopped work. All are needed down at the quarry to bring up more stones to the site.'

'Ah, I see. You seem to like this work,' she said, perching herself on a low stone wall.

'I am learning to be a master builder under the fosterage of my *aite*.' The boy spoke proudly.

'And where are you from?'

'I am of the Uí Briún Sinna, Sister.'

'Then you are from the Kingdom of Connachta. But isn't your foster-father from Laighin?'

'I do not know. I am told that he came to live among us just after I was born. My own father was a builder of mills and so Glassán and he worked together. When I was seven years old, my family, wanting me to train to be a master builder, arranged for me to go into fosterage with Glassán.'

Fidelma knew that the Law of the Fénechus determined that a mill-maker could charge two *cumals*, the equivalent of six cows, for a finely constructed mill. But a master builder was higher up the professional scale and could receive more money.

The boy added, 'My father pays Glassán a *cumal*, three milch cows, for my tuition.'

'And so you learn while working for Glassán.'

'I do. I came into fosterage at the same time that Glassán was invited here to start rebuilding this abbey in stone. Everything I have learnt so far, I have learnt here. Of course, I am not as strong as the men, so can't do the heavy work. But I have learnt how to do other tasks like woodworking. I can also use the plumb line and measuring rods to help position the stones.'

'That is clever,' Fidelma said. 'But dangerous work as well. That lintel that fell last night might have fallen while you were working underneath.'

The boy nodded solemnly. 'It must have been badly placed.' Then he added defensively, 'I did not measure the place for it. Anyway, sometimes accidents happen if you don't concentrate properly. Glassán taught me that.'

'A wise thing to remember,' Fidelma solemnly agreed.

'Indeed. Glassán was very angry when the Saxon Brother was injured.'

'Was he?'

'To be honest, there have been a few accidents here since Gealbháin left. I think Gealbháin used to go around the site every evening to ensure everything was in order. He was a very careful builder.'

'Gealbháin? Who was he?'

'He was the assistant to Glassán.'

'But I understood that Saor, the carpenter, is second-in-command here.'

'Saor has been with us only a short time. He replaced Gealbháin who quit the job several weeks ago.'

'Why did he quit?'

'I do not know, Sister.'

'So these accidents have occurred since Gealbháin left?'

'Saor is not as thorough as Gealbháin.'

'But isn't it the task of Glassán, as master builder, to check everything, to make sure it is safe?'

The boy shrugged and said, 'He has many tasks to perform. Saor is all right but I have not learnt much from him.'

'Oh? Why is that?'

'He does not seem to have time.'

'Who taught you your carpentry, then?'

'Gealbháin mostly.'

'Where was Gealbháin from? Connachta?'

'He was a local man . . . I think from a clan called the Uí Liatháin.'

'I see. Are the other workmen from around these parts or do most of them come from Connachta like you and Glassán?'

'Oh, no. Most of them are recruited from these parts. Although Saor is of the Uí Bairrche.'

'The Uí Bairrche? They are a clan from southern Laighin, aren't they?'

'So Saor has told me, Sister. I only know of my own lands and this place. I've never been out of sight of the abbey since we came here.'

'And do you stay in the abbey? I have only seen Glassán and Saor eating in the abbey *refectorium*.'

'We live in the wickerwork *bothans* we constructed outside the abbey walls by the river. That's where we all stay except Glassán. He has a special room in the guesthouse. The *bothans* are also where our stores are kept. That way, we do not interfere with the running of the abbey. Glassán explained that to us.'

A bell started to toll.

'That is the bell for the evening meal, Sister. I must go to join the others.'

Fidelma thanked the child before making her own way to eat. She was slightly annoyed for not having noticed the passing of time; she realised that she would have to miss the ritual of her evening bath before the meal. She paused at the fountain to wash her hands and face. Then she saw Eadulf walking slowly to the *refectorium* guided by Gormán.

'Eadulf!' Her voice was a rebuke as she greeted him. 'Is this wise?'

He grimaced before saying, 'I am hungry. A bowl of vegetable soup does not put strength back into one. I am all right. A slight headache still and soreness on the forehead but I have to admit that Brother Seachlann's noxious potion is doing the trick. But the aftertaste is awful.'

'Well, if you are sure.'

'I just hope that Glassán will not wax lyrical this evening.'
He smiled.

'I saw Glassán and his band of workmen leaving the abbey
a few hours ago,' Gormán offered. 'I haven't seen him return
since.'

'The young boy told me that they have gone to fetch stone
from the quarry,' Fidelma said, 'so we might avoid a discourse
on building.'

There was no sign of Glassán or Saor during the meal.
Several people, including the abbot, crossed to their table to
inquire after Eadulf's health. Even Brother Lugna asked, in
a sharply disapproving tone, as he passed their table, whether
Eadulf thought himself fit enough to eat in the *refectorium*.
Brother Gáeth and Brother Donnán raised their hands in
greeting and the Venerable Bróen, leaning heavily on a stick,
came across and said in a wheezy voice, 'I knew you would
be all right, Brother. The angel did not appear last night to
take your soul.'

Eadulf gazed uncomfortably at him and, with a forced
smile, said, 'I thank you for your concern, Brother.'

The Venerable Bróen leant closer, peering at Eadulf with
pale rheumy eyes, and whispered, confidentially, 'The angel
appeared in order to take the soul of poor Brother Donnchad.
I saw the angel, floating in the sky. But the angel did not
come last night, so I knew that you would be well.'

Brother Gáeth came across to take the old man's arm.

'Time to eat, Venerable Bróen,' he coaxed.

The old man peered round in bewilderment for a moment.

'Is it time to eat? Very well. We must all go to the *refecto-rium* to eat, must we not. Come on, then. Time to eat.'

Brother Gáeth gave them an apologetic smile and led the old man away.

There seemed an uneasy quiet in the dining hall that evening. Now and then they were conscious of surreptitious glances from the brethren. The atmosphere infected them and they exchanged little by way of conversation themselves. Afterwards, the three of them walked several times round the quadrangle of the abbey as a means of digesting their food. Fidelma ran over her conversations with the physician, who once again had not come to the evening meal in the *refecto-rium*, and with the boy. There was little to be commented on and Fidelma reminded them that she wanted to visit the fortress of Lady Eithne in order to ask her a few more questions. Eadulf assured her that he was fit enough to accom-pany her if she wanted to make the journey in the morning. Gormán was also enthusiastic. He was finding the stay in the abbey uninteresting and dull. It was agreed that they would make the journey in the morning.

A gentle tapping on her door woke Fidelma. It was still dark and she had the feeling that she had not long been asleep.

She frowned and swung out of the bed. She drew on her robe, thankful of the full moon which lit her chamber and saved the trouble of trying to light the candle.

'All right, Eadulf . . .' She began pulling open the door, for she expected no one else to arouse her at such a time.

Abbot Iarnla stood outside, one hand holding a lantern while the other seemed to be vainly attempting to shield its light.

Fidelma stared at him in astonishment.

'My apologies, Sister Fidelma.' The abbot was whispering. 'I need to talk to you urgently and without prying ears. That is why I have waited until the community are asleep.'

Fidelma held open the door without speaking and the abbot passed in. She peered out into the darkness of the passage but could see nothing, so she shut the door. She went to the solitary chair in the room over which she had hung her clothes, picked them up and laid them on the end of the bed. She motioned for the elderly abbot to sit. He did so, placing his lantern carefully on the table. Fidelma then sat on the edge of the bed and waited expectantly.

'I want you to know that I am not a fool, Fidelma,' he began.

'I did not think you were, Abbot Iarnla,' she replied. 'As you told me the other day, you have been a member of this community for thirty years and more, and abbot for a large part of that time.'

The abbot nodded absently. 'I know what you and Eadulf must be thinking. Poor Iarnla. He must be in his dotage. He has given up control of the abbey to this young upstart of the Uí Briuin Sinna. Do not deny it. I know many in this abbey, many among the brethren, are thinking the same thoughts.'

Fidelma smiled at him. 'You are certainly not in your

dotage, Abbot Iarnla. But there is a mystery here that needs to be resolved. Why would you give so much power to this young man. He only joined the abbey a few years ago and is so intolerant and fanatical in his beliefs – beliefs that seem out of step with the reputation of Lios Mór.'

The abbot shrugged expressively. 'I am not so blind as to be unaware how opinionated and dogmatic Brother Lugna is, nor how he is regarded by the brethren.'

'Then tell me,' invited Fidelma. 'Why give him such power?'

'I did not. He has taken it and I do not know how to extricate myself from the position I am placed in.'

'You will have to explain that.'

'When Brother Lugna joined us, as you know, he had spent some years in Rome. He came ashore at Ard Mór, presumably to journey back north to his homeland in Connachta. The road ran by the fortress of Lady Eithne who offered him hospitality on his journey. Her two sons were then on their pilgrimage to the Holy Land. She invited Brother Lugna to stay a while, eager to hear what such journeys were like. I think she wanted to be given hope for the safe return of her sons.'

'Understandably,' conceded Fidelma.

'Indeed. She seemed enthralled by Brother Lugna, his stories and his ideas. She even suggested that he join our community. He was, at first, a bright and likeable young man. My old steward had been weakened by a bout of the yellow plague. He had survived its worst ravages but he became ill again and died. That was when Brother Lugna, who was initially held in some respect by the brethren as one who had been all those years in Rome, was nominated to fill the office as steward.'

The abbot paused and licked his lips, which had gone dry. Fidelma rose and poured water from a jug by her bedside. The abbot swallowed it in two gulps.

'It was only later that we found that Brother Lugna was in fact sympathetic to some of the extreme sects in Rome. He began to change our native ways and methods of doing things. He even destroyed some of the books in our abbey that he did not agree with.'

'He is not a tolerant person,' agreed Fidelma. 'Why didn't you stand up to him? You could overrule him.'

'I cannot.'

'Cannot?'

The old abbot nodded mournfully. 'He has the full support of Lady Eithne. Everything that Brother Lugna does is deemed to be right by her. In her sons' absence on pilgrimage, he somehow fulfilled their role for her, and ever since he can do no wrong in her eyes.'

'How can you stand this? You are the abbot. You have authority.'

'Do I? You know the law, Fidelma. You know that the chief and the council of the clan on whose land an abbey is built have ultimate say over the fate of the religious community that serves their territory.'

Fidelma knew that in many parts of the country, the lands

of the religious communities were still tribal. In several places the abbot was also the chief of the clan or elected in the same manner. The position of abbot and bishop often went through the same family succession. But here, Lady Eithne retained ultimate authority over the community as their chief. It was a curious but not an unusual position.

'Let me get this right, Abbot Iarnla. Lady Eithne supports Brother Lugna and if you object she threatens the ultimate sanction over the community. Is that it?'

'The law is the law.'

'But she can't strip you of your position as abbot, surely?'

'No, but she can force the community from these lands or establish a new community under the leadership of Brother Lugna.'

'Does Abbot Ségdae of Imleach know of this situation?' Ségdae was also Chief Bishop of Muman. 'And what of my brother, the King?'

Abbot Iarnla shrugged. 'The law favours Lady Eithne. I disagree with the way my steward runs the affairs of the community but that is not an argument that carries weight in either the law or in the rules of the religious. They would merely say that in my old age I am fearful of fresh blood and ideas.'

'And fearful of appealing to my brother and his Chief Bishop?' Then she paused. 'Do you suspect these matters have anything to do with Brother Donnchad's death?'

The abbot's eyes widened. 'Heaven forfend! Do you think that when Brother Donnchad returned to the abbey,

Brother Lugna thought his position here weakened? That Lady Eithne would reject him in favour of her own son, Brother Donnchad? That Lugna murdered him in order to retain her support?'

'More terrible things than that have happened,' Fidelma replied quietly. 'However, it seems unlikely, for if that is what happened, I would have thought Brother Lugna would have been more subtle about the way he has been conducting himself. Nonetheless, I shall not discount it.'

'This used to be a place of happiness, even in the latter days of Maolochtair, when the old chieftain had become senile and saw threats lurking in every corner. Today, I walk through the abbey and see these new stone edifices rising but feel it has become a dark, evil and threatening place.'

Fidelma leaned forward and placed a sympathetic hand on the old man's arm. 'We will overcome this evil, Abbot Iarnla. *Dabit Deus his quoque finem* – God will grant an end even to these troubles. I am sure of that. Brother Lugna has tested his strength against mine and found that I am not wanting. I do not think he will be foolish enough to try to block my path in the future. But I will continue to keep a careful watch on him. However, I need to find out more from Lady Eithne. I mean to question her further about Brother Donnchad so tomorrow Eadulf and I, with Gormán, will ride to her fortress and speak to her.'

The abbot rose to his feet and took his lantern.

'This conversation must remain a secret,' he said sadly.

'Don't worry. Brother Lugna will not hear of it, and nor

will Lady Eithne. But I must confide in Eadulf. And at the end of this investigation I shall be duty bound to bring the matter to the attention of my brother and to Abbot Ségdae.'

Abbot Iarnla seemed suddenly very old. 'I thank you for that, Fidelma. I hate to think such thoughts but it is almost providential that Brother Donnchad's death provided the means to bring you to Lios Mór so that you can help restore the abbey and its community to happiness once again.'

'That, indeed, is not a good thought and best forgotten,' Fidelma replied. 'By the way, can you confirm my assumption that it was Brother Lugna who brought Glassán to the abbey? Did you know of the builder's work before he came here?'

'As far as I was aware, Lady Eithne recommended him. But then, as I have said, she supports Brother Lugna's choices in all things,' replied Abbot Iarnla with a frown. 'Is there something wrong?'

'Nothing that is relevant as yet,' Fidelma returned. She rose and went to the door, opened it quietly and peered outside. The passage was still dark and silent. There was no one about. She stood aside and without another word the abbot went out, shielding his lantern before him. For a moment Fidelma was left in darkness and then the moon raced out from behind a cloud, leaving her with light to shut the door and return to her bed.

Automatically, she picked up the bundle of clothes and returned them to the back of the chair and then sat down on the bed. She sat there for a long time, turning over in her mind what the abbot had said. Sleep took her unaware and the next thing she knew, the light that shone through the window was the rising sun and not the pale light of the moon.

CHAPTER THIRTEEN

An Dún, the fortress of Lady Eithne, lay no more than two kilometres due east of Lios Mór, overlooking the main road from Cashel where it forded An Abhainn Mór, The Great River. It had been built in ancient times to guard the roadway. Fidelma had passed it many times but had never visited it. All she had ever known of Lady Eithne was that she was very pious, a staunch upholder of the Faith, as befitted the mother of two sons who had become scholars of reputation at Lios Mór. The fortress lay a little way south of the river crossing, on a dominant hill. The track from Lios Mór ran through cultivated lands that belonged to the abbey, just north of a series of hills, to join Rian Bó Pádraig. The hills were no more than rounded hummocks, on which some ancient mounds, like carbuncles, rose. The fortress dominated. Its walls were imposing, a mixture of wood and stone.

Gormán, riding behind them, drew Fidelma's attention to the dark silhouettes of several figures on top of the fortress walls.

'There are many warriors there,' he observed. 'I thought this lady was more given to religion than to war.'

'There does seem more than the usual number of body-guards a chieftain is entitled to,' agreed Fidelma, looking towards the figures.

They had just turned up an incline where the track formed an avenue between yew trees, leading towards the great wooden gates of the fortress, when a harsh voice called on them to halt. A moment later a heavily armed warrior stepped from behind the cover of some trees. His sword was drawn and he examined them in a professional manner. His eyes came to rest on Gormán.

'Disarm yourself and dismount, warrior,' he snapped in an accent that they did not recognise.

'I am Fidelma of Cashel, come to speak with Lady Eithne,' Fidelma said sharply, edging her horse forward.

The man looked at her closely, and saw the torc emblem she was wearing round her neck.

'You and your religious companion may go on up, lady,' he said with more respect, 'but I am under orders not to allow any strange warriors beyond this point.'

'This man is no strange warrior. He wears the insignia of the Nasc Niadh, the King's bodyguard, and has the King's authority. Where I go, he goes,' Fidelma replied firmly.

'I have my orders, lady,' he said awkwardly.

'From your accent, I take it you are a stranger to this land.'

'I am a Briton in the employ of Lady Eithne,' the man said defensively.

'A mercenary?' sneered Gormán.

'My sword is bought by Lady Eithne,' admitted the man. 'She has the right to be apprehensive for her security. Her son has been murdered. To the south are the Uí Liathán and to the west are the Fir Maige Féne. She trusts neither clan. Even to the east, among her own people, the Déisi, there are some chiefs who cast envious eyes on this territory.'

'Are you telling me that Lady Eithne has been threatened from these sources and needs mercenaries from a strange land to defend her?' Fidelma frowned.

'It is not for me to say. I obey her orders.'

'Well, here is an order. I am sister to the King of Muman, a *dálaigh* of the courts. I order you to let me pass to the fortress with my companions. Is this order understood?'

The man looked as if he would argue for a moment. Gormán's hand was already on his sword hilt, his body tensed. Then the opposing warrior shrugged as if the matter were no longer of concern to him. He stood back and they proceeded at a walking pace until they came to the closed gates of the fortress.

They were uncomfortably aware of archers on the ramparts above them, with bows unslung, ready to be drawn. The dark oak gates of the fortress were forbidding. Gormán looked up at the figures on the wall and shouted, 'This is Fidelma of Cashel who comes to speak with Lady Eithne.'

There was movement and the sound of a whispered exchange above them. Then a voice replied, 'Wait.'

It seemed an eternity before they heard the noise of large wooden bolts being slid back. Then one of the gates creaked and moved. It swung open with a rasp of its hinges and another warrior appeared and gestured for them to enter. As they halted in the inner courtyard, they saw several warriors on either side with bows in their hands. The gate swung shut behind them with a crash. Then a warrior, who seemed in command, approached.

'The Lady Eithne will see you and Brother Eadulf,' he told Fidelma. 'But my lady says nothing of the warrior. He must await you here.'

Fidelma slid from her horse and glanced apologetically at Gormán.

'You will have to wait with our horses while we speak to Lady Eithne.' Then she turned to the warrior who seemed in charge. 'I trust you will see my companion is refreshed and our horses watered.'

'He can take the horses over to the blacksmith's forge,' the warrior said, pointing to where a smith was working his bellows in a corner of the yard. Then he guided them across the courtyard towards the main building. The wooden doors opened immediately into the great hall where Lady Eithne waited to welcome them with her sad smile

'It is good to see you both again. Come, be seated with me and take refreshment.'

She indicated two comfortable chairs adorned with cush-ions and coverings before a fire at the far end of the hall. She seated herself in a third chair before motioning with a slim hand towards a servant. Moments later wine and sweet pastries were brought and served.

'We are told that you fear some attack, lady,' Fidelma said after the courtesies had been exchanged. 'Who do you fear?'

Lady Eithne's eyes narrowed. 'Who says I fear attack?' she demanded softly.

'Your warriors proclaim the obvious. Mercenaries as well.'

Lady Eithne suddenly smiled and shrugged. 'What is there to say? My son is murdered and we know not how or why. My other son has chosen to remain in some foreign land. I am but a poor widow. In the days of old Maolochtair of the Déisi, both my sons were threatened, as you know, and perhaps the spirit of that threat lives on among certain chiefs of our people. Old Maolochtair was my husband's cousin and he thought my sons wanted to wrest the chieftainship from him. Some of his relatives who live beyond the boundaries of The Great River still think our family nurse that ambition. In such circumstances, and because of the murder of poor Donnchad, should I not take to myself some protection?'

'No blame to you for doing so, lady,' agreed Fidelma lightly. 'So there is no specific threat, for example from the surrounding clans – the Uí Liatháin and the Fir Maige Féne?'

'A flock of swallows is a good sign of rain,' she replied, using the old proverb that meant one should be prepared in case of trouble.

'Yet both clans owe allegiance to Cashel, just as you do,' Fidelma pointed out.

Lady Eithne stiffened slightly. 'This is true. But the Uí

Fidgente to the north are also supposed to be loyal and subservient to Cashel and yet their history of insurrection is well known.'

'There is no denying that,' agreed Fidelma. 'Therefore, it is good that your warriors train in preparation. I heard that one of them injured himself while training. I trust his wound is healing.'

Lady Eithne seemed slightly taken aback. 'Who told you this?'

'I believe that you had cause to send for the physician from the abbey.'

'Brother Seachlann?' She hesitated a moment. 'Yes, I did send for him. I do not have my own physician here. I have seen men die from small wounds that have been neglected.'

'So Brother Seachlann was able to successfully attend the man? That is good.' Fidelma smiled. 'It seems that he returned to the abbey after nightfall and his lateness in returning caused some concern.'

'I am afraid I sent for him in the evening,' Lady Eithne said. 'I am glad that he returned without mishap. Sometimes, one has to be careful of wolves in these hills. They come down to The Great River to drink at night. Even in the day they have been known to roam abroad without fear.'

'Brother Seachlann met with no mishap,' Fidelma confirmed.

'Good. But I am sure that you have not come here simply to ask about the health of one of my warriors.'

'Indeed. There are a few matters we need to clear up.'

'I have said that I would help you in any way to find the murderer of my son. Ask your questions.'

'I was wondering whether you could tell us any more about the intrigues and jealousies which your son feared within the abbey?'

There was a sudden brightness in Lady Eithne's blue eyes. 'My son, Donnchad, accused no one by name but I would look to those of a jealous nature.'

'People who were jealous of his learning?' queried Eadulf.

'Many were jealous of his piety and learning,' replied Lady Eithne. 'He could have been the greatest scholar of the Faith. Some were even willing to besmirch his reputation with false accusations of some heresy or other.'

'Do you suspect someone in particular?' pressed Fidelma.

'It is not for me to sow suspicion when there might be no grounds at all. I make no accusations. You will surely be able to pick out those who resent the young and talented.'

'Let me get this clear, Lady Eithne. Are you saying that there are some in the abbey who resent people younger than themselves who might be more talented than they are?' Fidelma asked in an even tone. It seemed clear that once again she was pointing a finger at Abbot Iarnla.

'I do.'

'Furthermore, do you believe that they might have killed your son out of jealousy?'

The woman's mouth hardened for a moment before she said, 'You asked for my thoughts. That had occurred to me.'

'What of Brother Lugna?' Eadulf asked with an innocent

air. 'He arrived at the abbey a few years ago when your sons were both on their pilgrimage. Might he not have resented the return of your son Donnchad? Brother Lugna seems to have created a powerful position for himself at the abbey.'

A dark shadow crossed her features and Lady Eithne spent a moment or two fighting some emotion.

'Brother Lugna is a pleasant and devout young man. He is the best thing to have happened to the abbey since my sons left. He has my full confidence and support.'

Fidelma nodded. 'You know him well?'

'I offered him hospitality when he returned from several years in Rome. He was returning to Connachta, which was his home.'

'I am told that you persuaded him to stay here and join the abbey.'

Lady Eithne did not deny it. 'I think he liked this place so much that he needed little persuading. But the abbey is lucky to have the services of such a talented young man. A learned man, a devout man, one who has such an aura of saintliness about him. He may one day become the most famous abbot of the community here.' Her voice had grown strident with enthusiasm. Then she paused and shook her head sadly. 'It was a role that I was hoping that one of my sons would fulfil. But this was not to be.'

Eadulf tried to keep his tone even. 'There is no point, then, in asking you whether you fully support the changes that Brother Lugna is making in the abbey. I mean the changes to the liturgy and practices native to churches here in favour of ideas emanating from Rome. For example, Brother Lugna tells us that he wants to introduce the Penitentials as the Rule of the abbey in place of obedience to the Law of the Fénechus.'

'I am sure that whatever changes he is making will strengthen the community there and make Lios Mór venerated throughout Christendom,' Lady Eithne firmly assured him.

'In spite of the resentment against his ideas?' Eadulf asked.

Lady Eithne grimaced as if in distaste. 'From small-minded people, that is all,' she replied curtly. 'I suppose it is in the nature of the old to feel jealous of the young. But I will support those ideas that will strengthen and propagate the Faith in this land with all my power. Brother Lugna's knowledge and piety are not to be questioned. God has sent him to us. I will tell you this: until Brother Lugna began to show me the true path, I did not know what the way of Christ really was.'

There was a silence while they digested the vehemence in her voice.

'He must be a powerful advocate of the Faith then,' Fidelma observed softly.

'He has persuaded me to seek the truth, a search which not even my sons were able to inspire.'

'I have heard that you have a dispensation to borrow some of the texts from the library. Brother Donnán brings you the epistles of the saints to read.'

Lady Eithne's eyes widened in surprise for a moment. Then she said, 'You have a sharp eye and sensitive ear, lady. Are there those at the abbey who now object to my borrowing these works?'

'I am told that Brother Lugna approves,' she replied. 'But I was merely going to ask what sort of books you borrow.'

'What sort?' She paused in surprise. Then said, 'The epistles of the founders of the Faith, that is all. Why?'

'I was just curious,' dismissed Fidelma. 'We have also heard that you are supporting the tremendous task of rebuilding the abbey.'

'It is God's work and I am privileged to be given the opportunity to help in it.'

'Yet it is expensive to commission a professional master builder and those that work for him in an undertaking that will last for many years.'

'You have doubtless met Glassán. He was master builder for the King of Laighin and came highly recommended.'

'Ah, yes. The King of Laighin.' Fidelma allowed a small smile to cross her features. 'I had heard that Glassán was unwelcome in the Kingdom of Laighin and had been exiled in Connachta for some years after being found guilty of being responsible for a building that collapsed and killed and injured many people due to shoddy workmanship.'

Lady Eithne's face went white. 'Where did you hear such a thing?' she demanded.

'Such information is hard to keep secret,' replied Fidelma smoothly. 'In spite of this, I am told that Brother Lugna recommended him.'

'All I can say is that Glassán is highly recommended and his work will be a great memorial to Donnchad.' She suddenly rose, trying to control her irritation. 'And now, if you will excuse me, I have pressing matters to attend to.'

It was nearly noon when they rode into the abbey grounds. Brother Echen, the stableman, who was waiting to take charge of their horses, greeted them with a worried glance.

'A short while ago Brother Lugna was asking whether you had returned or not.'

'Why did he want to know?' asked Fidelma, as she swung off her horse.

'Cumscrad of the Fir Maige Féne arrived with a small guard of warriors some time ago. He demanded to see the abbot. Perhaps that has something to do with it.'

Eadulf glanced curiously at Fidelma. 'The Fir Maige Féne? Lady Eithne's bodyguard mentioned them as one of the clans they felt threatened by.'

'Their main township is Fhear Maighe,' Gormán said, 'about twenty-four kilometres due west from here. I can't say they are my favourite people.'

'Well, let's find out why Brother Lugna was asking after us.'

They left Gormán helping Brother Echen tend their horses and walked slowly across the quadrangle towards the guest-house. They were halfway across when Brother Lugna appeared on the far side, calling to them with a disapproving expression on his face.

'Cumscrad of the Fir Maige Féne has arrived here and demands to see you,' he announced without preamble as they turned in his direction.

'Demands?' queried Fidelma mildly.

'He had no idea that you were at the abbey until he spoke to the abbot and now he feels he must see you,' replied the steward indifferently.

'Where is Cumscrad now?' asked Fidelma.

'Abbot Iarnla has received him in his chamber and requested your presence as soon as you returned.'

'Very well. Tell the abbot we will come immediately we have washed ourselves after our journey.'

Brother Lugna hesitated at this dismissal, then turned and hurried off. Fidelma turned to Eadulf with a shake of her head.

'I wonder why Cumscrad wishes to speak to me? The Fir Maige Féne are not exactly robust in their loyalty to the Eóghanacht of Cashel.'

'But surely they acknowledge the authority of your brother as King?'

'With the same reluctance as the Uí Fidgente. They are hostile to the Eóghanacht and one of the few clans in Muman who claim no relationship to the line of the Eóghanacht succession. Even the Uí Fidgente claim to be Eóghanacht. But the Fir Maige Féne claim their ancestry is far older and more distinguished than ours.'

'I seem to have heard that they are talked about as being involved in the black arts.' Eadulf tried to dredge up a memory.

Fidelma smiled. 'It is their claim that their ancestor was Mug Róth, a one-eyed Druid whose breath could raise a tempest and who flew like a bird on a chariot made of polished silver and lustrous gems, which made night shine as bright as day. It was called the wheel of light. Not far from Cashel, at Cnámhchaill, is a pillar of stone which local people say was once a fragment of that great wheel.'

Eadulf shuddered. 'How can they boast such an ancestor?'

'He was probably the old god of the sun before the coming of Christianity. When the Faith denied the existence of such gods, he took on human form in our eyes. In ancient times the clan were renowned for their knowledge of ancient lore and even supplied the kings at Cashel with their Chief Druid. This was before King Oenghus was converted to Christianity.'

They washed their faces and hands, refreshed themselves from the short journey and then made their way to the abbot's chamber.

Cumscrad was a tall man with a deep voice that made him seem intimidating. He was sallow of skin, with thick black hair to his shoulders and a beard to match. His eyes, also black, like shiny pebbles, were shadowed by a ridge across his forehead. But his features were well formed and his face had a handsome quality to it. His manner and bearing suggested a person used to command. Nevertheless, he rose with courtesy when Brother Lugna showed Fidelma and Eadulf into the abbot's chamber.

'Ah, the Lady Fidelma. I have not seen you since your marriage at Cashel.' His voice resonated in the stone chamber. He turned to Eadulf. 'We meet again, Eadulf of Seaxmund's Ham.' He smiled and inclined his head in acknowledgement.

Eadulf returned the courtesy. He vaguely remembered

meeting Cumscrad when all the nobles of the kingdom had come to attend the ceremonies at Cashel which had marked his official marriage to Fidelma.

'I trust we find you well, Cumscrad?' Fidelma inquired.

'Well in body but not in spirit,' he replied.

When Fidelma seated herself, he sank back into his seat next to Abbot Iarnla, who wore his usual worried expression. Brother Lugna and Eadulf remained standing to one side of the chamber.

'Cumscrad comes with disturbing news,' the abbot said. 'When I told him that you were here in your official capacity, he asked that he might make some representation to you.'

Fidelma turned to face Cumscrad. 'Representation?'

'I came to ask Abbot Iarnla's advice and now I find that you are here and I can ask your advice instead. Perhaps, through you, I can make an official complaint to your brother, the King.'

There was a silence while Cumscrad gathered his thoughts.

'You may know that my people trade along the river here,' he began. 'The Great River is a watery highway that runs from our territory, past this community and then turns south to the great sea at Ard Mór. Our people have traded along its reaches for centuries beyond measure.'

Fidelma knew well the geography of An Abhainn Mór.

'I know your smiths and metalworkers rely on the river for trade,' she acknowledged.

'Indeed, our smiths are dependent on it. As you well know, our territory is also known as Magh Méine, the plain of the minerals. Our mines provide the ores that allow our smiths to make their goods – goods that are eagerly sought as far away as Connachta and Ulaidh. Even beyond the great sea.'

'All this is well known, Cumscrad. Is there a purpose in reminding me of it?' inquired Fidelma mildly.

'There is,' snapped the chief. 'The complaint I wish to make is that two days ago, one of our barges was attacked as it came along the river. It was a vessel taking goods to the abbey at Ard Mór.'

'What happened?'

'The barge was not far out of Fhear Maighe when warriors, having blocked the river with their own vessel, attacked the crew and took over the barge.'

'Were there survivors of this attack?' asked Fidelma.

'Every one of the crew survived. A few were wounded in the attack but the crew were unarmed merchants. They were simply seized, bound and placed ashore, while the attackers continued on in the barge. They must have passed this community.'

Abbot Iarnla spread his hands in a helpless gesture and felt compelled to explain. 'None of the brethren working along the river noticed anything untoward. Some of them saw the passing of the river barges, but many barges use the river here so no one questioned what they saw.'

'The attackers who took charge of the boat disguised themselves as bargemen,' Cumscrad said.

'And you have no idea who these robbers may be?' asked Fidelma.

A grim smile spread across Cumscrad's features. 'Oh indeed, lady. We know right well who they are.' He paused, as if for dramatic effect. 'The attackers were our southern neighbours, the Uí Liatháin.'

'How do you know this?'

'I have said that our crew survived. The master of the barge, Muirgíos, as well as his crewmen, were able to identify them.'

'There was no mistake?'

'I trust Muirgíos. He has sailed the river for many years. The attackers made no attempt to conceal their identity. Furthermore . . .' He hesitated. 'Furthermore, one of our bargemen, Eolann, who also trades along the river, was returning from Ard Mór and saw Muirgíos's barge passing him on its way south. He was about to greet his comrade but found he did not recognise any of the crew. He felt it wise not to challenge them. Eolann is a clever man. He was in a small craft and so he backtracked along the river and saw the vessel turn west up the river Bríd that joins The Great River south of here.'

'I know it. It is the river which provides the boundary between your people and the Uí Liatháin,' Fidelma said.

'You are right, lady. Eolann tied up his craft and waited a while before setting off again upriver. He did not wish to be observed following. When he did set off, he had not far to go. He soon found the vessel tied up and deserted. Eolann came back and reported it to me and I came here to ask the abbot's advice. We must do something about the thieves.'

'This is not something the abbey is concerned with,' Brother Lugna suddenly declared.

Cumscrad looked at him in astonishment and then turned to Abbot Iarnla.

'Then if this is of no concern to the abbey, times have changed, Iarnla. More than once you have acted to resolve conflicts between the Fir Maige Féne and the Uí Liatháin. Do you tell me that you refuse to do so now?'

'I am the steward of this abbey,' Brother Lugna replied before the abbot could speak.

'And I am chief of the Fir Maige Féne,' snapped Cumscrad. 'Very well, I shall send my envoy to Uallachán, chief of the Uí Liatháin, demanding reparation for the act. And if I do not receive it, we shall know how to answer.' He had clamped his hand to his sword hilt, and made for the door.

'One moment, Cumscrad.' Fidelma spoke quietly but it had the effect of stopping the chief in his tracks. He turned to look at her. 'Return to your seat, so that we may discuss this within the bounds of the law.'

'I could raise my people and attack Uallachán and his robbers now,' Cumscrad said as he obeyed her. 'But I respect the law and so, before I do so, I shall send an intermediary. I will demand reparation first so that when we attack the Uí Liatháin it will be done in accordance with the law.'

Fidelma sighed and shifted her weight in the chair.

'You have not been refused the intervention of either myself, on behalf of the King, or of this abbey.'

Cumscrad frowned for a moment and then jerked his head

to where Brother Lugna was standing with a slightly belligerent thrust of his jaw.

'But he said—'

'He said he was the steward,' pointed out Fidelma. 'It is the abbot who makes such decisions.'

There was a spluttering sound and Brother Lugna went red in the face with anger. The abbot was looking at his feet with an unhappy expression.

'Before we come to what course of action should be taken, I presume the cargo in the vessel was valuable,' Fidelma went on, ignoring the reaction her words had provoked.

Cumscrad nodded. 'The total value of the cargo was thirty *seds*.'

Eadulf's eyes widened in surprise. 'Why, that is the honour price for . . .'

'For my own worth as chief of my people,' Cumscrad calmly agreed. A *sed* was the value of a milch cow.

'Was there much gold in this cargo, then?' asked Fidelma in astonishment.

'Not gold, lady. And in truth the metalwork was not of great value – cooking pots, horse bridles, agricultural tools and the like. That was worth no more than a few *seds*, and Eolann reported that it was all intact on the vessel, it had not been removed.'

Fidelma was bewildered. 'If this cargo was still on the barge when it was recovered, what was missing? How did your man identify what was missing?'

'Because he had come upriver from Ard Mór and he knew

that the barge was expected there and, moreover, what it was expected to deliver to the abbey there. It was carrying two books which the scribes in our *tech-screptra*, our library, had been copying. The library of Ard Mór, knowing we had these books, had commissioned our scribes to make copies for them. The work had taken one year and had just been completed.'

Fidelma pursed her lips thoughtfully. 'What were the books?'

'One was a copy of the poems of the great bard Dallán Forgaill, which we consider valuable.'

'And the other?'

'A Greek work. *The True Word*, I think they called it.'

'*Alethos Logos* by Celsus?' Fidelma gasped.

Cumscrad looked at her in admiration. 'You are well read, lady. Indeed, it was a work by Celsus.'

CHAPTER FOURTEEN

Fidelma cast a warning glance towards Eadulf before turning back to face Cumscrad. 'The theft of books is a great crime according to the law,' she said, 'but who would go to such lengths and risk so much for such a theft?'

'It was for the theft of a book that Colmcille was exiled from the Five Kingdoms,' Cumscrad pointed out.

Eadulf was astonished at the remark, for he had long held Colmcille as a great pillar and teacher of the Faith. This man appeared to be calling him a thief.

'What are you saying? That the Blessed Colmcille of Iona, whose abbey brought the new Faith to the lands of the Angles and Saxons, was a book thief?' he queried.

'The story is well known,' Cumscrad returned dismissively.

'Colm Crimthain, whom you call Columba, went to stay with Finnén at the abbey of Maghbhile,' explained Fidelma. 'Finnén had a copy of a gospel from the abbey of the Blessed Martin and Colm coveted it. So each night he went to the

PETER TREMAYNE

abbey library and copied the gospel. Finnén discovered what
he was doing and took his complaint to the High King
Diarmait mac Cerbaill and his Chief Brehon. The judgement
was given that just as every calf belongs to its cow, so every
copy belongs to its original. In making a copy without permission, he was in fact stealing the book.'

'But to be exiled for that . . .' began Eadulf.

Fidelma smiled and shook her head. 'That was not the
reason why Colm was exiled. He was not only a religious
but also a hot-headed prince of his people – the Cenel Conaill,
a sept of the Uí Néill of the north. He raised his clan and
physically challenged the High King and his Brehon over
their ruling. There was a terrible battle at Cúl Dreimne at the
foot of the mountain called Binn Ghulbainn. Many fell in
that dreadful clash but the High King's warriors prevailed
and Colm was banished from the Five Kingdoms as a punishment. That was when he went to Iona.'

'All that just because he copied a book?' said Eadulf in
amazement.

'Is not a book of more value than metal?' asked Cumscrad.
'It is the fruit of a person's brain and contains knowledge
and ideas; it has power greater than gold because knowledge
and ideas can change people.'

'And some books can be dangerous.' The comment came
ominously from Brother Lugna who had been standing quietly
all this time.

'I am sure the songs of the chief bard of the Five Kingdoms
cannot be dangerous,' Fidelma said with a smile, being

deliberately obtuse. She turned to Eadulf. 'Dallán Forgaill died nearly a century ago and was regarded by all as the greatest bard in the Five Kingdoms. But he was killed out of jealousy,' she added significantly. 'I would say that even the works of Dallán Forgaill are rare.'

'We have a library of several ancient works, lady,' Cumscrad said proudly. 'Fortunately, we even retain some of the books that were not destroyed by the early zeal of those proselytising for the new Faith. Works that reflect the mind and spirit of our ancestors, which would otherwise have been lost in the book-burning.'

Brother Lugna scowled and almost hissed, 'Heretical works. Works of pagan idolatry!'

'Works such as that of Celsus?' asked Fidelma innocently.

'Exactly so! There is only one book that should exist and that is the gospel bearing the good news of the Faith.'

Cumscrad regarded the steward with an expression akin to pity and said softly, '*Timeo hominem unius libri.*'

Fidelma gave the chieftain an approving glance, for the adage was: 'I fear the man of one book.' Trying to argue with someone who believed that the literal statement of one book was sufficient knowledge to form a dogma was difficult.

'The burning of books must surely be a crime against culture and civilisation,' Eadulf remarked.

'I agree with you, Saxon.' Cumscrad chuckled cynically. 'That should have been explained to Patrick the Briton who, according to his friend and biographer Benignus, ordered the burning of eighty books of the Druids.'

'Druidical books! Pagan idolatry!' hissed Brother Lugna again.

'Books that would have helped us understand our past, without which we are condemned to live in ignorance,' observed Fidelma quietly.

'Heresy!' replied the steward. 'I will not listen to such conversation.'

'Indeed, there is no need for you to remain,' Fidelma told him. 'The abbot and I will reach a conclusion as to what is to be done in this matter.'

It was a direct challenge to the steward. He stood for a moment, undecided. His chin was raised belligerently as he stared at her. He saw the sparkle of fire in her eyes, hesitated a moment more, then turned and left the room without another word.

Cumscrad grimaced in satisfaction. 'An unpleasant fellow, Iarnla. What possessed you to appoint him as your steward?'

Abbot Iarnla glanced at Fidelma and made a hopeless gesture with his hands. He was far from happy.

'You said that the books that were stolen were copies of originals?' Eadulf asked to distract the chief's attention.

'It took our scribes over a year to make them and in that lies their value.'

Fidelma turned back to Cumscrad. 'It will be my brother's wish to avoid the unnecessary spilling of blood, so I warn you not to raise your clan against Uallachán of the Uí Liatháin before I have had time to properly investigate the matter. We must then place the evidence before Uallachán and allow him to submit his rebuttal. Do you agree with that, Cumscrad?'

The chief thought for a moment and then gave a quick smile of agreement. 'I do, for I favour things being done in accordance with the law.'

'Then what I suggest is, after the midday meal, we set out for your township of Fhear Maighe so that I can question the bargemen and librarian. Then I shall ride to Uallachán of the Uí Liatháin and put the matter to him.'

Abbot Iarnla was frowning. 'But what of your inquiry here? This means you may be gone two days or so.'

'There are some things I must consider before making my report on the death of Brother Donnchad. But have no fear. I should be able to announce my findings soon.'

'Then you have come to a decision on the death of Brother Donnchad?' demanded the abbot in surprise.

'I will let you know soon.'

Cumscrad was shaking his head sadly. 'Ah, Brother Donnchad. He did not look a happy man when I saw him.'

'Did you know Brother Donnchad then?' Fidelma asked with interest.

'Who did not?' replied Cumscrad. 'He was well known even before he went off on his pilgrimage to the Holy Land. It was only a few days after he came to Fhear Maighe that I heard he was dead.'

'After he came to Fhear Maighe? Are you saying that you met him there a few days before his death?' demanded Fidelma.

'That is what I said. He spent the day at Fhear Maighe and only a few days later we heard of his death. It was a shock that . . .' He paused as he noticed the expressions of surprise on the faces of his audience. 'But you must have known of his visit, Iarnla. Brother Donnchad would have sought permission to leave the abbey to ride to Fhear Maighe, isn't that the rule?'

Abbot Iarnla nodded uneasily.

'It was noted that Brother Donnchad had disappeared for a day without telling anyone where he was going,' Fidelma told Cumscrad before the abbot could reply. 'That was four days before he was found murdered. So now we know. What was the purpose of his visit to you?'

'He did not come to visit me,' replied Cumscrad.

'But you said—'

'He came to Fhear Maighe but he went to visit our *tech-screptra*.'

'Your library?'

'Brother Donnchad came to examine some of the texts that we hold in our library.'

'Which ones?' Eadulf could not disguise the hint of excitement in his voice.

'I don't know. You would have to ask Dubhagan our *leabhar coimedach*.'

'How long did he spend at the library?' Fidelma pressed.

'I met him when he was departing in the evening,' admitted Cumscrud. 'But I was told that he had arrived early that morning.'

'So he spent the entire day in the library? He went nowhere else when he was at Fhear Maighe?'

'I don't think so.'

'Was his visit unusual? I mean, had he ever visited the library before?'

Cumscrad smiled and shook his head. 'I had encountered Brother Donnchad only twice previously, when I visited this abbey. However, he did employ my son to make copies at our library. My son, Cunán, is assistant at the library and has a reputation for the fairness of his copies. Not that Brother Donnchad approved of many of the books the library holds. He was somewhat like our friend the steward.'

'Like Brother Lugna?'

'He claimed that our library was full of profane and heretical works. He had never expressed a wish to visit us before he arrived on that day.'

'Didn't that arouse your curiosity?' Fidelma asked. 'The fact that he suddenly turned up at a place abhorrent to his thinking?'

'I gave it a passing thought, no more. I knew he was an intelligent man and thought that perhaps he had reconsidered his attitude.'

'And within a few days of his returning from your library, he is found murdered,' muttered Eadulf and immediately received another warning glance from Fidelma.

'What are you implying, Brother Eadulf?' demanded the chief quickly.

'Eadulf meant that it would be of benefit to know the reason why he visited your library. We may learn the answer by speaking to your librarian this afternoon.' She rose determinedly from her chair. 'As it is now well past the hour for the *etar-shod*, the midday meal, I suggest that we partake of refreshment before we set out with you, Cumscrad.'

'I have no objection to that.'

The *refectorium* was deserted and so the meal was a frugal one with just the four of them being served cold meats and cheeses with cold water from the abbey fountain. As they rose to leave, Cumscrad lingered a moment.

'I will see you at the gate shortly. I have one other small matter to speak to Abbot Iarnla about,' he said.

'We have some things to pick up from the guesthouse so we will meet in the courtyard in a little while.'

As they left, Fidelma caught sight of Gormán in the quad-rangle. He was obviously waiting for them. She felt a tinge of guilt in case he had not eaten but he assured her that he had gone into the *refectorium* when the bell for the midday meal had sounded.

'Ask Brother Echen to saddle our horses and be ready to join Cumscrad and his men. We may be away for a day or two.'

Gormán was surprised. 'Are we going to Fhear Maighe, lady?'

'We are.'

'I thought there was something in the wind because the steward came hurrying into the courtyard some time ago. He looked angry. He seized Glassán, spoke swiftly to him. Glassán took a horse from the stable and rode rapidly away.'

Fidelma frowned. She had forgotten about Brother Lugna.

'Did you notice which way Glassán went?'

Gormán shook his head. 'Only that he rode through the abbey gates as quickly as I have ever seen a man move on a horse. Whether he turned east or west, I did not see.'

'Well, no matter,' replied Fidelma. 'It may not be relevant. Get the horses ready.'

She and Eadulf went to the *tech-oíged* to pack a few things in case they were obliged to spend more time away than Fidelma expected. On their return to the quadrangle, they found Gormán and Brother Echen waiting in front of the stables with her white horse Aonbharr and Eadulf's cob already saddled.

Fidelma took the opportunity to ask Brother Echen about what he had told Gormán. 'You mentioned to Gormán the other day that your cousin told you that a building Glassán was working on in Laighin had fallen down and killed several people.'

'I did so,' the stableman replied.

'I just wondered if you knew where that building was located?'

'It was in the country of the Uí Dúnlainge,' Brother Echen replied immediately. 'In the south of the kingdom.'

'Can you be more specific?'

Brother Echen thought for a moment and then shrugged. 'Alas,' he said after a moment or two, 'all my cousin knew was that it was a chief who lived on the southern coast. Anyway, it was some ten years ago. Glassán was not held directly responsible; he was deemed to have neglected his contractual duty by not overseeing the work and then trying to blame others.'

Fidelma was about to ask another question when Cumscrad emerged from the *refectorium* with Abbot Iarnla. Brother Echen, with a muttered apology, hurried into the stables and returned with the chief's horse and led it across to him.

'Do you think that it is more than a coincidence that Brother Donnchad went to this library and that a copy of the book he was interested in was later stolen?' asked Eadulf quietly as they mounted up

'I do not believe in such coincidences, Eadulf,' replied Fidelma. 'But let us keep this between ourselves.' She glanced at Gormán; the young warrior was pretending to be absorbed in adjusting his horse's bridle. 'We'll explain later, Gormán.'

'I notice that Cumscrad does not call his *scriptor* by the Latin title,' Eadulf said.

'The library of Fhear Maighe is still a secular one.'

While the religious had taken over many of the professions, there were still some secularists fulfilling the roles of poets, doctors, lawyers and other official functions, and many libraries remained unattached to the new abbeys.

'That surprises me. I would have thought that Fhear Maighe was too remote to have a library, particularly one that is not part of a religious institution. I thought that the members of the Faith now controlled all the intellectual pursuits.'

'It would be a sorry day if everyone agreed on how we should think or what we should do,' responded Fidelma. 'There would not be much individuality left in the world. But there is a curious pattern emerging here. Brother Donnchad wanted to see a copy of Celsus's work. Brother Donnán tells us that he saw a response to that work by Origenes but that work has been sent to Ard Mór abbey. Cumscrad says the original of Celsus's work is in Fhear Maighe, but that a copy on its way to Ard Mór has been stolen.'

'Isn't Ard Mór in the territory of the Uí Liatháin?'

'It is in the territory of the Déisi but stands on the opposite side of the river to Uí Liatháin territory – the same Great River that flows from here.'

'I wonder how Brother Donnchad heard or knew that Celsus's book was at Fhear Maighe,' mused Eadulf. 'What about the other book – the poems of Dallán Forgaill?'

'It is of no consequence. The thieves were after the work by Celsus, I am sure. Dallán's poems are no danger to the Faith.'

At that moment Cumscrad came trotting towards them on his black mare.

'Ride alongside me, Fidelma. My warriors are waiting outside the abbey to escort us.'

Indeed, just outside, a group of half a dozen warriors were sitting on a grassy knoll indulging in a game of chance which involved throwing *dísle*, or dice. They scrambled to their feet when they saw their chief and hurriedly set about collecting their horses, which were tethered nearby. Within moments two of them had placed themselves at the head while the others fell in behind and the entire party was on the road, riding due west.

The afternoon's ride passed pleasantly enough and the group kept a fairly good pace leaving Lios Mór on the roadway that ran along the south bank of The Great River. Fidelma rode with Cumscrad, with Eadulf and Gormán behind. The pace was comfortable even for Eadulf. He enjoyed the ride in the mild afternoon sunshine. The hills to the south of them looked peaceful, large and rounded with thick woods carpeting them. There were plenty of rivulets and streams that tumbled and gushed down these hills to empty into The Great River, An Abhainn Mhór. There was no shortage of places to water the horses.

'I can see why you call it simply The Great River,' Eadulf observed, nodding towards the flowing water. 'It's large enough. Though in truth I have seen broader rivers in my travels.'

Gormán grinned, shaking his head, and replied, 'It is not named because of its width, Brother Eadulf.'

'Then it must be its length, for I understand it rises in the mountains a far distance to the west and bends southwards, flowing down to the sea.'

'Again, not so, my friend,' the warrior replied. 'It is called The Great River as a euphemism. It is not its real name.' Eadulf gave him a questioning glance and Gormán continued: 'In the old days, before the coming of the new Faith, the river was called the Nemh, which meant immeasurable, sacred and heavenly. In that lies its greatness.'

Eadulf recognised the word, which also applied to a saintly person. 'A sacred river?'

'Many of the rivers in this land are named after the old gods or goddesses. They are dedicated to sacred deities.'

'That is the custom in many countries I have visited,' Eadulf said.

'I have not travelled beyond the Five Kingdoms,' Gormán replied regretfully. 'But my people regard some rivers or places as being so sacred that their real name is never mentioned. As with The Great River here. There is a *geis* upon speaking its name.'

'I have heard of the *geis*. Isn't it a prohibition or taboo which, if broken, results in serious consequences?'

'Yes.' Gormán smiled grimly. 'Breaking a *geis* could result in death or bring misfortune on your family.'

'I had not realised that it could apply to uttering certain names.'

'Very much so. For example, the sun and moon were considered sacred objects in the old days and their real names were names of gods. But the Druids forbade those names to be used, so we have several terms for them. For example, as you well know, we call the moon simply "the brightness", or "the queen of the night", and many more names besides. No one is allowed to call it by the name of the goddess it represents.'

'So we can be sure that this river was named after a powerful pagan god?'

'Yes. I have heard that along its great length there are still spots where people gather to make obeisance to the spirits of the river.'

They were approaching a large hill to the south, which

Gormán told him was called the Hill of the Stone Ridge because of its obvious feature. Just before this point, the track they were following meandered away from the river. The river's path came directly from the north for a while but the track continued west through thick forests.

Suddenly one of the leading warriors gave a cry and pointed with his outstretched arm.

Some distance away to the south a band of horsemen was riding swiftly across the hills. They were a dozen or more. They were heading towards the south-east.

'Warriors,' muttered Cumscrad with narrowed eyes. 'Uí Liatháin, from the colour of the battle emblem their leader is carrying.'

Fidelma stared at the distant riders. Their small party had halted and they heard a distant shout. The warriors had seen them and the leader had halted them in turn.

'We are not enough swords to hold them, should they attack, lady,' called Gormán. 'Two, perhaps three, to one.'

The warrior band was still for a moment or two, seeming to return their observation.

'Be prepared to ride,' called Cumscrad, for he realised that discretion was the better part of valour.

Then suddenly the leader of the warriors raised his arm in a signal and, as one, the band turned and disappeared over the shoulder of the distant hill.

Cumscrad sniffed derisively. 'Cowards!'

'Are you sure that they were Uí Liatháin?' asked Fidelma, frowning at the place where the warriors had disappeared.

'You saw their battle standard,' Cumscrad replied. 'It was white with the head of a grey fox on it. That is their emblem.'

'My eyes are not as good as yours, Cumscrad,' Fidelma admitted. 'I saw only a white flag. But I accept that the odds are that they were Uí Liatháin. Whoever they were, I am concerned about the direction they were coming from.'

For a moment Cumscrad did not understand what she meant and then he looked to where the men had first appeared. An oath fell from his lips.

'Forward!' he shouted. 'Forward to Fhear Maighe!'

Abruptly, they were racing forward along the track into the straddling woods. As they rode through the woodland, the cries of birds seemed unusually loud. Even Eadulf raised his eyes to the dark canopy of branches spread above them. Something was exciting the birds, that much was obvious. They suddenly emerged on to the edge of some cultivated fields, which overlooked Cumscrad's main township of Fhear Maighe. It lay below them along the south bank of The Great River. Cumscrad let out a great shout.

It was but a fraction of a second before they saw what had caused it. Below them, near the bank of the river on the edge of the town, a building was on fire. They could see smoke billowing. Borne into the air on a southerly breeze, it was black and ominous. Even from this distance they could all see the red and yellow tongues of flame leaping into the air.

'The library!' cried Cumscrad, digging his heels into his horse. 'The library is on fire!'

CHAPTER FIFTEEN

Eadulf barely had time to catch his breath before they were racing down the track towards the inferno. Fhear Maighe was a large collection of buildings that clustered on both banks of The Great River. On the south bank, on an elevated section of land that was not really high enough to be called a hill, stood the fortress of Cumscrad. It was in no way as imposing nor as threatening as An Dún, the fortress of Lady Eithne. Not far away from this, the blaze was devouring a large building that rose almost on the edge of the settlement. It was a construction of both stone and timber with a curious tower at one end. It was rectangular, like a monastic hall. The tower seemed to be the centre of the fire. Great flames leaped around it and inside it, as if its very structure made it a natural chimney. But the flames were also racing eagerly along the exterior walls of the main building.

As they hurtled down the hill towards it, Eadulf was briefly aware that they passed a riderless horse in a field and, nearby, a prone body with an arrow in its back. There was no time to investigate. They swept on into the township. It seemed that the entire population, men and women and even children, had gathered in a vain attempt to combat the flames. Several young men were rushing back and forth through a door in the main building, emerging with armfuls of scrolls, manuscripts, books and *tiaga lebar*, the book satchels. Here and there someone would stagger out with a metal box called a *lebor-chomet*, or book holder, in which very valuable books were stored.

The people were so intent on rescuing the contents of the building from the hungry flames that items were simply dropped on the ground. Several of the precious books were trodden into the earth as people passed buckets of water from hand to hand in a line from the river. Alongside the human chain, Eadulf noticed a curious construction of wooden troughs, along which water from the river was being pumped by a strange mechanical contraption.

Fidelma and Eadulf could see that the people were fighting a losing battle against the flames. Cumscrad and his warriors had dismounted and were assisting but it seemed there was little they could do. Suddenly, there was a great roaring noise and sparks and flames shot into the late afternoon sky as the main roof collapsed, followed, moments later by the tower section imploding. The fire, having satiated itself, was beginning to die rapidly away to a collection of blackened, smouldering timbers. The implosion seemed to have stopped its spread more than the water that had been poured into the building. Only some of the walls and a large grey stone arch, blackened with smoke, remained standing.

Fidelma pointed to where Cumscard and a group of people were standing looking down at what appeared to be a body that had been dragged clear of the building.

'Can I help?' offered Eadulf. 'I have some training in the healing arts.'

'It's too late, Brother Eadulf,' replied Cumscard with bitterness in his voice. 'Dubhagan is dead.'

'Dubhagan?' Fidelma asked quickly. 'This was your *leabhar coimedech*, your librarian?'

A young man with a blackened smoke-stained face came forward.

'We were too late to save him,' he announced flatly, staring down. He seemed dazed and uncertain.

Cumscrad gazed at the young man for a moment and then asked sympathetically, 'How was he caught in the fire, Cunán?'

The young man shook his head. 'He was dead of a sword thrust before the fire started.'

Anger began to harden Cumscrad's features. Fidelma laid a hand on his arm.

'Let me ask this young man some questions.'

Cumscrad hesitated before saying, 'This is my youngest son, Cunán. He was training as an assistant to Dubhagan the librarian.'

'Cunán.' Fidelma spoke gently, for she could see that the young man was in a state of shock. 'Tell me what you know of this.'

Cunán ran a hand over his forehead as if to gather his thoughts. 'It was a short time ago. We were working in the copying section of the library. I suddenly smelt smoke and heard the crackle of flames. I raised the alarm and ran to find Dubhagan—'

'Where was he?'

'In his chamber in the tower.'

'And where is the copying section?'

'The twelve copyists work in the main hall, at the opposite end of the main library building to the tower. The tower is where Dubhagan kept his place of study and special books that are considered valuable.'

'Very well, you say you smelt smoke and raised the alarm. Then you hurried to find Dubhagan. Is that correct?'

'I rushed into his chamber, for it was no time to stand on protocol. The books and manuscripts in that room were already burning, the smoke was choking, but I saw our *leabhar coimedech* lying face down on the floor. He was already dead. There were two wounds, one in his chest and one in his neck. I knew it to be useless, but I seized him by the wrists and dragged him out of the building.'

Cunán paused and licked his parched lips. He nodded at the body of the librarian.

'By the time I turned back, the flames were already in control. They were leaping from the tower across to the main library room. One of the copyists was ringing the alarm bell and people were coming to our aid. But the flames were too strong. They seized and swallowed the books – they were just fuel to the fire. We formed a chain, trying to bring out the books, while others formed chains to bring water to douse the fire, but there was little we could save. All the priceless works consumed . . . irreplaceable!' He broke off with an uncontrollable sob.

'Are you saying that the place where the fire started was in Dubhagan's chamber? That he had been killed and then the place set on fire?' pressed Fidelma.

Cumscrad scowled and before his son could speak retorted, 'I clearly understood that is what he said. And we saw the culprits themselves riding away – the Uí Liatháin!'

Fidelma ignored him and kept her eyes on those of the young man. It was clear that she was expecting an answer from him and so Cunán nodded. 'That is so.'

'And there was no sign of an assailant or assailants when you found him?'

'None.'

'I saw them,' called a voice from the crowd. A slight man came forward. 'Our chief is right. I recognised them by the banner carried by one of their number. It was the grey fox's head, the symbol of the Uí Liatháin.'

'How were they allowed to do this?' shouted Cumscrad. 'Is there no man among you to take sword and shield to defend my people while I am absent? Who allowed these raiders to ride in without any attempt to stop them?'

A burly man pushed forward from the crowd. He was red in the face and spoke defensively.

'They rode in openly, Cumscrad. We thought that they

came in peace, for their swords were sheathed and they made no display of war. Their leader called out that they had only come to consult with Dubhagan.'

'What happened then?' asked Fidelma when she saw that Cumscrad was framing some angry retort.

'They did just that. Two of them dismounted from their horses and entered the library tower. The rest remained outside. We did not realise anything was amiss until there was shouting, a smell of burning and we saw the flames appearing. By then, the two who had gone inside re-emerged with swords in hand, leapt on their horses and they all galloped out towards the forest beyond before we knew what was happening.'

'Not all of them.' It was the slight man who spoke. They turned to him. 'I was mending my bow when they rode out. I managed to loose an arrow at one of them. I thought I hit him.'

'You did,' Eadulf replied, remembering the riderless horse and body. 'He lies in the field outside the town, his horse nearby.'

Soon volunteers went to retrieve the body and the horse and when they were brought back, they crowded round to see if they recognised the person. It was Gormán who turned with a serious expression to Fidelma. 'I think you should look at him, lady,' he said softly.

She looked down. The man was thin, with a head of hair that was as white as snow, and a pale skin to match. She glanced back to Gormán with a query in her eyes. He nodded. 'It is the *bánaí*. One of the two who tried to ambush us on the road to Lios Mór. And look at that.' He pointed to the man's neck where there was a dark mark, almost an abrasion, such as they had seen on the dead attacker on the road to Lios Mór.

'Does anyone recognise this man?' Fidelma demanded of those who were staring at the body. There was a shaking of heads and muttered denials.

'A warrior, that is clear,' replied the archer who had claimed his life.

'That he was part of a party of Uí Liatháin raiders is good enough for me,' Cumscrad said angrily. 'I regret no more of them paid a price for this crime.'

'What could we do?' It was the burly man again. 'Fight the fire or make ready our horses and ride after them? We fought the fire.'

'You made the better choice,' Fidelma agreed before turning to Cumscrad's son. 'You mentioned that Dubhagan's chamber was where special books were stored. What do you mean by special books?'

The young man gazed at her blankly. His face was black with smoke and his cheeks and forearms looked singed.

Cumscrad, now icy calm, answered for him. 'They were the ancient works, some of which many might condemn as heretical to the new Faith.' Then he added to his son, 'When you feel better, come to the rath, for we must talk further.' He turned to a woman who was helping to attend those who had exhausted themselves fighting the fire. 'Take Cunán and see to his needs,' he instructed. The young librarian allowed himself to be guided away by the woman.

Fidelma turned to Cumscrad. The chief's features were set and bitter and before she could speak he had turned to one of his warriors and issued rapid orders. Tasks needed to be done, assessing the damage, removing the bodies of Dubhagan and the albino raider, attending those who had been injured. One of the scribes had already volunteered to start listing what books had been saved and what had been destroyed. Other volunteers started removing the rescued books to a place of safety to store them. Cumscrad also gave orders to his warriors to arrange a special watch in the unlikely event of the raiders returning. Only when he was sure that all matters were being taken care of did he turn back to Fidelma and her companions. His expression was still bitter.

'Let us go to my hall and discuss this matter,' he suggested shortly. Without waiting for an answer, he turned and strode to where he had left his horse. They followed him and collected their mounts. The rath was only a short distance away and so the four of them walked in moody silence to the gates, where Cumscrad issued orders to his stable boys to take their horses and care for them. Then he led the way into his great hall where an attendant waited. He called for mead and refreshments and then invited them to sit in seats arranged before a glowing fire. When the drinks were brought, he gazed thoughtfully at Fidelma.

'It was deliberate,' he began. 'The place was fired deliberately and my librarian killed.' Cumscrad's features were hard. 'First they attack our barge and steal its precious cargo. Two books which our library had copied for Ard Mór. Then comes this attack on our library and its destruction. Yet I fail to see the motive. Why would they want these books? Why would they attempt to destroy the library? Why kill our librarian? It doesn't add up.'

'I can offer you no motivation behind these events as yet,' replied Fidelma. 'But we will find out.'

'I understand that this library is famous for keeping books that are not approved of by many members of the Faith,' interposed Eadulf softly. 'That might be the motivation.'

'You mean they attacked the books because they posed difficult questions for the Faith?' Cumscrad smiled cynically.

'Well, people have destroyed books for less,' Eadulf pointed out.

'It is certainly the unintelligent option to destroy that with which we don't agree rather than present our arguments and then decide what is the better argument.'

Gormán gave an embarrassed cough. He had been silent for so long they had almost forgotten he was there.

'But why would the Uí Liatháin be so fanatical about the Faith? I know them. They are not known for their piety.'

'Your warrior companion is right, lady,' Cumscrad agreed. 'But they are enemies of my people. That's why.'

'How much was this library of yours worth, Cumscrad?' asked Eadulf. 'What did it contain that made it as priceless as you claim?'

'It has existed since the time of Mug Ruith, long before the new Faith reached these shores,' replied the chieftain. 'It was famous. It was unique.'

THE CHALICE OF BLOOD

'Famous?' queried Eadulf. 'I have heard of many libraries but not of Fhear Maighe's.'

'That does not reflect on the fame of our library but on your ignorance of it,' the chieftain replied icily.

'You may be right, Cumscrad.' Fidelma smiled at his riposte, in spite of the mortified expression on Eadulf's features. 'But indulge our ignorance and tell us something about it.'

The chieftain was mollified. He gave a sigh and began to recount the history of the library. 'Four centuries or so ago, a scholar from the east called Aethicus of Istria wrote what he called a *Cosmographia*, a cosmography of the world. Aethicus sailed to our shores from Iberia because he had heard of the fame of our libraries. He speaks of the *volumina* of our libraries as noteworthy.'

'You say that this was four centuries ago?' Eadulf interrupted in surprise. 'But that would mean—'

'That would place the fame of our libraries two centuries before the new Faith came to this island,' finished Cumscrad. 'Furthermore, Aethicus writes of the *ideomochos* of our books, clearly indicating that the books contained a literature that he had not seen before and using a word that meant that it was particular to our people.'

'They were written on what we call the *flesc filidh*, or rods of the poets,' Fidelma said. 'The *flesc filidh* were wands of beech and birch. So you are saying that Aethicus actually came here and viewed these ancient books?'

'Indeed. But since the coming of Christianity, there has been a systematic attempt to destroy everything that went before.' Cumscrad gestured in the direction of the smouldering ruins of the *tech-screptra*. 'The destruction is almost succeeding. We are witnessing crimes against knowledge. Aethicus of Istria praised our libraries and we know that he came to this very spot to examine the ancient books. His *Cosmographia* tells us so.'

'I have never heard of this Aethicus and his *Cosmographia*,' said Eadulf.

'Have you not read Orosius Paulus's *History Against the Pagans*? Even he quotes passages from Aethicus about his voyage to this country. But Orosius was a Christian and wished to denigrate the pagans. He described us as cannibals.'

'You'll forgive us, Cumscrad,' intervened Fidelma, seeing the chieftain's anger just below the surface. 'It is in the nature of lawyers to be sceptical while gathering evidence.'

'Truth is great and will prevail. You are fond of quoting that saying of your mentor, the Brehon Moran, Fidelma of Cashel. But truth does not always prevail. I presume you know of our ancestor, Mug Ruith?'

'I was told that, in pagan times, he was regarded as a sun god who rode the skies in a chariot of burning light.'

Cumscrad grimaced sourly. 'The stories became embellished in the retelling. He did take his name from the solar deity but Mug Ruith was a man of flesh and blood and a great Druid of my people. My clan look to him as our ultimate ancestor.'

'So tell me who he was,' Eadulf asked, 'and forgive me my ignorance.'

'The zealots of the Faith claim he was a magician. That's

how they dismiss the Druids these days, they call them wizards and magicians. Now the fanatics of the Faith also claim that Mug Ruith went to the Holy Land to learn his so-called magic from someone they call Simon Magus.'

Eadulf stirred uncomfortably. 'That was Simon of Gitto who is considered the source of all heresies.'

'Exactly. Mug Ruith did not have to go to learn "sorcery" from anyone. He was a great Druid.'

'And Simon of Gitto is certainly not well regarded among those of the Faith.' Eadulf frowned. 'So it is a story to denigrate him.'

'Did your library hold a copy of the *Apophasis Megale* or *The Great Declaration* which Simon of Gitto is said to have written?' Fidelma asked suddenly.

'You would have to ask my son that question,' replied Cumscrad.

'There are many things we must ask Cunán,' Fidelma said quietly. 'I hope he will join us soon.'

'One thing I would like to ask now,' Eadulf said quickly. 'What was that curious contraption I saw which seemed to pump water from the river towards your *tech-screptra*?'

Cumscrad smiled sadly. 'It was something that Dubhagan was working on. He had not perfected it. It is a new form of water pump that relies on a plunger at the top of a cylinder creating a vacuum which draws water up through valves, pushing it along the troughs. Do not ask me the meaning of these terms for I heard them only from poor Dubhagan. I barely understand the purpose.'

'Dubhagan invented this machine for pumping water upwards?'

Cumscrad shook his head. 'He did not invent it. He told me that he found a description of the machine in one of the Latin books that came to our *tech-screptra*. Let us hope that it has been saved, for it was written many centuries ago. It was called *De architectura* and was written by a Roman, Vitruvius. Dubhagan said Vitruvius had seen this machine in Egypt and had adopted it when he served in the army of Julius Caesar.'

Fidelma was vaguely interested but more impatient to be about the work she had come for.

'Let us hope it is a book that has been saved. But you remind me that the books you had here in your *tech-screptra* were not only the ancient ones from the Five Kingdoms.'

'Our library made a practice of keeping religious books that were not written by the zealous, such as the book that was stolen – the one by Celsus. They were books it was felt might be destroyed because they were regarded as heretical.'

'Do you know what they were?'

'Only our librarians would know that.'

'Maybe I can help you, then.'

They looked up to find that Cunán had entered the hall. The young man was washed and looked more in control of himself. The scorch marks on his face were clearly visible now.

'Are you all right, my son?' asked the chief anxiously.

'I am now. I must apologise if I seemed dazed before. To

find poor Dubhagan murdered and then to see the destruction of all those priceless works . . . it is like seeing the destruction of all you hold dear.'

He came and took a seat with them while an attendant appeared with a jug of mead and poured a measure for him. He sipped it slowly and thoughtfully.

'I understand that the library contained books that were not entirely approved of by the Faith,' said Fidelma.

'It was the purpose of our library to save books from destruction which might otherwise be lost for ever,' Cunán replied sadly. 'Now many have been reduced to ashes. We shall not know the extent of our loss until our scribes have checked through everything. That will take many days.'

'Your library made copies of two books that were sent to Ard Mór library,' Fidelma began.

'At their request,' the assistant librarian said. 'It was some of our best copying work. And they were stolen.'

'Your father told us that they were the poems of Dallán Forgaill and a work by Celsus.'

'That is true.'

'It is the work by Celsus that interests me.'

Cunán's eyes registered surprise but he said nothing.

'Were you here when Brother Donnchad of Lios Mór came to visit this library?' Fidelma asked quickly.

Cunán nodded.

'Do you recall what sort of books he was looking for?'

'He spent his time with Dubhagan in his chamber so I do not know what they talked about, nor what he was seeking.'

'But you did say that the books in that chamber were those of special interest,' pressed Fidelma.

'I did so and they were.' He hesitated. 'I did have to go to Dubhagan's chamber while Brother Donnchad was there. I needed to seek Dubhagan's advice and found Brother Donnchad poring over some books.'

'I don't suppose you know what they were. Was it the work of Celsus?'

Cunán shook his head. 'Celsus? I don't think so. I know he was looking at one of the books from our section of works in Hebrew when I entered.'

'Hebrew?' Fidelma was disappointed.

'Indeed, we have copies of several works in Hebrew.'

'What sort of works?'

'Our prize possession is . . .' he caught himself and a look of bitterness moulded his features. 'Our prize possession was a parchment scroll of the *Sefer Torah* – all five books: the *Bereshit, Shemot, Vayikra, Bemidbar* and *Devarim*.' Seeing Fidelma's puzzled features, he explained. 'The Faith calls them the five books of Moses.'

'And these are all now destroyed?' gasped Eadulf.

'I imagine so. They were all in the tower room where most of the destruction was wrought.'

'Were these the books he was interested in?'

'I don't believe so. The book satchels were all in their correct place except one. Brother Donnchad was sitting by the Hebrew section. I knew that he was looking at a Hebrew book because I registered the space in my mind where that book should have been – in the small section we place those Hebrew titles in.' He shrugged. 'Librarians seem to develop an unconscious eye for such things.'

'And do you know what the book was?'

'I cannot be sure,' frowned the young man.

'Then let us hear your uncertainty,' pressed Fidelma. 'What book do you think it was?'

'I think the empty space usually contained the *Tosefta*.'

Fidelma looked blankly at the young man.

'It is a book of Jewish oral law which was compiled three or four centuries ago. We were told it was written in some rabbinical academy in Judea.'

'Jewish law? Why would Brother Donnchad be interested in such a text?' mused Eadulf.

Fidelma was looking a little uncertain for she was convinced that the reason for Donnchad's visit to Fhear Maighe had something to do with the Celsus text. She had been hoping for some easy connection.

'But didn't Donnchad also ask to see a work by Celsus, the same one that was copied and stolen?'

Cunán did not reply immediately. He looked slightly guilty.

'You hesitate. Why?' pressed Fidelma. 'I am right, am I not?'

'It is just that Dubhagan asked me particularly not to mention it. But I suppose it is all right, for now both Brother Donnchad and Dubhagan are dead.'

'Why did Dubhagan ask you not to mention it?'

'He came into the main library when Brother Donnchad was in the tower room and asked if he could borrow the text for a while. I was just finishing copying it for Ard Mór. He told me not to mention that he was showing it to Brother Donnchad as a special favour. Brother Donnchad did not want it to be known that he had examined it.'

'I suppose that is natural enough,' Fidelma said after consideration.

'We welcome books of every description. Many brethren, returning from journeys to Rome and to other places, come back with books; even critiques of the Christians by the Emperor Flavius Julianus, those of Porphyry of Pergamum – we had a copy of his *Adversus Christianos, Against Christianity* – and, of course, we had the work of Celsus, *Alethos Logos – The True Word*. Books in several languages are brought to us.'

'How many of these have survived the fire?' asked Eadulf. 'I don't suppose you know as yet.'

'Of the critiques of the Faith?' Cunán shrugged. 'I suspect that most have been destroyed. They were all in the tower room where poor Dubhagan was. Julianus's work, *Contra Galilaeos, Against the Gallileans*, was very rare, although I think we still have Clement of Alexandra's response.'

'As I have said, it is Celsus that I am interested in. Do you know what his criticisms of the Faith were?'

The librarian looked uncertain for a moment and then glanced around almost in a conspiratorial manner.

'I do. To be honest,' Cunán confessed, 'I found Celsus's arguments fascinating and do much to support the beliefs taught by our forefathers.'

'I have read neither Celsus nor Origenes' answer to him. Can you tell me what Celsus argued against the Faith?'

'Remember he was writing several hundred years ago,' the young librarian said. 'He argued that the idea of an incarnation of God as man is absurd. He asked why the human race should think itself superior to bees, ants and elephants . . . I have heard of those strange animals,' he added as an aside. 'The Roman Emperor Claudius took elephants to Britain to help him overcome the Britons.' He paused before continuing. 'Celsus asked why should Christians put themselves in such a unique relation to their creator as to make him one of them? And why should God come to men in the form of one nationality and of one distinctive faith? Celsus believed that the idea that the Jews had a special providence was nonsense. He believed that all life in the entire world was special. He likened the early Christians to a council of frogs or worms on a dunghill, croaking and squeaking, crying, "We are the rulers of the world and it is for us that it was created." He found that absurd.'

Fidelma was frowning. 'Does Celsus say what he did believe in?'

'He wrote that it is more reasonable to accept that each nation, each part of the world, has its own gods, its own prophets and messengers. He charged the Christians with preaching intolerance; he charged them with not understanding other religions. He asked why Christians could not find common ground with the great philosophical and political authorities throughout the world. He argued that an effort to properly understand mankind's belief in all the gods and demons was compatible with the purified monotheism that Christians preach. Unless they did this, he said, Christians had no hope of winning people to their Faith or hoping to attain anything like universal agreement on the divinity.'

'He was a harsh critic, indeed,' murmured Fidelma, feeling uncomfortable because she had often found it difficult to simply believe and not to question matters of dogma that seemed illogical to her.

'There is much, much more,' said Cunán. 'Alas, it is difficult to find anyone who will admit to reading a copy of Celsus's writings. I am told, however, that Tertullian and Minucius Felix knew his work and were influenced by it. I think the main thing Celsus was arguing for was that Christians should not remain aloof from other faiths and from politics. He apparently urged them not to claim another empire or any special position within the Roman empire but make peace with the emperors. He wrote, according to Origenes, that if all the other faiths followed the Christian example and abstained from the politics of the empire, the affairs of the empire would fall into the hands of wild and lawless barbarians.'

'You appear to know a great deal about Celsus's work,' Eadulf commented with a frown.

Cunán actually grinned. 'I have sat every day this year copying the text of Celsus. If nothing else, I know this work and its arguments. I was surprised that Brother Donnchad asked to see it. I have never met him, but we exchanged letters many years ago. I have a reputation as a copyist and I have also copied several of his own works. His reputation is well known.'

A thought suddenly occurred to Eadulf.

'I have heard that every scribe has what is called a special "hand", not just a way of forming letters but little idiosyncrasies in forming sentences and words. Would you know something about this?'

Cunán suppressed a smile of immodesty. 'It is true and I believe that I know the hand of most of the leading scribes in this kingdom.'

Eadulf glanced at Fidelma. She immediately realised what he had in mind. She took from her *ciorbholg*, comb bag, the piece of parchment that they had found under Brother Donnchad's window. She handed it over to Cunán.

'What do you make of that?' she asked.

'*Si vis transfer calicem istrum a me . . . Deicide. Deicide. Deicide,*' he read carefully. 'Take this chalice, or cup, from me. The last word written three times means god-killer, but you know that,' he added quickly. 'It is a claim that has often been levelled against the Jews by the Fathers of our Faith. It is as if Brother Donnchad was practising some phrase but it looks odd.'

CHAPTER SIXTEEN

Fidelma and Eadulf regarded Cunán in astonishment for a moment.

'Are you saying that Brother Donnchad wrote this?' Fidelma asked.

'As I have just explained,' Cunán said patiently, 'I was the chief copyist of this library. Who does not know the hand of Brother Donnchad, one of the foremost scholars of this kingdom?'

'Can you prove that it is his hand?' pressed Eadulf. 'After all, it is only a few words.'

'Any good scholar who knew his work will tell you so. This is a good enough sample to spot the individual writer. Look at the words *calicem* and *deicide*. Brother Donnchad formed his letter "c" and the "d" in a very distinctive fashion. See there?' His eyes lit up. 'Why, I can prove it further, if you like.'

He stood up and hurried from the room.

Cumscrad smiled approvingly. 'My son, Cunán, may not have the skills of governance to take over the chieftainship of the Fir Maige Féne but he has attended the bardic school for six years and achieved the degree of *Cli*, he knows the secret language of the poets, can recite the prescribed number of poems without fault and knows eighty of the ancient tales by heart.'

'Then he is a son to be proud of,' replied Fidelma just as the door reopened and Cunán returned holding a small scroll.

'This was sent to me from Brother Donnchad some years ago and you can see clearly this formation on it,' the young scribe explained.

Fidelma took it and examined it with interest. Cunán was correct. The same distinctive forms appeared in it. She could not help but read the opening: 'Donnchad, a humble servant and an apostle of Christ, Jesus, to Cunán the scribe. Grace and peace be multiplied unto you through the knowledge of God and of Jesus our Lord.'

'You knew him well, then?' she asked.

'Only by an exchange of letters. Our librarian knew him better,' replied Cunán. 'But he did ask me to copy some texts that we held.'

'When was this?' Fidelma asked.

'Oh, long before he went off on his pilgrimage to the Holy Land.'

'Can you remember what they were?'

'Some letters of Paul the Apostle, as I recall.'

'Nothing contrary to the Faith then?' Eadulf sounded disappointed.

Cunán shook his head, then looked carefully at him. The young man was not lacking in wit.

'Are you saying that there is some connection between the manuscript books he was examining here, his death and this attack on our library?'

'Books that speak of things and people before the Faith might be enough to cause these things,' intervened his father bitterly. 'Look at the way we are condemned by that young upstart Brother Lugna.'

'But it doesn't explain why the Uí Liatháin would attack our library or the barge taking the books to Ard Mór,' pointed out Cunán.

'That is true, Cunán,' said Fidelma after a moment or two of thought. 'I would like to speak to the bargemen about the attack on them and also to the man who found the barge.'

'Very well,' Cumscrad said, rising abruptly. 'Let us find Muirgíos.'

Muirgíos, as befitted someone whose name meant 'sea strength', looked every inch the sort of person whose profession had to do with the sea or the waterways. He was a stocky individual with sandy hair, sea-green eyes, and a weather-beaten face, and he had a habit of standing with his feet wide apart as if balancing on the deck of a ship. They found him on board one of the broad river barges that traded along The Great River. He was mending some of the rigging on the vessel.

He greeted Cumscrad with a gesture of his chin towards the still smouldering library building.

'A bad business. The Uí Liatháin have over-reached themselves this time.'

Cumscrad did not reply but indicated Fidelma.

'This is the Lady Fidelma, sister to Colgú. She has come to hear our complaint.'

It was clear that Muirgíos was not impressed for he did not rise from his seat nor interrupt his work on the rigging.

'Then you have come at the right time. Now you can see their viciousness for yourself.'

'At the moment, it is the attack on your barge that I want to talk about,' she replied, ignoring Gormán's look of outrage at what he saw as the man's discourtesy towards the King's sister.

'It is as we told our chieftain, Cumscrad,' the man replied. 'We were not far from Lios Mór when we saw a man lying on the southern bank of the river. He appeared to be in distress. So we pulled towards the bank. It was a ruse. The next moment, without warning, an arrow struck our steersman. Then warriors appeared from behind the trees and bushes and swarmed over the side. One of our men injured one of the attackers in the arm with his knife. But we were not armed as warriors. No reason to be. So we surrendered.

'Our steersman was badly hurt but is now recovering. The crewman who caused injury to one of the attackers was beaten severely. They took us from the barge and bound us, leaving

301

us on the river bank. Then they sailed off downriver. It was as simple as that.'

'How did you know that they were of the Uí Liatháin?' asked Eadulf.

The bargeman laughed bitterly. 'You are a stranger, judging by your accent. Well, it is easy to tell, stranger. Firstly, you should know that each clan has its own symbol, its own totem. The banner of the Uí Liatháin is the head of a grey fox on a white background. That banner was carried by one of those who attacked us.'

Eadulf nodded slowly and then said, 'And what else?'

The bargeman frowned. 'What else?'

'You began by saying "firstly" as you explained about the banner. I presumed there was a second point.'

'Well, you're right. As they were leaving us, one of them said loudly to his companion, "Uallachán will be pleased." Uallachán is—'

'We know who Uallachán is,' Fidelma said quickly. 'Can you remember the features of any of these raiders, anything distinctive?'

The bargeman regarded her curiously and shook his head. 'Nothing particular.'

'Was there a *bánaí* with them, a thin man with white hair and—'

'I know well what a *bánaí* is. I heard that one of the raiders was shot this afternoon and he was one. I cannot swear he was among those who stole the barge. All I know is that they were men of the Uí Liatháin.'

'Did you not consider it strange that these thieves made no attempt to hide their identity?'

The bargeman shrugged indifferently. 'All that is bad in this area is down to the Uí Liatháin. They have always had their eye on our fertile lands. It is not the first time they have crossed north over the Bríd River into our territory to attack and rob us.'

'Yet it is curious that they should do so openly. They know such attacks would bring down the wrath of my brother and his warriors.'

'Maybe they have no fear of the King at Cashel,' Muirgíos commented dismissively. 'He sits far away in a comfortable palace.'

There was a sharp intake of breath from Gormán and his hand gripped the hilt of his sword. Fidelma motioned with her hand to still him.

'It is well known that the Eóghanacht of Cashel are not well favoured by either the Uí Liatháin or the Fir Maige Féne. Nevertheless, Colgú is the King and you are both answerable to him. If the Uí Liatháin are in open rebellion then they must face the consequences – as, indeed, will any of the clans of Muman who disobey the law.'

Muirgíos stared in surprise at the authority in her voice.

Then Cumscrad interrupted the awkward silence by calling to a passing man to come aboard.

'This is Eolann, the man who found the missing barge.'

Eolann was almost a replica of Muirgíos. His story was also simple.

'I had been to Ard Mór to take a religious brother seeking transportation there. He had journeyed from Gúagan Barra, a little abbey to the west of here. I have a boat that I can manoeuvre single-handed. Having delivered the brother to the abbey, I was returning. I was not far beyond the point where the River Bríd enters into The Great River when I saw Muirgíos's sailing barge coming downriver. I was about to call a greeting when I saw the crew were all strangers. There was no sign of Muirgíos and there were no men of the Fir Maige Féne that I recognised. So I sailed on by with no more than a courteous wave as one bargeman gives another when passing on the river.'

He paused for a moment before continuing.

'I knew Muirgíos well, and he had told me that he was taking books to Ard Mór on his next trip there. I also knew that Ard Mór was expecting his barge. So I drew in my sail and turned back after his barge. I let the flow of the river take me after it, keeping as close to the bank as I could. I saw it manoeuvre into the Bríd. So I hove to and waited for a while in the shelter of the bank. Then I went more cautiously along the river but it was not long before I found the barge abandoned.'

'Which side of the river was it abandoned on?' asked Fidelma. 'I mean, was it on the side of the territory of the Uí Liatháin or was it on the side of the territory of the Fir Maige Féne?'

'It was on the south side,' confirmed Eolann immediately. 'On the side of the Uí Liatháin.'

'What then?'

'Seeing no sign of anyone, I went aboard. I feared I would find Muirgíos and his crew below, perhaps slaughtered. But there was no sign of anyone. Curiously, the cargo seemed intact, although I saw some chests broken open and empty. I have sailed with Muirgíos before and realised that was where he usually stored the copies of manuscripts and books that were often transported from our library to Lios Mór and Ard Mór.'

'How were you able to bring word here so quickly?' Fidelma asked. 'You could not crew the barge and to sail here in your small boat would have taken a while against the current of the river.'

Eolann smiled. 'I knew further upriver was a small settlement, a place where *compara* grows.'

Seeing Fidelma frown, Eadulf explained quickly: 'The henna plant, camphire.'

'I went there and sought out men who could bring the barge to the north bank into our territory. While they did that, I borrowed a horse and rode here directly across the hills, so that our chief could be immediately alerted to what had happened.'

Fidelma nodded approvingly. 'You did well, Eolann. One more question. Did you glimpse a *bánaí* with these men?'

'I heard one was killed in the attack on the library. I did not glimpse any such person, though.'

Fidelma turned to Cumscrad, glancing up at the darkening sky. 'I have heard enough. My companions and I will ride south at first light to confront Uallachán on these matters before returning to Lios Mór. So I ask you for hospitality for the night. I would like your word that you will undertake no action against the Uí Liatháin until Gormán brings you Uallachán's response and my advice. Do I have it?'

Cumscrad hesitated before agreeing.

'Excellent. Have no concern, Cumscrad. The Uí Liatháin will be made to account for any deeds that they have committed contrary to the law. They will be answerable to my brother, just as you will be if you attempt to take the law into your own hands.'

It was not long after daybreak that Fidelma, Eadulf and Gormán set off southwards over the forested hills towards the meandering Bríd, the river that marked the border between the two clans. The sky indicated fine weather for their journey, with only a few clouds spread like woolly sheep's fleeces across the blue. If the clouds grew larger, the innocent-looking fleece could turn into thunderclouds. But the early signs, together with the glorious red sunset the previous evening, gave them every expectation of good weather.

From Fhear Maighe to the River Bríd was only some eight kilometres. Taking the track south-east, they moved through a small valley and from there only one large hill lay between them and the river. Once across the hill, they would descend on to a plain towards a fortress that had once dominated the river crossing and had long been a subject of dispute between the Fir Maige Féne and the Uí Liatháin. The disputed fortress was regarded as Fir Maige Féne, but it was still called Caisleán Uí Liatháin after the southern tribe's claim. Ancient standing stones rose in the surrounding countryside.

The place was strangely silent as they rode by the deserted fortress walls. They could hear the distant sound of animals, the clucking of chicken, bleating of sheep and the occasional protesting moo of a cow, which they supposed belonged to an isolated farmstead further back on the hill. Yet Gormán was growing uncomfortable and Fidelma's eyes searched the deserted buildings.

'It's too quiet,' whispered Eadulf.

Fidelma did not reply; she had noticed a movement in the shadow of a wall.

'Gormán,' she said softly but Gormán was already reaching for his sword. Before he could draw it, a stentorian voice called out.

'Hold, warrior! Even breathe and you are a dead man!'

Gormán had spotted at least two bowmen with weapons levelled and he let his sword hand stay motionless in the air. Abruptly two riders came round the corner of the fortress wall, blocking the pathway. They edged their horses closer.

'Well, well,' the leader, clearly a warrior, sneered as he examined them. 'Who do we have here? More thieves and liars of the Fir Maige Féne?'

Neither Fidelma nor Eadulf made any response or movement. They were aware of several other people among the buildings now. It had been a simple and successful ambush and Fidelma was silently chastising herself.

'I advise you,' called Gormán, undeterred, 'that you stand in grave danger. This is Fidelma of Cashel, sister to King Colgú. Threatening her and her husband, Eadulf of Seaxmund's Ham, is an affront to her brother, your rightful King.'

'I serve only Uallachán, chief of the Uí Liatháin,' replied the man with a sardonic smile. 'I stand in danger only of his displeasure if I do not carry out his orders.'

He turned and waved to his men to close in. With growing apprehension, Eadulf saw that one of the riders carried a banner with a grey fox's head on it. Then another rider, dressed in the brown robes of a religious, moved forward.

'Is that Fidelma? Fidelma of Cashel?' The man clearly recognised her and turned to the leader of the warriors. 'It is true that she is Fidelma of Cashel, sister to King Colgú.' Then he turned to her. 'What are you doing here? Do you recognise me?'

Fidelma frowned slightly. 'I seem to know your face . . .'

'At Ard Mór when you were waiting to go on board the *Barnacle Goose* on a pilgrimage voyage.'

Her features cleared. 'You were the librarian of the abbey. Brother . . . Brother . . .'

'Brother Temnen,' supplied the man eagerly.

'It was some years ago,' Fidelma admitted.

'I also remember you during the summer that you solved the murder of poor Sister Aróc,' said Brother Temnen.

'This is Eadulf of Seaxmund's Ham,' introduced Fidelma, 'and this is a warrior of my brother's bodyguard, Gormán.'

'Of Eadulf I have heard,' acknowledged the librarian. He turned again to the leader of the warriors. 'These are not our enemies, my friend. They are not Fir Maige Féne.'

The man seemed undecided. 'My chief, Uallachán, should be here within the hour. It will be for him to decide what is to be done.'

'Uallachán is coming here?' asked Fidelma in surprise.

'We are an advance party to hold this crossing in case Cumscrad and his lying tribe attack us. I suggest that we all dismount to await his arrival in the fortress.'

Gormán looked questioningly at Fidelma but she shrugged her acceptance of the inevitable. Everyone dismounted and the horses were led into the abandoned fortress. Guards watched over them while others went to strategic points. The leader of the warriors then came to stand uncomfortably by them while Brother Temnen sat down with Fidelma and her companions.

'What brings you here into the country of the Fir Maige Féne?' she asked.

Brother Temnen's expression was serious and he made a helpless gesture. 'I wish we could have met in more pleasant circumstances.'

'What makes our meeting here unpleasant?'

'I have been asked to accompany Uallachán's war band.'

'War band?'

'He means to raid Fhear Maighe as a punishment.'

Fidelma's eyes grew hard. 'Means to raid it? Are you saying that he has not done so already?'

The librarian looked surprised. 'I do not understand your question.'

'We have just come from Fhear Maighe. While we were there yesterday, some warriors carrying the same emblem that you carry,' she indicated the man still carrying the clan totem, 'raided and burnt the library there. Dubhagan, the librarian, was killed. Many priceless manuscripts have been destroyed.'

'These are lies put out by our enemies the Fir Maige Féne,' snapped the leader of the warriors.

'Then we are liars too,' Fidelma riposted. 'Because we were there and saw the raid.'

'It was not my men nor any warrior of the Uí Liatháin. Uallachán rides an hour behind us, so it was not he.'

'It is true, Fidelma,' Brother Temnen chimed in firmly. 'He tells no lie. I have been with the Uí Liatháin and they have raided no one.'

'Among your warriors, do you have a *bánaí*, a thin man with snow-white hair and skin?'

'Not among my men,' replied the Uí Liatháin warrior immediately. Then a frown appeared on his features. It was clear that he recognised the description.

'But you know of such a man?' Fidelma asked quickly.

'I have seen such a man at the head of a band of warriors,' admitted the warrior, 'but not in Uí Liatháin territory. I saw them weeks ago landing from a ship in the bay below Ard Mór.'

'Landing from a ship?' repeated Fidelma thoughtfully.

'The fact that he was accoutred as a warrior yet was also a *bánaí* drew my attention. He wore a golden circlet round his neck but not of the style our warriors wear, such as that one.' He pointed to Gormán.

'I don't suppose you can tell us more.'

The Uí Liatháin shrugged indifferently. 'Little more to tell. A dozen men disembarked with him. They were all warriors. The ship had arrived from Britain, so I was told. Some outlandish kingdom – ah, a place called Kernow.'

'What happened to them?' asked Fidelma.

'They bought horses from the local traders and rode off north. They carried arms with them. I suspect they were *dílmainech*.'

'Mercenaries?'

'Exactly so.'

'What were you doing in Ard Mór?'

'Some of us often go there to see what foreign ships come in and what goods may be bought.'

Fidelma gazed hard at the warrior and then at the religieux and realised that their puzzled expressions were not false.

'Will you explain how you came here and for what purpose?'

'To teach Cumscrad and his fellow liars a lesson,' snapped the warrior.

'I will explain,' Brother Temnen intervened in a more moderate tone. 'Our abbot, Rian of Ard Mór, who is a kinsman of yours, contacted Dubhagan, the librarian at Fhear Maighe, with a commission. As you know, the library there has many works that are not to be found elsewhere among the great libraries of the Five Kingdoms.'

'And the commission was?' prompted Fidelma.

'To copy two works, one a collection of the poems of the great bard Dallán Forgaill, and the other a foreign work by a writer called Celsus.'

'And why would your abbey want to spend money on getting a copy of a book attacking the Faith?' queried Eadulf.

Brother Temnen said, 'So you know this work? One of our scholars had read a criticism of Celsus by Origenes and thought it could be improved on. He did not want anyone beguiled by the pitfalls Celsus had prepared.'

'Very well, continue.'

'Dubhagan accepted the commission and all was agreed by us in good faith. Then we heard word that the copies had been placed on one of the river barges which was due at Ard Mór. Not only did they not arrive but we also heard rumours that Uí Liatháin warriors had attacked the barge and stolen the books. Uallachán was summoned to the abbey but denied this. He claimed the Fir Maige Féne were liars. This war band is to demand reparation from Cumscrad and the Fir Maige Féne for spreading such lies.'

'And why are you, a librarian from Ard Mór, accompanying these warriors on this raid?'

'Uallachán believes that the books were never sent and that Cumscrad has engaged in some deception,' said Brother Temnen. 'He wants me to search the library during the raid and identify the books that he claims were stolen. I am to be a witness.'

'How could you tell who was the liar?' demanded Fidelma. 'Either chief could be lying.'

'When Abbot Rian called Uallachán to the abbey, he made the chieftain take oath before the High Altar that he spoke the truth. He did so and therefore we believe that no warrior of the Uí Liatháin has done this thing. Uallachán believes that Cumscrad is spreading lies to provoke a war in the hope of seizing the lands of the Uí Liatháin.'

'If that were so,' Fidelma smiled thinly and gestured to the warriors around her, 'Cumscrad has been successful. However, I don't think it is that simple, Brother Temnen. If you had witnessed the destruction of the library of Fhear Maighe, the near death of Cumscrad's own son who worked in the library, and the death of Dubhagan . . . I do not think Cumscrad or his men had a hand in it. Furthermore, the *bánaí* was killed when he tried to escape with the others.'

Brother Temnen shrugged. 'We will have to await the arrival of Uallachán. After speaking to him, perhaps you will be able to ascertain where the truth lies.'

'That is my intention,' Fidelma replied. 'If the Uí Liatháin did not attack either the barge or the library, then someone is trying to create a problem between Uallachán and Cumscrad. But why? Who would that benefit?'

Eadulf had been thinking. 'Who knew about this commission from your abbot to the library of Fhear Maighe?' he asked. 'I mean, who apart from your abbey and Dubhagan?'

'I suppose several people.'

'But would they know the titles and the nature of the books that were to be copied?'

'That was a matter that only we in Ard Mór and Dubhagan and his copyists would have known. But isn't there a saying that to tell a secret to three people makes it no longer a secret?'

'How did you learn that Fhear Maighe had these books?' asked Eadulf.

'I checked with them.'

'How?'

'I sent a messenger to find out. But that was a long time ago. It took many months to make the copies. It was only last week that we received word that the books were ready. We were to pay thirty *seds*.'

'A large price to pay.'

'Extortionate,' agreed the librarian, philosophically. 'But the Celsus book is very rare. I am told there is not another copy known in the Five Kingdoms because of the nature of the book.'

'You mean because it was an early attack on the founders of the Faith?' asked Eadulf.

'Exactly so.'

'So who brought you the news that the copies were ready and would be delivered?'

'One of the brethren.'

'The same messenger from your abbey?'

'Not from our abbey, no.'

'From Fhear Maighe?'

'A physician,' replied Brother Temnen. 'He paid us a visit to collect certain herbs that had been brought ashore from one of the merchant ships.'

The abbey of Ard Mór lay where The Great River emptied into the sea, just on the southern coast where merchant ships came and went to many parts of the world, to the island of Britain, the coast of Gaul and even south to Iberia.

'A physician?' Fidelma queried sharply.

'The physician from Lios Mór.'

'Are you speaking of Brother Seachlann?' she asked slowly.

'Seachlann, that was his name. It was Brother Seachlann who came to our abbey some days ago in search of herbs that had been lately carried from Gaul. He told us that the books were ready and being shipped by barge to the abbey. Thus we were forewarned to gather thirty *seds* to pay the bargemen, but the barge never arrived. Then we heard that the Uí Liatháin had stolen the books.'

'How did Brother Seachlann know that the books from Fhear Maighe were ready?'

The librarian shrugged. 'No one asked. What need was there to ask? We were happy to hear the news.'

There came a shout from one of the sentinels and the sound of approaching horses. The warrior commander went quickly to the entrance of the fortress just as a band of horsemen entered.

The leader of the newcomers was not an ugly man but he

could not be described as handsome. He was a bearded, middle-aged man, clad entirely in black, with burnished armour and plumed war helmet. He wore his weaponry in such a way that it was obvious that he was no novice in the use of arms.

The commander saluted the man respectfully and held his horse while he dismounted.

'So what have we here?' the newcomer thundered. 'Innocent wayfarers or spies from the Fhear Maighe?'

They had all risen and Gormán took an aggressive step forward but Fidelma held him back. But the young warrior paid her no attention and shouted in a firm voice, 'You stand in the presence of Fidelma of Cashel, sister to your King, Colgú, son of Failbe Flann. Do I, Gormán of the Nasc Niadh, need to teach you a lesson in respect?'

The newcomer stared at Gormán, then he saw the golden circlet round his neck that denoted membership of the Nasc Niadh. He turned his head to examine Fidelma and his eyes widened in recognition.

He strode forward with a grin spreading over his features but first he spoke to Gormán.

'Be at peace, young cockerel. You could not teach me anything.' Then he gazed at Fidelma for a moment more before he held out his hands. 'It is so,' he said quietly. 'Fidelma of Cashel. Was I not at your wedding celebration last year?' He glanced at Eadulf. 'And with Eadulf of Seaxmund's Ham. The Saxon whose fame is spoken of even in our tiny part of the world.'

Fidelma allowed herself to be caught in a bear hug and

then Eadulf found himself similarly smothered before the chieftain swung round to his men and thundered, 'Why are they held prisoners?'

The commander hung his head as if in shame. 'I thought—'

'Not clearly enough,' bellowed his chieftain, turning back with a broad smile again. 'Forgive us, lady.'

Fidelma did not respond to his smile but gazed evenly at him.

'Why do you ride in a war band, Uallachán of the Uí Liatháin, when my brother's kingdom is at peace?' she demanded. 'I am told you ride against Fhear Maighe?'

The big man raised one shoulder and let it fall. 'It is true that there is a score to be settled with Cumscrad. We ride to punish him for his lies.'

'Do you claim that you have not done so already?' replied Fidelma. Uallachán looked uncertain. Fidelma went on, 'We have just ridden from Fhear Maighe where I have seen the library attacked by sword and fire and it now lies in ruins with many priceless works destroyed. The librarian Dubhagan lies dead. Several are injured. The attackers rode in under your banner. One of the attackers was killed, he was a *bánaí*. Tell me, Uallachán, what score needs to be settled?'

There was no disguising the utter astonishment on Uallachán's face. The man was no actor and he was clearly shocked at her news.

'My people are not responsible for this. And I have, or had, no *bánaí* riding among my warriors.'

'Then we must discover who is responsible. The same people, under the same banner, took the barge of Muirgíos of the Fir Maige Féne and stole two valuable books from it. The blood of the Fir Maige Féne has been spilt enough.'

'But not by us,' protested Uallachán. 'Let us sit a while and you tell me the story as you know it.'

They did so and Fidelma outlined the accusations that she had heard about the Uí Liatháin. Uallachán did not interrupt but sat listening patiently. When she had finished, he shook his head slowly.

'As Christ is my witness, lady, I know nothing of this. What would I want with such books, let alone want to destroy them? How can Cumscrad demand retribution for something I did not do? Can you not persuade Cumscrad that he must defer to the judgement of yourself and your brother?'

'I would hope that both of you will accept such judgement,' replied Fidelma. She sighed and then suddenly asked, 'Do you know of a cousin of yours, Gáeth, who is currently a member of the brethren in Lios Mór?'

Uallachán looked surprised at the abrupt change of subject.

'Gáeth, the son of Selbach of Dún Guairne?'

'The same.'

'His father was my cousin and found guilty of *fingal*, the kin-slaying of my uncle, who was chief before me. He was judged harshly, in my opinion, and consigned to the fate of the wind and waves. But the night before the sentence was due to be carried out, he escaped. He took his wife and Gáeth, who was hardly more than a child. Why do you ask? What has that to do with this matter?'

'Probably nothing at all. Yet I am interested. In law, a wife and child does not have to share the fate of the husband. They do not have to become *daer-fudir*.'

'That is true but Selbach's wife chose that fate. She was loyal to her husband. However, if Gáeth has become a member of the community at Lios Mór, it means that he has freed himself from that stigma.'

Fidelma look at him curiously. 'You did not insist that even as a member of the brethren he be regarded as a *daer-fudir* and be consigned to work as a field labourer?'

Uallachán uttered a short laugh. 'Why would I do that? I thought the punishment given to his father was harsh enough at the time. Anything else is simply revenge.'

'You did not inform the abbot that, even if Gáeth joined the abbey, he must remain a field worker.'

'Doesn't the law in some place say that every dead man kills his own liabilities?'

Fidelma smiled and nodded. 'Thank you, Uallachán. Now, let us return to this matter between you and Cumscrad. This is my condition, and I will send Gormán here back to Cumscrad with a similar condition. I want you, Brother Temnen and a chosen warrior to go to a *bruden*, a hostel, on the Rian Bó Phádraig where it crosses the Abh Beag, the little river, south of Lios Mór. Do you know the place?'

'I do,' said the leader of the Uí Liatháin.

'You will wait there until I send for you to come to Lios Mór at a time when I am ready to render judgement.'

'And is Cumscrad to be there as well? How can I stay there if Cumscrad is there?' he protested.

'Cumscrad will be told to wait at another place, awaiting a similar message from me. You will not know where, and he will not know where you are. I do that for the protection of you both. I will send messengers to you at the same time, asking you both to come to the abbey, freely, without prejudice and with no warrior guards apart from your single bodyguard. Is that understood?'

'I understand the terms, lady, but not the reason.'

'You may have to await my message for several days but it will be sent and this matter resolved. A judgement shall be made about the tensions between your peoples. I begin to realise that there is a greater judgement to be made, of which your conflict is but a smaller part, although an important part – an attempt to distract me from reaching the truth.'

CHAPTER SEVENTEEN

It was Brother Echen, the keeper of the stables, who greeted them as they rode through the gates of the abbey of Lios Mór early the following morning. They had spent a night at the hostel by the Abh Beag where they had left Uallachán and his companions to wait until Fidelma was ready to call them. It was a short ride. Gormán had been sent back to Fhear Maighe to see Cumscrad and give him similar instructions. Now Brother Echen came forward and he was clearly agitated as they swung down from their horses. He began to speak excitedly even before Fidelma reached the ground.

'Glassán, the master builder, has been killed, Sister.'

'When?' demanded Fidelma.

'His body was found only a short time ago.'

'How was he killed and where?' Eadulf asked.

'Where else but on the building site?' Brother Echen replied. 'He has just been found by the little boy, his foster-son, as the builders were coming to start work.'

Before they could question the man further, Fidelma's name was called from across the quadrangle. They turned. Brother Lugna was striding towards them.

They left Brother Echen attending their horses.

'I presume that Brother Echen has told you the news?' was Brother Lugna's opening question. His expression registered no emotion.

'He has. What happened?'

'An accident. One of the stones of the building fell on him.'

'There seems to have been too many accidents on this building site,' Eadulf commented drily.

'Such things happen,' replied the steward in a terse tone.

'Let us see where this happened.' Fidelma turned and made for the half-finished building.

The body still lay where it had fallen. Brother Seachlann was examining it and beside him was Saor, the carpenter and assistant master builder.

Abbot Iarnla looked relieved as he spotted their approach.

'Thanks be that you have arrived back,' he greeted Fidelma. 'As you see, we have yet another tragedy on our hands.'

The group stood back while Fidelma moved forward to look down at the body of Glassán, the master builder. His body lay on its back under a small doorway amidst a pile of debris. Some large blocks of stone that had been dressed were nearby. One of them was stained with blood but there was no blood on the man's face or the front of his body.

'He has been moved,' Eadulf said, stating the obvious.

Brother Seachlann nodded. 'He was lying face down. A heavy stone crushed the back of his head. I turned him on to his back to see if he had any injuries to his front. As you can see, there are none.'

'It is sad,' offered Saor. 'But it seems clear what must have happened. Glassán came here to inspect the work early this morning and a loose stone fell as he was passing this wall.' He pointed upwards to where the wall was unfinished and some dressed stones seemed not to have been placed correctly. He shook his head. 'These accidents can some-times happen.'

'Sometimes?' Eadulf's inflection was cynical as he bent down beside the body. Then he raised his eyes to the physician. 'With your permission, Brother Seachlann?'

'I have finished my examination, Brother,' the man answered with a shrug.

Eadulf turned the corpse on to its front and examined the back of the skull. They could all see the massive injury. There was little doubt how the master builder had come by his death. To Fidelma it seemed that Eadulf spent a longer time than necessary peering at the injury before standing up. Then she saw from his expression that he had noticed something.

'Is it all right to remove the body now?' asked Brother Seachlann.

Fidelma glanced at Eadulf who nodded.

'I understand the foster-son, Gúasach, found the body,' Fidelma said. 'I will need to have a word with him.'

'He is being comforted by Brother Donnán in the *scriptorium*,' Abbot Iarnla told her.

Saor was helping Brother Seachlann lift the body of the master builder in order to carry it to the *bróinbherg*.

Brother Lugna looked on, still expressionless, as the two men began to carry the body out of the debris. He muttered a swift apology to the abbot and hurried after them.

Abbot Iarnla remained, looking helpless and undecided. 'Is there anything that I should do?' he asked.

'Just tell me what you know,' Fidelma suggested. 'I am told that it was not long ago that young Gúasach came to the site, presumably to start work. He found his foster-father here, already dead. What then?'

'I was not witness to this, Fidelma. I was in my chamber when Brother Lugna came to tell me the news.'

'How was Brother Lugna told?'

'I think the boy raised the alarm with Brother Seachlann. Then a passing member of the brethren told Brother Lugna. By the time I came here with Brother Lugna, I found the physician and Saor standing with the body. The physician had asked our *scriptor* to look after the boy. As we were contemplating the removal of the body, we saw your return to the abbey and Brother Lugna went to inform you of what had happened.'

Fidelma stood in thoughtful silence for a moment and then said, 'Very well. You had better ensure that the brethren are not alarmed over this. A second death in the abbey will be disturbing. It would be best to carry on with your routines without interruption.'

Abbot Iarnla hesitated, a worried expression on his features.

'You are right, of course . . . but surely there are no links between this accident and Brother Donnchad's death, are there?'

Fidelma smiled as if pacifying a child. 'What links would there be?' she countered.

Abbot Iarnla took this as a negative and, nodding slightly, he turned and hurried off.

Fidelma looked at Eadulf. 'What?' she demanded.

'He was murdered,' Eadulf replied simply.

'How did you make that out?'

Eadulf raised a fist and opened it. On his palm lay a number of bloodstained slivers of wood. 'No one seemed to notice that I picked these from the wound at the back of his skull. From these splinters I would say the wood was blackthorn, which is pretty hard.'

Fidelma looked closely at the splinters.

'Well done, Eadulf,' she murmured, appreciatively. 'How do you interpret the event?'

'I believe that someone came up behind him and hit him with a stick. He has been dead some time.'

Fidelma knew that Eadulf did not just make guesses on such matters.

'Because?'

'The body was stiff and cold.'

'So he came here in the dark?'

'Certainly some time before first light.'

As he spoke, Eadulf was looking around the area where

the master builder had fallen. His brow was creased in a frown of concentration.

'What are you looking for?' Fidelma asked patiently.

'That!' said Eadulf in triumph, pointing.

Just behind where she was standing was a piece of half-burnt candle and a battered holder. Eadulf looked back to where the body had been lying with its feet towards the candle.

'I think he came here after dark,' he said slowly. 'Why? I suspect he came to meet someone. Whoever was waiting for him could not replicate what happened to me – it had been tried once, and Glassán might well have been on his guard. So they hit him over the head – so hard their blackthorn cudgel splintered around the skull. But I would have expected the candle he was carrying to have been flung forward by the impact of the blow, not behind him.'

Fidelma regarded him with approval. 'Well spotted, Eadulf. How do you explain it?'

'Having knocked him out, they pulled the body to the place where he was found. This was to ensure he was under a half-finished wall. They smeared one of the stones with his blood so that it looked as if the stone had fallen and killed him. But they forgot the candle.'

'How can you be sure they moved the body?'

He examined the area just behind her and pointed without comment.

Fidelma saw that there were little spots of blood on the debris there and one tiny almost dried-up pool.

'In the dark, the killer did not manage to clean up all the evidence.' Eadulf paused. 'It seems clear that the attack on me was intended for Glassán. But when I held up the candle and was recognised, one of the killers pushed me out of the way of the falling stone.'

Fidelma nodded in agreement. 'There had to be two killers to accomplish that.'

'There were probably two attackers this time as well.'

'And don't forget that we have heard of other so-called accidents. These must all have been attempts to kill Glassán. After the last one, where you were nearly killed, the attackers probably gave up the idea of trying to make it look like an accident. They must have made sure he was killed first and then fixed things later to seem like an accident.' She looked around and then said, 'Let us have a word with the boy.'

'I can't see the connection between Glassán and Donnchad,' Eadulf said as he fell in step with her.

'Perhaps there isn't,' Fidelma replied.

'But it would surely be a curious coincidence.'

'Coincidence defeats a well-laid plan, Eadulf,' Fidelma remarked.

Eadulf thrust out his lower lip as he pondered this.

'I am inclined to think that the reason might lie in the master builder's reputation. Wherever a man goes, his character goes with him.'

Fidelma smiled at him but said nothing.

Brother Donnán met them at the door of the *scriptorium* with a sad face.

'Have you come to see the boy?' he asked, as they came up the steps into the building.

'Is he able to answer some questions?' asked Fidelma.

'He is young but he is strong. However, it was a shock for him and he is far from home.'

'Thank you for looking after him, Brother Donnán,' she answered. 'Where is he?'

The *scriptor* indicated a spot at the far end of the library where the boy was seated, staring before him. He held a mug in his hand, which he was regarding morosely.

'I thought, in the circumstances, a little wine might help to ease his distress,' muttered Brother Donnán.

Fidelma walked to where Gúasach sat. Eadulf followed with Brother Donnán.

'Hello, Gúasach,' she said as the boy looked up at her approach.

'Hello, Sister,' he replied, his voice firm.

'How are you feeling?'

'I do not know. I have been in fosterage to Glassán for three years. He was not a nice person. He did not treat me well but he was my legal fosterer and instructor. What am I to do now?'

Fidelma drew up a small stool and sat by the boy.

'Before you tell me all you know of this morning, let me assure you that you must not worry about that. You will be looked after. Now, what can you tell me about finding Glassán?'

'Not much to tell,' replied the boy. 'I rose at the usual

time, at first light. I came to the abbey to make sure all was prepared for the day's work. That is what I usually did.'

'You live in the workers' cabins outside the abbey walls, don't you?'

'By the riverside,' he confirmed.

'And Glassán lived in the guesthouse in the abbey. So you would not have seen him until you came to the site. Isn't that unusual for a foster-child?'

The boy shrugged. 'I would not know. It was the way things were. Glassán always treated me as one of his workers and told me what work I should do. It was the others who taught me their skills when they had time.'

The corner of Fidelma's mouth turned down in disapproval. It was not the custom of fosterage. The foster-child usually became part of the fosterer's family, lived, ate and slept with them as one of them and was given their education with them. It seemed Glassán simply treated the boy as one of his work-force from whom he expected a day's work as well as the fee from the boy's father for his training.

'So you came to the abbey at first light. Did you see anyone about?'

'Brother Echen was up and cleaning the stables,' the boy said. 'He is usually up first and he opens the gates of the abbey. The ugly brother was coming through the gates at the same time.'

'The ugly brother?' queried Fidelma.

'He has a name like "wind" or something similar.'

She frowned.

'He means Brother Gáeth,' interpreted Brother Donnán. Fidelma smiled as she suddenly realised the connection. The name Gáeth actually meant 'clever' or 'wise', whereas *gáith* meant 'wind'.

'Was anyone else about?'

'The steward was crossing the quadrangle.'

'Brother Lugna?'

'I do not like him,' the boy confessed. 'I don't think he likes me.'

Fidelma nearly agreed aloud but she remained silent.

'Did he say anything to you?'

'He never speaks to me.'

'So what happened next?'

'I came up to the building that we were working on to make sure the tools were all ready for when the men came to work. It was there that I saw the body. You couldn't miss it once you came into the building. I saw he was dead at once. The back of his head—'

'We know,' Fidelma assured him. 'Do not think about that. What did you do then?'

'I knew where the physician worked, not far away. I ran there immediately. He asked me what was wrong and I told him.'

'Brother Seachlann was already at work?'

'He was in that little place where the men sometimes go to get salves when they are cut or bruised on the site.'

'So you told him what was wrong. Then what?'

'When we came out, one of the brethren was passing by

and the physician called to him and told him to find the steward, that there had been an accident and that Glassán was badly injured. I had already told him he was dead,' the boy added after a pause. 'I am not that young that I do not know what death is.'

'Brother Seachlann went with you to the body?'

The boy nodded.

'Then what?'

'He confirmed that Glassán was dead, by which time the steward came and also the abbot. Then Saor appeared and he suggested that I should be taken to Brother Donnán here while they made a further examination. It was while I was coming here that I saw you and Brother Eadulf coming through the gates.' He paused and then added, 'I'm glad you came, Sister. Now that Glassán is gone and I am far from home, I do not know what I should do.'

Fidelma reached forward and patted the boy on the arm to comfort him. 'I have said that you do not need to worry. Back in your own lands, where Glassán lived before he came here to work on the abbey, did he have a house? Did he keep cattle?'

The boy nodded.

'Did he have a wife and sons?'

'He had a farm and employed a *saer-fudir* to watch over it as his tenant. But he had no wife or child.'

'In that case, I will see that you return to your father and I will send instructions to the Brehon of your clan so that the cows that your father paid to Glassán for your fosterage are returned to him. Then, if you and your father wish it, you might find another master builder to take you as a *felmacc*, or pupil.'

The boy seemed slightly relieved that he was not to be cast out into the country without anyone to care for him although he was clearly confused by the legal detail that Fidelma had given him.

Fidelma glanced at Brother Donnán. 'Perhaps it can be arranged for Gúasach to remain in the abbey until this matter is cleared up. I will ensure that things are sorted out for him.'

'I will arrange it with Brother Máel Eoin at the hostel.' The *scriptor* turned to the boy with a smile. 'There, did I not say you had no cause to worry? All is well.'

Fidelma and Eadulf bade farewell to the boy and left the library building.

'Will the young lad truly be looked after?' asked Eadulf once they were outside.

'The resolution of this situation is provided in law,' replied Fidelma. 'The boy was given in fosterage to Glassán, being a master builder. He was to instruct him in the craft of building. We have a set of laws called the *Cáin Íarraith*, the law on fosterage and fees. Basically, Glassán was his *fithidir*, his instructor, and he was a *felmacc*, a pupil. If a foster-child has to return prematurely to his father for whatever reason, then the foster fee, the *íarraith*, must be repaid in full. Only if Gúasach had been guilty of serious misconduct could Glassán or his heir be exempt from returning the fee. So, under law, the boy must be escorted back to his father with the entire fee and neither he nor his father loses by what has happened.'

'I see,' Eadulf said. 'So, what next?'

'We will have a look in Glassán's room in the guesthouse. Perhaps he has left an *audacht*, a will. Most people engaged in dangerous work do so. But first I want another word with Brother Seachlann while I think about it.'

Eadulf knew the custom of Fidelma's people to leave a will, a set of instructions covering the disposal of their property. It was apparently an ancient custom, which dated back long before the coming of Christianity, for it was believed that death was not an ending but the gateway into the Otherworld. So before one went on the *fecht-uath*, or grave journey, as it was called, those who could do so made a will.

They found Brother Seachlann alone in his *bróinbherg* and engaged in preparing the *racholl*, or winding sheet, to wrap the body of Glassán for burial.

The physician looked up with a frown.

'Do you need to examine the body again?' he asked irritably. 'I have already washed it.'

'It is not Glassán I needed to speak to you about,' Fidelma replied. 'I hear that you recently went on a trip to Ard Mór.'

Brother Seachlann looked surprised.

'I did,' he admitted.

'May I ask why?'

'It is no secret. I went to get some herbs for preparations. There is a market there where ships from over the seas land their cargoes and often you can find herbs of great benefit to—'

Fidelma raised her hand impatiently. 'You also visited the abbey with a message from Fhear Maighe.'

'What of that?'

'How did you come by that message?'

'How?' He frowned as if trying to think. 'From a young man from Fhear Maighe who knew I was journeying to Ard Mór.'

Fidelma suppressed a sigh. 'Who was he and how did he know you were on your way to Ard Mór?'

'I have no idea of his name. He was a young religieux who I met in the *scriptorium*. The *scriptor* told me that he often carried messages between the abbeys. He had come from Fhear Maighe and had an urgent message for the abbot of Ard Mór. He was worried for he had also to take an urgent message to the abbey at Fionán's Height, which is north across the mountains. As I was riding to Ard Mór that same day to get the herbs, I offered to help and we parted happily.'

Fidelma was quiet for a moment. 'What was the message?'

'Simply that certain books were being sent by river from Fhear Maighe to Ard Mór. I forget when the barge was due to arrive, although I was told at the time, and the name of the barge. The abbot was to have payment ready when it arrived. What does all this mean?'

'Perhaps nothing,' Fidelma replied quietly. 'Were you given the names of the books?'

'I cannot remember now. I recall that I had the titles written down by the *scriptor* in case I forgot them. He did so on a piece of bark. I gave that to the abbot at Ard Mór.'

'You definitely gave the list to the abbot at Ard Mór on your arrival?'

'I have said so.'

'Very well,' Fidelma said thoughtfully. 'I thank you for your help.'

'And you do not want to examine this corpse further?' Brother Seachlann asked, indicating the body of Glassán.

'I do not. When will he be buried?'

'It is the custom of this abbey to have a day of watching and then to bury the corpse at midnight. We did not find the corpse until the early hours of this morning but Brother Lugna has said that as he died in the night, the obsequies should be carried out tonight.'

Fidelma glanced at Eadulf. 'I thought the *laithina canti*, the time of watching and lamentation, should be a full day and night.'

Brother Seachlann sniffed slightly. 'He was not part of this abbey community. I suppose Brother Lugna takes into account that there appear to be few people willing to take part in the *aire*, the wake. But he has instructed that he is to be buried in the plot to the east of the abbey where other members of the brethren are laid to rest.'

'Brother Lugna seems to be in a hurry to bury Glassán,' observed Eadulf once they were outside. 'Surely some of Glassán's workmen will want to keep watch over the body according to the custom?'

'We will have a word with Saor about that. There are many things that Brother Lugna does that surprise me.'

'Well, I think we also have reason to be suspicious of Brother Seachlann.'

'He certainly took the news of the books coming by river to Ard Mór. We have established that. He might well have been part of the chain that caused the news to fall into the hands of those that attacked the river barge and stole them.'

'Why is this Celsus book so important and how is it connected to the death of Brother Donnchad?' Eadulf asked irritably. 'And to everything else that has gone on here? I don't understand it.'

'Didn't Julius Caesar comment, *In bello parvis momentis magni casus intercedunt*?'

'In war great events are the result of small causes,' he murmured in translation.

Fidelma nodded. 'In other words, Eadulf, pay attention to the small details. By doing so, you will find that patience will reveal the matter.'

'Well, I already feel exhausted,' Eadulf remarked, as they walked across the stone flags of the quadrangle. 'We have travelled a considerable distance these last few days.'

'If we had not then we would not now be as close as we are to a solution,' she pointed out. Before Eadulf could form his question, she began to walk to the guesthouse calling over her shoulder, 'Now, let us search Glassán's room.'

CHAPTER EIGHTEEN

As they passed the fountain in the centre of the quadrangle, the sound of raised, angry voices caused them
to look towards the gates of the abbey. They saw Brother
Lugna facing a band of men, whom they immediately recognised as the builders. Among them was Saor. Brother Lugna
was standing in a belligerent posture that seemed curiously
grotesque for a man of the Faith. Even as they looked, the
builders turned their backs on him and walked through the
gates. As they did so, Gormán rode into the abbey courtyard
and swung off his horse. Fidelma and Eadulf went to join
him. The steward had not moved from his position, standing
staring after the disappearing builders.

'Is all well, Gormán?' Fidelma greeted the warrior.

'Everything is as you instructed, lady.' Gormán smiled.
'The conditions are agreed. Both chiefs await your message.'

Fidelma glanced across to Brother Lugna. Anger had made

his countenance fierce. Suddenly aware of their presence, he tried to relax his features.

'There seems to be some trouble with Glassán's men,' Fidelma observed.

'True enough,' replied the steward through between clenched teeth. 'They are refusing to come back to work. They say there have been too many accidents on the abbey buildings for them to continue. They demand their wages and say that they are leaving.'

It was clear that the steward was more upset at the demand for wages than by the death of the master builder.

'Can you continue the work here without a master builder?' Eadulf asked.

'There is always someone who can take over,' replied the steward immediately. 'I am sure that Saor is qualified but he seems to agree with the workers. It is not that there is no one suitable; the problem is the stupid superstition of these country people. If this abbey were operating under the Penitentials, I would have every man of them flogged until they undertook the work with enthusiasm.'

He spoke with such vehemence that Eadulf could not disguise the distaste he felt. Like the Roman law they originated from, the rules of the Penitentials were based on physical punishment, bodily mortification and ritual maiming which even included the removal of limbs of those found guilty of breaking the rules. The discipline was completely at odds with the spirit and nature of the native Law of the Fénechus. Eadulf knew that Fidelma regarded them in abhorrence in those few abbeys where zealots of the Faith had managed to introduce them. Usually, they went with those communities of single sex where the rule of celibacy had been enforced. Eadulf shivered slightly. He had come to appreciate the Fénechus laws as being more humane and progressive, based on compensation for the victim and rehabilitation for the perpetrator. Physical punishment was simply bloodthirsty vengeance.

Brother Lugna regarded Eadulf's look of disgust with an arrogant expression of pity.

'One day all members of the Faith will fear God and the Penitentials,' the steward added. 'There is too much laxity in this land . . .' He paused. 'Fear is a great persuader, Brother Eadulf. How else can I get them back to work when it is fear that now causes them to run away? Confronted by superstitious fear, one must offer a greater fear.'

Fidelma shook her head. 'I will reason with Saor and his men. Not to keep them at work but because they must remain here until my investigations are complete.'

'I doubt whether Saor will listen to you. Anyway, I must go to inform the abbot. He seems to be in a state of panic about everything, as usual.'

'Glassán was legally required to present you with a list of his workers. Did he do so?'

'Of course. And if these men march off now, I shall consider the contract with the abbey broken and I shall not pay them.'

'Really?' she said quickly. 'Wasn't the contract with Glassán to employ the men he thought fit?'

'I paid them individually on behalf of the abbey. I did not trust Glassán to resist helping himself to a little extra.'

Fidelma regarded the steward thoughtfully for a moment. 'Well, Brother Lugna, I think I know an argument that will persuade these men to stay.'

Gormán joined Fidelma and Eadulf as she led the way determinedly through the gates of the abbey and towards the scattered collection of wicker and wattle cabins, called *bothan*, that the workmen lived in. As they approached there were signs of men moving about, collecting their belongings. A couple noticed their approach, stood still and fell silent.

'Where is Saor?' Fidelma asked the nearest man.

She received a shrug in response but after a moment or two the carpenter appeared from one of the huts. He did not meet her eyes but came forward, head down. 'The men have made up their minds, Sister. We have had enough of this accursed site.' Then he glanced at Eadulf. 'I am surprised that you are still here after your life was nearly taken. This is not normal. There are forces at work here that we cannot oppose. Dark forces. Lives have been taken. We cannot stand against evil.'

There was a muttering of assent among the men who had gathered round them to hear what Fidelma had to say.

'On the contrary,' Fidelma raised her voice above the hubbub, 'the forces at work here are man-made and if you run away then whoever did this killing might be among you and you are providing them with an opportunity to escape justice.'

Saor's eyes narrowed. 'Do you accuse one of us? Why would we kill our own master builder? This does not make sense.'

'All things make sense once the causes are known,' replied Fidelma. 'I am requesting that every one of you remain here until the truth is known.'

Saor shook his head. 'The men and I have had enough, Sister. Brother Lugna must pay what he owes and allow us to depart.'

'If you all walk away now then it will be you who are breaking the contract and you will have to go to arbitration over your payment. The abbey does not have to pay you if you break your contract. For once, I have to agree with the steward.'

This caused an angry muttering among some of the workmen. Gormán slid his hand to his sword hilt and eased his balance slightly. It was not a threatening movement but enough to remind them of his presence. Saor, however, was not persuaded by Fidelma's argument.

'Our contracts were with the master builder who is dead,' he said. 'So perhaps they are already terminated. The steward insisted on paying us individually, for he likes exercising power. But Glassán employed us. The abbey can't refuse what is due to us.'

'You speak like a lawyer, Saor,' interposed Eadulf.

The carpenter thrust out his jaw aggressively. 'I am no lawyer. But I say this job is over.'

This brought a protest from one of the men near him.

'Perhaps the sister is right. We have wives and children to feed and if we walk away now we shall not be paid. Arbitration will take a long time.'

Saor swung round to him. 'There have been too many accidents on this site. It is not a safe place, and now that Glassán is dead, there is no one to speak for us.'

'You are the assistant, you are now responsible,' replied one of the men.

'And I tell you, I am leaving,' replied Saor grimly. 'I have no wish to be associated with—'

'I suggest that you all stay here so that this matter may be sorted out,' Fidelma interrupted. 'The events that led to Glassán's death will soon be made clear. When it is, his contract with this abbey will be renegotiated so that you may come or go as you will and with the payment you are owed. There seems to be some disagreement among you as to whether you will remain . . .'

Saor replied: 'There is no disagreement, Sister. We will go with or without the money for we have no wish to remain.'

Some of the men looked doubtful but none spoke.

'Very well.' Fidelma was clearly exasperated. 'You seem to be rejecting my suggestion. Now I make it an order.'

Saor looked at her. 'An order?' His surprise dissolved into humour and he gave a short bark of laughter. 'What right do you have to give us orders?'

Fidelma regarded him with a long, cool look.

'Some of you know that I came to this abbey to investigate the death of Brother Donnchad,' she said firmly. 'You know that I am a *dálaigh*, a member of the Brehon courts, qualified to the level of *anruth*. Even the High King must respect my decisions.'

A nervous silence fell.

She glanced towards Gormán. 'The emblem this warrior wears proclaims him to be of the Nasc Niadh, bodyguards to the King of Muman. Know you further,' went on Fidelma, speaking in a deliberate tone, 'that I am Fidelma of Cashel, sister of your King, Colgú mac Failbe Flann. Someone has been killed here and I declare that you are all legal witnesses. You will remain here until this matter has been resolved or face the fine for contempt of the authority of the Law of the Fénechus.'

Saor regarded her, surprise and bewilderment crossing his features.

'You can't do that,' he said but there was uncertainty in his voice.

'But I can. Under the terms of the texts of the *Berrad Airechta*, I formally name you all as *fiadu*, witnesses. You are all called as witnesses and your *drach*, the legal term of your security to appear when called, will be your honour price. If any of you fail to appear when I call you, you will forfeit your honour price.'

Saor was shaking his head. 'You can't do that,' he repeated but he had no conviction in his voice.

'Try me,' Fidelma smiled grimly. 'Glassán handed a list of your names to the steward of the abbey, as the law requires, so do not think you are not known. If you do not report on the day I fix for the hearing of this matter, you will be hunted down by the King's warriors and forcibly brought before a Brehon who will strip you of your honour price.'

The men stood in silence and then one of them spoke up. 'We will stay, then.'

'That is good,' returned Fidelma with ill-concealed irony. 'Do not think that I wish you to remain against your will as a mere whim. The law can be hard but it is the law.' She paused, to let her words settle, then went on, 'I understand the physician is preparing the body of your master builder for burial at midnight. I presume some of you will be going to the *aire*.'

There was a shuffling among the men and no one replied.

Fidelma hesitated and said, 'That is your choice. Some might say that workers who do not respect their master builder in death could not have had any respect for him in life.'

She turned with Eadulf and they began to make their way back to the abbey. Gormán waited a moment or two, hand still on his sword hilt, before he followed.

'A miserable lot,' he said pleasantly as he caught up with them. 'They don't seem too keen on their employer.'

'Perhaps they have their reasons,' replied Fidelma drily. 'Someone certainly had reason enough to kill him.'

'I just can't see the connection between Glassán and Donnchad because the two murders must be linked,' Eadulf commented.

'Maybe we are looking for a connection in the wrong place,' she replied. 'And speaking of looking, let us return to our search in Glassán's *cubiculum*. There is no need for you to come, Gormán, but stay close, we may have need of you.'

They did not meet anyone on their way to the *tech-oíged*. Not even the hosteller, Brother Máel Eoin. They knew Glassán had occupied a *cubiculum* at the far end of the oblong building which they also shared. The hostel was quite deserted as they entered.

Glassán's room was almost featureless; the furnishings were sparse. If Glassán had occupied the place for nearly three years then he had not believed in many personal touches.

A crucifix alone decorated one wall of greying wattle and daub plaster. A bed, a table, a chair, and a trunk comprised the furnishing. The blanket on the bed was folded untidily. A few changes of clothes were hung in a corner, and two pairs of sturdy leather shoes of the type a builder would wear were on the floor in a corner. A couple of amphorae stood by the wall and the smell of stale wine came from them but they were both empty. A lantern, some candles and stubs, and a tinderbox were on top of the trunk. On the table were rolls of papyrus filled with lists, columns of figures and plans.

'The designs for the new buildings,' Eadulf announced after glancing at them.

'Check them through, Eadulf, just in case there is anything there of interest,' Fidelma replied, turning her attention to the trunk and beginning to remove the candles and items on top of it. Then she tried to open it. It was locked.

'Did you see if Glassán had a key on his body?' she asked.

Eadulf looked up from the papers and shook his head. 'He had nothing in which to carry a key or anything like that.'

Fidelma glanced round the room. She went to the head of the small bed and lifted the pillow. Then she bent and pulled back the straw mattress. Two keys lay there and a purse. 'Predictable,' she muttered. She returned to the trunk. It was clear that one of the keys was intended for it.

At first she thought there were just a few clothes in it and more building plans. Then she saw several leather bags at the bottom of the trunk. They were filled with gold and silver coins. Eadulf came to stand at her shoulder and gazed down with a soft whistle.

'Is it his own money, do you think, or money to pay his workers?' he asked.

'Brother Lugna paid the workers, not Glassán. This is his own money and he acquired a tidy sum.'

She counted three leather bags and, while each could be balanced in the palm of a hand, they were heavy. Then she took out a small scroll, tied with a coloured ribbon. She untied it and smoothed it out. Eadulf could see it was written in the language of the Five Kingdoms and headed *Cendaite Glassán*.

'Glassán's will?' he hazarded. The words were mostly unfamiliar, but he knew that there were three ancient words for a will.

Fidelma nodded and began to read.

'In the presence of the Brehon Lurg of the Uí Briuin Sinna, I, Glassán, originally of the Uí Dego of Ferna, declare myself a sinner before Christ. Being a sinner and exile, I am an outcast without kith or ken, with neither wife nor children to sustain me. Should I die with only a few items to redeem me, I declare that my farm in the country of the Uí Briuin Sinna will return to the chief of that people who gave me succour in exile. I rely on him to dispose of the claims of my clients and tenants as he sees fit. I have one boy in fosterage and if I die before he reaches the age of maturity and becomes qualified, the full fees of this fosterage shall be returned to his father, as is the law. Further, I deem that he be given, out of the funds I have acquired, his father's honour price so that he may be placed in another fosterer's care to achieve the qualifications necessary to become a master builder. I will die truly repenting all the ills that I have done in my life, the sins that I have committed by thoughtlessness and neglect. *Ego contra erravi, ignosco mihi, quaeso!*'

Peering over her shoulder, Eadulf grunted with derision.

'I suspect that bit of bad Latin expressing his guilt and asking for forgiveness was put in by the Brehon who drew up the will. I don't think Glassán knew much Latin.'

'Even so, Glassán was admitting his responsibility for his past and at least he was thoughtful enough to make provision for young Gúasach. He was not entirely a bad man.'

'I suppose not,' Eadulf admitted reluctantly. 'What happens now? I mean to the young boy.'

'The will and the boy, with these bags of money and Glassán's belongings, will be returned to Brehon Lurg in Connachta.'

'What are you doing here?' The voice of Brother Lugna

cut suddenly into the chamber. They had not noticed him standing in the doorway.

Fidelma was unperturbed as she glanced up to look at him.

'Glassán died in suspicious circumstances,' she replied, rising to her feet. 'It is my right to investigate anything that might cast a light on the circumstances of his death.'

'You came here to investigate Brother Donnchad's death, not that of Glassán,' the steward protested.

'As a *dálaigh* it is in my power to investigate anything I consider relevant. You should know that. The master builder's will is here, with money and possessions that belonged to him. I shall have them sealed in this trunk and removed to my room so that, when the time comes, it will be sent back to Connachta with the boy Gúasach. The will mentions that the boy is a beneficiary.'

Brother Lugna swallowed hard. He was clearly not happy that they had beaten him to an examination of the chamber.

'I suppose you are within your rights,' he admitted reluctantly.

'You may well suppose it,' Fidelma answered acidly. She stood looking at him.

'I came to ensure that his belongings were safe,' muttered the steward, dropping his eyes.

'They are safe enough.'

'The body has been transferred to the chapel and will be watched there until midnight when the *clog-estechtae*, the death bell, will sound and the members of the community will accompany the corpse to the funeral place,' the steward went on gruffly. 'He was not a member of our community, nor does he have blood family among us. So only two members of the brethren will bear witness at the *aire* in the chapel. Our evening meal must serve as the *fled cro-lige*, the feast of the deathbed.'

Fidelma inclined her head. 'We will be attending, Brother Lugna,' she said gravely.

He hesitated, made as if to say something, and then dropped his gaze, turned and left.

'He looks disappointed,' murmured Eadulf. 'Do you think . . .' He gestured with his head towards the bags of coin.

'Help me pack these things up,' Fidelma instructed, not answering his unfinished question. 'We'll move them into your room.'

Eadulf frowned. 'But you said you were putting them in your room.'

Fidelma gave one of her rare, mischievous grins. 'I did, didn't I? Well, just in case . . .'

Eadulf sighed and moved forward to help her with the trunk.

Two members of the community sat silently in the chapel by the corpse for the traditional watching of the body, the *aire*. The only movement was the flickering of the candles at the head and feet of the body as it lay on the wooden board that was the *fuat*, the bier, on which the corpse would soon be carried to the graveyard. The silence was unusual. There was none of the *laithina canti*, the lamentations, the clapping of hands or cries of despair that would normally mark the *aire*. Many members of the new Faith objected to these customs, which had survived from ancient times. Abbot Iarnla and Brother Lugna spent only a short time in the chapel to show their respect. Brother Donnán accompanied young Gúasach, who as foster-son was naturally expected to attend. But there was no sign of Saor or any of the builders when Fidelma and Eadulf entered to pay their respects in accordance with protocol. Gormán hovered at a discreet distance, keeping in the background.

That night, at the evening meal, the abbot made mention of the master builder in the opening prayers. As Brother Lugna had designated the evening meal the 'feast of the deathbed', he gave a short tribute to Glassán's work at the abbey. No one else came forward to praise the master builder or lament his passing. Once again, Fidelma and Eadulf noticed that Saor and his fellow workmen did not attend. She had been expecting that Lady Eithne might have come to pay her respects as she was the moving force behind the rebuilding of the abbey.

Just before midnight, the *clog estechtae*, the death bell, was sounded, its solemn tones echoing through the abbey. The brethren gathered in the quadrangle as the corpse was carried out of the chapel on the *fuat*, wrapped in the white *racholl*, or winding sheet. Several members of the community carried lanterns, lighting the scene with an eerie, flickering half-light which caused grotesque shadows to jump this way and that.

Fidelma, Eadulf and Gormán joined them and glanced
about, wondering if Saor and his builders were going to ignore
the master builder's funeral entirely. Belatedly they appeared
at the gates of the abbey with Saor at their head. They seemed
reluctant as they lined up behind the bier, carried by four of
the brethren. Abbot Iarnla took his place at the head of the
procession. In spite of the tensions they had observed among
the brethren, they found most of the leading members of the
community were there. Brother Lugna, Brother Seachlann,
Brother Donnán. Brother Máel Eoin, Brother Echen and even
the smith Brother Giolla-na-Naomh were in attendance.

Abbot Iarnla held up his staff of office and turned towards
them. He raised his voice to call the traditional instruction:
'The *fé* has been measured, we will proceed.'

The *fé* was a measuring rod for a grave. It was regarded
almost with horror by ordinary folk and only the gravedigger
was allowed to touch it, for it was thought to bring bad luck
and death to others.

The procession moved off with the brethren chanting.

> *Hymnum dicat turba fratrum*
> *Hymnum cantus personet . . .*

> Band of brethren, raise the hymn,
> Let your song the hymn resound . . .

The procession, guided by those holding high their lanterns,
made its way through the abbey gates and turned towards the

eastern side of the buildings where the graveyard of the abbey lay between rows of towering yew trees. The gravediggers stood awaiting them. As the voices of the brethren died away with the final verse, they gathered round the hole that had been dug in the ground and lined in the traditional fashion with branches of broom. The *fuat* was lowered and tipped, and the body slid into the grave. Then one of the gravediggers came forward and smashed the wooden bier and tossed the pieces into the grave. Once a *fuat* had carried a body to the grave, it could not be used again. Then the gravediggers threw in what was called the *strophaiss*, the birch branches that always covered the body before the grave was filled.

There was an expectant silence as the gravediggers stood back. Abbot Iarnla looked round, trying to pick out Saor and his comrades in the semi-darkness.

'Who among you will come forward to speak a few words in honour of Glassán the master builder?' he asked. 'Who will sing the *écnaire*, the song for intercession for the repose of Glassán's soul?'

There was a shuffling among them but no one spoke. No one came forward.

It was Brother Lugna who said coldly, 'All that should be said was said at the *fled cro-lige*. Let us proceed.'

Abbot Iarnla waited a few moments more and then uttered an audible sigh. He raised his voice. 'This is Glassán, sometime master builder of the abbey of Lios Mór. His work will be his memorial for as long as this abbey stands. May he be granted eternal peace.' The abbot gave the sign of the Cross and turned to the gravediggers. At his gesture they began to fill in the grave. The brethren waited a moment or two before beginning to move away, back to the abbey, in ones and twos.

Eadulf found his arm gripped by Fidelma.

'Let's pause a while,' she said softly. 'Let's stand in the shelter of those yews behind us.' She turned to Gormán. 'I need you to go back to the abbey, don't do it discreetly. Go to the guest-house as if you had accompanied us there.'

Gormán was quick to realise what she wanted.

Eadulf followed Fidelma into the darkness of the yew trees without anyone apparently noticing them.

They silently watched the burly gravediggers fill in the grave. They worked rapidly and soon finished their task. Obviously the men had no wish to hang about the cemetery longer than was necessary. Then they were gone.

'Well, that's that.' Eadulf turned to Fidelma. 'There's nothing else to see here and—'

He winced as Fidelma struck him on the arm. He was about to protest when a dark shadow emerged in the gloom. The figure was not carrying a lantern, relying on the moonlight that lit the graveyard. It approached the freshly filled grave and stood before it.

There came a chuckle from the figure. It was a chilling sound.

'Well, Glassán, at last. If you can hear me in the Otherworld, go with the memory that we are finally avenged. Those to whom you did wrong may now finally rest . . .'

They could not see the man's face. Eadulf moved forward

with the intention of seizing him and tripped over a root. He went sprawling. Stunned on the wet ground for a moment, he heard Fidelma call on the figure to halt. By the time he picked himself up, the figure had disappeared. Fidelma had given up the chase after a few steps and was returning to him.

Eadulf rose mumbling an apology for his clumsiness. 'Did you see who it was?'

'I did not,' she replied, her voice tight with annoyance. 'I did not even recognise his voice.' Then she added, 'Are you hurt?'

Eadulf shook his head and then realised it was a futile gesture in the dark. 'I'm all right,' he said. 'I'm sorry, a root—'

'I know,' she said shortly. 'We will have to find some other means of identifying the killer. Come on, let's get back to the abbey before the moon disappears behind the clouds. I don't have a lantern.'

'At least we know our killer is a man,' Eadulf said and then realised it was a silly thing to say.

'Then we have a wide choice of suspects,' Fidelma said wryly. There was no bitterness in her voice.

A tall shadow emerged from the walls of the abbey. Then a lantern glinted. For a moment they held their breath, only to realise that it was Gormán.

'Are you all right, lady?' he asked anxiously, holding the lantern high.

'We are so,' replied Fidelma. 'Has anyone just come back into the abbey?'

To her disappointment he replied in the negative.

'No one has come this way and Brother Echen has just closed the gates for the night. So I thought I would come to meet you and guide you in by another way.'

'So there are other ways the killer could gain entrance to the abbey?' queried Eadulf.

'I will show you.' Gormán said, setting off along the eastern wall, which formed part of the new stone building where Brother Donnchad and the Venerable Bróen had their chambers. Fidelma recalled that there was a small gap in the wall.

'Did you suspect the killer would come to the obsequies?' Eadulf said as they squeezed through the gap.

'I suspected the killer could not resist attending the funeral of Glassán,' she admitted.

'Then you must know who he is, or rather suspect who he is,' protested Eadulf. 'Wouldn't it be best to share that knowledge with me?'

'I still do not have the final link to put all this together,' she admitted. 'That is the frustrating thing. I can guess, but guessing is not proof.'

'So where do we go from here?'

'I need to have a further word with Lady Eithne. Have the horses ready tomorrow after we break our fast, Gormán. We will ride to her fortress in the morning.'

CHAPTER NINETEEN

T he clouds were piled high and fluffy against the blue expanse of the sky. Fidelma noticed several swallows flying high above them, their long pointed wings, deeply forked tails and acrobatic flight unmistakable. The signs were that the weather was going to be dry and sunny. In fact, it would be another month before the swallows would begin to flock together and disappear *en masse* towards the south. With Gormán leading, they left the abbey on horseback and began their journey.

The ride to Lady Eithne's fortress was a pleasant one. This time, although a few sentinels were still in evidence along the short route, they were not challenged until they reached the gates of An Dún. Even then, they were kept only a few moments before the gates swung open to allow the three of them to enter. Once again, however, it was only Fidelma and Eadulf who were allowed into the great hall to see Lady Eithne.

'Well, lady,' greeted the tall woman, standing in front of her chair in the great hall, 'I was told that you had abandoned the abbey.'

'Indeed?' Fidelma was puzzled. 'Then you were told falsely.'

'Did you not ride off with Cumscrad of the Fir Maige Féne to investigate some paltry complaint of his and abandon the investigation of my son's death?'

'No complaint is paltry, lady, when it involves death. Speaking of death, I was surprised that you did not attend the abbey last night.'

A look of uncertainty appeared on Lady Eithne's face. 'I do not understand.'

'I speak of the obsequies of your master builder, Glassán.'

Lady Eithne seemed irritated. 'Glassán? The master builder of the abbey? Why would I attend the funeral of an artisan?'

Fidelma was surprised. 'I thought Glassán was the creator of the memorial to your son.'

'Creator? He was merely a workman and, as such, of no interest to me. The true creator is Brother Lugna.' Her blue eyes were cold.

The woman's indifference chilled Fidelma.

'You feel it is not a matter of concern that the master builder has been killed while working on a project that you are financing?'

'The work of rebuilding the abbey is entirely in the hands of Brother Lugna, as I have explained before,' Lady Eithne replied distantly. 'I am not expected to be in communication with the workmen he employed to do it.'

'Did you know that there have been several accidents on the building site? Eadulf was knocked unconscious when a stone fell on the same site.'

'I am told that accidents can happen,' Lady Eithne replied unemotionally. 'Is this why you came here, to find out why I was not at this workman's funeral?'

'We came to clear up a few matters which I believe are related. You told us that the rebuilding of the abbey was meant as a memorial to your son, Donnchad.'

'I did. It is.'

'But the rebuilding started three years ago,' Eadulf pointed out. 'Did you not expect Donnchad to return from his pilgrimage when you commissioned Brother Lugna to start the rebuilding?'

Lady Eithne uttered a sound like a hiss. 'It is a lucky thing you are a guest in my house, Eadulf of Seaxmund's Ham.' There was ice in her voice.

'What Eadulf meant was that you could not have started out with the intention of rebuilding the abbey in honour of your son,' intervened Fidelma quickly. 'You will forgive him for his clumsy use of our language.' She knew that Eadulf spoke the language almost perfectly. But Fidelma shared his curiosity about the timing of the idea of creating the abbey as a memorial to her son.

Lady Eithne appeared slightly mollified. 'The decision to rebuild the abbey was made before the return of my son,' she said tightly. 'That poor Donnchad died merely made me decide to dedicate the rebuilding to his honour.'

'It is thought among the brethren that the idea for rebuilding came from Brother Lugna,' Eadulf suggested, unabashed by her previous rebuke.

'It may well have been,' she admitted coldly. 'Brother Lugna is such a clever and far-sighted young man. Needless to say, I am totally in agreement with his ideas.'

'I am curious as to why you did not negotiate the idea with Abbot Iarnla?' Fidelma made the sentence into a question.

'Abbot Iarnla has been a long time at the abbey and he is conservative in his outlook. I have already tried to suggest this to you. He would be happy if all things remained exactly the way they are or, rather, were. He has shown himself jealous of Lugna and his ideas. Indeed, my ideas. I would like to see, before I die, a great complex of buildings rising at Lios Mór as a beacon to the Faith, not just here but throughout Christendom. I am sure that your brother, the King, would approve of such tribute in stone to the Faith in his kingdom. A tribute that will last for all time.'

'*Nihil aeternum est*, nothing lasts forever,' came unbidden to Eadulf's lips before he could stop himself from uttering it.

The Lady Eithne turned to him with a disapproving scowl. 'You disappoint me, Brother Eadulf. I would not expect such a philosophy from a man of your cloth. The one thing that will endure is the Faith and this will be its greatest physical memorial. I am determined upon it.'

'Of course,' Fidelma said hurriedly, with a frown of warning at Eadulf. 'The buildings of Lios Mór are beginning to look impressive.'

'Brother Lugna has been a great asset to the abbey. In a few years from now, everyone will be speaking of the greatness of Lios Mór. I feel humbled that I have been able to play a part in its creation.'

'You have been and are most generous to the abbey,' agreed Fidelma.

'Is it not an edict from the Council of Nicaea that places of worship to the Faith should be built wherever possible?'

'I think that was meant as—'

'Indeed, lady, Lios Mór owes you much,' Fidelma cut across Eadulf. Lady Eithne did not appear to notice.

'I simply follow the teachings of Brother Lugna,' Lady Eithne said. 'He says that the Blessed Timothy taught that the rich should give generously to the Faith and in that way they will build themselves a good foundation in heaven.'

Once again, Fidelma shot Eadulf a warning glance before he could attempt to correct her interpretation of the writings of Timothy of Ephesus.

'It seems that you are lucky to have Brother Lugna to guide you in these matters,' she observed drily.

'Indeed, I am. For he has brought a refreshing wind from Rome. Here, we have fallen into lax and immoral ways. Under his abbacy, new rules will clear away all that is corrupt at Lios Mór.'

'Under his abbacy?' queried Eadulf.

'Abbot Iarnla, as I have said, is old and set in his ways. He must move with the times and give way to Brother Lugna soon.'

'I am sure that you take pride in seeing the development of the abbey. Your generosity must be appreciated by the brethren,' Fidelma went on before Eadulf could say more.

'I contribute what little I can.'

'I am told that you were always of a kind and generous nature.'

Lady Eithne frowned uncertainly. 'I have always tried to keep to the rules of the Faith and raise my two sons to praise the Lord and do His great works.'

'I was thinking of Brother Gáeth.'

'Brother Gáeth?' She blinked in surprise. 'What has he to do . . . ?' Then she smiled sadly. 'A poor creature. My husband had more to do with him than I did. He came as a refugee with his father and mother. Our Brehon advised us that we could give sanctuary but not freedom and so they became *daer-fudir* on our land.'

'There was no question that the father, Selbach I think his name was, was unjustly sentenced of the crime of which he was accused?'

'Not at all. The Uí Liatháin made representations to retrieve Selbach from our jurisdiction and presented testimony as to how Selbach killed the chief of the Uí Liatháin by stealth. We gave them assurances that Selbach and his family would remain as *daer-fudir* on our land and they went away, not happy but satisfied that Selbach would not trouble them any more.'

'And Gáeth was raised on your estate?'

'He was a field worker, that is all.'

'He was a friend of Donnchad, I'm told.'

She laughed derisively. 'Friend is not the word I would use. As a child Gáeth used to run after both my sons although it was Donnchad who showed him more kindness and compassion than Cathal.'

'I thought he became Donnchad's soul friend?'

'A matter which I thoroughly disapproved of. Even Abbot Iarna tried to persuade Donnchad to choose someone else.'

'Yet you allowed Gáeth to go with your sons to join the brethren in the abbey.'

'My weakness is that I indulged my sons, particularly my younger son, Donnchad. He pleaded with me and so I agreed. It was part of Donnchad's kindness, to keep the poor simpleton happy.'

'Surely he is no simpleton,' reproved Eadulf, realising that she was not the first person to use the word in connection with Gáeth.

'If not a simpleton, than a cunning young creature,' she sniffed in reply. 'He was much like his father, Selbach, and doubtless will end up the same way.'

'And was that why you instructed Abbot Iarnla to ensure, if he granted him the right to join the breathren, that he remained as a *daer-fudir* within the community?'

Lady Eithne smiled. 'The law is clear. Not until the third generation of the family of a *daer-fudir* can freedom be achieved. The Uí Liatháin made the judgement and we had to follow it. Abbot Iarnla agreed to the condition. When Donnchad returned from his pilgrimage, his sense of generous kindliness had altered and thankfully he realised that Gáeth could not be treated as anyone special.'

'You do not like Gáeth?' Fidelma put the question softly.

'Not like him? Why should I feel anything at all about him? He was just a field worker. I cannot be expected to like or dislike those who are nothing to me.'

'Yet Gáeth grew up with your sons and your son Donnchad believed him to be his friend,' Eadulf pointed out.

'I believe that in my stables there is an old workhorse who grew up with my sons,' replied the lady in a cutting tone. 'Am I suppose to like the horse too? It is just a horse.'

Fidelma rose to her feet. 'We have troubled you long enough, Lady Eithne,' she said decisively, glancing at Eadulf who also rose. 'We thank you for your time and your hospitality.'

Lady Eithne raised a hand and beckoned to one of her attendants who had stood quietly in the background awaiting her orders. The man came forward.

'My steward will see you out,' she said. 'I hope you find the culprit. When you return to Cashel, remember me to your brother, the King, and tell him something of the great work being done here at Lios Mór.'

'When I return to Cashel, lady, I hope I shall be able to

report a resolution of this matter,' Fidelma said solemnly and bade Lady Eithne farewell.

On the road back to the abbey, Fidelma called a halt, ostensibly so that they could water their horses by a tiny stream. While Gormán led the beasts to the water, Fidelma sat on a nearby boulder. She seemed deep in troubled thought.

Eadulf guessed what she was thinking. 'She seems a cold sort of woman,' he observed.

'She certainly does not like Abbot Iarnla,' agreed Fidelma. 'And is enamoured of Brother Lugna.'

'Does not like Abbot Iarnla?' grunted Eadulf. 'Last time we saw her she more or less accused him of being her son's murderer because he was jealous of young talent.'

'It's not beyond the realms of possibility,' sighed Fidelma. 'I have known such things happen before. In fact, the thought crossed my mind the night he paid me a visit to claim how powerless he is.' Fidelma had told Eadulf of her night visitor.

'Abbot Iarnla told you that it was almost a good thing that Donnchad was murdered so that he had an excuse to send for us to tell us about the problems with Brother Lugna and Lady Eithne,' said Eadulf. 'Do you think he precipitated the cause to send for you?'

'It occurred to me.'

'Well, now, we are told that the plan is to replace Abbot Iarnla with Brother Lugna as abbot.'

Fidelma did not reply. 'I think I can work everything out but it's the basic motive that confuses me. There is just one thing I am not clear on, something that does not fit correctly here. Something that I am overlooking and I can't quite put my finger on it. It is the linchpin, it holds together all the parts.' She shrugged and stood up. 'Let me think for a while and then I will tell you what I believe happened but it is all supposition.'

They remounted their horses and continued in silence. They had just passed the spot where the roadway branched southward to Ard Mór when a figure moving up a hill to the south of them caught Fidelma's attention. It was scrambling up towards a mound near the top of the hill. It was a man. He had his back to them and so he didn't notice them. Fidelma halted to stare up at him. When he reached the mound he disappeared behind it.

'Did you see who that was?' Fidelma asked her companions.

'A religieux,' offered Gormán.

'It was Brother Gáeth,' Eadulf announced. 'He is beyond the borders of the cultivated fields of the abbey. Aren't *daer-fudir* supposed not to leave the lands of their community?'

'Perhaps he has permission to do so,' replied Fidelma. 'Anyway, he is still on the lands of the Déisi so I am not going to report such a silly infraction of the law.'

She stared up at the mound behind which Brother Gáeth had disappeared. There were many such ancient burial mounds scattered across the countryside.

The thought occurred to her in a sudden flash.

'Gormán, what would you call that place?' she asked.

The warrior looked up. 'Don't they call them the mounds of the dead?'

A broad smile spread across Fidelma's face.

'I think we may have found the solution.' She swung off her horse.

'Stay here with the horses and wait for me,' she told an astounded Eadulf and Gormán. 'We do not want to intimidate Brother Gáeth.'

'Wait,' protested Eadulf. 'You cannot go up there alone.'

'Of course I can,' she retorted. 'Stay here and do not follow.'

'But you might be in danger,' Gormán said. 'I'll come with you.'

'You will both stay there. I am in no danger from Brother Gáeth.'

'But you never know, he is—'

'He is not a simpleton,' snapped Fidelma, guessing what was passing through Gormán's mind. She began to climb the hill. As she approached the mound on its summit, she saw that, although it was mainly earth-covered, it was certainly man-made. It was formed of large stones placed as a circular cabin over which sods of earth had been placed. She walked slowly round the circular stone wall and, as she expected, came to a small entrance. There was a flickering light inside. She halted and bent down to peer in.

'Stop!' cried an echoing voice. 'This is a place of the dead.'

She halted, bending in the entrance. 'Yet it is where you come, Brother Gáeth. Why are you here?'

Brother Gáeth was sitting in the centre of the small stone hut. It smelled of that strange mustiness that she associated with the graveyard. There was an oil lamp on a stone ledge to one side. She noticed that there was also a bright polished crucifix perched on another stone ledge behind him. It was ornate and reflected the light of the lamp. There were some small boxes and other objects piled along the walls, and among them she noticed two funerary urns of baked clay.

'This is a place of my dead,' replied Brother Gáeth softly. 'They are here, here beyond harm.'

'And I have no wish to harm them or you, Gáeth. May I be allowed to enter?'

Brother Gáeth stared at her for a moment or so, as if trying to make up his mind what to do. Then he shrugged. 'You have been kind to me, Sister. You may enter.'

She crawled in and sat down near some boxes. The interior was no more than five or six metres in diameter. She coughed a little in the musty air. Then she glanced towards the ornate crucifix. It was of silver with several semiprecious stones in it. She had seen similar workmanship before.

'Brother Donnchad brought that back from the Holy Land, didn't he?' she said softly, inclining her head towards it.

'It was his gift to me,' Brother Gáeth said defensively.

'Indeed.' Fidelma glanced at the funerary urns. Brother Gáeth saw her look.

'My father and my mother. I . . . Donnchad and I rescued

their ashes and brought them here. This was an ancient chief's mound. They deserved to rest here and not in the grave of paupers. My father was Selbach of Dún Guairne, a chief of the Uí Liatháin.'

'I know,' Fidelma replied softly. 'Yet cremation is frowned on by the churches of Ireland. I thought the practice had ended.'

'Because my parents were *daer-fudir*, Eochaid said it did not matter for there was no place to set up a memorial to them anyway. But they rest here now.' Brother Gáeth reached out and touched one of the urns. 'Those I have loved rest here. Donnchad helped me bring them here when I was a boy, just after they died.'

'Ah, Donnchad knew of this place.'

'We often played here. It was,' he paused, searching for the right word, 'it was our special camp. No one dared come near the mound of the dead. That's what we called it. It was our secret.'

'So Donnchad requested you to bring some things here before he died.'

Brother Gáeth's brow creased. 'How did you know that?'

'He asked you to bring them here because he feared that he would die and they would be stolen. Isn't that it?'

Brother Gáeth made a movement with his right hand that encompassed the interior of the mound. 'Donnchad gave me things to bring here for safe keeping.'

'Of course. You were his friend.'

'I was. Whatever they say.'

'You need take no notice of them,' Fidelma assured him. 'You were his friend but he gave you something particular for safe keeping just before he died, didn't he?'

'You know about that too?' Brother Gáeth looked worried.

'I know,' confirmed Fidelma.

'They do not know, do they? Those who harmed him?'

'They do not. But now we must use what he gave you so that they will be punished for what they did to him. I give you my word on this.'

Brother Gáeth shook his head. 'He asked me to come to his cell one night and told me to take it and keep it safe. I was never to give it to anyone.'

'And you have kept it safe all this time?'

'It remains here safely.'

'But now he is dead. Do you know what a Brehon is?'

'Of course.'

'You know I am here to find out who killed Donnchad. The King, who has great authority over this land, sent me. He wants those who killed your friend Donnchad to be discovered and punished.'

Brother Gáeth was thoughtful for a moment.

'The King has greater authority than Brother Lugna?'

'He has.'

'And greater than the abbot?'

'He has. Do you understand that this thing Donnchad gave you will help uncover the person who killed him?'

'But I was never to give it to anyone,' repeated Brother Gáeth in a dull tone.

'You do not want his killer to escape without answering for that evil deed, do you?'

Brother Gáeth looked uncertain.

'I was never to give it to anyone,' he said again but now there was confusion in his voice.

'Never until it was needed to help poor Donnchad find rest and make those who killed him answer for their crime.'

'You think that Donnchad would wish me to show you?' He was wavering. He needed guidance.

'I do.'

Brother Gáeth sat thoughtfully for a few moments and then moved to a corner where there was a pile of stones. Methodically, he began moving them to reveal a small hole in the ground. There was a box inside which he lifted out. Then he opened the box. Inside lay a scroll of papyrus.

Fidelma took the papyrus carefully from the box and unrolled it. It was written in a firm hand and in the language of her people. The title was *Do Bhualadh in Brégoiri – The Hammering of the Deceivers*. She swallowed nervously and held the lamp higher. '*Ni rádat som acht bréic togáis . . .*' She began reading aloud. 'They speak only lies and deceit . . .' She paused and licked her dry lips before she continued reading to herself.

A short time later she stopped reading and sat back. It was not a long manuscript but it was one whose contents chilled her to the marrow. She rolled up the papyrus, replaced it in the box and handed it back to Brother Gáeth. He was looking at her with troubled eyes.

THE CHALICE OF BLOOD

'What did it say, Sister?' he asked. 'I do not have the ability to read it. It is too complicated for my poor learning.'

'It tells how distressed Brother Donnchad was.' She smiled quickly. 'He was confused and concerned.'

'But will it help track down who killed him?'

'It does. Continue to hide it safely, Brother Gáeth,' she said. She crawled towards the entrance and paused. 'A time will come in the next few days when I shall ask you to bring that box and papyrus to me. Then I shall reveal who killed your friend.'

'You won't tell anyone of this place, Sister?' Brother Gáeth asked anxiously.

'Have no fear. Your monument to your dead will not be violated again.'

She left him and walked slowly back down the hill where she found Eadulf and Gormán waiting with the horses, their impatience and anxiety plain to see.

'Well?' Eadulf demanded anxiously. 'What happened? Are you all right?'

'Why would I not be?' she answered evenly.

'Then what did you discover?'

'The final piece of the jigsaw.'

'You know who killed Brother Donnchad?' asked Gormán.

'I wish I did not,' she replied grimly. 'I was certain before but unable to understand the motive that could drive a person to such a crime. Even so, it must stand the test of argument and that might prove the most difficult part of the entire puzzle. Gormán, I must ask you to ride directly for Cashel with some instructions for my brother—'

'*Instructions?* For the King?' asked the warrior, astounded.

'It will be up to you to impress on Colgú that he must obey these instructions to the letter, otherwise danger may ensue, a danger that might result in a threat to the security of the kingdom.'

'A threat?' stammered Gormán.

Fidelma was irritable. 'Gormán, I thought more of you than to see you impersonate a newly landed salmon, opening and closing your mouth like that,' she snapped. 'When you ride for Cashel you must ensure that you go by a route that is shrouded from the main paths so that no one will know that you have gone or in which direction.'

'Very well, lady.'

'Good. I will now tell you what you must say to my brother.' She spoke rapidly and clearly. Gormán nodded that he had understood the instructions. When he remounted his horse, she stood back and smiled at him. 'I will expect you back at the abbey in three days' time.'

Gormán raised his hand in salute and sped northwards.

Fidelma watched him go with an expression of satisfaction.

'I presume that you are going to tell me what these curious instructions meant?' Eadulf asked, almost petulantly.

'Indeed I shall. And then we shall have a few days to occupy ourselves until my brother arrives, so we will be able to prepare our case. The presentation will fall entirely on me, Eadulf, as only a qualified *dálaigh* will be able to do this. But you must stand ready to find references to back me. This will be a difficult case to present and I fear there will be few precedents.'

Eadulf knew that any judge needed to see precedents in law before making a judgement.

'I will do my best,' he said.

Fidelma looked suddenly tired. 'We have to be well prepared, Eadulf. I swear that I would never have believed that virtue was the cause of so much evil.'

ChAPTER TWENTY

Three days after Gormán had left for Cashel, he returned late in the evening to report that everything had been accomplished as Fidelma had instructed. Fidelma immediately made arrangements with Abbot Iarnla and Brother Lugna that at midday, the next day, she would present her report in the *refectorium*. Word was then sent to Lady Eithne, to Uallachán and to Cumscrad so that they could attend at the same time.

Fidelma and Eadulf rose at first light on the day and made their way across the quadrangle. It was a peaceful morning, the dawn sunlight giving the promise of another warm day ahead. The early morning birdsong, however, was eclipsed by the sounds from the chapel. They could hear the raised voices of the brethren singing Colmcille's famous hymn *Altus Prosator*.

Regis regum rectissimi
Prope est dies Domini:

Dies irae et uindicatae
Tenebrarum et nebulae . . .

King of Kings, of Lords most high
The day of judgement comes nigh:
Day of wrath and vengeance stark
Day of shadows, cloudy dark . . .

Eadulf smiled as he glanced at Fidelma. 'That seems appropriate in the circumstances.'

Fidelma paused, head to one side, listening. Beyond the gates of the abbey the sound of horses came to their ears. It was the movement of several mounted riders. She smiled with satisfaction. 'Indeed, the strands are finally coming together to complete the tapestry.'

Gormán appeared from the direction of the stables and a moment later Brother Echen hurried to open the gates. The leading horseman, a warrior, carrying the rampant stag banner of the Eóghanacht, came trotting into the quadrangle. Behind the standard bearer they saw Caol, the commander of the Nasc Niadh, bodyguards to the King of Muman, and behind him rode Fidelma's brother, Colgú, with Ségdae, Abbot of Imleach and Chief Bishop of Muman. His steward, Brother Madagan, rode behind, with an elderly man, while two more warriors of the bodyguard brought up the rear.

Fidelma and Eadulf hurried across to greet them. Brother Echen seemed to be wringing his hands, at a loss how to cope with so many distinguished visitors. Caol dismounted with a brief acknowledgement to Fidelma before beckoning Brother Echen and giving instructions about the care of their horses. Colgú slid from his horse with a broad smile at his sister and a friendly nod to Eadulf.

'Did you carry out my instructions?' were Fidelma's first words to her brother.

He chuckled at his sister's single-minded approach.

'A sharp greeting for your brother,' he rebuked. Then he nodded seriously. 'The instructions have been carried out to the letter, sister. I told our main body to rest last night at Brother Corbach's place at Cill Domnoc in the mountains. As you suggested, our party left them there and crossed the mountains to the woods on the north side of the river and encamped there for the night. We forded the river as dawn was breaking. I doubt anyone has seen us.'

'Who is in charge of the main body?'

'Dego and Enda,' replied her brother, naming two leading members of the Nasc Niadh. 'The orders were given to them, just as you decreed.'

Fidelma heaved a sigh of relief. 'As a *dálaigh* I have encountered much evil, Colgú, but never to the extent that I have in this place. I am glad you are here.'

Only then did she greet her brother with a hug. She and Eadulf greeted Abbot Ségdae and Brother Madagan in turn and then Colgú introduced the elderly stranger.

'This is Brehon Aillín, he will sit in judgement on this matter.'

Fidelma had heard of the elderly judge, who was Chief

Brehon of the Eóghanacht Glendamnach, and she knew his reputation to be that of a thorough and a fair man.

'Do you know who killed Brother Donnchad?' he asked, as he came forward to greet her.

'I have suspected for a while,' Fidelma replied quietly. 'The question was the main motive. Without the motive, this horrendous crime made no sense at all. When I discovered it, I sent word to Cashel.'

'And who is the killer?'

'*Tempus omnia revelat.*' Fidelma smiled thinly. 'Time reveals all things. I have sent messengers to summon several people to come here. Cumscrad of the Fir Maige Féne, Uallachán of the Uí Liatháin, who are staying within two kilometres to the west and south of here, and, of course, Lady Eithne at An Dún to the east. I have told them that the court will convene in the abbey *refectorium* at the *etarthráth* – noontide.'

'Are our guards enough if there is trouble?' Colgú asked her.

'So long as Dego and Enda do not move before the hour stipulated.'

'They won't,' her brother assured her.

'Excellent.' She glanced across the quadrangle. 'Ah, the first service has ended and here come the dour-looking steward, Brother Lugna, and an anxious-looking Abbot Iarnla. They will be worried by your presence, particularly that of Abbot Ségdae.'

Colgú chuckled. 'Then we better put them out of their anxiety.'

Eadulf noticed that Fidelma was now walking with a lighter step and he actually heard her singing a snatch of song beneath her breath.

> *Diesque mirabilium*
> *Tonitruorum forium*
> *Dies quoque angustiae*
> *Maetoris ae trititae*

> Thunder shall rend the day apart
> Wonder amazes each fearful heart
> Anguish and pain, deep distress
> Shall mark the day of bitterness

The *refectorium* was so crowded that many of the brethren were forced to stand. The table at which the abbot and his senior advisers usually had their meals was occupied by Colgú, with Brehon Aillín on his right and Abbot Ségdae on his left. Behind Abbot Ségdae, who was there in his role as Chief Bishop of the kingdom, sat his steward, Brother Madagan. Caol, as commander of the Nasc Niadh, stood directly behind Colgú, with the King's standard bearer. Facing them, but in the main body of the hall, were Abbot Iarnla and his steward, Brother Lugna. Lady Eithne, who had arrived with three of her bodyguards, sat to their left. Clustered behind the abbot were all the senior members of the abbey. The two rival chieftains, Cumscrad, with his son Cunán, and Uallachán, with Brother Temnen of Ard Mór,

plus their two bodyguards apiece, had taken seats on opposite sides of the hall. Standing where they could were Saor
and his group of builders, with the young boy, Gúasach.
The rest of the hall was filled with as many members of
the community who could squeeze in. Gormán and the two
remaining warriors of the Nasc Niadh had positioned themselves at the door.

Fidelma had taken her position at a small table to the right
of the raised platform. Eadulf sat with her, with notes and
papers, to aid her if needed. But the arguments before Brehon
Aillín had to be made by a qualified *dálaigh* and so Eadulf
could be of no assistance to her in the direct presentation of
the case.

Brehon Aillín glanced at Fidelma and then stood up. He
raised his staff of office and banged it on the floor three
times.

'At this court we are here primarily to attempt to discover
cause and responsibility for the death of Brother Donnchad.
However, there are other matters that we must consider. The
raids on the Fir Maige Féne and death of Dubhagan of the
tech-screptra at Fhear Maighe. We shall also attempt to
discover cause and responsibility for the death of the master
builder Glassán.'

There was a ripple of subdued but surprised voices. Most
knew only that Brother Donnchad's death had been under
investigation, while Glassán's death had been thought an accident. As for raids and the death of Dubhagan, little gossip
had infiltrated the abbey.

Brother Lugna immediately rose, protesting. 'Are these not separate matters? How are they to be heard all at once? Sister Fidelma's only responsibility is to tell us who killed Brother Donnchad.'

Brehon Aillín regarded him with disapproval. 'This is now a court of law and I have proclaimed the matters it will consider. Fidelma of Cashel, will you proceed?' he added solemnly.

'I shall.' Fidelma bowed her head towards the Brehon, as protocol demanded, before turning to face the assembly.

'We shall deal first with the murder of Glassán. For that is a separate matter.'

When the astonished murmur died down, Fidelma raised her voice a little. 'Yes, it was murder even though it was made to look like an accident. Glassán was bludgeoned from behind with a blackthorn stick, dragged to the wall and the scene made to look as if one of the stones from the wall had become loose and fallen on him. This murder had long been in the planning.'

She held the audience's attention completely now.

'Sometimes,' she continued, 'when one has been so long investigating murders, one becomes too used to looking for the complicated and the unexpected. With the killing of Glassán we were, in fact, dealing with the obvious but thought we were looking for something deeper, more complicated and not so obvious; something that we thought would link up with the murder of Brother Donnchad. We nearly missed what was staring us in the face.'

'And that was?' prompted Brother Lugna, unable to restrain himself.

Brehon Aillín rapped on the table and snapped, 'There are to be no interruptions. I have already pointed out that this is now a court of law and protocol is to be followed.'

'I shall respond to the steward, with your approval,' Fidelma replied mildly. 'This was an act of vengeance, part of a blood feud.'

Fidelma waited for the hall to grow silent again before continuing.

'The most serious offence in any society is for one person to deprive another of their life. I have travelled in many lands and found that the laws governing what punishment should be given varies.'

Once again, Brother Lugna was on his feet.

'In Rome it is considered that the execution of the offender is the only just punishment. Among many members of our Faith beyond the seas, this punishment is supported because this is the justice that Faith proclaims. Is it not written in the ancient texts that life for life, eye for eye, tooth for tooth shall be the punishment? Even if death is caused by negligence, death must be returned as retribution.'

Brehon Aillín had reached for his staff of office, anger on his brow, but Fidelma held up her hand.

'I will respond, with your permission. Let us make allowance for the fact that Brother Lugna has been so long in Rome that he has forgotten how our courts of law are conducted. We do not believe that the teaching that you have cited is compatible with the Faith, for did not Christ tell us to ignore it? Perhaps, Brehon Aillín, you would allow Brother Eadulf, who has also studied in Rome, to remind us of Christ's teaching?'

At a nod from the Brehon, Eadulf rose. 'It is to be found in the Gospel according to Matthew: *audistis quia dictum est oculum pro oculo et dentem pro dente . . . ego autem dico vobis non resistere malo sed si te percusserit in dextera maxilla tua praebe illi et alteram.*'

'You have heard that it has been said, an eye for an eye, and a tooth for a tooth. But I say to you . . .' She stopped translating. 'I am sure that Brother Lugna knows the passage, as do we all. I rejoice that we live under more enlightened laws, though some would have us adopt the Penitentials of Rome where we must cut off the hand that steals, blind the eye that is covetous, kill the person who is responsible for the death of another directly or indirectly.'

Brother Lugna was looking outraged. He exchanged a glance with the grim-faced Lady Eithne.

'The basis of our law,' went on Fidelma, unperturbed, 'is that we allow someone who has transgressed to atone for his crime, even if they have caused the death of another. Moreover, our law says that as well as being given the opportunity for rehabilitation in our society, compensation must be given to the victim or the relatives of the victim. What use is the dead body of the killer to a wife left without a husband, a child left without a mother or a father? Vengeance has but moment-ary satisfaction. Only in extreme circumstances, where a killer is shown to be incorrigible, unrepentant and unwilling to provide the compensation and pay the fines required by law, do we say they should be placed in the arms of fate, that they should be cast adrift in a boat without sail or oar and with food or water for one day. Their fate is left up to the winds and the waves.

'Perhaps some of you have heard the story of Mac Cuill, the son of the hazel, who was a thief and killer in the Kingdom of Ulaidh. His crimes were so heinous and he was so unrepentant of them that he was cast adrift on the sea from the coast of Ulaidh in an open boat. After drifting for some time, he was washed close to the shore on the island that is named for the god of the oceans, Mannanán Mac Lir. There were only two members of the Faith on the island at that time but they took him from the sea. He realised that Fate had saved him for a more useful life. He travelled the island with them, preaching the Faith and founding an abbey now named after him, for he is known by the Latin from of his name – the Blessed Maccaldus. He ended his life as abbot and bishop on that island. Is that not a better contribution to life than having his dead, rotting body forgotten?'

She paused and Brehon Aillín took the opportunity to intervene in a mild tone. 'I am sure that those gathered here do not need to be reminded of the basis of the Law of the Fénechus, Fidelma.'

She turned to him with a quick smile. 'With due respect, I believe that you will find some who do need reminding.

We believe that our native law has more in keeping with Christ's teaching than those who support the Penitentials from Rome. However, I shall come to that later. I do need to outline the law a little more before I come to the main point. I would like to remind people of the *Cáin Sóerraith*, that is the law pertaining to all those who have a duty to the ruler of their clan.'

Colgú raised his head in surprise and glanced at Brehon Aillín before asking. 'What has that to do with the matter in hand?'

'This law, as some may know, states that a *sóerchéile*, a free clansman, has a duty to assist the lord of his clan. Whatever art or profession he follows, when his lord calls for help, he must obey on penalty of fines. If his lord wants him to help hunt down horse thieves or wolves, or protect the clan's territories, the *sóerchéile* must obey and answer his call. He even has a duty to assist his lord in the prosecution of a blood feud. Is that not so, Saor?'

The assistant master builder jerked nervously and he licked his suddenly dry lips.

'Do you recognise the law, Saor?' she pressed.

'I do,' he answered after some hesitation.

'And you thought you were obeying the law?'

Saor was looking confused.

'Are you saying that it was Saor who killed Glassán?' intervened Abbot Iarnla nervously. 'But he worked for Glassán. Technically, that made Glassán his lord.'

'Not so,' Fidelma replied before Brehon Aillín could rebuke

the abbot's intervention. 'Glassán was not the lord of Saor's clan. Saor was the *sóerchéile*, the clansman, called on to prosecute a blood feud. He did help his lord to kill Glassán as he was bound to do by his interpretation of the law. Therefore I have to say that Saor is exonerated from bearing the full blame for this crime of murder.'

Brehon Aillín made to intervene but Fidelma held up her hand. 'Better if I came to the truth in my own way.' The Brehon conceded and gestured for her to continue.

'Glassán, as you know, was a master builder. What some of you may not have known was that he was master builder to the King of Laighin until ten years ago. Ten years ago he undertook to build a hall in stone for one of the King's relatives in the south of the kingdom. However, he was a vain man who undertook many tasks at once. He did not fulfil his obligation and duty to the King to act as overseer on the building. Mistakes were made. The building collapsed, killing relatives of the King.'

'Then why wasn't he brought before the King of Laighin and his Brehon for this act?' demanded Brehon Aillín.

'He was,' Fidelma replied calmly. 'He argued that it was his assistant at the site who was to blame and not himself. This was technically true and the assistant had to pay the honour price of those who died to the families of the victims. But because Glassán tried to shift the blame for his own responsibility, the King and his Brehon dismissed him from the King's service and ordered him to pay the court fines. Glassán went into exile in the kingdom of Connachta where he settled down among the Uí Briuin Sinna. He began to build up a reputation again as a builder.'

'The Uí Briuin Sinna?' Abbot Iarnla intervened. 'But that's where—'

'Where your steward, Brother Lugna, comes from, yes,' Fidelma said. 'Brother Lugna knew of Glassán and his work before he went to Rome. When Brother Lugna returned from Rome and was given permission to rebuild this abbey in stone, he naturally called for someone he knew – he brought Glassán here as his master builder.'

'No crime in that,' snapped the sullen steward.

'Of course not,' Fidelma agreed. 'But in bringing Glassán here as your master builder it did open the path that was eventually to lead to his death.'

'How so?' demanded Brother Lugna.

'We are not far from the borders with Laighin and eventually Glassán's presence here was noted. Brother Echen, for example, is from Laighin.'

Heads turned towards the stableman who stood frowning.

'Am I being accused of involvement in killing Glassán? I am innocent. Was it not I that actually told you about his background?'

'Indeed it was,' replied Fidelma calmly. 'Brother Echen had a cousin who was in charge of the stables of the King of Laighin. He knew the story of Glassán and when his presence here was mentioned in conversation, that knowledge spread to certain people. Sit down, Brother Echen, you are not to blame, although, like Brother Lugna, you also prepared the path to his death.'

'But you have said that Glassán paid his fines to the King of Laighin and exonerated himself before the law,' pointed out Brehon Aillín.

'It is true that he paid fines to the King but there were members of the families of those who perished who felt that Glassán had not answered to them for the deed. He was the person who designed the building and should have overseen the work. The relatives of the dead received no compensation from him and did not believe he had repented. Eventually, the word came to the son of the chieftain who had perished in that building. As a young man he had sworn that his role would be the *díglaid* – the person who would take vengeance on behalf of his clan. He came to this abbey, ascertained that it was, indeed, Glassán who was working here and then sent for one of his clansmen to help him. That clansman was Saor.'

She paused and looked at Saor.

'I was told that it was not long after Saor arrived that several accidents began to happen on the building site. No one was badly injured until Eadulf went to look at the site because of something that had occurred to him. Thankfully, he had a lantern with him. As he came under a half-finished doorway, he heard a lintel being pushed. It would have fallen on his head had he not raised his lantern to discover the source of the noise. The light on his features showed he was not the intended victim. One of the two would-be vengeance-seekers recognised him in time and gave him a hard shove in the back, just as the lintel fell. The lintel missed him but Eadulf smashed his head on a wooden support which knocked him out.'

Saor was looking at the ground.

'Am I not right, Saor? You were the person who pushed the lintel.'

The assistant master builder shrugged but said nothing.

'I accept that you felt duty bound, under law, to assist your chieftain in pursuing this blood feud,' went on Fidelma. 'You told young Gúasach that you were from a clan called the Uí Bairrche in southern Laighin. That was where the building collapsed, wasn't it? Your chieftain demanded your help in pursuing vengeance against Glassán. Since that is the reason for your actions, you will not feel the full weight of the law.'

Saor looked up with a resigned expression. 'It was not only that I obeyed the call of my chieftain,' he said slowly. 'My brother was the carpenter working on the building that fell. He was killed. I was willing and pleased to help against Glassán.'

'So when you were called by your chieftain, you came willingly?'

'Of course.'

'Thank you for confirming that your chieftain is here with us. Was it him or was it you who paid Gealbháin, the previous carpenter and assistant master builder on this job, to leave the site so that you could present yourself to Glassán as his replacement?'

Saor's lips compressed and he shook his head. 'I will say no more.'

'No matter.' Fidelma swung round and looked at the physician, Brother Seachlann. 'Your chieftain can speak for himself.'

The physician stood up and gave her a curious half bow.

'I am Seachlann of the Uí Bairrche,' he said quietly.

There were several gasps round the hall.

'Do you deny these charges that are levelled against you?' demanded Brehon Aillín.

Seachlann stood erect, his head held high.

'There is no need to deny them. I am the *díglaid* and, as such, I claim that the law supports me. When the perpetrator does not compensate the victims and their families, the *Críth Gabhlach* says that the *díglaid* can pursue a blood feud even into other territories where the perpetrator might seek refuge. I have done so and I rejoice that I have fulfilled an obligation to my family and clan.'

'Are you, in truth, chief of the Uí Bairrche and therefore related to King Fáelán of Laighin?' queried Colgú in surprise.

'I am. Both my parents perished in the building that Glassán was supposed to construct. My brother, who was heir to my father, also perished, along with fifteen others of my people, including Saor's brother. I was a young man and had newly entered the religious. I was just finishing my studies in the healing arts at the abbey at Sléibhte.

'Glassán showed no remorse for his negligence. He claimed he should not be held responsible in any way. He complained when the King imposed the fines and exiled him, although we whose family members perished felt it was a mild punishment. Glassán was clever and he disappeared quickly and for years we could not discover where he had fled. I had been inaugurated chieftain. My *tanist*, my heir, was chosen, and so I left the affairs of my people to him while I continued in the practice of medicine. Then I heard from Brother Echen's relative at the palace of my kinsman, King Fáelán, that Glassán was here. As you rightly deduced, Fidelma of Cashel, that is why I came.'

'And is everything else correct as Fidelma has charged?' demanded Brehon Aillín.

'Everything else is correct. But, as the *Críth Gabhlach* states, I acted as the *díglaid*. I acted under the law and therefore no charge can be brought against me.'

'Except that you may have overlooked one thing,' Fidelma said quietly. 'In my preamble, I explained carefully what the basis of our law was. Recompense and rehabilitation. The matter of blood feud can only be enacted against an incorrigible, one who refuses to come to law and be judged. Under special circumstances, a king's Brehon could approve of the *díglaid*. Glassán had been judged and paid the requirements of the law.'

There was a murmuring throughout the hall and then Fidelma approached Brehon Aillín and whispered to him. He nodded slowly and she returned to her place. The murmuring dissolved to silence as the Brehon spoke.

'There may well be exonerating circumstances, Seachlann. But a judgement cannot be pronounced as a legal finding until you have argued it before the Chief Brehon of Laighin and your King. Glassán was judged before them and paid the fines imposed on him. Technically, according to the law, he was then a free man and entitled to the protection of his freedom. My advice to my King,' he glanced at Colgú, 'would be to have you and Saor escorted to the King of Laighin and for him and his Chief Brehon to consider your case accordingly.'

Seachlann acknowledged the authority of the Brehon with a slight bow. 'I am most willing to accept that course of action. Our main task here is done and I am prepared to answer for all my actions.' He glanced at Saor who nodded slightly. 'And so is my companion in this matter.'

Colgú leant forward to Brehon Aillín and held a whispered conversation before the judge turned to Seachlann and Saor.

'The recommendation has been accepted. After these proceedings are over, and a record made of these events, two of the King's warriors will accompany you and your companion to Ferna, where the King of Laighin may sit in judgement on this matter. As victims and perpetrators are men of Laighin, it is no longer in our jurisdiction and the matter is turned over to Laighin for judgement.'

Seachlann glanced to Saor and smiled encouragement before reseating himself.

Brehon Aillín sat back and looked at Fidelma. 'Are you prepared to proceed on the other matters?'

Fidelma allowed a moment of silence. Eadulf gave her an encouraging smile.

'I am. I am now ready to proceed in the matter of the murder of Brother Donnchad.'

CHAPTER TWENTY-ONE

'Brother Donnchad was the victim of extreme virtue, or should I say intolerance disguised as virtue,' began Fidelma. 'He was a great scholar. Had he lived, he might have been one of the greatest scholars of the Five Kingdoms.'

'His name will be remembered in such a light,' came the stern voice of Lady Eithne. 'That is why I sanctioned the rebuilding of this abbey. By these stone buildings, he will be remembered as a great teacher of the Faith.'

Fidelma allowed the murmuring to die away. Then, without looking at Lady Eithne, she said loudly, 'Is that what he would have wanted to be remembered as?'

There was a stir of surprise among the brethren.

'Truth is great and will prevail, so let us consider what the truth is. For some time I did not know why Brother Donnchad was killed. Without a motive, I could not present a case against the killer. Finally, I discovered that motive.'

Everyone was hanging on her words now, leaning forward in their seats in silent expectation.

'The reason why he was killed was because he had lost his Faith.'

There was immediate uproar. Lady Eithne shouted in outrage but her words were lost in the hubbub. Abbot Iarnla was white with shock and Brother Lugna's features were drawn into a mask of barely controlled fury.

'It is well known that Brother Donnchad was a great scholar of the Faith,' Brehon Aillín admonished. 'I cannot allow such a statement to be admitted in this court.'

Even Abbot Ségdae looked astounded at her words.

'You can if it can be proved,' protested Fidelma.

'I must accept the proof, as we know it. The knowledge and respect accorded to Brother Donnchad and his known writings on the Faith constitute proof of his views and are a precedent, a *fásach*, which cannot be challenged.'

Eadulf stood up and coughed nervously. 'I am not qualified to speak here, Brehon Aillín, but could I bring to your attention, through the *dálaigh*, that the *Uraicecht Becc* states that among the *senfásach* there is this admonition: that a Brehon cannot expect to find all truth contained in a *fásach*. It empowers the Brehon to consider any argument designed to overturn the precedent.'

Fidelma turned to Eadulf in surprise. He passed her the text and she read it rapidly. Then she approached Brehon Aillín and handed it to him. The Brehon read it, pursed his lips and shook his head.

'I cannot accept the statement you have made without proof. But I am willing to follow this admonition from the *Uraicecht Becc* and hear your evidence, Fidelma. If you cannot prove your claim then I must impose a fine on you. Will you attempt to prove it?'

'It shall be proved,' Fidelma replied, 'and in the words of Brother Donnchad himself.'

'How can that be?' called out Brother Lugna, with a sneer. 'Are you going to practise witchcraft and conjure him from his grave?'

There were gasps of horror at his words and several of the brethren performed the sign of the Cross.

'That is unworthy of you, Brother Lugna,' snapped Brehon Aillín. 'There should be no need to remind you of the reputation of the learned advocate in this kingdom and even beyond.'

'I will explain,' Fidelma said. 'The words of Brother Donnchad were written down before his death and hidden because he feared, correctly, that someone might kill him and destroy them. They certainly did their best to do so. They removed all traces of his writings and documents from his room, just in case his words were hidden among them. Thankfully, they were not and they have survived.'

'Do you mean to present them before us?' asked Brehon Aillín.

'I will do so although I am loath to as Brother Donnchad presents some disturbing arguments as to why he lost his Faith.'

There was some confusion in the *refectorium*.

'And have you proof that they were written by him?' pressed the judge.

'I can present someone who can testify to the handwriting of Brother Donnchad for I have learnt that each scribe forms letters in his own way and has a particular style of writing. Further, I will present the person to whom Brother Donnchad gave this writing, with the request that it be hidden.'

There was now silence.

'Very well,' Brehon Aillín said after a quick consultation with Colgú and Abbot Ségdae. 'You may sum up what Brother Donnchad said in this work on condition that the work is afterwards presented to us and verified to be his work.'

'I can do that simply. I do not have to remind you that Brother Donnchad was a talented scholar, able to read and write several languages. The librarian of this abbey, Brother Donnán, has pointed out on several occasions that Brother Donnchad was most interested in the works of the early believers in the Faith – indeed, in the very origins of how the Faith spread from the Holy Land across the world.'

'That is not denied.' Abbot Iarnla was frowning. 'He was always interested in those origins.'

'For Brother Donnchad, his pilgrimage to the Holy Land was a golden opportunity to further his studies. What concerned him were the references to James in the scriptures, particularly in the gospels according to Mark and Matthew, and in the epistle to the Galatians. James was said to be the brother of the Christ and executed by the Romans some thirty years after the execution of Jesus. The references were to James Adelphotheos, Brother of the Lord.'

'That's nonsense!' cried Brother Lugna, standing up. 'The name was miswritten, it was mistranscribed. The name should have been James Alphaeus, who—'

'I cannot debate the translation,' cut in Fidelma. 'I do not have that scholarship. I am merely stating what Brother Donnchad said and believed. He had pored over the texts of the Faith that were translated into Latin by the Blessed Jerome who was also called Eusebius Hieronymus. Donnchad found references that confused him, references not only to James as the brother of Jesus, but also to Joses, Simon and Judas, and to sisters, one of whom was called Salome. They were all clearly identified as brothers and sisters of Jesus.'

Brother Lugna, still on his feet, began to argue.

'Sit down, Brother Lugna,' ordered Brehon Aillín. 'This is not a scholastic debate.' He turned to Fidelma. 'I am allowing these statements, Fidelma, only on the grounds that you are presenting what Brother Donnchad's thoughts were and that these thoughts have a direct bearing on his murder.'

'I have said as much,' agreed Fidelma firmly. 'I am not as authoritative as Brother Donnchad so merely I repeat what he says. Brother Donnchad records that the relationship of those I have mentioned is termed *adelphos* throughout the texts. *Adelphos* means brethren in the blood relationship sense. Had the writer wanted to suggest brethren as in the meaning of the brethren of this community, the word he would have used is *suggeneia*.'

She paused but no one spoke.

'I repeat, I am no scholar in this regard. Brother Donnchad believed that he would be able to find out more when he went to the Holy Land. He made inquiries and then, when he was waiting in Sidon, which I understand is a port on the coast of the Holy Land, he began to hear stories that truly shocked him. He found that he could not even discuss them with his own brother Cathal, who remained untroubled and secure in his Faith. This he comments on in his record.

'He heard one story that particularly distressed him. The story referred to Jesus, and we must remember Jesus is but the Greek form of the Hebrew name Yeshu or Joshua. The story was about a Yeshu ben Pantera.'

'Yeshu was a very common Hebrew name of the time.' This came from Brother Donnán. He glanced apologetically at the Brehon. 'I am sorry, but I had to mention that, just in case it was thought that the name Jesus is a unique name. Its meaning in Hebrew is "red-handed hero".'

'You are no doubt correct,' Fidelma replied mildly. 'However, Donnchad was directed to a work called the *Tosefta*, which is a collection of Jewish oral law, and in it is a reference to Yeshu ben Pantera. The text makes clear that this was none other than Jesus of Nazareth. The word "ben" signifies "son of", as in our own word, "mac".'

She had to wait while the cacophony of voices that greeted her statement subsided.

'I will not go on to recount the research that a distraught

Donnchad continued to conduct. I know that he was also led to a work by a Greek philosopher named Celsus who wrote that Mary, or Miriam, the original Hebrew name, was a girl who lived in Sepphoris in Galilee. The Romans marched through the town and she was raped by a Roman soldier of Phoenician birth called Abdes Pantera and bore him a child—'

There was a gasp and Brother Lugna was first on his feet, shouting, 'Sacrilege, blasphemy!'

'I am only recounting what Celsus wrote. I do not claim that he speaks the truth or that I agree with him,' Fidelma went on determinedly. 'Celsus wrote that the parents of Mary, who many other sources claim to have come from this city near Nazareth called Sepphoris, drove her out from their home in shame. But eventually Joseph, a carpenter, accepted her and her son.

'In Sidonia, Brother Donnchad found other sources that spoke of a local man from the city called Abdes Pantera. He was an archer and he had joined the Roman army some years before the birth of Jesus and when he became a Roman citizen, he took the name Tiberius Julius Abdes Pantera. It is said that his regiment took part in the destruction of Sepphoris under the command of the Governor Quinctilius Varus.'

'This is ridiculous!' cried Brother Lugna in outrage. 'It is profanity against the Faith. Are we to sit here and hear our Faith insulted?'

'Once again I say that I do not offer this as fact,' Fidelma continued doggedly. 'It is what Brother Donnchad discovered in his research, came to believe as fact and formed his opinion.'

'I have already ruled that it may be presented for that purpose,' added Brehon Aillín. 'If understanding this leads to the discovery of who killed him, then I am prepared to hear it.'

'Brother Donnchad discovered that the name Abdes in the language spoken in Sidonia meant a "servant of Isis", a god of the Egyptians. Abdes joined the first cohort of archers and rose to be the standard bearer, a *signifer*. Abdes served forty years in the Roman army and Brother Donnchad discovered that his regiment, the *Cohors Primus Sagittariorum,* was stationed in Judea until Jesus was nine years old. Then the cohort was moved to the northern frontier in Germania Superior along the banks of the River Renos. Abdes was stationed in a fort called Bingium where, at the age of sixty-two years, he died and where he was buried.'

'You say all this was written down by Brother Donnchad?' demanded Abbot Ségdae, then he turned to the Brehon. 'Forgive me, Brehon Aillín, I want to be absolutely sure on this point.'

'It was,' replied Fidelma. 'His written account will be presented to you as evidence. I know nothing of these places or their history. All I know is that Brother Donnchad wrote this down and was influenced by it. On his return journey, when he landed at Tarentum, he bade farewell to his blood brother, Cathal, and continued his journey north. He crossed the mountains. Finally, he arrived in Bingium by way of the

River Renos. There, so he recounts, he found a guide who led him to the grave of Abdes Pantera. The Latin inscription was still clearly legible. He recorded it word for word.'

'But all this proves nothing about who killed him,' Brehon Aillín interjected.

'What this is meant to prove is the state of Brother Donnchad's mind – and a motive for his killing. As I have frequently said, I do not vouch for its accuracy one way or the other. But Brother Donnchad found himself troubled by the story, which is known to the people of Judea, the story of a rape in Nazareth, mentioned in a Jewish law text, recounted by the Phoenicians in Sidonia, and by Greek and Latin writers like Celsus. The story Celsus tells was even rebutted by Origenes who took the arguments seriously enough to argue with them. Brother Donnchad went so far as to trace the tomb of Abdes in Germania. Brother Donnchad was a great scholar. True or not, this was the matter that troubled him.

'What he had uncovered created such doubts in his mind that he was losing his belief in the new Faith. He was a very logical man. But, at times, belief calls upon us to shed our rational minds and simply accept that which we are unable to prove. *Credo quia impossible est*, I believe it because it is impossible, as many of our priests would say. Well, faced with evidence of a rational story about Christ, Brother Donnchad found he could no longer believe what logic told him was impossible.'

There was another ripple of angry mutterings in the

refectorium. Eadulf looked round uncomfortably. Fidelma was only presenting arguments that had caused Brother Donnchad to slip away from the Faith but to those who sincerely believed, it was as if she was preaching heresy or attacking the Faith itself.

Brehon Aillín rapped his staff of office. 'And you maintain that his doubts provoked such anger in someone that that person killed him?'

Colgú intervened. 'We have only to witness some of the emotions that this story has provoked here to realise that such an anger is not beyond possibility,' he pointed out.

'Exactly so,' replied Fidelma, nodding. 'Who in this abbey is so fanatical in their belief that they would do anything to stop a scholar of Brother Donnchad's reputation from proclaiming his views that might harm the Faith? Many of our people have not yet entirely accepted the Faith. It is only two centuries since the Five Kingdoms began to hear and accept the Word of Christ. What, then, if Brother Donnchad, recently back from the Holy Land, began to tell this story?'

There was an unhappy murmur and many of the brethren looked at one another awkwardly.

Abbot Iarnla's face was pale. He said slowly, 'Everyone in this abbey is of the Faith and to proclaim a disbelief in the Faith is a great sin.'

'But we are a tolerant people for we are but newly come to this new understanding with God,' Brehon Aillín declared. 'We tolerate and seek to persuade others to the Faith, especially those who are reluctant to make the leap into a new world that has come upon us from the East.'

'We cannot afford tolerance,' Brother Lugna snapped. 'The Faith is inviolable and every soul lost is a soul condemned to the fires of hell.'

'Brother Lugna is dogmatic on such points,' pointed out Fidelma mildly.

'I am only dogmatic when people deny the truth of the Faith.'

'Indeed. One would say that you have a fanatical belief.'

'I am zealous for my Faith, that is true.'

'And if someone disagreed with your Faith?' prompted Fidelma.

Brother Lugna opened his mouth to respond and then snapped it shut as he realised where Fidelma was leading him.

Fidelma watched him. 'Your sect does not hold with dissension, does it?'

Brehon Aillín had given up trying to make people accept the protocol of the court. Now he turned to Fidelma with a question. 'His sect? What do you mean?'

'I once talked with Brother Lugna about the rules of Pope Celestine.'

'Persecutions!' Brother Lugna almost spat the word.

'It was ruled by Celestine that certain philosophies were not consistent with the Faith.'

'He persecuted the Manichaeists and Donatists.'

'And the Novatianists,' added Fidelma. 'That is the sect you follow, isn't it?'

Brehon Aillín was clearly puzzled, as were several others.

'Novatian was a religious and teacher in Rome,' Fidelma explained. 'In fact, he is regarded as the first member of the Faith to write his work in Latin instead of Greek. But he opposed the election of Cornelius as Pope on the grounds that Cornelius was too gentle and forgiving to lapsed Christians. He held that those who did not maintain the Faith, even under torture and persecution, should not be received back into the Faith, whether or not they repented. He also argued that if a widow or a widower remarried, their second marriage was unlawful and they should be publicly accused of fornication and punished. His mistake, however, was in setting himself up as a rival head of the Church in Rome. He claimed that he was Pope. He was immediately excommunicated at a Council in Rome. His teachings were deemed heretical.'

'I have not heard of this,' admitted Abbot Ségdae. 'When was it?'

'About three centuries ago, according to the annalists.'

'If Novatian and his followers were declared heretics three centuries ago, how can you claim that Brother Lugna is a member of their sect?' Brehon Aillín demanded.

'Oh, the Novatianists still exist. Novatian was executed in the massacre of Christians in Rome by the Emperor Valerian. But his sect spread rapidly after his death. They were numerous in many lands and they called themselves *katharoi*, which is the Greek for "puritans", to denote that they kept themselves pure from what they saw as the lax and forgiving ways of the Roman popes. Some demanded that even those born and raised in the Faith must be baptised again before they could join the Novatianists and be considered saved. Of course the Novatianists are still regarded as heretics but I am not sure that they have been censured with any force since the time of Pope Celestine.'

Abbot Iarnla turned to glare at his steward. 'Is it true that you follow the teachings of this Novatian?'

'Why should I deny it?' retorted Brother Lugna with arrogance. 'I hold the Faith pure and untainted. There is no room for those who are half-hearted about declaring their beliefs.'

'And that is why you were concerned when Brother Donnchad returned from the Holy Land and you discovered that far from being strengthened in his Faith, his mind was full of questions for which he tried to find answers?' said Abbot Iarnla.

'The devil had tempted Donnchad while he wandered in the wilderness,' Brother Lugna replied calmly. 'He was not strong enough to fight the devil and fell into the greatest sin of all. He denied the Faith. There is no room in Christendom for those who deny the Faith even if they eventually come seeking forgiveness on their hands and knees. They should be turned away and punished.'

'Just as your founder Novatian preached,' said Fidelma.

'Just as he taught,' agreed the steward. 'Such sinners are condemned in this life and in the next. Those who give them forgiveness and succour are the real heretics. They will not receive forgiveness of the Lord when the time comes. They will be made to answer at the awful Day of Judgement.'

'There is a day of judgement come today,' Fidelma pointed out. 'We are here to judge who is responsible for Brother Donnchad's death.'

'I shall not deny my Faith,' Brother Lugna replied stubbornly. 'At least I will not die a sinner and a blasphemer as Donnchad did.'

'So you killed Brother Donnchad!' Abbot Iarnla accused, his voice rising. 'You admit it!'

The *refectorium* erupted once more.

'I deny it!' shouted the steward, red with anger.

Brehon Aillín stamped his staff of office loudly but it took a long time before he was able to quell the noise of surprise and outrage that had arisen.

When some degree of quiet was restored, Fidelma held up her hand.

'Let us come to the answer in the proper order,' she said, glancing at the Brehon.

Brehon Aillín was looking anxious and said, 'There are contentious matters here and in view of what you have told me, I am prepared to let you proceed for a little while longer in the manner you wish. But I urge you, for the sake of peace in this abbey, come to the point as quickly as you can.'

'I shall proceed as quickly as the matter allows.' Fidelma's voice was grave. She turned back to those gathered in the *refectorium*. 'The views expressed by Brother Lugna are part of the intolerance that I believe we must fight against. Beliefs are things to be cherished but we cannot be intolerant of others whose beliefs we disagree with. That intolerance can lead to war and even murder. It did lead to murder in the case of Brother Donnchad.

'As with the killing of Glassán the master builder, two people were involved in the murder of Brother Donnchad. Both parties to his murder were zealots for the Faith and could not tolerate someone who, rightly or wrong – for I make no judgement – began to ask questions instead of simply believing.

'When it became known to these two people that Brother Donnchad was researching writings that were critical of the Faith and meant to produce a scholastic work on them, they decided that he should be silenced. He was not to be allowed to proclaim his doubts or voice his questions because of the shame, as they saw it, it would bring upon this abbey.'

Many heads turned to Brother Lugna and to Abbot Iarnla. They both sat with expressions of defiance.

Brehon Aillín leant forward. 'Do you accuse the abbot or his steward? Or both of them? There is no one in a higher position to protect the reputation of the abbey than they are.'

'A moment more of patience,' Fidelma urged. 'One of the two people planned the murder and the other was their accomplice. But we must first comment on the circumstances of the murder. One of them entered Brother Donnchad's *cubiculum* and killed him. They had to remove all the manuscripts that Brother Donnchad had in his *cubiculum* that would show what he was working on. They could not allow the papers to be known.'

'How are you going to demonstrate that?' snapped Abbot Iarnla. 'There was only one key to the *cubiculum*, which Brother Donnchad had, and that was by his side when he was found. And no one came out of his *cubiculum* bearing any papers before his body was discovered.'

'That was where the second person was involved. It was the Venerable Bróen who gave me the clue with his story of seeing an angel in white fluttering in the sky. The Venerable Bróen occupied the *cubiculum* beneath Brother Donnchad. What he actually saw was a large piece of parchment fluttering down. The killer, having despatched Donnchad, threw the precious manuscripts out of the window. The window, as you will recall, faces the wasteland that lies just before the abbey graveyard. The window is too small for anyone to enter or exit through it. But it is large enough to throw out the manuscripts to the second person waiting below to collect them.'

She suddenly swung round.

'What happened to them, Brother Donnán? Have they been destroyed, given to your confederate, or have you hidden them away in the library?'

Brother Donnán turned white, stood up quickly, sat down again and then slowly rose to his feet once more.

'I . . . I deny it!' he gasped but there was no conviction in his voice.

'The first mistake you made was over a piece of parchment written on by Brother Donnchad. We found the piece below the window. You neglected to pick it up; it was such a small piece, you probably did not notice it. There were only a few words written on it anyway. You, who are certainly an expert on his writings, denied it was Brother Donnchad's hand. Yet Cunán, the assistant librarian at Fhear Maighe, who is also an expert, not only identified it as Brother Donnchad's, but was also able to prove this by the particular way letters were formed, by showing us writings received from Brother Donnchad as example.

'Donnchad wrote an entreaty that the chalice be removed from him. What chalice? The chalice of his knowledge. Brother Donnchad had also written *Deicide* several times; he was not referring to the Jews killing the Christ but to himself, to his own research, which was killing his Faith. He knew what was happening and he used the words written in the gospel of Luke when even Jesus doubted: "Father, if you be willing, remove this chalice from me . . .' It was to be a bitter chalice for Brother Donnchad.

'Brother Donnán also tried to lead us away from the books Donnchad was researching. Then he discovered that the original book by Celsus was in Fhear Maighe. By coincidence, the abbey of Ard Mór had asked and paid for a copy of it, having read Origenes' answer to it, which this abbey had lent them after Brother Donnchad had read it. A messenger arrived at the library with the news that the copy was ready and that it would be sent by barge. As the physician, Brother Seachlann, was going to Ard Mór, he volunteered to take the message. Brother Donnán overheard this and even wrote down the titles of the books. However, he thought it was the original that

Fhear Maighe was sending. He passed that information on to someone on the barge, who arranged for it to be attacked and the copy stolen.'

There was a deathly hush in the great room. Everyone was sitting spellbound.

'The attack on the barge was made to appear as if men from the Uí Liatháin carried it out. I will explain why, in a moment.'

Uallachán and Cumscrad stirred uneasily in their seats but they made no comment.

'Brother Donnán's accomplice, or should I say the person who was the main instigator of all these events, then learned that Fhear Maighe still had the original of Celsus's work. An attack on the library to destroy this copy and, indeed, to kill the librarian who might have read the work was arranged.

'Why were you involved, Brother Donnán?' Fidelma asked the *scriptor*. 'You have been at this abbey a long time. I suppose you have pride in your library, your *scriptorium*, and pride in the abbey which you hoped would become one of the great teaching abbeys of Christendom. Did you fear that if a scholar of Brother Donnchad's merit declared his doubts, it would destroy your ambitions for the abbey and tarnish the reputation you took such pride in?'

Brother Donnán resumed his seat and folded his hands before him. He was shaking his head. His face was set, his mouth compressed into a firm line.

'You will not tell us who the instigator was in all this?' Fidelma shrugged and turned towards Abbot Iarnla. 'Who, more than most, wanted to protect the reputation of this abbey and make it, as I have said, renowned for its Faith and learning throughout Christendom? Who wanted this abbey to rise as a great monument to the Faith that would last forever?'

Many in the *refectorium* were now looking with open hostility at Brother Lugna, while a few were casting suspicious glances at Abbot Iarnla.

'Who,' declared Fidelma, speaking in a slow, deliberate tone, 'has the ultimate power here?'

The eyes of all the brethren now focused on the abbot. Abbot Iarnla stared at her for a moment, and then his eyes suddenly widened. An expression of horror crossed his face and he turned to look at Lady Eithne. Everyone followed his gaze.

'This is a scandalous accusation!' she declared, immobile in her seat. 'Am I being accused of killing my own son? I cannot and will not stand for it.'

'Did you kill your son, Lady Eithne?' asked Fidelma coldly.

'I loved my son. Anyway, it would have been physically impossible for me to do what is claimed here. There was only one key to the cell, which was found by my son's body, in the locked cell after I had left him on that final visit when Brother Lugna called me to the abbey.'

'You had another key made,' Fidelma asserted flatly.

'How could I have done that?'

'Simple. I had overlooked that you made two visits to his cell. Brother Lugna told us about the day.' She turned to Brehon Aillín. 'Brother Donnchad disappeared for a day but came back in the evening and locked himself in his chamber. That was four days before his death. Brother Lugna told me that he sent for Lady Eithne the next day and she came and saw him. That was three days before his death, and later that same day Donnchad went to the *scriptorium*. Brother Máel Eoin remembered that he was upset because he had mislaid his *pólaire*, the wax tablet for making notes. He had not mislaid it, Lady Eithne had taken it during her visit.'

'Why would I take his notebook?'

'You pressed the key into it so that the shape of it was made in the wax. Donnchad was too preoccupied to notice your actions, or maybe you distracted him somehow. You took the tablet out concealed in your robes. I saw that you had your own smith at your fortress. It was easy to get him to make a key from the impression. The original key never left the cell. When I handled it later, when Brother Gilla-na-Naomh showed it to me, it was still slippery with wax.'

'That is true,' declared Brother Gilla-na-Naomh.

Lady Eithne's mouth thinned.

'You returned to see Donnchad on the day of his death. You returned specifically to kill him. After you had killed him, thrown the papers and books through the window to your accomplice, Brother Donnán, you were able to exit his chamber, leaving his key by his body. You locked the door with your newly made key. It was realising that you made two visits that put everything in perspective for me.'

In the brief moment of silence that followed, Brother Lugna cried out, 'I was not involved in any of this!'

'In a way, you are the person mainly responsible for this,' Fidelma replied harshly. 'Oh, you will not be found guilty of the killing nor of conspiracy to kill, but you were the malign influence over that woman,' she indicated Lady Eithne. Then she turned back to the Brehon. 'She had developed a fierce pride in the Faith. That pride increased when she encountered Brother Lugna and she saw in him the means to build up this abbey as a shrine to her sons Donnchad and Cathal. But Cathal chose to remain in Tarentum as its Bishop. Only Brother Donnchad had returned here. So this was to be his shrine, a beacon for the Faith, as she called it. But, to her horror, her son was having doubts about the very fundamentals of the Faith. He was even researching and writing an essay on the matter. That could not be allowed.'

Fidelma addressed Lady Eithne again. 'Who could you turn to to stop your son ruining your great plans for the abbey and, by association, your self-aggrandisement? Brother Lugna was actually too pious. I suspect he also thought he was making a shrine for himself. But you knew the *scriptor* was proud of the abbey, proud of the library that he had built up, and proud of its reputation. So you drew him into the plan, the plan to take the documents your son had gathered and to destroy them and any trace of writings that questioned the Faith.'

'I was not told that she was going to kill Brother Donnchad,' Brother Donnán suddenly said, loudly and clearly. 'I would not have agreed to that.'

'Shut up, you fool!' cried Lady Eithne.

'By the time Brother Donnán knew Donnchad had been killed, he was too involved and too frightened to do anything but continue as Lady Eithne's accomplice.' Fidelma looked at the librarian. 'What did you do with the books and papers Lady Eithne threw from the chamber?'

'As you said, I gathered them up and later took them to Lady Eithne's fortress.'

'You met Brother Gáeth along the way and said you were simply taking books from the library to her. But how were you able to alert her about the copy of Celsus's book at Fhear Maighe just as we were setting off there?'

'I was on the road outside the abbey, on my way to see Lady Eithne, when I saw Glassán riding off on some errand. He paused long enough to tell me that Brother Lugna had just seen Cumscrad and was in a rage, for he had learned that the library at Fhear Maighe held the Celsus book. I knew Lady Eithne would be interested.'

'Interested to send her warriors to Fhear Maighe. So all Brother Donnchad's papers are now destroyed?'

Brother Donnán shrugged.

'One thing that Lady Eithne and Brother Donnán did not know,' Fidelma said to Brehon Aillín, 'was that her son had already written a brief account of his findings and his thoughts. Oh, not the great reference work that he was planning, citing those writers of centuries ago who presented their criticisms against the new Faith. This was only a short account of his ideas. He included the fact that he had tried to talk to you, Lady Eithne, his own mother, about his doubts. Instead of discussing them, you threatened him if he spoke out. He believed that you would attempt to steal his work and suppress it. He mistakenly believed that your accomplice was Brother Lugna. He even thought Brother Lugna might contemplate physical violence against him. That's why he asked Abbot Iarnla for a key to his cell.'

There was a deathly silence as Fidelma paused, shaking her head.

'There were other matters to be considered along the way. When Lady Eithne heard that Abbot Iarnla had sent for me, she sent two of her mercenary warriors to waylay us on the road here. They were to ambush and kill my companions and me. They did not succeed and one of them was killed by Gormán, and the other, a *bánai*, fled. He was later to die in the attack on Fhear Maighe. It seemed he was the leader of a band of mercenaries from a kingdom called Kernow on the island of Britain. A band of mercenaries that you hired, Lady Eithne. I have since found that your clan, the Déisí, has a small settlement in that kingdom. The mercenaries were disguised as Uí Liatháin. Then, of course, there was the earlier attack on the barge by warriors dressed as Uí Liatháin. One of these attackers was wounded. And you felt you should send for the physician, Brother Seachlann, to attend to the man's wound. That was part of your undoing, lady. You have more than once demonstrated to me your complete lack of concern for those you consider beneath your rank. That is why you did not attend the funeral of Glassán.

'You told Seachlann your warrior was wounded practising

with his sword. So it was Brother Seachlann who provided me with an important piece of information. The two knife thrusts that killed Brother Donnchad showed some knowledge of anatomy, in that they were struck in points in the back where death was fairly certain. Brother Seachlann, when exami ing your warrior, realised you possessed a good knowledge of anatomy. You could have treated the man yourself and not aroused suspicion.'

Colgú was frowning. 'Why the subterfuge? Why would Lady Eithne have her warriors disguised as Uí Liatháin? To create war between them and the Fir Maige Féne? To spread alarm and dissension?'

'For an even more sinister purpose,' replied Fidelma. 'She knew of the tensions between the Fir Maige Féne and the Uí Liatháin and she knew they were often blamed for many things. Her intention was to create a conflict between them. She had hired an unusual number of mercenary warriors. I believe that she intended to use the ensuing conflict to step in as a peacemaker and claim, as a reward, some of the territories of the two clans to extend her own power around this abbey. Moreover, she needed the extra revenue from the new territories to finance her rebuilding of the abbey.'

Fidelma turned to Brehon Aillín.

'I have rarely encountered a crime that sickens me so to the depths of my soul. This is the crime of *fingal*, or kin-slaying, which strikes at the very heart of our society, based as it is on kin, on clans and our relationship with one another. Our laws stress that this is the most horrendous crime of all.

It is impossible to atone or compensate for such a crime. It is said that the fortress of a leader who has committed the crime can be erased so that all memory of it may be lost. It is a crime of such malevolence that—'

As she was speaking there came the sound of horses clattering through the abbey gates. Lady Eithne rose from her seat and glanced around. Her companions, the three warriors she had brought with her, drew their weapons and defensively closed around her.

The brethren began to move away from her but Brehon Aillín seemed unperturbed. 'I presume this gesture is an admission of guilt,' he said.

Colgú had signalled to Gormán and his two companions at the door, who had drawn their swords, as had Caol, standing behind the King.

'You will have to deal with my warriors before you can walk out of here, Lady Eithne,' Colgú warned. 'There is no escape.'

Lady Eithne laughed harshly. 'I am afraid you have not been very clever, Colgú of Cashel. While you may have a few of your bodyguard with you, they are not enough to challenge my warriors. Fidelma was right. I have increased my war band by hiring some of the best professionals I could find. Do you think I entered here with just these few men without making a plan? I suspected your sister might stumble on the truth.' She turned to Fidelma. 'Unfortunately for you, lady, when you came to see me a few days ago, I read the distrust in your eyes. Your companion, Eadulf, almost confessed your suspicions. Forewarned is forearmed. My warriors now surround this abbey. A moment ago, you heard my advance guard enter.'

Cries of alarm rose from the hall but Colgú remained relaxed in his seat, a curious smile on his face. Brehon Aillín called for quiet. When the hubbub had died away, he said softly, 'So what do you intend, Lady Eithne of the Déisi? You say you have surrounded this abbey with your hired bands. Now what? You intend to kill me? To kill all the brethren here?'

'As you leave me with no option,' Lady Eithne replied evenly. 'There will be an attack on this abbey by the Uí Liatháin who have long coveted the abbey and these lands.'

'That is not true,' cried Uallachán, springing from his seat. 'I have no hand in this. My warriors will not attack this place.'

'There will be enough evidence left to identify the attackers as your men,' replied Lady Eithne icily. 'Your own body will be found slain at the head of your warriors, bloody sword in hand. In the attack, you will have slain your arch-enemy, Cumscrad. Indeed, even the King and his retinue will not survive.'

Abbot Iarnla was staring at Lady Eithne in horror. 'You are mad, lady. You intend to wipe out all these brethren, your kin and the others gathered here? You intend to kill the King and his advisers? How do you think you can get away with it?'

'I am quite serious. Everyone will perish. This abbey will be cleansed of the faint-hearted. Purified, it will rise again under the leadership of its new abbot – Lugna. I appoint him as the new abbot.' She gestured to Brother Lugna who was sitting in a state of shock, white faced, as if unable to comprehend what was happening.

It was only then that Fidelma realised that not only was Lady Eithne a fanatic for the Faith, she was completely insane.

'It will be reported that the Uí Liatháin are the culprits and they will be punished,' Lady Eithne said gleefully. 'And now—'.

The door of the *refectorium* swung open and several warriors stood there. The cries of alarm began to rise. Lady Eithne's malicious smile faded when she saw Colgú grinning broadly. He rose and held up his hands, palm outwards. She swung round and noticed that the warriors at the door all wore the golden torc emblems of the Nasc Niadh, the bodyguard of the King of Cashel.

'It is done, Colgú,' called the leading man, his voice booming over the panicking hubbub. Brehon Aillín started calling for calm, telling the brethren that they had nothing to fear. The noise started to subside.

Colgú glanced at Fidelma and he inclined his head before turning to the now bewildered Lady Eithne, whose guards still stood ready to defend her.

'There was just one problem with your plan, Lady Eithne,' Colgú said. 'You were right that my sister suspected you. When she sent for me she had specific instructions. This morning, after you and your escort had left your fortress for this place, a full *catha*, a battalion of my army, moved from the mountains across the river and surrounded your fortress just as your men were getting ready to follow you here.'

The leader of the newly arrived warriors approached the King and spoke urgently in his ear. The King smiled and nodded. 'Thank you, Enda.' He looked at Lady Eithne. 'I am pleased to say, lady, that your mercenaries thought the better of fighting and surrendered their arms.'

Lady Eithne's face was white.

'I don't believe you,' she whispered.

'Oh, your *lucht-tighe*, your personal guard, those of your own clan, put up a brief resistance. But when you pay men to fight your battles, when it comes to fighting to the death, they will often choose life, for they cannot spend money when they are dead.'

Brehon Aillín looked grave. 'You should remember the words of the *Audacht Moraind* on nobility, lady. The noble who takes power with the help of foreign warriors can expect a weak and fleeting lordship – as soon as the warriors leave or surrender then that noble's dignity and the terror it inspires will decline. So has it in this case.'

There was a silence.

'You do not respond?' the King asked drily. 'I suggest, lady, you order your companions to put down their swords. I do not want to sully this abbey and this court with any more blood.'

With a gesture from Colgú, Caol and his men moved forward, weapons ready to meet any aggression. But without waiting for any order from Lady Eithne, her companions dropped their swords and raised their hands.

'Excellent,' approved Colgú. 'Caol,' he called to his commander of the Nasc Niadh, 'escort the Lady Eithne and her companions to a safe place until Brehon Aillín decides how best to resolve this matter.'

Fidelma watched as Lady Eithne, her head raised in arrogant fashion, left with her escort, looking neither to right nor left.

'I will never understand how a mother can kill her son even if she is insane,' she commented softly as Eadulf rose and laid a hand on her arm.

'I am sorry I could not help you more,' he said. 'That was one of the most complicated presentations you have ever had to give.'

'And the most difficult I have ever had to understand,' said Fidelma. 'But we might not have been allowed to proceed had you not found that legal maxim from the *Uraicecht Becc*. For that alone your help was indispensable.'

Eadulf shrugged with mock indifference. 'I suppose I have my uses after all.'

EPILOGUE

Fidelma and Eadulf were resting on the bank of a stream on the road to Cashel. Gormán had ridden on ahead to the next tavern where they were due to meet him. They were taking a more leisurely ride back and decided to rest a while and water their horses. Eadulf was chewing thoughtfully on a stem of quaking grass, watching the eddies and little whirlpools as the water splashed and gushed its way over the shallow stony bed. He had been thinking a lot since they left the abbey of Lios Mór and crossed the mountains on the way north.

'I have never been so depressed by events in an investigation before.'

Fidelma gave him a searching glance. His expression was dark and moody.

'Do you mean because a mother killed her own son? Indeed, it is a terrible thing.'

Eadulf stirred uncomfortably. 'There is that, of course,' he conceded. 'But I was thinking, what if the story related in Donnchad's document is true? What if he was right?'

'Maybe he was wrong,' Fidelma said lightly.

'Donnchad believed it to be true,' pointed out Eadulf. 'And his mother was so fearful of it being true that she killed him rather than let him pronounce his views. Had she been confident in her Faith, she would have had no need to defend it by silencing criticism in that way.'

'A good point, Eadulf. Yet, again, fear of it being true does not make it true. In the end it comes down to what you believe.'

'And there are countless who believe in the Faith, they cannot all be wrong.'

'But in that case, what makes the countless others who believe in the other faiths across the world wrong? That's the conundrum.'

'If Donnchad had not gone to the Holy Land on the pilgrimage, he might not have encountered the stories that caused him to doubt his Faith. He might have continued to be a great scholar of the Faith.'

'Perhaps, perhaps not.' She smiled. 'We can conjure many things with that magical word "if".'

'There is one other thing that bothers me.'

'Only one?'

'Brother Donnchad's own text was remarkable. But we never found out what the other works were that he brought back from the Holy Land, those works he kept protected in his cell, which his own mother killed him for, and which were destroyed by her. What did they contain that would have shattered the Faith of a scholar such as Brother Donnchad?'

Fidelma hesitated for a few moments before she turned to him, her expression serious. 'I am certainly no theologian, Eadulf. My expertise lies in the law, as I have often said. That is why I have determined to leave the constrictions of the religious to others and apply myself only to the law.' She paused and added quietly, 'Even if I do not become Chief Brehon of Muman.'

Eadulf's expression did not change, he remained gazing firmly at a dragonfly hovering above the water of the stream before him. Then he sighed deeply.

'I wonder what will happen to Brother Lugna.'

'I understand that he will return home to Connachta, taking young Gúasach with him. He could not remain at the abbey, especially not now his true views have been revealed.'

'You do not call him heretic?'

'I told you, I am no theologian. It is not up to me to pronounce on heresy. All I know is that I do not like anything he stands for. Maybe he will fulfil his ambitions and create some great abbey in Connachta one day. For the time being, Abbot Iarnla does not have to walk in fear of the malign influence of Lady Eithne. He can govern his community with a stronger hand.'

'And Lady Eithne, she has been judged insane. I am not familiar with how that judgement is carried out. It seems to be exile.'

'Not exactly. She has certainly been judged a *dásach-tach*, the worst condition of madness, one which might lead her to inflict harm on others. She will be sent to a place that we call Gleann-na-nGeilt, the glen of lunatics, in the west of the kingdom. There she will be looked after. The law not only protects society from the *dásachtach*, it also protects the *dásachtach* from harm from uncaring members of society. Eithne's rank and position mean that one-third of her land will be used to provide for her during her lifetime.'

'Do you think that the abbey of Lios Mór will ever rise as Eithne and Lugna envisaged it would?'

'I would hope it will rise but not as some stone shrine to commemorate mythology, rather as a living shrine to a belief in the ultimate goodness of its people, to their intellectual pursuits and the attainment of knowledge.'

'The rebuilding will surely end now, will it not?'

'My brother has confiscated one-third of Lady Eithne's lands in fines and this land has now been turned over to the abbey with all its wealth. I suspect that Abbot Iarnla will use that wealth to complete the work with a new master builder and workforce.'

Eadulf sighed deeply. 'I feel sorry for Brother Donnán. I think he was caught up in Lady Eithne's web of murder and intrigue without realising where it was leading.'

'Brother Donnán has agreed to make reparation and spend it rebuilding the destroyed library at Fhear Maighe. However, when a book that has no copies is destroyed, it is like the destruction of a human life. The book is no more and will never be again. It is just like murder. But the real person to feel sorry for is Brother Gáeth. He has lost most in this terrible affair. He lost his only friend, Donnchad.'

'But he is no longer condemned to be a *daer-fudir*, for Uallachán made his views known and Abbot Iarnla no longer has to obey the constrictions of Lady Eithne.'

'You are right. He is a freeman in law. But Fate has been harsh to him. He will continue his life as a field hand, working at the abbey. He is not prepared for anything else in life. At least he will have nothing to fear there but had things been otherwise . . .'

'What will happen to Donnchad's account of why he lost his Faith that he asked Brother Gáeth to keep?'

'Brehon Aillín has seen it and accepted it as proof of Donnchad's state of mind. But it can neither be destroyed nor proclaimed. For the time being, it will remain undisturbed in the Mound of the Dead.'

Eadulf rose to his feet and threw his piece of quaking grass into the stream, watching it swirl away in the eddies for a moment. Then he shook his head and looked up at the sky. There were some feathery-looking clouds high in the sky, the wisps almost blending together to form high ripples.

'A mackerel sky,' he remarked. 'There might be some changeable weather ahead. It has been warm for so long. We might have rain soon.'

Fidelma rose to join him. 'Let us hope that there will be no storms before we reach Cashel.'

'And when we reach Cashel?'

She regarded him sadly. 'I have made my decision, Eadulf. You must now make your choice.'

hISTORICAL AFTERWORD

The reader does not have to study the history of the early Christian movement to understand the doubts and conflicts that Brother Donnchad was faced with in this story. Nor does the reader have to accept or believe in the veracity of them. The point being made is that these matters influenced him as they influenced others of this period. Fidelma argued that, whether Donnchad was right or wrong in losing his Faith over the material he had discovered, it was a matter of personal choice.

But for those readers who are interested in that material, it is a matter of record that once Christianity took over as the official religion of the Roman empire, many works that were contemporary with the birth of Christianity and its early years were amended or destroyed when they were found to contradict and challenge the changing dogmas of the leadership of the Christian movement.

Some texts survived such as the comments of Pliny the

Younger (AD 61/62–AD 113) who saw the early Christians as just a *hetaeria*, or political club. The Neoplatonist philosopher Porphyry of Tyre (AD 234–305) saw them as 'a confused and vicious sect' in his *Adversus Christianos*. The scholarly Roman Emperor Julian, known as Julian the Apostate, who ruled from AD 355–360, wrote a discourse called *Contra Galilaeos* (*Against the Galilaeans*), which survives only in fragments. He called all Christians 'Galilaeans' and did not hold their philosophies in high regard. Galen of Pergamun (*c.* AD 129–200) gave his criticisms as part of his essay, 'On the Usefulness of the Parts of the Body', written *c.* AD 170, in which he expressed his belief that the Christian philosophies were 'unreasonable'.

The critical writings of the second-century Greek philosopher Celsus, essential to this story, have not survived completely. However, they are almost entirely reproduced in quoted excerpts given by Origenes in his counter-polemic *Contra Celsum* (written in *c.* AD 248). Celsus wrote his work *Alethos Logos* (*The True Word*) as a polemic against Christianity in approximately AD 178.

Sadly for historians, many works similar to these were burnt in the enthusiasm of zealots for the new Faith whose ideas and philosophies were then evolving.

Some very early Christian traditions had it that Joachim, of the House of Amram, and Anna, of the House of David, were the parents of Mary, mother of Jesus, and that they were natives of Sepphoris (Hebrew, Tzippori), which is in the centre of Galilee, six kilometres north north-east of Nazareth.

The *Protoevangelium of James* (sometimes referred to as the *Infancy Gospel of James*) was written in *c*. AD 150, although the earliest surviving copy dates from the third century AD. It is in the Martin Bodmer Foundation Library and Museum, in Cologny, near Geneva, Switzerland. While this text was not accepted in the final version of the New Testament by its compilers in the fourth century, St Anne and St Joachim are accepted in the Christian faith. When the Council of Laodicia, *c*. AD 363, made their final choice of the texts that would form the New Testament, with the exception of *Revelations*, it took a long time before all the branches of the Christian movement agreed on the choice. By the time of the Council of Rome in AD 382, there was general unanimity in the Western churches. The twenty-seven books, now including *Revelations*, that constitute the New Testament as we recognise it today, were accepted in the West. The Eastern churches accepted them the following century. St Jerome's Vulgate Latin Bible became the standard text of the Western churches through the medieval period.

The city of Sepphoris was the centre of Jewish religious and spiritual life in Galilee. Early texts said that Anna or Ch'annah (Hebrew 'favoured') and Joachim (Hebrew 'Yahweh prepares'), were living there with their daughter Miriam. Miriam was an ancient Hebrew name meaning 'rebellious' and 'disobedient' and was written in Greek as Maria and thence passed into Latin. The people of Sepphoris rose up against the Roman colonial administration in the Roman year 750 *ab urbe condita*, which is 4 BC in the Christian calendar. Because of calendar changes, this is the year now accepted as the birth year of Jesus. Under the Governor Publius Quinctilius Varus (46 BC – AD 9), Roman troops burnt the city to the ground as punishment for the insurrection and sold many of its inhabitants into slavery. Varus's campaign was brutal and he also crucified two thousand Jewish insurgents. The story is recorded by the Jewish historian, Flavius Josephus (AD 37 – after AD 93), who also mentions the death of Jesus's brother James, the name coming from Iakobos, the Greek form of the Hebrew Jacob.

A story circulated that during the sack, rape and burning of Sepphoris, a Roman soldier named Abdes Pantera raped Miriam. The child born from this rape, Yeshua ben Pantera, was mentioned in early texts. Yeshua (Yehoshua) was a common name among the Jews of the Second Temple Period (516 BC – AD 70). It is argued by some scholars that the name means 'cry to God when in need' and is the same name from which Joshua is transliterated. Jesus is the Graeco-Latin form. Celsus, with other early text writers, identified Yeshua ben Pantera with Jesus of Nazareth.

There was, indeed, a real soldier named Abdes Pantera who was a Phoenician from Sidon. He served in the Roman army and his unit could well have been one of those who sacked Sepphoris at this time. He later became a Roman citizen and was able to add the Roman *praenomen* of 'Tiberius Julius' before his own.

The tombstone of Tiberius Julius Abdes Pantera, who served in the *Cohors I Sagittariorum*, and lived *c.* 22 BC – AD 40, was rediscovered during the construction of a railroad in Bingerbrück (formerly Bingium), on the River Rhine, along with other monuments, in 1859. It is currently in the Schlossparkmuseum in Bad Kreuznach, Germany. The inscription on the tombstone of this Phoenician archer from Sidonia is still readable.

It is of coincidental interest that Varus had been given command in Germania and took three of his legions, the XVII, XVIII and XIX, into the Teutoburg Forest in AD 9, where the German prince, Arminius, annihilated them. Varus himself was killed. The three eagles of the legions were never recovered.

The writer who first commented on these connections in modern times was the Italian Biblical scholar Dr Marcello Craveri in *La vita di Gesù*, 1966, which was translated into English in 1967 as *The Life of Jesus: An assessment through modern historical evidence*, Panther Books, London, 1967.

Now you can buy any of these other bestselling
books by **Peter Tremayne** from your bookshop
or *direct from his publisher*.

FREE P&P AND UK DELIVERY
(Overseas and Ireland £3.50 per book)

The Subtle Serpent	£6.99
The Spider's Web	£6.99
Valley of the Shadow	£6.99
The Monk who Vanished	£6.99
Act of Mercy	£6.99
Hemlock at Vespers	£6.99
Our Lady of Darkness	£6.99
Smoke in the Wind	£6.99
The Haunted Abbot	£6.99
Badger's Moon	£6.99
Whispers of the Dead	£6.99
The Leper's Bell	£6.99
Master of Souls	£6.99
A Prayer for the Damned	£6.99
Dancing with Demons	£7.99
The Council of the Cursed	£7.99
The Dove of Death	£7.99

TO ORDER SIMPLY CALL THIS NUMBER

01235 400 414

or visit our website: www.headline.co.uk

Prices and availability subject to change without notice.